THE GUNTHERS
They were men and women of daring and heart . . . of fierce pride and smoldering passions . . .

THE GUNTHERS
Cunning traders and bold adventurers, they roamed the wide wilderness and the far-flung seas . . . culling the lustrous furs from a virgin land, and China's gleaming treasures from the shrouded East . . .

THE GUNTHERS
Theirs was a destiny that time would test and love would challenge . . . the mink-lined kingdom of the Gunthers . . . a dynasty of golden pioneers on a continent of giants . . .

THE GUNTHER HERITAGE

VOLUME THREE IN THE AMERICAN DYNASTY SERIES

*DO NOT MISS THE
FIRST TWO VOLUMES IN THE AMERICAN
DYNASTY SERIES:*

**THE VALLETTE HERITAGE
THE VAN RHYNE HERITAGE**

THE
GUNTHER HERITAGE

LOUISA BRONTE

A JOVE BOOK

Copyright © 1981 by Series International, Inc.

All rights reserved. No part of this publication
may be reproduced or transmitted in any form or
by any means, electronic or mechanical, including
photocopy, recording, or any information storage
and retrieval system, without permission in
writing from the publisher.

Requests for permission to make copies of any part
of the work should be mailed to: Permissions,
Jove Publications, Inc., 200 Madison Avenue,
New York, NY 10016

First Jove edition published February 1981

10 9 8 7 6 5 4 3 2 1

Printed in the United States of America

Jove books are published by Jove Publications, Inc.,
200 Madison Avenue, New York, NY 10016

*To the industrial families
that helped make America great . . .*

PART I
1780–1800

Chapter 1

Ludwig Gunther leaned forward on the plump sofa, his hands dangling between his long sturdy legs. His reddish-blond face was serious and intent as he listened keenly to the impressive, precise tones of his former schoolmaster, Augustus Voss. The older man was reading the letter he held.

"'This is a green and pleasant land. The earth is so rich that grains spring forth with little effort. Virgin forests cover the hills and valleys. A man may cut what timber he chooses, asking permission of no one and hunt game freely also. The land belongs to no king or lord!

"'We march on to the West tomorrow. The Colonials are ragged and have little ammunition. I have seen them fight with their fists when they have no more bullets. They fight on and on. We whisper to each other—it is possible these tough men may win this war! The king of England, his officers, our Hessian troups cannot always defeat them. Out of the earth, behind a fence of rock, they will spring out once more and fire at us, or jump on us from above.'"

Mr. Voss lifted his shining gaze to Ludwig's rapt face.

"Is it not splendid?" he asked, thumping his fist on the table in front of him. He removed his small spectacles and rubbed his eyes automatically. Though he was aging, in his late fifties now, still some fire burned in him.

"Why do they fight on?" mused Ludwig. "What do they hope to gain? The rulers always win, the powerful ones always crush those who revolt. That is what history teaches us."

"This time—it could well be different!" said Mr. Voss in a slow, wondering voice. His dreamy eyes shone with fervor. He had the face of a dreamer of dreams, yet he had known little but disappointment in his life. "Think, Ludwig! For once in the history of the world the masters will be overthrown. These are no slaves, no timid rascals. These are men of substance: farmers, artisans, gentlemen who own land and property! They are printers, writers, bankers, shopkeepers! And they have armed themselves for the struggle against the king across the waters!"

"What if a miracle happens and they do win?" Ludwig flung back his large head. "We talked in school of the Greek democracies. They failed before the conquerors of Rome. Freedom—a man's ability to rule himself—can it truly work?"

Mr. Voss sobered a little and sighed. After folding the thin papers with his trembling hands he listened for a moment to note if their voices had roused his ailing parents whom he had cared for most of his adult life. "My gentle chains of iron," he had once said of them with a sad smile.

"Ah, Ludwig," Mr. Voss said now. "If I were young and sturdy, with none to lean on me, I should go to America to find out if a man can be truly free. I would know if a man like myself can earn wealth such as our soldiers have seen, to win a fortune by his own labors. To marry as he pleases, to raise a family with no lord's permission, to move about—*to live free*, Ludwig! Can it be truly possible—for a man to live free?"

Ludwig looked down in silence at his huge red hands. He seemed to see blood on them, the blood of his work. As a lad of fourteen, his schooling finished, he had been put to work in his father's thriving butcher shop, and there he had worked four years. His father found him clever at carving, smart in sums, and polite to the housewife at the door or in the shop. Business was ever improving.

He knew his father would not let him go. Never! Not to some madcap adventure such as this! To sail to the New World, to make his way in a strange land...

"Ludwig. Does it not appeal to you, my lad?" asked the gentle voice of his schoolmaster. "If I were eighteen, free, and strong as you—strong like an ox—"

"Ox, yes," said Ludwig bitterly. "My father will have me remain home to carve that ox! I have brothers and sisters, all young, all needing help now. Most in school, but for the baby. Mother works hard in the flower market. My sister left school to care for the youngest ones. How can I leave them?"

Mr. Voss sighed, then glanced again automatically toward the door to listen for his parents. "Ah, yes, we owe them much, our parents," he said. "But do we not owe ourselves something as well? Do we not owe it to our souls to free ourselves from chains? In Germany, in Hess," and his voice lowered. "In our state no man is free from oppression. If you remain, you may be conscripted."

The two, the young man and the older, were silent for a time. Both were all too aware that even in their small remote village in the mountains, the hand of the lord of Hess would reach out and tap a man on the shoulder, and point. And that man must leave home, family, wife, children, and go—where he was sent. For his lord had complete charge of his life. Many never returned; others came back crippled in body and in mind, eyes blank from the horrors they had seen, heads injured, limbs shaking in palsy.

"Freedom," whispered Ludwig. "What is freedom? I cannot even imagine what it might be."

Mr. Voss looked at him with compassion. "We cannot know it here," he said. "But there—if the colonials win their war— it may be different from any place in the world. A man may pick up and leave and walk a league away and begin to construct a house, as Hendrick said. Or he may leave the army, and take a wife, and ride a horse a hundred leagues, and there begin to create a farm for himself, and none to say him nay! I have read the letters over and over. Otto does well. He exults in his new life. There is a militia, but no man serves more than three months! Imagine—three months! And no man, no man, must ask permission of a lord to marry! He asks the girl, and her parents, and if all agree, they walk to the parson!"

Ludwig shook his head slowly several times. With no wish to marry, he looked with indifference on the coy ways of the village girls. He had enough burdens on his shoulders—he did not wish to add to them, he thought bitterly. And he had no wish for a farm, for the farmers worked even harder than the butchers, early morning to late at night, at the mercy of the elements.

He wanted...he wanted a new life. Something different. Something that meant every day was not like the next. A life that held adventure, new horizons, new scenes, strange creatures, people unlike himself. He could scarcely express even to himself what he wanted. There was some deep hungry yearning inside him that rebelled fiercely against the dullness and sameness of the days.

Was there nothing else in life? Could he do nothing but go to the shop, add sums, chop up raw beef, and kill chickens? Day after day, with no change but on Sundays, and then only to attend church most of the day? So desperately dull a life that young men his age stole out to meet girls and married them only to find themselves trapped in another, more difficult life—with a family to support! That was no escape; that was putting one's neck in the noose!

Freedom. He tasted the word, he rolled it around his tongue. He whispered it. He did not know what it meant. How could a man be truly free? Was not some lord over him always? Did not a man have to bow down to someone else all his days? How would he act if he could do exactly what he wanted, from one day to the next?

Mr. Voss was scanning another letter, his eyes shining like a boy's. "Otto says there will be even more opportunities once the war is over. He believes the Colonials will win, and then once the British have left, they will all be free! Otto means to join with other farmers and open a market of their own, to sell their own produce to the people in town. They will keep the profits themselves! Imagine, Ludwig!"

"Freedom," muttered Ludwig. He was not thinking of farms and markets. He was thinking of the woods and fields, the mountains and wild streams of which one soldier had written. They had met wild painted Indians who had melted into the woods like shadows. No cabins for a hundred miles! "Freedom, to wander..."

Mr. Voss set down the pages again and leaned toward Ludwig, his favorite pupil. It was the schoolmaster who had encouraged Ludwig to think, to read more books than in the curriculum, to understand history, to debate with other students. It was Mr. Voss who had made his own home a refuge for Ludwig, when his father would have insisted on taking every free hour after school. They talked, drank tea, read philosophy, and discussed the new ideas that floated about Europe.

"Ludwig, you are smart, you are determined, you have courage. Leave! Do not be caught as I was," he said sadly. "The chains of love are so strong and binding. Leave before you are trapped. Let the others remain. You must go—and make your own way to freedom!"

Ludwig was thinking, rubbing his blond thick hair. "I must have a few clothes, warm and sturdy," he muttered. "I must have some money; I have none."

Mr. Voss was shaking his head impatiently. "A man such as you has his youth, his strong back, his will! You can work your way to the coast, to Holland, to the ports. You can exchange your work for passage to the New World. Ludwig— go, I urge you!"

His words finally set Ludwig on fire. The lad was a slow, thorough worker, a strong worker, but half of him wanted to go, to adventure, and half wanted to remain in safety, with his family. To go out alone into the world—it was to make one shudder with both apprehension and excitement.

Ludwig went to his father. On Sunday afternoon, while the older man smoked his pipe and mulled over his sums for the week, he spoke respectfully to him.

"Father, there is something I would discuss with you."

"Eh? What is it then? A new suit?" The older man frowned.

Bernardine Gunther looked up from her rocking chair before the fire. Sundays were the only days she had a bit of time to herself. She sat with the Bible on her lap, but Ludwig had noted that some day the pages were not turned, and a wistful dreamy look was on her face as she gazed into the flames. Had she herself dreamed once, before she had married a hard-working butcher and had child after child?

Ludwig had gathered up his arguments, just as for a school debate. He had rehearsed in bed, lying awake beside his two brothers who shared the bed in the loft, going over and over his speech. Now he began.

"Father, letters have come to our village from soldiers who serve in America. They say there is much good land there, and many jobs for the taking. Good wages are paid. A man may take fields, and have his own farm—"

Hans Gunther did not listen for the rolling sentences to conclude. He scowled at his son. "Nonsense. Drunken talk," he said briskly. "I know how soldiers talk! Do not deceive yourself; it is all the talk of fools in their beer."

Ludwig swallowed and tried to go on with his speech. His mother was listening, her faded blue eyes alert, fixed on his face. "Father, there is a land of freedom there, where no man owes his lord anything. There *are* no lords and slaves, no masters and underlings. A man may live as he wishes, in town or country, as schoolmaster, or farmer, or artisan."

"Ludwig, you displease me with this foolish talk! You have been too much to the schoolmaster. He makes you dissatisfied!" said Hans shrewdly. "No, no, no, you remain here. You are a good butcher. I bet you have an eye for a girl, eh?" and he chuckled. "That makes a man sit up and take notice of the world, eh? Who is the girl, eh?"

Ludwig was flushed with anger. However, when he caught his mother's eye, she gave a slow shake of her head and a warning look. He waited until his temper was in control. His father was working at his pipe, filling it, getting it to light properly, a slight triumphant grin on his face. A married man was a tied man, that was his philosophy, Ludwig remembered.

Not for Ludwig! Not until he was master of himself and his work!

"No girl, Father," he said quietly. "I think of the future. There is a world beyond the village, and I would find it. I would go to another world, to other work and another life. I am eighteen—"

"A boy!" His father was furious now. "You are a child! For eighteen years I have fed you, clothed you, taken care of you. Now you are grown up, you think? I think no! You owe me much! You will stay and work for your father! The world outside is just like the world here, there is no difference! You'll stay!"

He would hear no more. Hans was so angry at his son, Ludwig could not even talk to him for days.

His mother cautioned him, "Wait, Ludwig. Wait, and work well. Let him calm down. In another year your brother Johann will be out of school. He will work in the shop. Your sister will marry soon, I think. When the children are older, that will be your time."

"How long must I wait, Mother?" Ludwig asked grimly. "Until I am old and gray?"

"When you are twenty-one, your father cannot stop you," she said softly. "Wait, Ludwig. Be patient. Read of the New World. Do not allow anyone to stop you from visiting with Mr. Voss. You can tell your father you go to the village. Let him think you drink with the boys. Eh?" And she gave him a slow, lovely smile and a pat of her hand on his shoulder.

So the year went by, and his father forgot what Ludwig had said. But Ludwig did not forget. He visited Mr. Voss regularly and read the letters eagerly. The war changed. Battles were fought, and the Colonials began to win them. The British grew weary of a war taking place so far away. On the sea, they lost ships, and the Colonials were trading boldly with both the French and the Spanish.

Another year went by, and Johann joined his father and brother in the butcher shop. But the boy was careless and disliked the long hours. He would wander off to make a delivery and not return for two hours. His father scolded him. "Watch how Ludwig works, my boy! He is faithful, quick. No, no, not so sloppy in the cutting! Make slow smooth clean cuts, that looks so much better. The good housewives like the clean, nice-looking cuts of beef."

8

Johann grumbled. And Ludwig was afraid. If his brother did not work well, his father would be all the more reluctant to let Ludwig go. His mother worked daily with her flowers and took them to market on Saturday, selling them for good prices. She turned over the money to her husband, like a good housewife, but he grumbled.

"Come, come, Bernardine! You should have made more money with the flowers this week!"

"The cost of the booth went up, Hans," she said, her hands folded meekly, her eyes down. "And by the heat of the day, the flowers wilted early. I had to sell them for less than I had planned."

"Ah well, ah well, make sure to water them more during the day," he grumbled, putting the coins into the money box and giving the lid a pat as he closed it.

"Margerite needs a new dress for courting," said his wife gently.

Hans scowled but brought out a few coins reluctantly. "You can make the dress, that would be cheaper. Do not go to the dressmaker."

"Thank you, Father," said Margerite, prompted by her mother.

Though they all worked hard, Ludwig's father kept the money. Ludwig watched and listened, and more rebellion swelled in his heart. His mother worked as hard as his father, but his father took all her earnings! And he himself got not a pence for his hard work six days a week, ten to twelve hours each day. He had to beg for money to buy new shoes, or a suit. And his father begrudged it all to them.

"When I am a man of my own, I shall not be so to my loved ones," vowed Ludwig to himself. "A man and a woman are worthy of their hire, so says the Good Book. That means, they should be paid as they work." Yet he had not a pence of his own to put in his pocket.

During the next two years the only times Ludwig enjoyed were those he spent with Mr. Voss, reading the letters from his old pupils from America. The war went well. More Hessians had deserted and fled from the hated British officers. They had gone west, found farms, and made friends among many peoples.

"'There are Quakers who are very good to us,'" wrote one man. "'They hid me from the officers who came searching, fed me, and hid me in a wagon. They drove me many miles

9

away, where other Friends—which is what they call each other—hid me again. Thank the Good God for such men and women of courage! I tell them I want only freedom to live as I will, and they pat my shoulder and say that in the New World there is such freedom.'"

Ludwig talked to Mr. Voss, discussing what he would do, where he would go. Mr. Voss knew little more than his young student, but he would make suggestions eagerly. Where to go, how to get work, how to live.

"And always work with honor, my young friend," he would say. "Give a good day's work for a good day's wages. Be generous to your family and loved ones and friends. Honor another man's freedom, and own no slaves when you have money for that. Do not do to others what you would not want them to do to you."

Ludwig absorbed all he told him, still wondering wistfully if he only dreamed. Finally he turned twenty-one. His brother Johann worked well now in the shop, if not eagerly.

Ludwig went again to his father. This time he did not ask.

"Father, I shall leave you now, I am twenty-one," he said, standing before him on his sturdy legs like young tree trunks, his huge hands folded in front of him. His vivid blue eyes met those of his father steadily. "I am for the New World."

"You are a fool!" said his father angrily, but this time he could not hold Ludwig back, not with threats nor by withholding money.

"I can earn my way there," said Ludwig and prepared to depart. He folded a few clothes into a cloth bag he had asked his married sister to make for him. Into it he also put his own silver flute. They were all the possessions he had in the world.

On the morning that he left, a number of people walked to the edge of the village with him. His mother had come to his room as he finished dressing and put a cloth belt into his hand. "Wear it about your waist, Ludwig," she murmured softly.

He felt the cloth. Into each of various portions she had sewn a coin, and he felt about a dozen. Painfully saved over three years, about six florins, he thought.

"Mother, I cannot take this!" His vibrant blue eyes met her faded ones.

She smiled and nodded, her eyelashes blinking back the tears. "I saved them for you, my eldest and beloved son," she whispered. She gave him a quick hug, a final embrace, and studied his face. "Be good, my son, be honorable. I will pray always for you."

10

"You are good. It is hard to leave you," he choked.

"There is adventure in you, a longing for wild places," she murmured. "I saw this early. Once I also—but no mind. You must go. Oh, Ludwig, be happy, and stop not for dullness. Search the far places, follow the wind!"

His father called angrily. "Why do you stay up there? Come down, if you will go!"

Ludwig gave his mother a quick shy kiss on the cheek. Caresses were rare in the family. He took her hand as they walked down the stairs. His father stared at them suspiciously. They all walked into the street then, where Johann waited, and some of Ludwig's school friends, along with Mr. Voss, a storekeeper, several housewives and some neighbors.

They walked soberly to the edge of the town. There they halted, and Ludwig thanked them, shaking hands with each of them. They gave him their good wishes. All too often this had happened, as someone from the village left to go where the Hessian regiment took them. But this was different. Ludwig was alone.

Mr. Voss's hand closed strongly on his. Tears shone from his eyes, but his smile beamed on Ludwig. His boy was going at last out into the wide world. "Write to us," he said. "Write, and tell us of your adventures!"

"His failures, and begging for money, more like," grumbled his father. "You can come back and work for me," he added, surprising his son by his suddenly gracious tone. But Ludwig's mind was set, and his plans were made. There would be no turning back, not now, not ever.

He gave his last farewells and, after looking his last at his mother's set smile, he turned to walk down the long dusty road. He looked back once and waved, only to see the people distant and small. Then he turned the bend in the road and followed the river.

He walked all day, pausing only to eat bread and cheese and drink from a farmer's well. He slept at night in wheat fields. He walked until his food was gone, then he paused to ask for work to do. After sawing logs for several days, he earned enough to walk further and eat something.

He worked and walked through the long summer. Holland was further than he had thought, and the trip far lonelier than he had dreamed. The farmers stared suspiciously at times, and once a housewife, terrified, set her dog on him. But he continued, sleeping in the fields or by the river, working, eating, walking, and proceeding doggedly through the countryside,

11

north and to the west. And he took care to cross the borders through fields and over fences, avoiding the customs posts and the soldiers who walked there, watching for sturdy young men to take into the army.

And finally he came to Rotterdam in Holland. He stared with wide eyes all about him as he walked to the port. He had a few coins, all his mother had given him, but those he must save for the New World. Though he wanted to sail at once, he knew it might be necessary to stop and work for a time.

Mr. Voss had taught him a little English. Other than that, he knew only German. Painfully he studied the notices in the windows on the dock. He found a ship that was going to New York, but it did not leave for a week. Another was going to Philadelphia.

Philadelphia. That was where the Quakers were. Perhaps that would be a good place to go. He thought about it and studied the posting. Did the notice say the ship was going today?

A man wearing blue paused at the window to stare at the same listing.

Ludwig regarded him warily. Tall, he sported a blue cap pushed back from brown hair, and his brown eyes were steady. His face was tanned heavily, and his eyes squinted in the sunlight.

"I beg pardon," Ludwig ventured in German.

The man responded in hesitant German. "Yes, what is it?"

"This ship—does it go maybe soon?"

"It went yesterday," answered the man. He looked at Ludwig, slowly, up and down, noting the sturdy body, the anxious face, the sincere blue eyes, the shabby clothes and worn shoes. "Where do you wish to go?"

"To the New World," said Ludwig.

"Aye." The man nodded slowly. "Everyone wants to go to the New World," he said in English, absently.

To Ludwig's delight he could understand the man when he spoke slowly. Ludwig answered in English. "There is work in the New World! A man can be free!"

"You speak English!" said the man and stuck out his hand. Ludwig shook it heartily, relieved, beaming.

"I speak English a little," he said.

"And you want to sail to the New World," commented the man and laughed a big booming laugh. He was but a few years older than Ludwig, but he had such assurance. He put his hands on his hips. "So. Our ship over there sails in a week. You want to go with us?"

"Oh, yes, yes, yes," said Ludwig. He almost could not contain his excitement.

"We need men. The English have pressed some of our seamen. Can you work on a ship?"

"I will do anything you tell me!" Ludwig said quickly.

"Come and have lunch with me. We will talk about it." The man touched his arm and nodded to a bar nearby.

They talked over beer and hot beef. Ludwig, slowly and in broken English, told him of his years of planning, how he longed to go to freedom in the New World.

"There are many chances to work in New York," said the man. Ludwig learned that his name was Roderick Dindorf, and he had been sailing before the mast since he was fourteen. He was now first mate on the ship going to New York. "You can get a job anywhere. Butcher? Sure. Or baker, or candlestick maker! Or shopkeeper, printer, teacher."

His words made Ludwig's eyes shine with enthusiasm. What Mr. Voss had told him of opportunities in the New World must be true!

Roderick Dindorf paid for the meal, waving aside Ludwig's protests. "I'll take you to the captain and get you signed on," he said. "One way only, eh?"

And he laughed at the expression on Ludwig's face.

They went to the captain, who was talking to some men in a shipping office. They turned as Dindorf and Ludwig came in.

"Got another sailor for us," said Dindorf with a grin. "Doesn't know sailoring, but he's young and husky." He held out Ludwig's sturdy right arm. "Like a young oak tree."

"Good, good," said the captain heartily. "Sign him up. We'll put him to loading crates right away. Damn it all, I lost half my crew to the British." He turned back to the other men to complain.

Ludwig listened to the conversation, part in English, part in German, as the Dutch merchants arranged for shipment of their goods. The American seemed so informal, so easy, in talking either to the frock-coated wealthy Dutch merchants, or to himself in a dusty blue suit. Were all Americans so easy in manner?

The talking finished, the captain and first mate took Ludwig back to the ship, signed him on, and gave him a wooden bunk

13

in the hold. There wasn't much room for his big body and long legs, but Ludwig determined that nothing would bother him. At long last he was on his way!

Ludwig worked hard that week, watching the other sailors and imitating their ways. He caught on quickly, and they taught him well, as well as some other young Dutch and German boys who had signed on for the first time. They all learned how to handle the lines, how to climb to fix a mast, even to stand a watch.

The sailors found Ludwig dependable, always sober and obedient. Dindorf leaned on him more and more, explaining a sextant to him, the ways of the stars, and the importance of the wind. Dindorf explained that they must avoid British ships for fear of impressment of the seamen whom the British claimed were their own.

"The war is won," said Dindorf angrily, his brown eyes flashing. "But they will not admit it. Damn their arrogance! They will soon see how well we can get along without Mother England! Once free of their taxation and officials and soldiers tramping all over our streets, you'll see how we get along!"

The ship sailed. Ludwig was too busy pulling at lines and running about the deck to note the shoreline pulling away from them, until suddenly he realized the ship was rocking easily under him and the smell of salt in the air was stronger. The wind filled the sails, and he paused for a moment to stare upward, exultantly. The wind was blowing him away from the old country—and toward the new!

The sun burned hotly on him during the day, the cold wind bit into his bones at night. But Ludwig endured and even thrived on the ship. Dindorf was kind to him, a "good officer," said the men. Ludwig swabbed decks, threw out swill, helped to cook when others got seasick. His butcher training came in useful, as he cut slabs of beef skillfully and sawed the dried-beef chunks into pieces for cooking.

He would do any work the seamen asked, and with intelligence. No one had to tell him twice how to work, and the captain spoke of him to Dindorf. "Get him to sign on. We'll make a good sailor of him!"

But there Ludwig refused. He knew his life was not to be a sailor's. He was going to America to find adventure. What kind, he did not know, but he would find it, along with wealth and his most cherished goal—freedom.

He kept his ears open. Many of the passengers were men

14

of wealth. American, Dutch, German, even French, they talked freely to each other, these merchants and bankers. They spoke of their work, where money could be made, how to manage a company, what was the price of goods, what would happen now that the war was over.

Ludwig, often swabbing the decks near at hand, listened with all his attention. While waiting on tables for meals, patiently and in silence, he took in the free-flowing conversation. He heard better English and practiced it with the American sailors. He listened to their stories, and he listened to the businessmen, and he thought, and thought.

"Once the English are out of our country," said one American, "wait till the West opens up. There is opportunity! I've already made one trip out to the large lakes, and you should see the beaver, the wolves, the foxes. Furs, man! Enough to provide a beaver hat for every businessman in Europe!"

The other men laughed and teased him, but Ludwig stored away that imformation. Another man spoke of land. "The land is free now for the taking. Later on the government will want to keep control of it. All governments want to do this," he added in disgust. "A few wealthy men will get hold of the land, and others will be nothing but tenant farmers. If a man wants land, now is the time to take it! One day there will be none left."

How some of the others laughed! "None left!" one cried. "Why, there is all of the West, to the Mississippi River! Enough for every man for centuries to come!"

But others looked wise and shook their head. "Not with the way men are coming from Europe, men who want land. Be all snapped up," said one.

And Ludwig stored all he heard into his big blond head and tried to sort it out at night when he lay awake in his hard bunk. He listened to what they all said, the quiet ones and the noisy ones. By the time he reached New York, Ludwig could speak English fairly well, though with a heavy German accent. And he had a better idea of what he wanted to do with his life.

Chapter 2

The ship landed on a chilly autumn day. After shaking hands with the captain, Ludwig walked away from the ship with Roderick Dindorf. The first mate led him to a sailors' lodging house and helped him through the first formalities of being in a strange country.

"I'll see you again," he said cheerfully on parting. "And if you can't find a job you like, you'll sign on again with us. Right?" He laughed, patted Ludwig's big shoulder, and went off whistling.

Ludwig paid out one of his precious coins for a week's lodging, ate a hot meal, then set out at once to look for a job. He gazed in shop windows, walking further away from the docks. He did not want a job with a shipping firm.

As he walked further into New York City, he would often stop and stare. What an immense city! Buildings crowded against each other, and the streets were full of horses and carriages and people walking and stopping to talk to each other. What noise, what confusion! Several times he almost bumped into peddlers crying their wares, and when he saw carts set up with flowers in them, he thought at once of his mother with a pang of homesickness. But what amazed him most were the shops, their windows crammed with goods from all over the world.

He got lost and had to ask his way back to the dock, to his lodging house. He paid another coin for his dinner, and went to bed, soberly thinking that he must find a job soon, for the city was expensive.

He started out again the next day, in a different direction, to the north and west. He searched in every shop window, studying what goods they sold. He labored over every "position open" sign, and peered inside through glass windows to see what the work might be. Though he stopped in several places, some jobs had been filled and the others he did not want. He even passed several butcher shops, but he shook his head to himself. He had not come to the New World to begin the old work once more.

Then he saw it. "Position open." And it was in the window

of a music shop. He peered inside and saw silver flutes, horns, trumpets, bassoons.

He was ready. He had brushed his suit, cleaned his shoes, and wore fresh underclothing and a shirt he had washed the night before. Taking a deep breath, he opened the door and walked inside.

The clerk was tall and neat, with a long somber face. He attended to a customer, and Ludwig waited, listening with all his attention. The man was demonstrating how to play the bassoon to the customer, who was undecided. The stout woman finally shook her head and left.

The clerk then turned his attention to Ludwig.

"Yes, sir?" he asked, folding his hands and staring at the blond young man.

"I am asking about the position open," Ludwig replied, indicating the sign in the window.

The man's face tightened, and he frowned at Ludwig. "Any experience?" he barked.

"I can play the flute. I have played it all my life. Also I know something of other instruments—the bassoon, the oboe, the piccolo." Ludwig named them as he indicated them in the case.

"Ah," said the man, relaxing. He went to speak to a man in the back office.

Both men returned and talked with Ludwig. He took care to use his best English and spoke slowly, though his accent was thick. "You are German," noted the owner, nodding. "That is good. The Germans are a musical people."

The man had other fixed ideas, as Ludwig found out. He was hired only after he had demonstrated the instruments he could play. He worked six days a week, from nine to seven in the evening. Ludwig learned how to demonstrate the instruments and, just as important, how to show the customer how to play it. He learned little tricks of selling; how to find out who was going to play the instrument, and to insist on having that person be the one to play it in the store. And when the student was a child, Ludwig talked glowingly of the pleasures of being able to play music.

His life was now going well, but Ludwig found his situation to be not as pleasant as he would wish. The lodging was not clean, and it was very noisy. Sailors came in and out night and day, and the man who shared his room was not always discreet. He wanted to bring up a woman from time to time. Ludwig protested, in vain.

17

And he discovered that the wages barely paid for his living. He had little over. But when Ludwig talked to other men, they merely shrugged. Wages were good, they admitted, but expenses were high. "Get a job on a farm," they advised.

No, that was not for him. He kept searching. On Sundays he walked the wharves or in town. He noted that there was always one or more drunken Indians wandering about, with a fur or two or three on his arm. Curious, he paused to try to speak to one of them.

"Give money, get skin," said the Indian. He wavered before Ludwig. "Give money, give you skin." He held out one skin.

Ludwig noted the skin was fine and lustrous. He offered a small coin. The Indian seized it, thrust the skin into his hands, and lurched on down the street.

Ludwig took the skin back to the lodging with him. It was beautiful, and he brushed it, then scraped the hide a bit carefully with his knife, the way he had done in butcher shops. There they had often sold the leather when it was well cleaned.

He tucked the fur away in his locked suitcase. He bought another and another, giving coins for them. The Indians were usually drunk, and he felt sorry for them, strangers in the city, lurching about. Did they miss their freedom? Why did they come to New York? He wondered about them, but they never stopped to talk, only stared at him with somber black eyes if he tried longer speech with them.

He acquired a small pile of furs, and his suitcase was full. The room began to smell, and his roommate complained.

Ludwig walked further about town and finally noticed the sign he wanted. "Dealer in furs. Furs bought and sold. Inquire within. Franklin Baines."

Ludwig went inside. Though it was early morning, the shop was open. His eyes opened wide at sight of the bales and stacks of many furs, sorted by type and length.

A man came from the back room, alert bright green eyes studying Ludwig. "Yes, young man?" he asked briskly.

"I have some furs to sell," said Ludwig.

"Where are they? You get them from the woods? How far do you go?"

Ludwig was confused by the rapid-fire questions. Seeing his confusion, the man slowed down and asked his questions one at a time. Ludwig explained how he had bought his furs.

"Bring them in, and I'll have a look at them," promised the man.

Ludwig took him the full suitcase the next morning before going to work. Mr. Baines, laying them out on the work table, studied each one, brushing up the pelt, running his hands over the fur, studying the other side of them. Ludwig eagerly watched his face for a sign of what he thought.

"Not bad," he said finally. "You don't know how to treat furs, do you?"

He had asked in a kindly way, and Ludwig nodded ruefully. "You are correct. I used to work as a butcher in Germany. I do not know these furs."

"Hm. Well, I'll give you what they're worth to me. After this, don't brush them like that, brush up." And he showed how to do that. Ludwig watched keenly, but he could not take it all in, at once. The man's brisk movements were too fast, his speech rapid.

Ludwig bought more furs and brought them to Baines. Finally he took a part-time job with the man, arriving after his day's work at the musical-instrument store. Baines adored furs. His face would turn radiant, like that of Augustus Voss, as he talked of furs, of traveling into the woods and past the Great Lakes to buy them from the Indians. Lovingly he stroked the furs as he eagerly explained how to treat them, clean them, beat the dust from them, and how to present them beautifully, so they would bring in much more money.

Baines, a bachelor with no family, liked Ludwig. He admired his slow thoughtful thoroughness and the way he listened and learned.

Ludwig soon began coming to Mr. Baines's shop early in the morning, to work for an hour or two before his music-store job. The older man approved of his eagerness. When he had a new load of pelts, he let Ludwig work over them with him. Explaining the differences between the various furs, he showed him how to work with beaver, marten, fox, wolf and bear pelts.

In his eagerness to arrive early, Ludwig found a shortcut to the fur dealer's workshop. In doing so, he found that every day he went past a white two-story house with a sign for lodgers in the window.

If he went early enough, about seven-thirty, he would see a tall sturdy blond girl, who wore her hair in long braids almost to her waist. She would be clad in a white apron over a blue or a green or a rose challis dress, briskly scrubbing the front veranda, the porch steps, the walk before the house. She would take a pail of water and sprinkle water on the dusty road in front of the house and settle the dust. Then she would scrub the porch, sometimes going down on her knees.

He noticed that she had a sober pretty face, and she never looked at the men. If someone called at her, a fiery blush spread over her face, and she would duck down her head. She never looked up but kept scrubbing fiercely, and she would scurry inside the house with a bang of the white door.

Ludwig liked to watch for her, and he went early many a day to see her working and moving about. She was tall and graceful, and so blond that she looked German to him. But there was something about her that was different. She was not slyly watching for men. Her blue-green eyes were dreamy as she brushed at the front walk. Her arms were bare sometimes even in the chill morning, and she had round white graceful arms, a rounded sturdy body, and long legs.

One morning another, older woman was also on the veranda, her hands on her hips. The two spoke to each other. The older one said, "Agatha, I think we best let Mr. James go. I am sure he had a woman here with him last night."

Agatha looked up at the woman. Their faces were so alike they had to be mother and daughter, thought Ludwig, pausing in his walk as though to gaze admiringly at the flower bed of scarlet and yellow blossoms along the front walk. "I think so," she said slowly. "We can get another lodger soon, I am sure of it."

Ludwig walked on, his brain busy. Decent women, and alone. And nice, like his mother and sisters. And this seemed a quiet street. There were no noisy sailors rolling along it bellowing out their sailor songs in the middle of the night.

He went to the fur store, to work his two hours before his instrument-store job began. Mr. Baines had two more bales there, and the older man's tongue was as busy as his hands, as though the sight of the bales had set him off again to singing the praises of the fur trade.

"Ludwig, one day you must come with me on a fur-buying journey," he said with enthusiasm. After spreading out the first bale, he passed his hand lovingly on the thick bushy pelts. "One can never see such sights in the city! How beautiful are the forests! I have walked for many miles and never met anyone. The peace and stillness reaches to the soul."

"Did you never get lonely?" asked Ludwig curiously as he

opened the second bale and spread it out as Mr. Baines had the first.

"Lonely?" The other man laughed a little, as though to himself. "Ludwig, I have been lonelier in a crowd of fellows in a bar than ever in the wilderness! Nights I have sat beside a campfire, and sung to myself, and heard the sleepy birds echoing my songs so sweetly. I have heard the rustle of small animals and caught glimpses of their bright curious eyes. I have walked along streams of white swirling waters and watched the fish jumping, so thick one could reach in and pick out a fish and have it for dinner! And the Indians! One needs to know one tribe from another, for some are enemies of the whites, and others are friends of ours. I have found that fair treatment is remembered, and the good word about me must go from one tribe to another. For when I return, they are often kind and cordial, whether I have met that particular tribe before or not."

Ludwig urged him on eagerly, his mind thrilling to adventure. "And it is rugged traveling? Or are the roads easy?"

"Roads?" chuckled Mr. Baines, shaking his head even as he shook the pelt in his hands. "No, no, Ludwig! You cannot comprehend how the wilderness is! There are no roads there! Sometimes you find a short wagon path to a logging camp. Or the Indians have made a faint path through the thick forests. Mostly one walks where one can, along the rivers, the beach of a stream, or the edge of a lake. Sometimes I must walk a long way around a lake, or carry my goods for miles up a cliff and down again to avoid the thick dangerous rapids near a waterfall. But you always make your way through the forests, hoping to find the Indians, who will have pelts for sale."

"And do they always have the pelts?"

"No. Some sell their pelts to the men of the North, in Montreal. But further south and to the west of us, below the huge Great Lakes, there are other tribes who do not venture above the lakes. These tribes will sell to me what they have. The best time to take a pelt is after the first frost of the autumn," he went on, picking up another skin to examine it critically. "For the fur is then thickest on the animal which has not begun to get thin from the winter's cold and lack of food. Some animals sleep through the winter, and emerge in the spring, thin with poor furs so that they are almost worthless. Yes, yes, the best time is the autumn."

Franklin Baines could continue in that manner for hours, and Ludwig eventually came to hate the time when he must lay down his work, wash up, and run off to the musical-instrument shop. Much as he loved music, and enjoyed playing and demonstrating the instruments, he enjoyed Mr. Baines and handling the furs much more.

Mr. Baines had so many stories of his adventures through the years, the Indians he had met, the friends he had made in Canada among the fur-trade men, the disasters, the humorous episodes, that Ludwig wanted to go on and on listening.

But even as he showed an interest in the new land, his living arrangements were getting worse. On Saturday night the evening was rent with the yells of a fresh lot of sailors just off their ship. Ludwig tossed and turned, and just as he got off to sleep, healthily weary from his two jobs, another yell would burst out, along with laughter from the street, and songs. Again he would be awake.

By Sunday morning he was furious and determined. He went first to the Lutheran Church nearby, listened to the sermon in German, shook hands afterward, and went to eat at a restaurant. He waited a time, strolling along the streets, but finally ended up at about three o'clock in the afternoon at the house where the two blond women lived. He saw the sign in the window, and just below it was another sign, "One room available."

Firm footsteps sounded inside at his knock. The older lady came to the door. "Yes, sir?" she asked, in a slight German accent.

His hat came off his head, and as he spoke, he held it in his hands. "Madam, my name is Ludwig Gunther. I have come about the sign there. You have a room?"

She gave him a long keen look that lingered on his face and clean scrubbed hands. "Come in, Mr. Gunther," she invited him politely, showing him into a neat, clean-swept parlor with a stiff sofa and several chairs. In one corner was a pianoforte, and a harp stood nearby.

His heart fair jumped in his chest. Could they be musical as well as decent folks? It would be too great good fortune!

She indicated a chair. He sat down on the edge of it, placing his hat neatly on his knees. She sat down opposite him.

"You work, Mr. Gunther?" she asked politely.

"Yes, Mrs.—" he hesitated.

"Mrs. Colin Dindorf," she replied.

He stared. "Would you be related to Roderick Dindorf?" he asked bluntly.

Her blue-green eyes opened wide. "We are related, yes. He sent you?"

"Ach, nein, nein, gnadige Frau," he said, so excited he could not speak English. He explained quickly how he had met Roderick Dindorf on the wharf in Rotterdam, how he had sailed with him, and especially how good Roderick had been to him.

As he finished speaking, the tall girl came into the room. Ludwig jumped up and bowed.

"My daughter, Agatha," said Mrs. Dindorf. "Agatha, just think, your cousin Roderick brought him to America!"

They exclaimed over the coincidence, and sat down in friendly manner. As Ludwig spoke of his two jobs, they listened and approved. Quick glances were exchanged between the two ladies. He learned Mrs. Dindorf was a widow, Agatha her only child. The two managed the lodging house, taking in three lodgers, one for each of the upstairs bedrooms.

Mrs. Dindorf took Ludwig upstairs to view the room. "It is the smallest of the three," she said with apology.

He examined it, delighted. Though small, it would be his alone. It held a nice-sized bed, long enough for his long legs. There was a mirrored dresser and a table with pitcher and basin. A tall wardrobe for his clothes completed the furniture. There was no room for a chair, but a handmade rag rug decorated the scrubbed pine floor, and a quilt covered the white sheets. It was clean, neat, and quiet.

They agreed on terms, and he moved in that very day. He was most happy with his new circumstances. Mrs. Dindorf would give him breakfast every day in the week, with dinner added on Sundays. He would pay by the week, in advance. No ladies as guests, no loud singing at night, and the door was locked by midnight.

During the Sunday dinners, when there was time for conversation, Ludwig learned that Mrs. Dindorf had come to America from Germany at the age of twelve. She had married an Englishman, Colin Dindorf, related to Roderick Dindorf, and they had been most happy for several years, until his death in a carriage accident. The street had been icy, the horse had panicked, and he had been flung into the sea on the wharf. Being unable to swim, he had drowned. She had been left with Agatha, and the house.

He admired them both. They were honest, hardworking,

23

sober, church-attending ladies. Agatha had gone to school, a private school, as her mother had insisted on her having some education. She could read and write in English and German, as well as do sums. She kept the lodging-house books and did the shopping for meats, vegetables, flowers. Both took in sewing and did mending as well for the lodgers. For another small sum they would do the laundry for their guests as well.

Ludwig asked Agatha if she would help him with his English. They discussed the idea with her mother, and she agreed on the sum he would pay. So every Sunday afternoon Agatha would instruct him in English. He would read an article aloud, slowly, and she would correct his speech. Then he had to write down a composition explaining the meaning of the article. The work was long and sometimes difficult, but it taught him much. And it kept her in his company.

At Agatha's suggestion he would buy a paper twice a week and read it aloud to both ladies in the late evening, after he returned from his fur work. As they sat over their sewing, Agatha or Mrs. Dindorf would gently correct his pronunciation. They also talked about the news items, and from this he learned much about his new country.

Ludwig had never been so happy. He was coming to admire deeply the lovely Agatha. Serious and a hard worker, she was gentle and admirable in every way. Highly moral, she would not walk out with any young man. He must come to her house and sit in the stiff parlor on Sunday evening. Ludwig cleverly managed to be around at those times, innocently coming in to write a letter to his parents.

This had begun when Mrs. Dindorf discovered him sitting on his bed, awkwardly attempting to write a letter by holding a pad on his lap, with the inkstand on the windowsill.

"My dear Mr. Gunther, what do you do?"

He had jumped up and caught the inkstand just in time to prevent it tipping over on the scrubbed floor. "Mrs. Dindorf, I write to my parents," he said.

"But you have no lamp there, just the candle. And you cannot write well that way! Come to the parlor where you can use the table and the lamp."

He thanked her sincerely and went down to the parlor. It was ten o'clock, and Agatha was sewing on a dress for some lady. He bowed to her and apologized for disturbing her.

"You do not disturb me, Mr. Gunther," she said with her quiet smile that reminded him of his mother.

He sat down to scribble the letter, eagerly. It was to his mother and father, and he wished to reassure them of his safety and his happiness.

They waited until he was done. "You write to your parents often, Mr. Gunther?" asked Mrs. Dindorf approvingly.

"Once day a week," he said.

Agatha murmured a correction. "Once a week, Mr. Gunther, or else one day a week."

He repeated, "Once a week," and smiled and bowed to her. "And I also write to my old schoolmaster, Mr. Voss. It was he—him? who encouraged me to come to America."

He told them of his family, briefly, and then went upstairs to bed. Whenever he had a letter to write, which he made sure he would do every Sunday night, he would come to the parlor, with his inkstand, his paper and quill, and write away. If Agatha entertained a young man, he would turn his back discreetly, but make his quill scratch and mutter under his breath the words he was writing, so that they were disturbed.

He chuckled a little to himself. Was he falling in love? All he knew was that he resented these scrubbed, scowling young men who came to call on her.

Ludwig wrote the longest letters to his schoolmaster. He knew the older man would show the letters to Ludwig's mother, and she would keep silence about them, so his father did not know of it.

"Adventure!" he wrote one evening. "How marvelous a country is this! Mr. Baines has promised me that one time he will take me with him into the interior of America. There are such marvels to be seen. The silent woods, the dense forest where no tree has been cut ever. And the red-faced Indians creeping through the trees! They do no harm, if one does no harm to them and makes no threatening gestures. Mr. Baines is a kind man. They know him and do not menace him.

"Mr. Baines tells me of his life. He was an orphan boy but received a good education. When he was fourteen, he went to the forest with a trapper, who taught him much of the furs. He now teaches me how to trap, which I shall do one day. He teaches me to clean the pelts, to make sure they are scraped well, and how to prepare them for sale at the best prices. I could like this work the best of any in my life. And the profits!"

He hesitated, meditating. Should he tell them the full truth? He had been stunned and shocked when Mr. Baines finally showed him his books and accounts.

And Mr. Baines had said to him, "I want you to come with me, Ludwig, on my next journey. Should the pelts sell well in England, we shall go together, and purchase and carry twice as many pelts as I was able to the last journey! Consider giving up your job, and working for me full time! It will be well worth your time."

Ludwig considered the offer, and the fabulous amount of money it was possible to earn in the fur trade. Mr. Baines would buy a pelt for a few shillings at times. Then he would prepare it, clean it, shake it, dust it, fluff up the fur—and resell it for a hundred times the money he had paid for it! One hundred times! It was so incredible that Ludwig had not believed it at first.

But he saw the accounts, since Mr. Baines was frank with his pupil. "It is a good business," Ludwig wrote. "One can sell the pelts after preparing them for goodly sums. I think one day I may go entirely into this business."

He finished the letter, added his warmest greetings to all in the village, and ended, "May I thank my good schoolmaster once more, for his encouragement and advice? You were very good to tell me to come to this new country. For I truly think that here I shall make my fortune, as I never could in the old country. Would that you might come here, dear friend! How you would revel in the sights and sounds, the stories and opportunities of this great country! Thank you, thank you, dearest friend, for telling your pupil that he must go out into the world and make his fortune!"

He ended, sanded the letter, and folded it carefully. Tomorrow he would post it on his way to work. He smiled over it, thinking of the eagerness of Mr. Voss on receiving the letter, how he would read it again and again, how he would show it secretly to Ludwig's mother and eldest sister, how they would discuss it.

"You are happy over your letter, Mr. Gunther," said Agatha's soft voice behind him. He turned about in the chair and smiled at her. How pretty she was in the lamplight as she folded her sewing neatly.

"Yes, I write to my schoolmaster again. How he enjoys the letters. If only he might have come to the new country when he was young! His soul was made for adventure, and he encouraged many of us to set out and find what the world was made of."

"That must have been his delight," she said thoughtfully.

26

"Since he could not go himself, he would send out ships, like a merchant of rich spices, and find his pleasure in thinking of them in some foreign land."

He set his chin on his arm, gazing at her with peculiar pleasure and rapture. What a mind she had! And she was so good, her speech so beautiful. "Yes, that is how it is," he said at last, softly. "Your understanding of people is very deep, Miss Dindorf. Do you long for adventure?"

She blushed and shook her head. "No, I think I would be like your schoolmaster, Mr. Gunther," she said at last, her head bent. "I would not go out myself into foreign and frightening places. I like my home, my work, the streets where I am comfortable, the shops and my church and friends. But I would send forth many ships, full of spices and silks and rich goods, hoping to find that they give pleasure wherever they go."

Ludwig gazed at her again and again, until her mother came in and gently bade her to go to bed. He went upstairs himself, only to lie awake for a time, his arms under his head, gazing out the small window to the snow on the grass. It was winter, and at home his mother would be preparing for Christmas, thinking of her eldest son so far from home. The church would be preparing for the feast of Christmas, the decorations would be hung, the Christmas tree prepared.

Yet he had no longing now to go home, though he would have seen all his family and his friends eagerly. He felt comfortable here, in this white house, with the silence closed serenely about him, the snow softly falling outside, ice crystals on his window, a few lights from neighboring houses glimmering like orange stars. This was his new home, and he was falling in love with a fine lovely girl, and all the future looked bright and promising.

Chapter 3

Mr. Baines had sent a large load of furs with a merchant friend on a ship to England. With the furs he had included a load from Ludwig, furs he had purchased from Indians and sailors on the wharf. Ludwig's furs had made a respectable two bales, and he hardly dared hope how much he would receive for them.

After Christmas they began to wait eagerly for Mr. Baines's friend to return. And one cold snowy January day the front door blew open, and in strode a big man in a dark blue suit, with a thick overcoat of sealskin.

Mr. Baines held out his arms and embraced the man. They laughed and chattered together so fast in English that Ludwig could not understand them. It was time to go to the music shop, but he could not tear himself away.

"We shall have some coffee," said Mr. Baines and began to heat the pot of coffee he kept in his storeroom. He set out three cups and smiled at Ludwig and gave him a wink of his bright green eyes. "You will not go to work today, Ludwig? No, no, there is too much excitement."

Ludwig hesitated but could not resist. He had not missed one day of work so far, and it was a cold icy day. Surely not many customers would come to the music store today. "No, I must remain and hear the news," he said in his thick German accent.

The coffee was prepared, and they sat down to drink the thick dark brew. The other man talked on eagerly, about his voyage, the storms they had run into, the situation in London.

"Franklin, my friend," he said. "They beg for more furs. How they exclaimed over your pelts. Not only were the furs beautiful, but they were in such good condition, all ready to be made up into fine coats and beaver hats. And what a market there is for them in England and in all of Europe!"

They talked on through the morning and went to lunch together, the three of them. Ludwig scarcely said a word, intent on understanding their speech, their quick, excited words.

They returned to the store and got down to business. The merchant pulled out papers, and they went over the amounts. Mr. Baines gave Ludwig a beaming smile and a wink. Ludwig could scarcely contain himself to wait decently for word of what his furs had brought.

The merchant departed in the late afternoon. Baines lit another lamp and sat down at his desk. "Well, Ludwig, you are anxious to know how much money you receive, eh?" he drawled.

"Ach, ja, ja," sighed poor Ludwig with all the patience he could muster.

Baines handed him several sheets. "There are the statements, with listings. The martens, the beaver, and the fox are listed separately. The sum in English pounds is six hundred forty-three."

Ludwig stared at the papers in stunned silence. Was this a joke? He had paid not over ten or eleven pounds for the furs.

"It is not so good a profit as I would have hoped, but it is not bad," Mr. Baines continued, lighting his pipe. "The furs are not so good as those we can obtain directly from the Indians in the woods. My profits are closer to one thousand percent."

He grinned at Ludwig and showed his papers to him. Ludwig examined them, still unbelieving.

"But—but this is—a fortune," he gasped in a low tone as though the wind could hear him. "A fortune! I have never earned such in my life. It is—it is ten times what I would earn in the instrument store in a year!"

Mr. Baines nodded complacently. "Ludwig, by the time of my next trip you will give up that other job," he said. "You will come with me into the forests and return with a wagonload of furs! I will share with you one third of the profits. I have ordered many trade goods for the Indians, and you shall help me drive the wagon. We will take with us some iron pots, which they much prize, some thread, cloth, necklaces, mirrors, trinkets. I have many such goods from England and will go to the docks tomorrow and collect them. In the early spring we shall set out," he concluded and gave a decisive nod of his head.

Mr. Baines went with Ludwig to his bank to help him open an account. When they saw the amount of his receipts they were most cordial, and a young clerk bowed him out the door when their business was completed.

Ludwig went then to the instrument store, still dazed, and apologized for his absence that day. The owner was displeased, but very curious, because Ludwig was the kind to come early and remain late, and he was never, never absent, as the man said.

"What kept you, the icy street? Did you fall down?" he queried over and over.

"It was—most important business," said Ludwig soberly, and he went about dusting the shelves of the store to avoid more questions.

The next morning he went early to the wharves, found Mr. Baines, and helped him to claim the crates of goods he had ordered from England. He was especially curious about the iron pots.

Mr. Baines finished with the customs agent and helped Ludwig to load the goods onto a wagon from the warehouse. "Well, you see, Ludwig, the Indians must make their household goods slowly and painfully from whatever they can. They may make a pot from a hollowed-out log. They must buy at high prices any goods such as these. Their tomahawks are crudely fashioned from iron they dig from the earth and heat over a fire. Or they may pay a high price to buy one from the British."

"So—they think they have a bargain, do they?" asked Ludwig, trying out one of the new words he had learned.

"My dear fellow, they *do* have a bargain. We trade them what they cannot purchase because they have few coins. From them we receive what is cheap to them—the furs of animals they can trap. We are both satisfied, you see," said Mr. Baines, pushing a heavy crate onto the wagon and grunting as it finally settled. "It is fair. We trade to the other what each prizes."

Ludwig had much to think about that day as he went to work in the store. He was so excited, he was tempted to quit the job at once, but his sober German temperament was too practical for that. This might be a once-in-a-lifetime payment for furs he would never have again.

Troubled, he talked with Mrs. Dindorf and Agatha. Seeing their interest in him as a person, he went on to explain what his problem was.

"You see, I came to the New World for the great opportunities here. If I wanted a job to make a living, I would have remained in the butcher shop of my father and lived all my days in a village in Hess. But, I took the chance, I wanted the adventure, I came to America, not to be a dull stodgy fellow all my days. I wish to make a fortune," he said earnestly, twisting his big thick fingers together. "I do not wish to live lavishly, I do not wish to cheat anyone. But a fortune is in the Colonies; it is a new bright world. Shall I take chances? Shall I go out into the wild wilderness, and risk my life, my all?"

Agatha listened soberly, but said nothing, deferring to her mother. Mrs. Dindorf listened, sighed a bit, then said, "Mr. Gunther, nobody can make up your mind for you. Nobody can tell you, do this, do that, it will come right for you. Am I a teller of fortunes? Am I a gypsy? No, no. But I will say this. I have known you for some months. And what you say you will do, you do. You have determination and courage. Also you are not reckless, you do not take foolish wild chances."

She paused and looked down at her sewing as though not seeing the neat stitches.

"Such wild young men come about here," she continued in a low tone. "Such stories they say. They will dig for gold, they will make a fortune, they will live on champagne and oysters, and marry the beautiful girls, and be happy forever. Do I know anybody who is happy forever? I do not. They talk wildly, and do nothing. They run about, telling stories to themselves, and achieve nothing. But you are not like this, I am thinking. You are sober, conscientious, you have feelings for people."

Ludwig listened with puzzled brow, feeling as though she took him apart and put him back together again. He studied her face anxiously. Could she see into the future for him?

She half smiled. "Mr. Gunther, you will make up your own mind, I think," she said gently. "You remind me of our cousin, Roderick. He comes here and talks to me and to Agatha. 'Shall I go out,' he asks? 'Shall I take this risky voyage?' And always he answers his own questions. 'Yes, I shall go,' he says." She nodded her head. "You talk aloud, to hear what your head will say to you. That is good. I am glad to listen, and so is Agatha. You will talk to us all you wish, and we will listen. But we cannot say to you, this is right or this is wrong. It is your mind that will tell it to you."

Agatha smiled at the puzzled face of the big German. "Mama is right," she said gently. "You will find the answer for yourself. However, you will talk to us, and we will say nothing to anybody of what you say. It is your decision."

"I thank you very much for listening," he said politely. He was not at all sure what had happened. Yet he felt better.

As the winter wore on, the winds blew everlastingly across New York City, from one side to the other and back again. The raw winds made him bundle his woolen scarf more closely about his throat and bend his fur hat to the gusts of snow. But one day the ice in the rivers melted, and the ships began to go out once more without the little tugs making such an effort.

Mr. Baines began to load up his wagon with iron pots, mirrors, bolts of cotton and woolen cloth, blankets of gay stripes, iron knives, even tomahawks, and needles and pins.

"Well, Ludwig, are you coming with me?" he asked one day. "I will leave next Monday. Monday is a good day to go. I pray in church on Sunday, for a safe and prosperous journey, and on Monday I set out."

As spring had come on, the adventurous sap had seemed to rise in Ludwig's veins, like life-giving fluid in a tree. He nodded and said simply, as though he had not agonized over the decision, "I will come with you, Mr. Baines. I am grateful for the opportunity. Thank you."

And that day he told his employer at the instrument store that he would come in for the last time that Saturday, and then no more.

"But why? Do you wish a higher wage?" The owner was willing to pay more, now that he was losing Ludwig.

Ludwig thanked him politely for his kindness and merely added, "I am going on a long journey. I do not know when I shall return. You had best hire another clerk."

The Dindorfs were not surprised. They nodded placidly, though there was an excited, tense look about Agatha. He paid them ahead for two months for his room, begging them to keep it for him.

"I could not bear it, not to return to your home and your hospitality. You have been more than friends to me," he said with more emotion than he usually showed. His blue gaze went to Agatha anxiously.

"We will keep your room for you, no matter how long you are gone," Mrs. Dindorf assured him. "When do you depart?"

"On Monday," he said and drew a deep scared breath. He was excited, yet hot with anxiety. Thrilled, yet terrified, he knew that this was the opportunity of a lifetime.

It was for such a chance that he had left home, family, friends, his own village. It was for this that he had dared to cross an ocean, knowing nobody at all. It was for this that he had worked and dreamed. But now that the opportunity had come, it was scary.

The Dindorfs and Ludwig went to the German church on Sunday and sat together in the pew. The minister preached on the journeys of Paul, and to Ludwig it was a significant sermon, a symbol. Agatha thought so also and touched his hand at several moments.

And on Monday morning, early, Ludwig set out. He had taken Mr. Baines's advice and gone shopping with him in the stores of lower New York. Now he wore rough clothes, a woolen shirt and underwear, thick woolen trousers, stout boots, a thick mackinaw, and a fur cap on the thick blond hair. It was hot as he stood in the hallway of the Dindorf home and received Mrs. Dindorf's solemn blessing.

Agatha added a word of her own. "Be safe and careful, Mr. Gunther," she said and put her sturdy strong hand on his. He pressed it hard and muttered his thanks.

Then he went out into the cold winter air. The ice had broken on the Hudson River, and word had come that the Indians were stirring. It was time to go.

They drove the wagon as far as they could go, then ferried it across the river into New Jersey. Once on the wagon road to the north, they settled down to a routine.

Mr. Baines would drive for several hours. Then they would stop, get down, prepare coffee, water the horses at a stream, relax and smoke a pipe, then proceed. Ludwig would now drive for a time, as Mr. Baines watched alertly for the slight signs of the road he knew so well from his travels.

They always stopped at nightfall, near a stream or lake, or near the farmhouse of a friend. They would make a campfire, cook a hot meal, drink coffee, talk, and go to sleep early. No need to keep watch yet, said Mr. Baines, not until they came to the great St. Lawrence River.

It was more like winter again as they drove north. Some smaller streams were blocked with ice, and few canoes were seen. One day in mid-March they finally came to the great river, and Ludwig had his first sight of canoes filled with Indians, all going toward Montreal.

"This is nothing. Most of the Indians come from the West," said Mr. Baines, smiling at Ludwig's awe and excitement. But nevertheless they stopped their wagon and bargained a time for trade goods against furs.

They drove on, turning away from the river. "The British in Canada resent us," Mr. Baines told him. "They will prevent us from trading with the Indians, if they can stop us. So—we drive to the south, out of their sight, and in American territory."

"But they come south to our land," said Ludwig, already identifying with Americans.

"Aye, they do. But they think it is still their land. They believe Mother England will protect their rights to the lands around the Great Lakes," said Mr. Baines.

On they drove, day after day, and came at last into forests so thick one could not see an end to them. There was no break in the woods that Ludwig could see. Mr. Baines patiently pointed out the faint trail and showed where he could drive in and out of the trees where the trail was wide enough for the wagon.

"There is a tribe near," he said suddenly and pulled into a clearing. "Ludwig, take the rifle and your pistol and stay near the dark trees. I will wait and see if they are friendly or not."

Ludwig's heart thumped in his chest so loudly it sounded like a drum. He obeyed his mentor at once, and stood to one side, while out of the woods came one Indian, then another, then a dozen! They came so silently, on deerskin moccasins, painted, with few clothes on them, all indifferent to the cold. They did have blankets slung about their bronzed shoulders, and some wore deerskin trousers. The paint around their eyes made them seem strange, their black eyes piercing. They caught sight of Ludwig, and scowled, pausing. He was a stranger to them.

Mr. Baines greeted them in a friendly manner and pointed to the campfire. Several came to the fire and sank down with him on the ground, greedy eyes gazing toward the loaded wagon.

After a time others came to sit. Mr. Baines motioned to Ludwig to join them and elaborately introduced him as a friend.

Ludwig sat down, rifle at hand. He was so intent on listening to Mr. Baines and his slow speech with them, that he paid no attention to the Indian stealing up behind him. Mr. Baines said sharply, "No, not the rifle. Ludwig, take the rifle!"

Startled, Ludwig turned about, just in time to see the Indian behind him putting his hand on the rifle. Ludwig grabbed the rifle just before the Indian could get a firm grip on it. The Indians muttered in a guttural fashion and scowled at both the white men. Hands went to the tomahawks and knives in their leather belts.

Mr. Baines spoke soothingly. "We come to trade, not to fight. But we not trade our weapons. We need them against *bad* Indians, and also wolves and bears."

They finally calmed down. Mr. Baines got out several iron pots, their eyes glistened. One Indian, taller and more stately than the others, motioned. Several Indians went back into the woods and returned, lugging great bundles of pelts.

Then the bargaining began. The pelts were spread out, examined and criticized. The iron pots were set out, along with some knives, some thread, a couple of mirrors, and several cheap necklaces. A bargain was finally struck about midnight, and Ludwig began to feel more and more tense.

But Mr. Baines was satisfied, relaxing and smiling. The men prepared food, dried meat, coffee, some dried beans, and one Indian did some cooking in a new iron pot, grunting to show his satisfaction.

Then as they drank their coffee and settled down to the satisfaction of full stomachs and a good bargain, one of the Indians caught sight of Ludwig's silver flute. He had stuck it into his pack at the last minute, not quite knowing why, but it was light, and he liked to play it.

"What that?" the Indian demanded.

"Music," said Mr. Baines. "Play for them, Ludwig."

"They like my kind of music?" asked Ludwig.

Mr. Baines shrugged. "Can't tell till you try."

So Ludwig drew out the flute and put it to his lips. He tried a few tentative notes, then began to play a lilting German folk dance. The Indians sat and listened, all eyes and ears, some grinning with pleasure.

When he had finished, they said, "More play! More music!"

So he played again, and again, the German songs he knew, and an American one he had picked up in the music store. He played for almost an hour, while his eyelids began to close in sleep.

Some of the Indians had curled up at the campfire and lay sleepily to listen. One slept, frankly snoring on his back.

"Enough," said Mr. Baines softly, and Ludwig nodded, and put away the flute, and took care to keep his rifle with him as he lay down to sleep.

In the morning he wakened to find the Indians had crept away with their trade goods. He and Mr. Baines were left with two great packs of furs. Mr. Baines beamed with satisfaction.

"You did well, Ludwig," he said, and Ludwig glowed.

They drove on into the forests and had to drag and push the wagon up and down hills, then even a small mountain. Ludwig grew bronzed and dark in the sunlight as the spring came on. They met more Indians, made more trade, and acquired five more packs of soft beautiful lustrous pelts.

And each night Ludwig played his flute, sometimes for the Indians, sometimes just for himself and Mr. Baines. It was a pleasure and a satisfaction, soothing to the tense nerves after a session of trading.

What an adventure! Mentally he composed letters to Mr. Voss describing what they had done and seen. They trudged through thick glades, where the pine needles made the ground soft and difficult for the wagon to pass over. The horses pulled and strained at the heavy wagon. They pressed on, as Mr. Baines was reluctant to turn back.

"This trip, I will go on until we have traded all our goods," he bragged in excitement. "It will be the best journey ever!"

They did go on to the Great Lakes, and traded the last of their goods. Then finally, reluctantly, they turned back. Being late spring, the rains came, and many a time the wagon sank into mud. But their sturdy shoulders and the pulling of the horses drew out the wagon again, until the next bog.

It became increasingly difficult to sleep at night. The ground was often wet and soggy, the mosquitoes bothersome. Ludwig was bit and stung until his skin was a maze of cuts and scratches. Mr. Baines was more immune, having made this journey so often. But he too felt the many stings.

They approached the great St. Lawrence River again. This time the trees were green and fresh, rather than gray and winter-laden with snows and ice. Wildflowers grew in the shadows of the trees and bushes, and some bushes were covered with flowered boughs. Some were so fragrant that one could smell tham over the keen raw smell of the fur pelts.

Ludwig liked then to get off the wagon and walk alongside it, pausing to gaze intently at the flowers, to study the bushes, to lift up his face to the vivid blue sky and the fluffy pattern of white clouds. This country was so beautiful! And he often did not see a single person from day to day, but for an occasional settler in a crude log cabin.

"One day soon, all these places will be full of people," said Mr. Baines from the wagon seat. "There will be great towns here," he predicted, indicating a small crude settlement down in the valley near the river. "That is a good location, on the river. Many ships will come from the oceans, and Indians will come to trade on our side of the river, not only the Canadian side. Yes, many people will come."

Ludwig listened and asked questions and kept everything in his head, sorting and thinking and storing the information. Mr. Baines was good to him, imparting information, and advising, and teaching him without seeming to do more than casually talk.

Toward evening they were growing weary, when the horses stumbled, and went to their knees. "Damn it all," said Mr. Baines, hastily getting down from the wagon.

"What is it?"

"Bogs, hidden by bushes," said Mr. Baines briefly. "Help unload the wagon."

They began to unload, but the horses sank deeper, along with the wagon, into the hidden stream that flowed full under the deceptive marsh flowers and bushes. They tugged and pulled at the reins, but the horses neighed and sank deeper as they struggled in terror.

The two men were so intent on their task that the small band of brightly dressed men were upon them in the dusk before they saw them approach.

"Hey, there! You, what is the trouble?" cried one man in a thick accent that Ludwig could not place.

Ludwig turned about, startled that they had come up so quietly, where nobody had been. He stared at the scarlet-clad men, their fur hats with tails falling to their broad shoulders. They were not Indians. They had red hair or brown hair, though their faces were as bronzed as those of Indians.

Mr. Baines had a strange look on his face. He said, graciously enough, "We are caught in this bog. If you will aid us, we would be most grateful."

He was more formal than usual, not his usual friendly self. The men laughed and said something to each other in some foreign tongue, then spoke English to Ludwig and Mr. Baines.

"We'll unload ye, then see about the wagon. Poor horses! Half-mad with terror," said their leader who waded into the stream in spite of his moccasins and long leather breeches. He lifted out one pack with his strong long arms and tossed it to a fellow who caught it and waded to firm land to set it down.

Mr. Baines kept watching them, so intently he scarcely helped unload the wagon. But finally the wagon was unloaded, and the men unhitched the frantic horses and pulled the wagon to ground.

Two of the eight men were holding the horses, soothing them with hand and voice, until they could be rescued also. Then they led them to dry land, urging them, cajoling them with soft speech, and patting their sturdy backs.

37

"There—all set now," said the leader and grinned at them. It was totally dark now, and they could scarcely see each other's faces. "Come to my cabin, it is not far from here. You'll need to get dry. It's too cold to sit about on wet ground with soaking garments."

Mr. Baines hesitated, to Ludwig's further amazement. Then he finally accepted. Each of the scarlet-clad fellows lifted a heavy pack to his bronzed hard shoulders and carried it off. They all followed, with Ludwig in charge of one horse, and the leader of the men with the other.

"My name is MacCameron," said the tall, red-haired fellow. "Blaise Bruce MacCameron, late of Scotland. And what would be your name, my lad?"

The man was not much older than Ludwig himself, but he was bigger, sturdier, and a definite leader of men. Ludwig offered his hand. "My name is Ludwig Gunther, late of Germany," he said, copying the speech.

"Oh, aye? Germany? Far from home, ye are," said the man. "I'll warrant you came to America to make your fortune," and he laughed softly. "Aye, weel, so did we, to Canada to make our fortunes. 'Tis a merry and bountiful land."

"Yes, it is, a strangely beautiful land, and full of plenty," said Ludwig soberly.

They talked a bit as they walked across the boggy marshy land, until they came to a small cabin. The door opened, and there stood an Indian girl in buckskin, with long black shiny hair down her back. MacCameron came up to her, let the horse go, and hugged her. Ludwig watched in awe and disgust. Was she his *wife*? Was he one of those fellows who had taken an Indian girl to wife?

There was not room for all of them in the small cabin. The Indian girl gave them hot soup, fresh bread, and cheese, and then hung out their garments to dry while they crawled into blankets to sleep.

There was a small lean-to beside the cabin. MacCameron slept there with the girl, and in the night Ludwig, lying against the wall of the main room, heard giggling and movements that told what they were doing.

In the morning, early the men were up. The Indian girl came to fix breakfast for them, ham slices cooked over the fire, hot coffee, and more fresh bread.

One of the men had brushed down the horses, and they looked fine as ever, free of the mud. They hitched up the horses for Mr. Baines. Then out came the huge packs of pelts. Mr. Baines and Ludwig helped load the packs onto the wagon, and Ludwig counted them silently. One, two, four, eight, ten, eleven. Yes, they were all there.

"You'll come to Montreal one day," said MacCameron as they stood ready to depart. "My wife and me will be happy to welcome you. She gave me my first son last year," he told them, his bronzed face lighting up.

Ludwig looked involuntarily at the Indian girl. Her face was downcast, and she seemed to droop.

MacCameron laughed and gave her a squeeze. "Not this girl! She ain't my wife! My wife is a French girl, Yolanda by name, and my son is named Etienne! He's a fine lad, and he'll be a big man one day, with red hair and blue eyes! Just like me!"

The Indian girl turned away and entered the cabin. MacCameron gave them his address in Montreal, adding, "It's near the Catholic cathedral. Ask anybody where MacCameron lives! And I'll welcome ye, American fur men though you be!" And he boomed his laugh after them.

"Thank you for your aid," said Mr. Baines soberly. "I will not forget it."

They set out and went on about three miles. Then Mr. Baines pulled the wagon to a stop and got down. His face was grim. He motioned to Ludwig, and they pulled down a pack of furs.

Ludwig could not contain his curiosity. "What are we doing, Mr. Baines?" he asked as they began to open the first pack.

"Those were Canadian fur traders, our rivals, Ludwig," said Mr. Baines with a sigh. "I did not want to stop the night with them, with the pelts outside in the wagon. But to question them or refuse them would have made them furious. But now we shall see if they be honest men or no." And he opened the fur pack.

They went over one pack and another, Mr. Baines examining each pack with care. At the end of it, eleven packs worth, he said sheepishly, "There, now, I am ashamed of myself! All in order and not touched, not a one of them. They were honest men, or at least MacCameron was. He must not have let them touch the packs."

"And they might have?" asked Ludwig in amazement. "They seemed so friendly."

"They laughed at us," said Mr. Baines ruefully. "I knew

39

it, and it worried me. Now I realize they laughed because I worried. MacCameron had passed the word not to take our skins. He must be an honest man, for all he has taken an Indian squaw. Well, now I know I can trust him. Let us be on our way."

Ludwig helped load the last of the packs and got up with him on the wagon seat. The ground was firming, away from the river, and into the forests. They drove on, for it would be a long drive yet of another two weeks back to New York City.

Ludwig looked at the thick huge trees, never cut by man, at the dainty wildflowers never seen before by any except wild Indians. He gazed at the rivers and streams, where no log cabin stood. And his heart was full of wonder at the scenes. He had come into the wilderness, a little afraid, wondering, and yet the wilderness had been good to him. He had met wild Indians, and not been very afraid. He had traded with them, as well as played the flute for them. And he had met some of the wild teasing adventurous Canadians, and been their guest, and perhaps made a friend of one of them. A Scotsman! A squaw man, who bragged of his French wife and his new son in Montreal!

He could like the man. Yet . . . the Indian girl had smelled of grease and something wild. So had MacCameron, thought Ludwig. Yet he had kindly worked hard, he and his men, and gotten their wagon and horses out of the swamp, and asked not a penny for it! And as Mr. Baines said, he must be honest, for he had not taken their furs, while he had them at his mercy.

"A strange new world, eh, Ludwig?" asked Mr. Baines presently.

"That it is," said Ludwig, nodding his head. "A world of riches, and wild beauty, terrible beauty in which one must take care. I would not have missed this experience for any pot of gold in the world!"

Mr. Baines laughed heartily and slapped Ludwig on the knee. "Aye, you're bitten with it!" he said. "The adventure of it, the wild lands, the Indians, the animals, the men who are wilder than any in the cities! And look at that sky, Ludwig, and the land before us! From one end to the other, it is all new earth. Those trees are virgin timber. No plow has ever cut this earth. But one hundred years from now, mark my words, it will all be plowed, and cabins and houses will sit there beside the road where we ride alone. Mark my words. It will be true."

Chapter 4

Ludwig Gunther and his employer arrived back in New York City the third week of May, 1784. They had bathed in a stream the night before, but their clothes stank of the wild scent of animals, their own perspiration, and weeks of living in mud.

They went first to the warehouse and unloaded the eleven packs of furs. Mr. Baines locked them securely away, grinned, and said, "Now I shall go home and take a long bath! You come tomorrow, Ludwig, when you wish. We will start to clean and brush the furs. I think I must go to England myself this year."

Ludwig walked "home" to the Dindorf house, and never had he felt so anxious to be somewhere. He walked in the door. Mrs. Dindorf started up, staring at the dark-faced man in the muddy filthy ragged clothes, and seemed about to cry out.

Agatha was gazing at him with shining blue-green eyes. "It is Ludwig!" she cried out. "Mama, Ludwig has come home!"

And she was laughing while a tear spilled down her cheek. Ludwig beamed at her, so happy he could scarcely speak. Mrs. Dindorf bustled about.

"Your room, it is ready!" she said. "We kept it clean and neat. Agatha thought surely you would come home soon!"

"Ah, it is good to be home," sighed Ludwig. "Aye, but I am not fit to go into a clean room! So filthy am I!" he added ruefully, looking down at himself.

"Agatha, heat the kettles. Mr. Gunther, you shall have a bath in the big tub tonight. Leave your clothes on the floor. Tomorrow we shall scrub and cleanse them in the sunshine!"

The two ladies hurried about. Ludwig sang in the big tin tub in the room set aside for bathing on the first floor. Usually only the ladies used it, since for the men it was enough to have a basin and a pitcher of hot water each morning. How good to sit in a tub, and scrub away at his filthy body! To be clean and sweet smelling again!

Mrs. Dindorf tapped on the door and called through the panels. "Mr. Gunther, I leave here some salve for the bites! Use all you wish!"

"I thank you heartily!" he called back, smiling with pleasure. How good they were to him, and, most important, Agatha's blue-green eyes had smiled at him, and she had called him by his first name, like a true friend! He hummed and sang and splashed in the tub for half an hour, before dragging himself reluctantly from the cooling water.

He rubbed the ointment all over his bronzed face. How soothing it was, to cover the mean bites of mosquitoes and other insects. He used it on his shoulders, his body, his thighs and legs, grimacing at the amount of ugly bites on his body. He had been well bit.

He dressed in fresh clothing for the first time in almost three months. He came out, to find Agatha preparing a place at the kitchen table for him. Hot soup steamed on the stove, and there was fresh bread, real butter, a glass of chilled milk and a plate of cheese and cured ham.

"For me?" he asked, unbelieving. She smiled shyly at him and nodded.

"You must be hungry, Mr. Gunther," she said primly, her cheeks flushed with happiness. Her eyes sparkled so, he could scarcely take his gaze from her.

He sat down to eat, thanking them. They sat with him, and waited eagerly for what he would say. He managed to tell them something of what had happened, between bites of the delicious food. They gazed and gazed, as though not to miss an expression, a word, a tone.

"It was such a marvel," he concluded, pushing himself back from the table, and wiping his mouth carefully with the napkin. "Never did I see such forests, such skies, such wild beasts, Indians, the Scots and Canadians. I cannot believe yet that I saw all that I have seen."

The two ladies sighed with satisfaction. "You will tell us more another day," said Mrs. Dindorf with a sharp nod of her graying head. "Tonight you will go to bed early and rest. You must be most weary."

Oddly he found it difficult to get to sleep. The warm little room was stifling after the wide outdoors with the sky his roof. He finally slept, to waken late in the morning. Birds were singing in the nearby trees. Light shone into his bedroom window, and he heard Agatha singing outdoors.

Curious, he rose and peered out the window, to see Agatha busily pegging his rough clothes to the line. She had them in a basket at her side, and as he watched, he saw her shake them out, lift his trousers to the line, and peg them. Then she hung his thick shirts that had been so stiff with mud and sweat. She had been up early, washing his clothes.

He gazed down at her, the golden head in the sunlight, the lithe movements of her sturdy body. Love welled up in him. He loved her, he knew it now. How her eyes had shone when he returned! And he had felt as delighted to see her as though he had been gone a hundred years!

Could he offer to marry her soon? He sat down soberly on the edge of the bed and thought. He frowned. He had no idea what the furs might bring. And could he count on this job? Mr. Baines had been kind to him. But he could not lean on Mr. Baines forever. No, he must find a way to be self-sufficient, to be able to go out for the furs, and trade for them— by himself!

And soon, he thought. Agatha was too beautiful, too fine, for her to remain unmarried many more years. He had no time to waste!

He washed and dressed and went down to breakfast in the kitchen. Late though it was, the coffee pot was boiling, the eggs and ham sizzling in the pan. Mrs. Dindorf prepared a plate for him and patted his wide shoulders like a mother as she put his coffee cup beside him.

Agatha came in and blushed at his long look. It was difficult to leave her that morning, with words unsaid. But he had not yet the right to say anything. He was a man with a job of such uncertainty, and no family nearby. No, he must have more to offer her than he had at present.

He went to the warehouse, where Mr. Baines was already working on the furs, opening the packs, smoothing his hand lovingly over the rich lustrous chestnut-brown fur of beaver, the smaller chestnut of the muskrat, the silky rich dark fur of the Canadian sable, or marten, and the fine dark brown of the mink. There was also red fox, black fox, and even several pelts of the silver fox, which Mr. Baines handled reverently.

"This one comes from the far north," he explained. "In the winter they are very silvery and bring a high price."

He talked about the furs to Ludwig, explained where each probably came from, and what kind of money each brought as they brushed and shook the furs, hanging some outside to blow in the fresh May wind. They worked all that day, and for days to come, hurrying, because Mr. Baines had booked passage on a ship to Europe in mid-June.

43

Then on Sunday evening Ludwig had a great shock. He had brought his quill pen downstairs, and his pad of paper, to write to his parents and to Mr. Voss. He had not written for months, and they would be anxious.

And in the small neat parlor he found a man—Roderick Dindorf! He was seated across from Agatha as though he belonged there.

Ludwig gazed in shock at the man. He wore a smart blue uniform, new by the looks of it, the uniform of a first mate. Dindorf beamed at him, his brown eyes sparkling. He was so handsome, so rugged looking and tanned from the long sea voyage.

"Well, my old friend, Ludwig Gunther!" he said heartily, standing to hold out his hand. "I have just returned from a long journey to England and Italy. And you—I understand you have but returned from a fur trip to the Great Lakes!"

"Yes, just returned," said Ludwig. Agatha was sitting on the thick plush sofa, wearing a lovely long blue gown with white lace demurely in a fichu about her beautiful white throat. Were they courting? Ludwig could not believe it. He stared from one to the other.

After the amenities were said, and they had exchanged news, Roderick sat down, this time beside Agatha, and turned to her, speaking in a low tone. He said something that brought a blush to her cheeks. Mrs. Dindorf was not there, and Ludwig assumed that she must be in her own little sitting room at the back of the house.

Ludwig sat down at the table, in a daze, his back to them, politely. But he could scarcely concentrate on his writing. His mind was awhirl.

Agatha's soft laugh went through him like a bullet. Roderick laughed also and said something else in a low tone.

But they were cousins! Ludwig thought about that, his hand pausing in the writing. He stared at the lamp until he had to blink. They were second cousins, he thought. He must ask Mrs. Dindorf, oh, so very casually, about that.

Second cousins were allowed to marry in America.

Oh, Lord!

And he liked Roderick Dindorf, but not as a rival! The man was tall, handsome, a fine fellow, generous, good—

But not if he took Agatha from him!

All the more need for haste, thought Ludwig, and bent his attention again to the letter. So disturbed was he that his words scarcely made sense. He read them over, frowning. Perhaps his parents and Mr. Voss would think it was his excitement over the adventurous journey.

He managed to remain until Roderick reluctantly departed about eleven o'clock. Agatha saw him to the door, and they were alone in the dark hallway, for quite five minutes, thought Ludwig gloomily. He sanded his letter and folded it.

On her way to the back parlor, Agatha stopped for a moment. "Mr. Gunther, you will put out the lamp and lock the front door?" she smiled.

"Yes, Miss Agatha," he said quietly.

"Good night, then, Mr. Gunther."

"Good night, Miss Agatha."

She had called him Ludwig on the evening of his return!

He went upstairs to bed, having seen all doors locked and the downstairs windows securely bolted. They had but one lodger now beside himself, an elderly man who retired early. The sign was out for another lodger.

Roderick Dindorf seemed to be about all summer. He had signed on another ship, but it did not depart until September, for the Orient this time. His brown eyes shone as he told the Dindorfs and Ludwig about the upcoming trip over Sunday dinner. He seemed to come more and more often, and Ludwig was worried.

How did a man start to court a girl, when she was courting with another man?

Mr. Baines went off to Europe, in mid-June as planned. Ludwig went about New York, bargaining for some furs with Indians, but they seemed a poor lot now that he had seen rich full shiny pelts from deep in the forests. He kept the warehouse clean and neat, brushed and hung out the pelts they had acquired, and took care of two bundles which a man sold to them. He worked conscientiously from morning to night, six days a week, until the hour of six came, and he felt free to lock up and go.

Then he would go out to a nearby restaurant, eat the food offered on the blackboard menu, usually ham or pork or bacon or beef, potatoes boiled or fried, greens fried in pork, with some peaches or plums for dessert. He walked the streets afterwards, thinking and planning.

His mind was always busy. He read the journals, by himself now, for Agatha had said firmly that he did very well and needed no more lessons. He missed the instrument store but

45

would not go back to it. He played his flute softly in his room, and at times if he returned home early, he would hear Agatha playing the harp or the pianoforte in the little parlor.

He was lonely, and he was love-sick. He wanted a wife, he wanted Agatha smiling at him in the lamplight. But he did not yet feel secure enough to offer her his future.

Mr. Baines returned in August, beaming and happy. He had sold their fine furs for the highest price yet, and Ludwig deposited the biggest check he had ever seen made out in his name.

Then he told Mr. Baines his plan. "I would go out alone this autumn," he said. "Just at the time of the first frost, when the animals have fine pelts. If I am fortunate, I may be able to buy them from the Indians early, and get some fine ones. Will you allow me to purchase from you some iron pots, some knives, and such, and go alone?"

Mr. Baines studied his young assistant thoughtfully. "Ludwig, why do you wish to go alone? You have gone only once, the country is new to you. Why not wait until spring, and we will take the wagon? The backpack is very heavy."

"I wish to prove myself," said Ludwig. "Mr. Baines, I wish to marry. Until I can go alone, and prove to myself that I can manage alone, I cannot marry."

"Ah—marriage," said Mr. Baines, a shadow on his face. He took off the small spectacles he used for doing accounts and rubbed them briskly on his shirt. "To marry," he said.

"Yes. There is a fine girl—but I do not deserve her—not until I can support her. I must prove to myself and to her mother, that I am not a wild fellow, that I am dependable."

Ludwig was worried about his main rival, Roderick Dindorf. The man was fine, handsome, dependable, yet a sailor who loved the sea. Though he was gone for months, sometimes a year at a time, Ludwig knew that Agatha was the faithful kind. Had she promised to wait for him? It was a big concern for Ludwig.

He did not want to risk losing Agatha to Roderick. He must speak to her, yet he could not ask for her hand in marriage until he had more to offer, a more certain future. Yet—if he waited too long, she might become engaged to Roderick, or one of the other young men who hung about her hopefully.

His thoughts were interrupted by Mr. Baines.

"Ah," sighed the older man. "Well, Ludwig, you shall do it. But take care. At this time of year storms may come up out of the blue sky. This is the season of sudden heavy rains and winds that can blow a man to the earth. Worse, they can blow a heavy tree right down on you. I remember one year, the winds howled for many days, and nights, and I was soaked and sick. If you should see such a wind, creep into the fallen logs and make a shelter from the wind and rain, and hide there until the storms are gone. Or seek shelter from Indians, or those in cabins."

Plainly anxious about Ludwig, he gave him much advice. Ludwig prepared a backpack and insisted on paying for everything, the knives, mirrors, cloth, blankets. And he took with him metal coins, knowing the Indians would accept them greedily for their pelts. He decided against taking iron pots, since they were too heavy.

Roderick Dindorf departed on his own long journey. He would be gone perhaps a year, certainly over the winter. Ludwig waited until he had left, then spoke quietly to Agatha one evening in the small parlor. She had been playing the piano, and he had played his flute with her.

"Miss Agatha," he said. "I would like to speak to you about a—a serious matter."

"Yes, Mr. Gunther?" Her wide blue-green eyes gazed up at him. She wore a lovely blue dress with white trim. Her face glowed in the yellow lamplight.

"I am going a long journey," he said carefully. "I will probably return in late November or early December. When I return—if I succeed in my mission of buying furs by myself— would you consent to—to being courted, by me?"

She caught her breath, her face grew grave. She turned over a music page with shaking hand. When he grew more nervous at her silence, she finally said, "I will consider it, Mr. Gunther. I—I did not know—did not think you—thought so—of me."

"Yes, I have long—thought of you," he said. He wished he had a tongue of honey, but he did not. "I have long dreamed that one day I might have a wife, such a fine wife as you would be. So lovely, so kind, so good. That is my dream, to be worthy of you."

She gave him a tremulous smile, but that was all. When he departed several days later, she shook him by the hand and said, "Ludwig, you will be careful?"

"I will be careful," he swore to her, and it was a kind of oath. She had said nothing of being promised to Roderick Dindorf!

47

The journey was as difficult as Mr. Baines had warned, and more so. Soon after Ludwig started out, the rains came, and many a night he had to take refuge in some fallen stand of trees, as the bears did, making a nest for himself in thick fallen leaves and a couple of logs. And it turned cold, oh, how bitterly cold it was. He wrapped a couple of trade blankets about himself and trudged on, with the bitter wind biting through his trousers, and across his face, until it was red and burnt by the wind.

He made his way up through New York State, and across to the large St. Lawrence River. Then he turned to go south again, searching for signs of Indians. Still they surprised him. At his campfire one cold snowy night half a dozen Indians suddenly appeared behind him.

He started but stood up and greeted them gravely, leaving his rifle at his feet. One of them pointed to his opened pack, and put his fingers to his mouth, and began to whistle. Ludwig smiled in relief and nodded. *"Ja, ja,"* he said. "Play music!"

They had furs, and the furs were fresh pelts, scarcely dried, thick and fluffy from the first frost. Some still had snow and ice deep in them. He traded for them carefully, offering a fair exchange, and sticking to it until they gave in. They took the coins eagerly, and asked also for mirrors. They were disappointed he had no iron pots and pans, but he showed them how he had no wagon. He carried all on his back, he indicated, with his hands.

After the sales were completed, Ludwig played on his pipe for them. They listened in grave admiration, nodding their heads, one trying to hum along with him.

In the morning they were gone, leaving the furs, taking only their coins. They had not wakened him, but nothing else had been touched, not even his rifle.

Ludwig felt very happy about that. They trusted him. With renewed confidence he set out. The pack of furs was heavy on his back, along with the smaller pack of trade goods, and a change of clothing. But he persisted, moving slowly through the thickening snow that sometimes came up to his boot tops.

More snows came, and the winds howled. He lost time, having to shelter once in an Indian camp. They made him welcome but had no furs. They had sold them all. They looked longingly at his trade blankets. "Wait," they said. "Wait with us."

He waited. Some of the warriors went away, to return in

three days with some fresh prime mink and fox furs. Though pleased and excited, he tried to match their gravity.

He studied the pelts, and gave the Indians a firm offer. They tried to haggle, but cheerfully, and soon gave in. The snows let up, and he went on his way, the two packs of furs heavier and heavier.

He met another small wandering group of Indians, eight in number. These were hard of eye, suspicious of him. But they also traded with him. They had some fine furs, fresh and lustrous minks and some lynx. He traded the last of his goods for them.

The first day he had cut a foot-long piece of wood, and each day he had notched a cut with his knife on it. Now he knew he had been gone forty-two days, and it must be December.

He would turn back. He watched the sun, but some days he lost sight of it behind thick clouds of rain or snow. More snow came, and at times he trudged on with his packs heavier and heavier on his back, until he thought his spine would break with them. Ice clung to his eyebrows and new beard.

The days were shorter, and when the sun did shine, it glistened on the white snow and hurt his eyes. He bound a cloth over his head and shadowed his eyes somewhat. His boots would grow wet, and dry on his feet, until they bound his legs like iron. Had he been mad to attempt this journey into winter?

Yet, how beautiful were the woods! The trees had been stripped bare of their red and golden leaves, except for the evergreens, tall and stately among the barren trees. After a snowfall the branches of oaks and maples were lined with rows of white, and the smaller boughs were like flowers of white. How they shone in the rising or setting sun, reddish-gold, and the lakes glistened with ice crystals. Small animals slid across the ice. Ludwig wasted an entire day in December, hidden in a thicket, watching a family of river otters making a slide down a slope, then taking it in turn to race up to the top, and slide down. He could have sworn they were laughing to themselves, like children at play.

The day of rest revived him for the remainder of his hard journey. The snow had ceased, the sun shone, and his boots crunched on the thick snows and ice. He strode on, smiling as he remembered the clever otters and how they played. How nature smiled at times! He chewed on the dried deer meat some Indians had given to him and reflected on his future.

He came to a small town, and with a start he knew the easiest part of the journey was ahead. He caught a ride with a hearty farmer and talked with him as the man drove him more than forty miles to where the farmer would buy some more stores against the winter. They talked of the way America would grow, how towns would spring up in the wilderness. The man was about sixty.

"Even in my day," he said, drawling out the words, "I have seen forty, fifty, sixty families come out to settle near me. Some have gone on, and I heared they settled a hundred miles west. Think on it, when my grandsons are grown, they also may go West, and settle on better land, not so many stones in the fields. Why, men come from the West, young like you, son, and tell us of the rich fertile lands out there."

"*Ach, ja, ja,*" said Ludwig, nodding. "Not a plow in the earth, not a tree fallen by the ax, not a horse to be seen but the wild Indian ponies. And the Indians are good souls and sometimes friendly, if one is good to them."

The kindly farmer shortened Ludwig's journey by three days, and he came into the city of New York about two weeks before Christmas. As he walked up the street to the Dindorf house, he had the contented sense of coming home. He did not go to Mr. Baines's warehouse. Before leaving New York, Ludwig had asked Mrs. Dindorf for the use of her empty outbuilding and had whitewashed it inside and out. Now he came to the house, and as he looked at it in contentment, he saw the yellow lamp of the front parlor there, lit as though for him.

He stamped his booted feet free of snow on the edge of the porch, and at once the door flew open.

"Ludwig, you have come home!" cried Agatha. He dropped the heavy packs to the ground and pulled her into his arms. He forgot his smelly person, his clothes thick with dirt, he forgot formality, dignity. He pulled her to him, and when she raised her blond face and smiled up at him, he put his lips on her mouth and kissed her.

"Oh—Ludwig," she breathed.

"Agatha. My love. I could not ask for a sweeter welcome!"

Mrs. Dindorf came to the door, exclaiming in excitement, and Ludwig returned to himself. He took the packs around to the whitewashed building, put them inside, and locked the door. Then he came in the back way, into the warm fragrant kitchen, and was greeted over and over again by the women.

They greeted him like one of the family, and he accepted their reaction with pride and joy. How they laughed and talked that first night. He took himself to Mr. Baines's warehouse the next day and told him what he had done. Mr. Baines nodded and watched the expressions on Ludwig's face with a faint smile.

"So—now you are a man and have proved yourself, my son," he said and patted his shoulder and gave him hot coffee.

Ludwig did not take the pelts to him. He would handle them all himself. He set up a table in the yard, and there pounded the raw pelts and brushed the furs, and shook them out, and hung them on Agatha's washing line. He worked with them, then brought Mr. Baines to see them, proudly. The older man looked them over critically and said, "Good, good. You have a fine lot. We could sell them this time in New York. There is a big market for such furs now. No need for us to send to England and wait for the next journey, since you are in a hurry for the money."

Ludwig took Mr. Baines's advice. He did not want to wait for the money. He had been courting Agatha every evening, and he could scarcely wait to get married.

Ludwig and Agatha were wed two days before Christmas, in the German Lutheran Church, with the lovely white building filled with the odor of pine and cedar, the beauty of a tall Christmas tree with candles and ornaments and dolls on it. The elderly lodger had moved away, to be with a daughter, and the rooms were kept empty, by Ludwig's wish. "I can take care of both of you now, no need to work for others," he told them.

Agatha had prepared two of the upstairs rooms for them, one as a bedroom, one as a beautiful parlor where they could be alone. Many a night Ludwig worked on his accounts with a lamp, while Agatha sewed. Or they would go downstairs, to the front parlor, and play the piano and flute while her mother listened, and smiled, and made embroidery. No need now to sew and clean and wash laundry for others. Ludwig would take care of them the rest of his life. He had vowed it.

He had found joy in his bride. He never forgot his wedding night. He had gone to bed in a new white nightshirt, to find Agatha in the wide bed, her sturdy strong body so beautiful in a white gown with lace about the shoulders. She lay there, her blond hair in two long braids to her shoulders. It had been

51

his pleasure to unbind her hair and draw it about his own bronzed sturdy shoulders, and bend down to her, hidden in her hair.

"Ah, Ludwig, what a fine man you are," she said shyly. "What a man I have! What you have done in the one year you are here in America!"

"It is nothing compared to what I shall do for us both," he whispered. "I shall make a fortune for you and our *kinder*, our children. Never shall you know want or fear. I shall care for you, and dress you in silk and satin and the finest mink! You shall have a maid, and a carriage."

She had put her fingers gently on his broad lips. "Mine Ludwig," she whispered. "Do not make such big promises. Do you not know how happy I am, to have such a fine husband, such a good man? Does a woman need more?"

"You shall have everything in the world that you wish," he promised and drew her close to himself. How lovely she was, how beautiful in the lamplight. Shyly she blew out the light.

He had found her lovely in his hands, so lovely, so rounded and firm, so close fitting to his body. He had been gentle with her, satisfied to kiss and caress her the first nights. He knew little about women. He had not gone to any of the cheap women in town to learn. He and Agatha would learn together, he had said. Her mother had told her what she needed to know, and she knew more than Ludwig.

By the end of a week they had come together, in surprise and ecstasy for Ludwig. There was some pain for Agatha, but she protested that it was nothing, that she did not mind. He kissed her for that.

"You are a joy to my heart," he murmured in German. "My body, my mind, and my soul adore you, and ever shall."

She had smiled at him and drawn him down to her firm breasts, and he had slept with his head on her, hearing the soft pulsing of her generous heart.

Ludwig had worked so long and hard on his furs that there was little else to do that winter. Mr. Baines needed him a few days, but not for long hours. Ludwig worried that he had no work to do, and was tempted to return to the instrument store. Yet they had enough clerks now.

"I would like to start a store of my own," he said to Agatha one day. Her mother looked up alertly.

"You could make a store of our second parlor; it is large enough, *ja?*" she asked. "Why not? Agatha or I are always here, and you could put a jingling bell at the door to sound when someone comes in. What about that, Ludwig?" And her eyes sparkled.

"You would not mind, Mama?" he asked. "It might be a burden to you both."

"*Nein, nein,* my son. No burden. You have taken away all our work," she joked. "What will I do all the days until you have a child?"

Agatha blushed, and Ludwig smiled at her tenderly. He had never felt so happy. Such a beautiful loving kind wife that he had!

And so they opened a store. Ludwig went out and bought a few instruments to begin, and sent to Germany for more. A ship brought them by spring, and the store was in full operation. But by this time Ludwig was ready to start out on another fur-buying journey with Mr. Baines.

From this trip, said Mr. Baines, each would earn one half of the profits. He was getting older and was glad to have a sturdy young man like Ludwig to go with him on the journeys. "And we shall take a large wagonload of lighter goods," he said. "We shall return with more packs of furs, maybe twelve, maybe fifteen!"

Ludwig nodded. "No buying of poor furs, only the best. Much mink, and lynx, that is going well in London. And the beaver brings good price."

They talked about it, as equal partners. Ludwig had proved himself by going alone, and succeeding in bargaining and returning with excellent furs.

The instrument store did well also. Agatha had learned to play, in an elementary basic style, the flute, the bassoon, and oboe. She was already familiar with the harp and piano. They could assist purchasers in the buying of any musical instrument by using catalogs of British and German firms.

The drawing room had now a fine counter and shelves for the smaller instruments, comfortable armchairs for the customers, and a sign in the window, "Gunther's Musical Instruments. All fine German-made instruments. Inquire within, ten to five o'clock, weekdays."

No more lodgers, no more sewing and laundering for strange men, no risking sailors and other seedy characters for the two women. Their home was their own, and they were contented, as was Ludwig.

Chapter 5

Agatha Dindorf had always seemed to herself to be a sturdy practical girl, a hardworking girl. She had rarely allowed herself to dream, especially not of the future.

Her father had died early, and all her days she had known what it was to work, study, plan for the following day, shop for a shrewd bargain, sew and cook and launder clothes, and scrub the front steps and sidewalks. Work, work, and plan only for the work of the next day.

When Ludwig Gunther had come along, and talked of his dreams, while his vivid blue eyes shone, and his accent became thicker in his excitement, Agatha had been drawn to him. He dared to dream! He had come from his home, leaving everybody he knew, to cross an ocean and start a new life.

What it must be to be a man of courage, daring, and dreams! Somehow she knew he would succeed. From the first he had been different from any man she had known. Her cousin Roderick was similar to him, yet he stuck to the known ways. He sailed with men he knew, followed their directions, and was calm, solid, and predictable.

But Ludwig! No, he was different. He would work for others, to learn a trade, to understand the country. But he chafed to be his own man, his own boss.

Cousin Roderick had sometimes hinted of marriage, and he came courting and visiting whenever he was in port. He considered his Aunt Constantia and Cousin Agatha as his own family, and they both loved him, as a kind man, a good nephew. Yet Agatha had been wary of talk of marriage.

He was not full of the same dreams and desires as Agatha. He enjoyed the sea and could be away for a year or more, and she scarcely missed him. He was not like her father Colin Dindorf. Now there was a dreamer of dreams! He had had big ideas, and had eagerly talked them over with his wife and small daughter. Agatha's eyes grew sad as she thought of his brief life, snuffed out so soon. What could her father have done, what might he have accomplished if he had lived? An Englishman, he had cut loose from a fine family and come to the Colonies to make a new life. As a younger son in Europe, he had been stifled. Everything went to the elder son, the younger ones having to join the army or enter the clergy.

Agatha had compared Roderick unconsciously to her father, and he had not measured up. Roderick had had too many things handed to him by his parents. And he loved the sea, his mistress—he would gladly live on a ship for months at a time. Could any woman rival the sea in his affections?

She had put off Roderick whenever he came too close to proposing. In order not to hurt him, she would murmur that she did not feel ready for such a decision, hoping he would forget the matter by the end of the next voyage. Agatha hoped that Roderick might find another girl, and that she herself might find another man, a good one. She dreamed of a strong, kind man, with adventure in his heart, with a spirit that did not make him cruel and thoughtless.

Her mother had warned her since her early teens. "*Mein Kind*, you must be careful of men," she had said over and over. "These are rough times; they encourage rude men. They will take a girl, use her and then leave her, if she is not careful. I married a good man, we were happy together for as long as he lived. I would wish such a marriage for you, but longer, happier, more full of joy and pleasure, and many children. Be careful, my child!"

Agatha had been taught to be so careful that sometimes she felt cold inside herself. She smiled at men, but did not believe their fine speech. She did not walk out with any man. She insisted that he come to her, at her own house, with her mother in the same room or the next room. She did not even go out to dances, unless they were neighborhood events, and her mother with her, to walk home with friends together.

Sometimes a man would take advantage. He might slip his arm about her waist, squeeze her, and whisper to come out into the darkness and see the moon. Agatha would only laugh and say, "I have seen the moon already, sir, it is very lovely, but I do not go outside with you!"

They reproached her and called her cold. Perhaps she was cold, she thought, her hands idle on the sewing in her lap as she gazed into the heart of a fire for a time. Then she would pick up her sewing again with a short sigh. She was a practical girl, but all that she had wanted was the moon.

She was shrewd. She knew that some idle lazy men would look for a hardworking girl, marry her, then live off her all their days. Look at the laundress two blocks away. Mrs. Murphy, with five children, was but thirty, yet stooped and gray as a woman twice her age. She worked six days a week and went to the Roman Catholic Church on Sunday, with her children trailing behind her, the youngest by her hand. Her husband, frequenting the saloons, laughed about how he had married a fine woman, who did enough work for the both of them! Agatha shuddered in disgust.

It was splendid to marry a man who would support her. It was better for both to work hard for the good of the family. But a man who would lie back and let a woman work her hands to red, cracked skin, whose back was stooped with worry and sadness and weariness, and laugh about it . . . Agatha had only contempt for such.

She would never be caught in such a trap, she had vowed. She studied men with a keen though demure gaze. She would like to love a man, as her mother had loved her father. But if she could not do this, she would at least marry a man she could respect and honor, or she would not marry at all.

Should she marry, and her man become lame, she would continue to work for them both, as the women did whose men had fought in the War of Revolution. She knew many such men, those who had lame bodies, or heads with no brains left in them, with wild, dazed looks. Everyone felt sorry for them and respected them for having fought. Their women were helped by the church and by neighbors.

However it was quite another matter to marry a man who was wild and fickle, who wished only to roam the world, or laze away his days in taverns, telling laughable stories of what he might do one day!

Then Ludwig Gunther had come along. From the first Agatha and her mother had sensed that this man was different. His head was held high, and he worked hard from morning to night—and beyond. He honored learning and strove to learn more. He wanted so much to learn English correctly, that he would study when his young sturdy body was so tired, it would slump in the chair until he jerked himself erect again.

She admired the way he wrote to his parents, and his friends. Though he might never see them again, he kept the old honored ties. She liked his courtesy to her mother, the way he jumped up when she entered the room, the way he held her chair at table, the way he listened thoughtfully to her sage advice, and never mocked or laughed at her old-fashioned dignity.

Agatha smiled over her sewing that night. She was making a new shirt for Ludwig. He would be leaving soon on another

56

fur trip, and she wanted to make him a fine comfortable shirt of wool for warmth, with big pockets in it to hold his gear. She would make three shirts for him, enough for the fall journey he would make also, probably. She stroked the material with her hand, then picked up her needle to thread it once more. They would be sturdy, sewn with two seams, to hold together against the stress of the journey.

Her mother gazed across at her from her chair under the other lamp. "You smile, my child! You are happy?" she asked softly, her eyes glowing also.

"So happy, Mama," sighed Agatha and turned her hand to admire the gold ring on her wedding finger. Such a fine wide gold band. She had chosen it with Ludwig's urging to take the best ring there.

She had feared the wedding night a little. She had known it would bring pain. But Ludwig, how he had surprised her.

"You are weary, my darling girl," he had said. "We will just lie together, and you will allow me to kiss you, yes?"

Surprised, she had agreed, and he had kissed and stroked her soft body, with a kind of reverence, whispering his love for her. She had slept in comfort, in her man's arms, with no pain, no terror for that first night. How thoughtful he had been!

Closer they had come, closer each night, until a week later they had come together, and the pain had been strong. But Ludwig's gentle ways had held no terror for her. She had been relieved that he was so good to her, and in response her body had softened for him, and she had wanted to hold him to her breasts.

In January several days with thick snow and biting winds came. None of them had gone out for two days, and Agatha and her mother had been urged by Ludwig to remain indoors longer.

He came in from shoveling the walk free of snow, going back to make sure the horse was all right and the furs safely locked inside the outbuilding. He had gone each morning, and each night, tramping through two feet of snow, to the horse, to soothe it, take water to it, and feed it. But he would not let Agatha do this.

"No, no, you shall not go out in this, it is too deep, my darling wife," he had said. "What do you wish? I will get it for you from the pantry," and out he would go again to the cold storehouse some feet from the back of the house, returning with flushed red cheeks and sparkling blue eyes.

How strong he was! And good to her and her mother. He

57

had taken over the house, and not even her mother minded. Her mother said with contentment, "Ludwig, you will decide about the roof, does it need tiling? How happy I am that you will take care of all matters!"

And she had said to her daughter, "It is good to have a strong man about the house. I worried for many years, trying to make the right decisions. I would trust Ludwig to my dying day."

"So, Mama, you are happy in my choice, eh?" asked Agatha, teasing her mother gently. "Always you told me to be so careful, yet I decided in two weeks to marry! And you said not a word of opposition!"

"My dearest, you did not decide in two weeks. You decided in one day, when he first came!" said her wise mother, laughing. "And so did I. When I first met him, I thought, this is a man! And soon I thought, this is a man for my Agatha. I watched the two of you and prayed that it would happen."

The March wind was wild that night, and Agatha kept looking up from her sewing, anxiously, as the howling storm raged outside.

"He does not come early," said her mother. "Now, he will be fine, my dear."

"It is so near to the ocean, that warehouse," said Agatha, remembering her father.

"Ludwig walked, he did not take the carriage," said her mother, knowing her thoughts. "And he walks inland, within the shelter of the houses."

Agatha nodded and gazed out the windows, drawing aside the draperies. In the rain and wind she saw the tall sturdy figure drawing near, the walk that was like no other, so rapid and firm, head bent only slightly against the wind, the fur cap on his head, the rain streaming down his face.

"He comes—he comes," she exclaimed and went to the door, ready to fling it open for her husband.

Ludwig's step sounded on the veranda. Agatha flung open the door, and his smile warmed her heart. He came in, but held her off with his two dripping hands.

"I am wet to the skin, my love," he said. "Let me dry myself and put on a warm gown before you touch me." He turned, closed the door against the storm, and bolted it shut.

He gave her a grin, his white teeth slashing against the bronze of his skin. In spite of his blond hair and blond beard and moustache, he was now such a dark man, for the sun had burned him thoroughly summer and winter. He went upstairs, dripping as he removed his boots and put them to dry in the kitchen.

He returned in fifteen minutes, in fresh clothes, with a dark red velvet robe on him. Agatha had made it for him, and he admired it and wore it often.

"There, I am human again, and not a wild animal out in a storm," he said, grinning at them. "How do you ladies endure my ways? I could have come home two hours ago, but instead I lingered to hear Mr. Baines talk of the forests and its ways, and this afternoon we did little work because two men came to tell us of opportunities for trading in the Orient!"

"Ludwig, your dinner is here," said Agatha, shaking her head at him. She had set the hot tray on the small table beside the sofa. "How can you go for so many hours without eating?"

"Your scolding is but music to my ears," he joked and sat down hungrily to eat the good hot food, the thick meat and vegetables in soup, the thick-sliced dark brown bread, the way he liked it. She had spread butter thickly on the bread, made also to his liking. He ate and drank the hot spicy coffee. He always insisted on the best coffee and bought it on the docks when it came in, right from the captains of merchant vessels from South America.

He talked between bites, chewing his food, then pausing to talk, eat again, then talk, enthusiastically, his blue eyes blazing with his excitement.

"A man took his furs to the port of Canton, and there he sold them for much trade!" he was saying. "The Chinese merchants despise us, and usually insist on gold or silver coins in trade. But for the furs of the sea otter and the mink, and the seal, they did trade in much tea, barrels of tea, and silks so fine that the merchant told us he could slip the silk cloth through a wedding ring of gold! So beautifully woven were the silks, I would have bought a length from him, but he would not sell. I must have some of these silks for Agatha!"

"No, no," she protested, her cheeks flushed with some of his excitement. "I need not silks, Ludwig!"

"You shall have silks, my love, silk brocade, silk velvet, and porcelains also. You should see the vase he brought to show us—so fine that one could see the light through it!"

Presently he stopped talking, and they closed up the house, made sure of all the bolts, and went upstairs to their rooms. In the lamp-lit bedroom, with the wide bed waiting for them,

Agatha removed her dress and underclothes, then modestly slipped into her warm woolen nightdress with the lace on the neck and sleeves. He was lying in bed, his hands under his head. She thought he still was with the merchants in his mind, but when she turned, she met his gaze and knew he thought only of her.

He looked at her lovingly, his hand held out to her. She bent and blew out the lamp, and slipped into bed beside him; he drew her at once against his heart.

"Such desires I have," he murmured with a sigh. "I long to be only with you. But when I hear the merchants of the fur trade, and the China trade, then how I long to be off on my adventures again! It is not fair to you, my love."

"Oh, fair!" she scoffed. "Do you not know—do you not remember, my dearest Ludwig? I would send out merchant ships, for spices and silks and China ware, and have them return again to me? I would wait for my love to come sailing back to me, with excitement in his eyes, and adventure in his blood, and happy with the joys of conquering his world!"

"You do understand," he marveled. "Oh, such a wife that I have! How did I come to be so fortunate? Such a beautiful wife, with such skin, softer than silk, richer than the finest velvet," and he stroked his big hand over her breasts to her waist, making her thrill with his touch.

Gently he opened the nightdress down the front and bent over her as his lips went down to follow his hands. She caught her breath and grew giddy with the ecstasy of his kisses. He was learning so well what caresses pleased her, and he would move his lips over the soft tips of her breasts until they hardened to peaks of pleasure. He would nibble at her soft rich breasts until her back arched with desire.

And his big hands that he called rough were not rough to her. She would feel them stroking over her thighs, the hard skin catching on her softness, and he apologized, but the touch thrilled her. He worked so hard, for her and her mother, and he would do so for the children to come. She was not ashamed of those rough red hands. She was proud of them, and she thrilled to their touch on her.

His fingers went to her thighs and teased softly. He had just learned recently that he could thrill her with this, and she caught her breath, and he laughed softly against her breasts. "You like this, my beautiful love?" he whispered, teasing her with his fingers, again and again.

"Oh, Ludwig—it is so—exciting. Oh, darling—" She caught his hard shoulders and drew him closer to her body. Her hands stroked up and down his spine, and he shivered with pleasure and pressed himself closer to her. She felt her body grow hot under the covers, under her man.

He rubbed his hard body against hers, slowly, so she felt the hard masculinity of him against her feminine curves. She knew he was growing hard in desire, and that rapture would come soon. She smiled in the darkness, her gaze blurring, so that she scarcely saw the rain that beat against the windows nor heard the howling of the wind outside.

Her ears were drumming with the blood that rose in her veins. He pressed against her, his leg holding her thighs apart. She shifted on the bed, to take his weight, and he moved directly over her. He supported himself on his elbows, always worried that he was so heavy he would crush her. She found delight in his heaviness on her. And the hardness of his thighs.

He came to her and pressed softly. He found her ready, and she tingled as he came inside her and moved up. His arm was under her body, and his other hand on her breast, cupping it for his lips. He seemed all over her, caressing every part of her. How hard his arms were, like iron, yet so gentle with her. She relaxed into his grip and let them come together like a hot poker into a bed of fire—and then smoke and flame and explosion.

She cried out softly, rising to his hips, lying back again, the convulsions of rapture flaming through her. She shivered without will, gripped in helpless response to his thrusts.

He did not draw out. He held high and tight in her, and she felt the growing tension of his body. She came again, exploding helplessly against him, her hands on his thighs, tugging at him, begging wordlessly for more.

He thrust, drew out slowly, and thrust again, again, and again. And in her third explosions of rippling waves of feeling came his own bursts. He came hard into her, and she felt the spurts against her very womb.

He finished and groaned helplessly, falling against her. It had been such a tremendous burst, and she held his head against her breasts, until his hard breathing had eased somewhat. He rolled over and drew her with him, so her head in turn was on his broad, hairy chest.

His hand stroked softly through her thick long silky hair, drawing it to cover his head and shoulders, and she felt him

61

kissing her head, and her forehead. "My—beautiful—marvelous—darling," he breathed.

"I love you, my Ludwig," she responded, and her legs wrapped about his, her arms twined about his thick sturdy body. They slept lazily but wakened in the night to begin again, desire so strong in them they cared for nothing else. It was a desire that had to be answered, and blaze up like fire, and die down again into the peacefulness of their bed—peace in the heart of the storm.

Ludwig went on a fur trip during April and May; by the time he returned, Agatha had known for a while that she was pregnant.

When she told Ludwig, he veered from sober responsibility to wild joy and back again. "You will have my child? When, Agatha? What joy, what delight!" He held her closely against him.

"In mid-November, Ludwig."

"Ah." As his face shadowed to thoughtfulness, she knew he thought of a fur trip. "I shall come back by that time, if I go at all," he said musingly.

"You must go when you wish, Ludwig. I shall manage. Mother will help me, and I can also depend on our good kind neighbors."

"*Nein*, I shall not leave you at that time," he said firmly.

She knew in the summer, as he worked with the thick load of furs, that he mused over whether to make the autumn journey. The furs brought so much money that she caught her breath over the amount when Ludwig explained the finances to her. Since she was keeping their books now, he told her everything. He still worked with Mr. Baines, and they split both their expenses and the earnings half and half.

She also learned that summer how to work with the furs. Ludwig and Mr. Baines were gone for months at a time, and the furs would accumulate in the warehouse with no one to look after them. So Agatha agreed to learn how to beat the furs, and how to clean them carefully, scraping the raw skin on the back, then hanging them up to let the wind blow out the dust. She learned their value and how to bargain with those who brought furs to her during Ludwig's absence.

Ludwig wanted to get together enough money to make a great venture with his furs. She thought he was considering a journey to China, and her heart almost failed her. But Ludwig was careful as well as thoughtful. He did not dive recklessly into ventures.

She urged him to take the autumn journey. The child would not come until mid-November, and even if her husband had not yet returned, she would manage.

"I shall come back before the child comes, I swear to you," Ludwig told her anxiously, kissing her mouth gently. She was growing large now, and her waist was quite thick.

She did not mind. It was his child in her. She put her hand to his rough cheek as she bade him farewell and sent her blessings with him.

In September the men set out, and Agatha and her mother settled to work in the instrument shop in the front parlor. Agatha would continue to work with the furs which were accumulating in the outbuilding. She was pegging out some furs and scraping some on a table in the backyard when Roderick Dindorf appeared.

He came around the corner of the house, a dazed look on his bronzed face. "Agatha," he called out. "What in the name of heaven are you doing?"

He was tired from his long journey, and his handsome blue uniform hung on him. His brown eyes were gentle and anxious as he gazed at Agatha, obviously pregnant, working over the furs.

"Cousin Roderick, how good to see you." She did not offer her cheek for his kiss, as he usually expected. She held out her hand to him, with a smile of a matron.

"Agatha, I am overcome—you are married?"

She showed her hand with the gold ring. "As you see," she said simply. "I married Ludwig Gunther last Christmas. But come into the house. Mother will wish to know you are here. You are well, the journey went well?"

He helped her put the furs into the outbuilding and lock them away. Questions filled his face, but he said little until they were inside. Agatha went to wash away the fuzz and dust of the furs, took off her apron, and returned to the little parlor on the other side of the instrument store.

Roderick and her mother came from the store. "And now you also run a store," he said, accusation in his tone. "Ludwig works you very hard!"

"Not at all," said Agatha, fury in her heart. She looked at him coldly. "The work is not half so difficult as caring for three lodgers. We take in no sewing or laundry. We work as

63

we please. Come, Roderick, sit down and be comfortable."
She indicated an armchair and seated herself in another, carefully, because of her bulk.

"And where is Ludwig Gunther?" he asked. "Off on another long journey?"

"Aye, yes, the furs sell so well," smiled Agatha. "And you—how long were you gone, dear cousin? One year this time?"

Agatha's mother gave her a look which said severely that the girl was being rude to her cousin. She changed the subject and asked smoothly about his mother, his family, his journey. Agatha listened in silence, until it came time to make some tea. She moved to the kitchen, and prepared it as she heard the voice going on and on, as Roderick told of his adventures in the China trade, the long journey around Cape Horn which was so dangerous.

She carried the heavy silver tray back to the front room. Roderick jumped up to take the tray, but he was too late; it was already on a small table. Ludwig would have followed her to the kitchen and carried the tray for her, thought Agatha. His thoughts were always ahead of others, and his consideration of her was genuine, not an afterthought.

"I did not know you were considering marriage with Gunther," said Roderick, ignoring his tea. His brown eyes were full of reproach and some anxiety. "I tried to speak—you knew my feelings."

Agatha answered lightly. She was fond of Roderick, she did not wish to hurt him. "La, Roderick, you were always considerate. But you know that you are a restless sailor, and that the sea alone is your true love!"

She hoped to save his feelings, and he accepted that, bowing his head briefly. "Well—well, it is done," he sighed. "You are happy, Agatha? He treats you well?"

"As you see," she said, indicating the room and the house with a wave of her hand. "No more lodgers. The shop of musical instruments is easy to take care of. Ludwig set a bell at the door, and when it rings, we go to the customer. No need to wait about there. As for the furs, they are here only part of the time, and I work with them only when Ludwig and Mr. Baines are off on a journey. The rest of the time, I sew clothes, do some cleaning, some cooking. I have an easy life."

It was not all that easy. Some days she went to bed weary to the bone, but she would never say so, not to Roderick! And

64

it was a good weariness, a satisfaction, to work with and for her man. Ludwig worked even harder.

She was quietly satisfied, for Ludwig loved her. He was so farsighted and ambitious, she knew he would take good care of her, and of the children to come. She left him no cause to be dissatisfied with her. She loved him deeply. And in turn he adored her and let her know day and night of his feelings. And to her mother he was a son, solicitous of her, ever welcoming to her, never making her feel she should leave them alone. He called her "Mama" just as he had called his own mother, and was anxious that she should not have heavy work to do.

"And tell us of your journey. Roderick," said Agatha, encouraging him as she had always done, naturally. "You went forth in September? Where did you get trade goods?"

Roderick relaxed and settled down to tell them of the trip. "We took on a full load at Boston Harbor," he began. "We took cloth, nails, needles and pins, many items for the Russian settlement in Alaska. Yes, we went there first, for I had heard that they are often short of goods and impatient with their government for leaving them so long. They were suspicious of me at first, but I reassured them. I wanted only the furs they were willing to trade, and for it they might choose what they wished of my cargo. They took most of my goods."

He spoke on and on, talking of how they had then gone to the Sandwich Islands to take on sandalwood, then sailed to the port of Canton, China. There the Chinese merchants had haggled with them, but their eagerness for ginseng and for the sandalwood and furs was so great that Roderick and his crew were able to take on a full load of China tea, silks in great lengths, crates of the China ware, and other such fine goods.

"I have saved some for you, Agatha," he told her, giving her a reproachful look. "Some lengths of silk, much tea—"

"You must speak to my husband about this," said Agatha tartly. "He will wish to say whether you are allowed to make us presents!"

Roderick looked pained, at the brusque remark. Agatha's mother had a little quirky line about her mouth that meant she wanted to laugh. She left the matter to them to argue about.

Roderick insisted that the beautiful goods were a Christmas present from last Christmas and for this one. Agatha still insisted that he speak to Ludwig, and he finally left rather sulkily, his presents still in his carriage.

"You were a little hard on your cousin, *nein*?" said her mother mildly, rising to clear away the teacups.

"He must know I am married now. It is not the same thing, Mother," said Agatha. She added thoughtfully, "I am beginning to know Ludwig's pride also. He wished to give me silks and taffetas, and whether he will permit me to accept some from Roderick, I do not know. Anyway, I am with child, and a silk dress at my state . . ." She indicated herself with a little mischievous grin.

"Yes, yes, I think you are wise, leave it to your husband, and let him decide," said her mother. She gave a satisfied sigh. "You have a good man, my Agatha!"

"I know it, Mother," said Agatha softly, and her blue-green eyes shone. Ludwig had promised to come home by the first of November, sooner if they could manage. And after that the child would come.

Chapter 6

As Ludwig drove the wagon north, that early September, Mr. Baines kept glancing at his burly young partner. He was coming to know Ludwig well, and the young man was deep in thought and planning.

"The first frost has not come yet, it has been a warm summer," said Mr. Baines finally.

"*Ja, ja,* that is what I think also. There will be no furs yet in the land below the Great Lakes." Ludwig clucked at the horses and they pulled willingly along the dry earth.

"So—where do we go, Ludwig?" asked Mr. Baines, troubled. "You said you wished to return by the first of November, for the birth of your child."

"*Ja,* for the birth of my child," said Ludwig absently.

Mr. Baines stopped speaking and turned his attention with some exasperation to the fresh fields of ripe corn, almost ready for the cutting, to the fields of wheat, the long lines of green vegetables, and the reddening apples in the small trees that gave such sweet crisp fruit.

When Ludwig was thinking, there was no talking with him. He would talk when he was ready. Nights they lay before their campfire on the earth, wrapped in blankets, and slept early. Little talking was done.

Steadily Ludwig drove north. When Mr. Baines was driving one day, about one week out of New York City, he began to turn off to the west. Ludwig caught at the reins, and shook his thick blond head.

"*Nein, nein,* to the north, Mr. Baines!"

Mr. Baines followed his directions, but he was puzzled and worried. "North? Ludwig, are you mad? The Canadians will not let us have furs there. You know the laws."

"*Ja.* After the war the British kept the old laws. No boats but theirs may go on the Great Lakes. They keep their fur trade posts in our Northwest Territory! *Ja,* I know that. The laws are wrong," said Ludwig.

"But they are the laws! Customs men wait on the borders, along the lakes and rivers!"

"They are wrong," said Ludwig stubbornly. "Mr. Baines,

do you know any men along the river? Do you know any man who would be a good friend to us?"

Mr. Baines was gasping at the thoughts swirling in his brain. Ludwig meant to cross the river and go into Canada for furs!

"Aye," he said finally. "There is a man, one Kurt Aronhold. He fought during the Revolutionary War and lost a leg. He is a farmer along the river who fought to keep his land, though some almost succeeded in taking it from him. He is not married. He keeps to himself."

Mr. Baines looked at the blond man beside him in the wagon. He knew Ludwig was a shrewd man and a cunning one. So far he had known him to break no laws. But Ludwig was also a strong, stubborn man. If he said the laws were wrong, then he might not be willing to obey them.

And the laws *were* wrong! Over the conference table the Northwest Territory had gone to the United States. The Canadians hated to admit it, they refused to concede the land, they kept police posts and fur posts in the Ohio Country. Did they think the British could get all that rich land back for them? They tried to keep American fur traders from "their" lands.

And now Ludwig would invade the Canadian land!

"You will direct me?" asked Ludwig the next day as they drove north toward the St. Lawrence River.

In resignation Mr. Baines told him where to go, and by nightfall they had reached the farm of Kurt Aronhold, right on the river. They drove into his farmyard, and out from the barn came the one-legged farmer, limping on his peg leg, his rifle held before him.

"Who goes there?" he barked gruffly.

"It is Franklin Baines, Mr. Aronhold! May we put our wagon and horses in your barn?"

He peered up at them both, then nodded curtly and led the lead horse himself by the bit into the barn. Silently he helped them unhitch the two horses and took a good look at the trade goods loaded in the wagon. He said nothing until they were in the small cabin, sitting at the kitchen table.

Aronhold had coffee on the stove, and he poured some out for them; then he moved about slowly on his peg leg to prepare some beef and cabbage. He put it before them and set a plate down for himself.

"I thank you for your courtesy," said Ludwig and fell to his eating with no more ado.

Kurt Aronhold was watching him shrewdly. They ate in

silence, finished their coffee, ate several small apples apiece, and sat back to smoke their pipes.

"So," said Aronhold. "You go north, eh?"

"I wish to," said Ludwig. "You see how it is. No frost yet. If we wish furs, we must go into Canada."

"Rash young man," said Aronhold dispassionately, puffing at his long clay pipe. His eyes were half-shut under the shaggy, thick eyebrows. In his mid-forties he was turning gray. Tough, grumbling, he was alone but self-sufficient. "Think you can get past the Canadians, the British, the Indians?"

"I want to meet the Indians and buy the furs from them, intercepting them before they come to Montreal."

"Um," was all Aronhold said. Ludwig eyed him warily.

They all sat in silence for a time. Then Aronhold spoke. "What is your plan? To leave the wagon and horses with me?"

"*Ja*," replied Ludwig. "Do you have friends across the river? We would go on foot, or borrow a carriage and horse, gather packs of furs, and leave them with friends. Return as often as we can, until mid-October. Then cross the river again, pick up our own wagon, and return to New York City. I will pay you well, in gold."

Aronhold's eyes opened wide in surprise, and so did Mr. Baines's. "Gold, is it? That would not go amiss."

"I have it with me. Half in advance, ten pounds now, ten pounds when we return."

Aronhold nodded, and the bargain was made. In the morning he got out his sturdy boat from under some reeds and bushes. He crossed the river with them, for it was a foggy day, and most boats had left the river. He knew that river and its narrower places. He landed just below the farm of some friends, Mr. and Mrs. Perrine.

Ludwig and Mr. Baines met the Canadian couple and were pleased to find them dour, French, and hating the British. Ludwig made them the same offer for gold that he had to Aronhold. They agreed to loan him a wagon and a horse, and to store the packs of furs and some trade goods for them as they traveled.

Mr. Baines protested once as they set out again, with one third of their trade goods, and innocent farmers' hats on their heads. "What if we cannot trust them? What if they betray us to the soldiers?"

"They will not," said Ludwig. "One knows whom to trust. I like their speech and their manner."

Mr. Baines nodded. He did also, but he had not thought young Ludwig was mature enough to know this. He put those thoughts out of his mind and concentrated on watching for small bands of Indians.

They left the roads and traveled across country, having to skirt large lakes and drive around to fords. Mr. Baines did the talking since a German accent would be suspect.

Halfway to the Great Hudson Bay, they came across two bands of Indians. Ludwig bargained briskly and had iron pots for them, tools of axes and knives, blankets. The black eyes glistened. Ludwig was generous with them.

He also was careful about which furs to buy. He looked over the pelts and chose only the best ones, the finest mink, otter, and beaver. He turned down the wolf, the bear and the muskrat. The Indians muttered among themselves, but accepted his word, especially when he added some silver coins to the deal. Ludwig and Mr. Baines then turned back with a carriage full of furs and left them at the barn of the Perrines.

They made three trips to pick up their trade goods, leave the furs, and start out again. Grimly determined to continue, Ludwig muttered furiously when they had to hide out one full day while some soldiers blocked the road they wanted to take. He was losing time, and he seemed to be driven by a demon against the calendar.

But finally, near the end of October, they arrived a final time at the Perrine farm. The good people were surprised at how rapid a trip the two men had made the last time, only four days up and back.

They paid the farmers, and Mr. Perrine rowed them across the river at night. Ice was forming, but the sky was clear and a midnight-purple blue with many stars and a moon. They skulked from ice pack to ice pack, pausing to listen for sounds of the customs boats, for great canoes which might come from Montreal, for any sound that did not belong to the quiet night.

The boat reached the farm of Kurt Aronhold at dawn. He was waiting there on the bank, an empty pipe clenched in his teeth.

"So, you come when you say," he said, grunting approval. He helped unload the nine thick packs of furs, and carried them to his barn.

"Did anybody come asking questions?" asked Ludwig.

Aronhold grunted. "Customs man once. He asked about the horses and wagon. I told him I was thinking about buying them, using them for my corn harvest."

They slept soundly all through the day. Aronhold woke them at nightfall. "Time to go," he said gruffly. He had a packet of meat and bread and cheese for them, and he gave them hot coffee before they departed.

Ludwig paid him more than he had said, and the man grunted. "Too much," he said.

"We shall come again," said Ludwig with a grin. "I wish to make many such trips, and I like a silent partner."

Aronhold made a sound that was rather like a laugh and waved to them as they departed into the night.

There was a customs post not far off. Ludwig drove off the road, and skirted it cautiously, letting the horses walk slowly through the empty fields. They managed to get past and did not return to the road until they were twenty miles south of the river.

Then Ludwig returned to the road and urged the horses on faster. The first couple of days they slept by day and traveled by night, until they came to the main road to the Hudson River.

Down they drove along the river, by daytime this time, with the packs of furs hidden under blankets. Shocks of corn stuck out under the blankets as though they carried farm products to market. They were not stopped.

They arrived back in New York City on the first day of November. Ludwig drove right to the warehouse, and they unloaded the packs of furs and locked them securely inside.

Agatha met him at the door and flung her arms about him. She could scarcely reach him, she was so plump with child.

"My dear one, I am in time," he said tenderly, drawing a deep breath of relief. There had been occasions when his mother had given birth as much as a month early.

"Yes, but so anxious for you! Oh, Ludwig, Roderick said the frost was late this year! Where did you go for furs?"

"Roderick talks too much for his own good," said Ludwig. "Let me do the worrying for the family!"

He had never spoken so sharply to her before, and she started and went red. But Ludwig was deeply annoyed at Roderick Dindorf and resolved to speak to him.

"So he hangs about you yet, does he?" Ludwig added with a scowl.

"I know somebody who is jealous," said Mrs. Dindorf, smiling to ease the tense atmosphere.

"*Ja, ja*, I am! Tell that young man you are my wife, as I tell him myself!" And Ludwig kissed his wife tenderly and said, "How glad I am to see you, beloved."

Her face relaxed, she smiled up at him radiantly.

They worked on the furs at the warehouse, and added those that Agatha had prepared while the men had been gone. Twelve good packs of furs they had. Mr. Baines and Ludwig talked about how to sell them but decided not to take the furs themselves to England. They sent them off with a trusted merchant friend.

At the end of the second week of November Agatha was put to bed with child. It was a long time of birthing, thought Ludwig, though Mrs. Dindorf said it was normal for a first child. But as ten hours passed, then twelve and fifteen, Ludwig began pacing the hallway downstairs, intensely worried.

After twenty hours, the child was born. Ludwig heard its lusty cry, and the laughter of the women helping. He raced up the stairs, then dared not enter the room. They washed the child, wrapped it in a blanket, and Mrs. Dindorf brought out the bundle.

Ludwig stared down at the red wrinkled face. "This is a child, this small thing not as large as a mink?"

Mrs. Dindorf shook her head at him, her face wet with sweat, yet serene for all that. "You have a son, Ludwig, praise God," she said. "And healthy and good. Your wife does well."

He went in to see Agatha as soon as they let him. They had made her comfortable in a fresh white gown. She smiled sleepily at him and pressed his hand with weak fingers. "A son, Ludwig," she managed to say.

"My wonderful wife," he said, his voice shaking, and he bent to kiss her fingers, then her cheek. He held her hand until she slept.

The full knowledge of the miracle did not come for a while. Then it came to him—he had a son! He, Ludwig Gunther, stranger in a stranger land, had fathered a son who was an American! A free man, American, not German, not sworn to serve any master!

They named the boy Colin Hans Gunther. Colin was for Agatha's father, and Hans was for Ludwig's middle name and the first name of his father. He wrote to his parents at once with the joyous news and had quick responses of pleasure from them.

But his father added, "You should come home to us! Times are good here. You can have a job in my butcher shop once more."

Ludwig showed the letter to Agatha and laughed. "How my father would open his eyes if he knew what we earned in a single month here with the furs! Even the instrument shop earns more in a year than the butcher shop does!"

"You will not say so to your father?" asked Agatha anxiously. "His feelings would be hurt, I am sure of it."

"*Nein.* But I will write and ask them to come to the New World, for it is much more exciting here, and with more opportunities to make one's fortune than in the old!"

But his father replied sharply that he was not such a fool as to leave a good job for the unknown. And his mother wrote to say that her children were becoming settled in their lives and had no wish to roam, as her eldest had. She sent her love, and he sensed a wistfulness to come—but she would not leave her family. She could not.

In March, 1786, Ludwig set out alone, early. He wanted to find out some matters for himself. And Mr. Baines had wearied on that rough Canadian journey. Ludwig did not like the worn look on the face of the older man. Up in years, he could not take the bitter cold, the sleeping on the ground, the cruel winds that blew.

"*Nein*, you remain home this journey. I will travel out into the Northwest Territory by horseback," said Ludwig. "I will take but small tools and some coins with me, no heavy trade goods. I wish to learn the true situation, and a man on horseback may travel without stirring up much notice."

Mr. Baines argued a little and insisted on paying half of the coins, but willingly remained in his warm apartment over the warehouse, dealing happily with the few fur dealers who came his way during the harsh winter.

Ludwig set out in mid-March. Snow still lay on the ground, and the rivers were full of ice. The horse was a heavy, sure-footed animal, placid and strong-hearted. He rode directly west this time, across the Pennsylvania woods and farms, ignoring the farmers, sleeping in fields and along the roadside. He went deep into the Ohio wilderness, crossing mountains, down cliffs, as the spring came on.

It was a beautiful land, he noted. The wild flowers sprang up in lush fields. The timber grew high, untouched by ax. But already here and there a log cabin sat on a cliff, and smoke from the chimneys traced gray wisps in the blue sky. Ludwig rode past them, not stopping to talk.

He came across a few bands of white hunters, Kentucky rifles on their arms.

"Watch out, stranger," they warned, shifting plugs of tobacco to other bulging cheeks. "Shawnees are on the warpath, looking for horses like that fine critter you got. Miami are mad too."

"Why are they angry?" asked Ludwig, lounging beside their fire. He noted they had set it cautiously in the lee of some high rocks, and someone was always on guard.

"White folks moving in. Crossed the mountains in wagons and are settling. Injuns don't like it. They raid at nights, steal the horses, burn the fields, sometimes carry off the children."

"What about furs?" asked Ludwig.

One man laughed and shrugged. "Furs done going away, stranger," he said. "It used to be, ten year ago, there was plenty beaver, wolf, bear, lynx, fox. Now I ain't seen a beaver for four years. No mink to speak of. Few foxes. Nope, reckon the furs are gone from here. Have to go further."

"Have to go to the Mississippi River," drawled one soft-spoken man in smoke-burnt buckskins. "Furs done gone. Trade posts closing."

"Traders moving further west," said another.

"But the further west you go, the wuss the Injuns are," drawled one old-timer, gray of hair and bald on top. He noted Ludwig's curious look at the long scar on his bald head. He touched the scar in gingerly fashion. "Want to hear how I got this mark on me?"

Ludwig nodded, the others laughed or groaned, "Not that story again!" said one of his companions. "Gives me night-mares!"

But the man told the story anyway. "I was traveling with just one partner. We set traps up in the hills near the Canada border and built a small cabin for the winter. Fixed fine, we were. Then some Injuns come busting out of the hills, mad as fire, 'cause some white trapper stole one of their gals and took her off as his squaw. Well, they burned us out, and my partner got an arrow in his back. Dead as dead. They caught me and took my hair off with a tomahawk, left me bleeding for dead. It took me a time to get over that. I crawled to a fort, and even though they was British, they took care of me. Surgeon sewed me up, said I was lucky to keep some of my hair." And he laughed, while another man shuddered.

"You talk about the British being good!" he said. "Maybe they was good to you, 'cause you was sick to death. But me—well, I didn't get such fine treatment! They caught me trapping up on the Abitibi River, that flows into Hudson Bay. Tarred and feathered me and put me on a horse headed south! I complained to one of their law officers. He just looked at me and said I got off easy!"

"Wal," drawled another man, "all in all, we get into trouble wherever we go. But what is a fellow to do? The furs are getting scarce hereabouts. We have to go west or north! Toss a coin, throw the dice, you decide that way. Trouble either way!"

"Wherever the furs are, I got to go there," said one man philosophically. "When the furs are gone, then we got to go further to get some. No other way to live, for me. I like the wild. I'd die in a city."

Ludwig listened to them, traveled with them for a week, then thanked them and moved north. He had sober thoughts to carry with him. No more furs! The Indians were moving across the Mississippi River where the furs were more plentiful.

What a few short years, and then the furs were gone. Had they trapped too much? What had happened? Or did the fur-bearing animals leave an area when the white man moved in? He saw cabins almost every day, with clearings about them.

He would stop at some of the cabins now, identifying himself as a fur trader. He would be welcomed, after the first suspicious moments, and given a place to sleep beside the hearth. They would feed him, ask hungrily for the news from the East. He told them what he had read in the journals, the political news, the farmers news, what went on in New York. To them it was like the news of around the world, distant and unimportant, yet some touch of home for which they longed.

He patted the heads of the tow-headed children and said proudly, "My son was born November. We named him Colin."

"Aye, a baby son? Congratulations!" and out would come the jug of home brew. He would drink a little with them, smoke a pipe, and be off the next day, wondering how a woman could live in such wilderness. Not for his Agatha! No, he wanted a fine mansion for his wife, fine silks and satins, a carriage, an easier life.

He reached the edge of Lake Erie and blundered right into a customs post. A single agent was there, bold-eyed and dark, Jack Smithson by name.

He was not fooled by Ludwig's story of wandering in the wilderness. "Got trade goods, have you?" he grinned. He was a young man, restless, about twenty-five.

Ludwig waited for him to ask the right questions, then he

told the man, "For ten pounds in gold, would you let me cross the lake here?"

The man blinked, then winked at him. "Why not? I'll take you across in my barge." He laughed, "Tell you what, I'll go with you and help carry your packs for another ten pounds in gold! I don't see that much in two years!"

It was Ludwig's turn to swallow. He studied the man. Could he trust him? He thought so. The man lived alone and was obviously left to himself too much. They struck a deal.

Jack Smithson got out his barge and chose a calm day in April. They went across the lake in two days, taking turns poling and rowing, and made it to the other side. Smithson did the talking. He was showing a friend the lake, how grand it was, and how good the fishing was. They paused to fish and were cooking the fish over an open fire when another customs team came up. They shared the fish, and some jokes, and the other men moved on.

The barge was left with a friend of Smithson. Then the two men walked on up toward Lake George, and there met with some Indians just coming in with a full canoe of furs. Ludwig paused to bargain with them. The trading took two days. Ludwig wanted them to open every pack, and he studied the furs so keenly that the Indians blinked in wonder.

He bought only their best furs, those his horse and himself could carry. He paid them well, giving them all his trade goods and some of the coins, though letting them think he gave them all the coins. At the greedy look in their eyes, it would not do to allow them to believe he had more gold in his belt.

Smithson chuckled again and again as he led the way back to the barge. "If I had knowed you were such a smart trader," he said, "I would have asked for half the profits!"

But he stuck to his bargain, amiably, and waved Ludwig off as he departed from the small lonely customs post. "Come again, anytime, friend!" he called.

So Ludwig had made another friend on the lonely border, and he made a mental note of the place so he might find Smithson again—if the man's restless feet had not caused him to move on. Smithson was twenty pounds in gold richer, and Ludwig had furs worth more than twelve thousand pounds in London.

He returned to New York, this time avoiding lonely hunters and trappers, cabins, and farms. He would share his furs with no man. He traveled often by night, his horse carrying three packs, and he himself carrying two lighter packs on his back.

Ludwig had to travel slowly, since the packs were heavy and he wanted to move secretly. And traveling over the Pennsylvania mountains with five packs was certainly no easy matter. He trudged on day after day, grateful when it did not pour down rain. The snows and ice were finally gone from the rivers, and the fertile green sprang up. He could eat berries to vary his diet of dried game. His coffee was long gone.

He came to the Hudson River and paid for a passage downriver on a small boat filled with farming produce. It was late May, and the first lettuce and cabbage had come up in the fertile farmlands. A farmer sold him some apples to eat, and Ludwig ate them greedily. How delicious they tasted!

He returned to New York during the first days of June, with the rich, lustrous furs and much knowledge. The knowledge disturbed him and caused him and Mr. Baines to talk for many a day.

The men now realized that they must either prepare to travel many long miles out past the Mississippi River, to deal with strange Indian tribes they had never met, or they must dare the laws and customs agents and secretly move up into Canada, to trade for furs up in the northlands.

That decision would come slowly, as they worked on the furs that summer. By autumn they must make up their minds.

Chapter 7

Ludwig thought long and carefully about what he should do. He had heard stories about the American West and the Northwest Territories. The Indians there were of many different tribes and often fought fiercely among themselves.

The white man was their enemy. Some had formerly lived among the Colonists and been gradually pushed westward. They had lost their homes, and some had been victims of massacres, and lost brothers, fathers, wives, children.

Others further west had known the bitterness and cruelty of Spanish conquerors. They had taken some of the methods of the Spanish invaders who had used the techniques of the Spanish Inquisition to torture their Indian prisoners in an attempt to discover the sources of gold. The gold of the Seven Cities, the Spanish sought eagerly for it, and death lay wherever they stepped.

The British were conquerors also, thought Ludwig. But they used—and he smiled grimly—more "civilized" methods. They were arrogant, thinking that all of North America would belong to them eventually, as they drove out the French, the Spanish, the Russians. But they had not counted on being defied by the Americans! Still—the two peoples spoke the same language, they had a similar background of customs, law, and beliefs. Ludwig thought that he did not care yet to risk the furious Indian tribes, and their hatred of all white men, except the few trappers who had won their confidence. He did not want to lose his scalp to them.

He thought he would risk his chances with the British. The Canadians were a wild, carefree lot, laughing and singing. They would be furious for a time with an intruder. But with care, he could win them over or persuade them he was not much of a threat to their way of life. They could understand a man wandering alone in their woods—if he presented his case well.

And he might be able to evade them.

The lesser of the two risks—the Canadians or the Indians of the West—seemed to lie with the Canadians. It would be a difficult journey either way.

*   *   *

Autumn came, and Ludwig had made up his mind. Mr. Baines protested, but with evident relief, when Ludwig said, "I shall go alone this time."

The man was ill, his face pale and drawn. He was reluctant to go to a doctor, but Ludwig asked around until he found a physician with a good reputation among the people. He took Mr. Baines to him for an examination.

The doctor told them, "It is the heart. It is not strong, the beat becomes irregular. It is not safe for him to lift heavy loads, nor travel long distances."

That settled the matter. Ludwig told Mr. Baines, "You will remain at home in the warehouse, then, and take care of all the matters here. Our new young clerk needs training, which will take much time. But do not work long hours. I intend that you shall rest much! See to it!"

Mr. Baines looked uneasy. "But I shall not earn our partnership. Perhaps I will take less now, yes?"

"No, for I need you here to take care of the orders. Watch for the captains on our trusted ships, commission them to buy trade goods for us, and send off our furs only with those you trust most. This is most important."

That made Franklin Baines feel better. Ludwig privately gave instructions to the new young sturdy clerk, not to allow Mr. Baines to lift any heavy packs or carry crates about.

"Do all the heavy work for him. That is why I wish you to live in the apartment with him. Take care of him. His mind is most important to our business!"

The clerk promised to obey him implicitly, and Ludwig went back home. A more difficult farewell awaited him.

How he adored his Agatha and little Colin! He could scarcely endure to leave them. The lad was a year old, staggering about on plump young legs, gurgling in answer to teasing questions, flinging plump arms about Ludwig's neck when the father scooped him up. "Da-dada," he would cry out when he saw him come in the door and run to him.

And Agatha, with her gentle smile, and the look in her blue-green eyes just for him. That secret look that told of the passion inside her cool appearance. He was more and more reluctant to leave them both.

But he must go off. And he did, in mid-September, into the far north. He went by way of Kurt Aronhold's land, and the farmer made him welcome. All went well. Ludwig gathered up the best furs be could purchase from the Indians, managing

79

to meet the bands before they went to any of the British trading posts, and choosing the best mink, ermine, blue fox, silver fox, and marten. He stayed alert and had no trouble on the journey.

He came home by Christmas with a rich load, and sold most of the furs in New York. The markets had increased for the furs as men became more wealthy and craved the signs of wealth for themselves and their wives. A mink coat with an ermine collar—ah, that looked nice in society! And Mr. Baines and the clerk worked hard on the furs, as did Ludwig when he was not out dealing for their sales. They sold them to good furriers, with high prices for the best ones and had the pride of knowing their work was known and in much demand.

The beaver hats were more in evidence than before. Every man of any importance wore one. Whatever style of hat he favored, be it military, curved brim or tricorn, it must be of the smart beautiful shining beaver fur, not only warm in the winter but also of the highest style.

Ludwig brooded quietly during the winter as he went about the city. He listened to the talk. Furs were more in demand, yet he knew they were more scarce in the West of America, in the Northwest Territory. And there was more talk of war. Even in the cities of the East it was said that war must come. The Indians were enraged that more and more white settlers were coming out to the fertile lands of the Ohio River. Treaties were broken, they said, and the whites had no right to build cabins and make fences for their horses and cattle, and break the land for farming.

Up north, above the Great Lakes, the canny Scots and the easygoing French had made friends of the Indians of the East. Few were militant, and only the Blackfeet and other tribes of the West still attacked the fur trade posts. And Ludwig need not worry about the far west of Canada.

Nor did he wish to go west of the Mississippi, not yet. It was too unsettled, too dangerous, for a man alone. Fur trade parties were made up of many men, companies with keen sharpshooters, not afraid of battles with whole tribes of Indians, to obtain the beaver and even the strange huge buffalo.

Ludwig still worked alone, but for Mr. Baines and the clerk. He would travel alone, in secret and stealth. That was the best way for now.

So in the early spring, in March, he set out alone, with a horse and wagon, and made his way this time to the post of

Jack Smithson. He approached the customs post warily, knowing that the young man might not be there.

But the dark-eyed, bold man was still there and glad to see him. "Ah, my friend, Mr. Gunther!" cried Jack, flinging up his arms. "I was in despair! If you had not come after this horrid lonely winter, I was going to give up and find some other occupation!"

He made Ludwig welcome, putting hot soup before him and questioning him eagerly about the news of the East and the world. He was restless, ready to give up the lonely post and the low-paying occupation of agent. Ludwig resolved to hire him and put the idea to him as they sat long before the hearth fire.

Smithson was to leave his job, giving it to a friend who had been applying for it. The friend was of the same restless ilk as Smithson and would help them slip across the lake and back again. It was decided that Smithson would travel with Ludwig so he could carry back to the lake twice the packs of furs as before. Each would drive a wagon back East. And two could keep track of the Indians, their approach, the British soldiers and their posts.

Arrangements were quickly made, much less formal than in the Eastern cities. Smithson's friend was installed in days, and Ludwig and Jack Smithson headed north across the Great Lakes. They hid their two wagons and horses with the same French friends as before, and they set out on foot.

They looked like two young tough wanderers, not businessmen. They traveled with rifles at hand, eyes sharp for any strange movement in brush or trees. They avoided the bands of soldiers easily. The "scarlet coats," as the Indians called them, could be seen for miles.

They intercepted some bands of Indians, opened the packs of furs, and over the firelight in the evening they would go over the packs, picking out the best furs only. Ludwig had not bothered with many trade goods. He had only the smallest, lightest with him—needles and pins, thread, small sharp knives, half a dozen flutes, and some gold and silver coins. When a trade was struck, and the talk finished, he would sit down and play for them, for the Indians enjoyed it enormously, that music from old Germany, performed before the warm fire in the cold spring night. The stars blazed overhead in the midnight-blue skies, and sometimes there would be odd flashing lights in the northern sky. The Indians would gaze at the

81

lights solemnly, the streaks of green and rose and orange, and tell long strange stories about them, and their legends of how the world was made.

"They like you," said Smithson thoughtfully as they started out one morning. The Indians had silently gone hours before.

"I do not feel one way or another," said Ludwig, puzzled. "I deal honestly with them, I give them knives or silver coins, and the price is what they would get from the British, or higher. That is all."

"No, that is not all," said Smithson, his dark eyes glancing about automatically to the land about them. He strode lightly, his boots scarcely made a mark on the thick grassy turf, his buckskins melted against the undergrowth. "They trust you, they like to bargain with you, they smile more with you. And when you play—my God, do you see their eyes?"

Ludwig was silent, since he had not thought much about the matter. He did what pleased himself, and if the Indians also liked the music, well and good. He had noted their pleasure, but it meant little to him, just being a pleasant way to end the day. He lived for his family, his Agatha and little Colin, for his partners and for his future. That was all that mattered to him.

He dealt honestly with men, because that was the way he lived. Principles had been instilled early in him. One gave honest goods for honest pay. One did honest work for that return. One dealt with men as he wished to be dealt with. In this world it paid to be careful, and shrewd, and not to trust too much. Care, prudence, hard work and honesty, those were the ideals by which he lived. Laws were another matter. He had seen the injustice of the laws of his lord of Hess. He had seen the men go off to war, unwillingly, reluctantly, for no reason of their own. And when they had returned—if they returned—many were blinded, crippled, mentally deranged.

No, laws were not made to be obeyed. They were made by powerful men, and imposed on other men but only if they could so impose! So Ludwig obeyed only those laws he must, and for himself, he would quietly do as he thought best.

He liked his new land, his America. A man could be truly free. No man had the right to stop him from earning as much of a fortune as he chose. Only physical limits could stop him. And Ludwig was young, strong as an ox, and clever. He figured he could make thousands of dollars, maybe hundreds of thousands of dollars, for himself, and his family, within another ten years.

Then he would build a mansion for Agatha. He would dress her in silk. His sons and daughters would go to the best schools. Education was a good thing. A man needed to be smart, and his Agatha was living proof that it was good for a woman to be smart also. He believed in education, cleverness, honesty and paying honest wages for honest work. But he wished to owe no man or king or lord any scrape of the foot or bend of the head.

He lay awake that night, thinking of the mansion he would plan. Because he was awake, he heard the snap of a twig, the quiet slither of a footstep near to him. He was up in a flash, his rifle to the ready.

From the darkness came the whine of an arrow!

"Up, Smithson!" he said in a low tone and shook Jack awake. He half dragged the dazed young man into the shelter of a huge oak.

"What is it?" Jack was rubbing his eyes, shaking himself from the deep first sleep of the night. Another arrow whined and struck into the tree bark, sending showers of bark over their heads.

"Listen." Ludwig hushed him, holding up his hand.

How many Indians were out there? Ludwig faced toward the last remains of the campfire and tried to peer into the thickness of the trees. He could make out nothing, but someone was there.

Jack Smithson faced the other direction, peering into the trees all about them, the thick bushes. Leaves were in full growth on the tree boughs, making it difficult to see far. They sat quietly, listening, rifles ready, heads alert.

Finally out of the darkness crept one Indian. Smithson lifted his rifle, but Ludwig put his hand on the barrel. "Wait," he cautioned.

Another Indian joined the first. They muttered together. In keen profile, they revealed proud heads, with long high tufts of hair, the rest shaved. Were they ready for battle?

Ludwig made Jack wait, though he himself longed for the first shot. Finally a third Indian joined them, grumbling. Ludwig still waited, and finally the Indians sat down at the campfire and began poking around the packs. One drew out the flute and talked to the others about it, fingering it curiously.

Ludwig called out, startling them. "Friend! Friend!"

They scattered like autumn leaves, fleeing to the trees again. "Friend!" called Ludwig again. "We are fur traders! Do you have furs to sell? Give good price!"

Silence. Finally one Indian came out, warily. "We have no furs," he said in a fairly good English accent.

Ludwig stepped out, motioning to Jack to stay where he was, his rifle trained on the Indian.

He held his own rifle loosely in his hand, barrel pointing down. The other Indians came out slowly, glancing toward the tree where Jack stood in shadow.

"You are trappers?" asked Ludwig slowly, clearly.

The one Indian nodded, gloomily. "Fur stolen," he said. "Injun take. All traps empty!"

They were lean, obviously hungry. Ludwig gazed at them thoughtfully.

"We sit, eat together, friends," he said.

They exchanged somber looks, but nodded to Ludwig. "Come out, Jack," he said. "We will fix food for friends, talk some."

Jack came from under the trees, got out some meat, and set it on sticks over the fire. One Indian tended those, with wary glances at Jack. Jack got out his battered coffeepot and fixed coffee; they drank together.

The Indians could not wait until the meat was cooked. They grabbed the sticks, and ate it, gnawing and gulping at the meat until it was finished. Ludwig put more meat on the sticks as they ate, and prepared some biscuits, heating them in the fire. He had thought to have them for breakfast, but this need was greater.

When they had eaten and drunk their fill, he said, "Talk now?"

The leader nodded. His legs folded beneath him, he said, "I am Red Hawk. Miami Indians, us. We come north, hunt. Bad Indian take mink from trap, take all furs. We shoot, use up all bullets. They run off, take all. We not go home to people. No food, no fur. People hungry." He scarcely glanced up, but his tone was low and ashamed. He had gone out hunting, and he had nothing to take home.

"How much food you need to take home, maybe?" asked Ludwig slowly, painfully searching for words. "How many people?"

"Old men, old women, wives, children, no more hunters. We are twenty, maybe more."

Ludwig nodded. It was a small remnant of a tribe. Drifting away from a main body, perhaps. Or thrown out for some tribal reason.

He thought carefully. If he gave them bullets, they might

shoot him and Jack for their packs of furs, the coins and the rifles.

"Morning come, we hunt together," he said. "We sleep now."

Black eyes glistened in shock and pleasure. They nodded, accepting that. The Indians lay down, and so did Jack. Ludwig sat at the rebuilt fire, until morning. He could go for several days and nights with little sleep, being young and husky, and he was accustomed to it from other journeys.

In the morning Ludwig gave each Indian three bullets, and loaded his own rifle. They set out, soon finding a small herd of deer. With good aim they brought down four deer. Ludwig and Jack helped them skin the animals and cut them up in large pieces. They then found some young willow trees, cut poles, and helped the Indians string the meat on the poles.

"You can cross river, the great river?" asked Ludwig.

"We have big canoe," said the lead Indian. "How we pay you? No furs."

"I hunt here, many times. I come again, buy furs. I know your name, ask for my friend Red Hawk. Maybe next time you have furs, we sell, we friends. That is good?"

He held out his hand, frankly, his rifle in his left hand, hanging loosely. The Indian's hand met his, clasped hard.

"You come again, you stay at my tent. You welcome. Next time, many furs!"

"You take more bullets, some coins. I buy furs next time," said Ludwig conclusively, in relief. They could have been murdered by hungry men. Instead they had made some friends in this wild territory.

He got out the coins he had ready, in a small deerskin pouch, and handed them over with a dozen bullets. The Indians thanked him gravely, and soon were on their way, the poles over their shoulders.

"Wow," said Jack in relief, his shoulders showing his tension. "We got out of that one!"

"And with our scalps," said Ludwig, touching his blond hair.

"You'll never see them again, not that lot!"

"Maybe so, maybe not. In any event we made some friends, not enemies. They will remember, and maybe pass the word around, that not all white men are bad and greedy."

"What do you care what an Injun thinks of you?" Jack frowned, puzzled.

"They are men. We live in this world together. I would

rather men thought well of me, than evil. I'll live longer, maybe," said Ludwig dryly.

Jack Smithson and Ludwig wandered far that spring. They had great good fortune, as Smithson put it. Ludwig thought their success came from hard work but did not argue with him.

They took back eight packs of fine furs, the best, as spring wore on. Jack became jubilant and talked wildly of what he would buy when he returned East. But Ludwig said nothing. He did not count his money until he had it in his big tough hands.

Chapter 8

On the next journey north they veered a bit to the west. Voyageurs were returning from the far west with packs in their long canoes, bearded, weary, clothes worn from the winter in the wilds. Ludwig and Jack hid in the bushes beside the wide rivers and watched as the men bent to the paddles, and made the laden canoes swing around the dangerous rocks, and over the rippling white waters of the rapids.

"That is hard long work," said Jack in a murmur.

Ludwig nodded. But would they have to go through that to get more furs one day? He wondered. The days might pass when a man could go out alone into the wilderness and bargain with the Indians. One might have to go far and hard, in the company of other men, organized, humbling oneself to carry the packs around the portages, working for some big company like Hudson's Bay Company. He did not want that. He wanted to work only for himself, and would do anything to retain his freedom.

Jack and Ludwig were resting and at their ease at a campfire late one night, their new packs of furs resting under their heads, when a twig snapped. Ludwig was up and alert in moments—but too late.

A dozen Canadians in their woolen shirts and plaid hats came into the clearing. They scowled at the two Americans.

In the lead was a familiar figure—tall, red haired, and now wearing a thick red-brown beard, grimy and ragged with a long winter of traveling. Blaise MacCameron!

"So! You are the one who has been stealing our furs!" he growled at Ludwig. Jack Smithson's hand reached stealthily toward his rifle. A Canadian kicked it from near him, and a pistol flashed in the firelight.

"Calm yourselves," warned Ludwig, as much to his partner as the Canadians. "I have stolen nothing. I traded with Indians and gave always fair value."

His cool voice chilled the hostile air. MacCameron relaxed a bit and nodded to his men. They leaned against the trees, and a couple slid down to rest on the thick pine-strewn ground.

MacCameron crouched on his haunches and plucked a twig to nibble on as he studied Ludwig thoughtfully. "You have no right to come up into our lands and take our furs. All right, ye say you bought them. I say, all right, you bought them. But those are furs we would have bought for our fur company! You had no right to dicker for them."

Ludwig studied him thoughtfully, letting silence calm them all. "You work for the Hudson's Bay Company?" he asked.

MacCameron shrugged. "Like hell!" he grumbled. "I have my own company! They don't own all the wilderness."

"The Hudson's Bay Company says they own all, by king's charter," drawled Ludwig placidly, his eyes narrowing shrewdly. "Yet you go about the forests and travel the lakes, and take the furs you can buy for your own."

There was a little silence, broken by a brief chuckle from one of the bearded shaggy men behind MacCameron. The big Scotsman scowled.

"Words, words, you are clever with words, you German with your heavy accent. I heard about you," he growled. "I heard about the big blond man who plays his pipe for the Indians after a sale. I remembered you, and figured you was about."

Ludwig was silent again. His body seemed relaxed on the pack of furs behind him, but his hand was not far from his pistol. At the odds of twelve to two, he knew it was no good to struggle. He must talk, and talk.

Smithson said, "We trade fair. And what about you, coming south across the Great Lakes? That land came to us after the American Revolution. We are free of England! She no longer rules us! The land is ours, yet you come south and hunt and trap, and trade for furs in our land!"

"*Ja*, the land is ours," said Ludwig slowly, as MacCameron seemed to blaze up, his blue eyes like fire. "Yet the British still have posts in our land. Why is that?"

MacCameron seemed to hesitate, frowning. He had probably not thought much about that. "Why—the land is always ours. That revolution—pah! Britain will take you over again, I have heard talk. You won't last long on your own. You need trade with us. I'll warrant you sail to England to trade with your furs, or send them over!"

"True, but at our wishing," said Ludwig. "I will tell you this, MacCameron. I came to America from Germany, for I would be a free man. In my German state a man was not his own man. He must go to war if his lord said so. He must pay high taxes, he may marry only if his lord permits, he must give

88

part of his money from his trade, his farm, his any work, to his lord. That to me is not just or fair or right. If a man cannot keep the money earned by the sweat of his brow—why, he is not a man, but a slave."

"Ah," said MacCameron, and there was a murmur from behind him. MacCameron relaxed and sat down more easily on the ground. "So, you came to be a free man? But an Englishman is a free man."

"Are you?" asked Ludwig. "I had heard that Scots were turned off their lands and sent to America to fight against us. I have heard that some are driven from their homes, forced to labor in factories. Even their small children are taken from them and forced to work unto death, is this not so?"

"Where did you hear this?" growled MacCameron uneasily.

"I read it in the gazettes. There are articles from the newspapers of Glasgow and Edinburgh. A few protests, stifled. Who owns you, MacCameron? Why did you come to Canada?"

The man leaped up to his full height, glaring fiercely. "No man owns me!" he cried. "A shipload of us came to Canada, and now we are free men! We work as we please, we own land—"

"Land in Scotland?" asked Ludwig dryly. "Land in your own Highlands? Or did the English drive you out and send you to a new wild land, to risk your necks for them? Do they send you to test the land, to see if it will support the English in comfort? Will they allow you to keep your house after they decide to come out to Canada? Will you own land? Will you pay their taxes? Are you truly a free man?"

"Curse you," said the Scotsman without heat. "Curse you. I had put all that behind me."

"A man taught me to read, to think, to understand," said Ludwig dispassionately. "A schoolmaster taught me, God thank him. In Canada I think you are not free. In America I shall be free, or die for it. Never will I live under another man's rule, never will another man be my master! Can you say the same?"

"I am a free man!" cried MacCameron. "I am—now. I own my house, my land. I have a company which I have formed. I pay taxes, yes, but—"

"But your wife and son died on voyage, MacCameron," reminded a deep burred voice behind him.

The dark red shaggy head drooped, and a bronzed hand went to the bearded face. "Aye," he said, muffled. "My wife, my beloved—beauty—my son—my son. Now I am married to a French girl, and I have a new son. Etienne is his name, a French name. She would not even give him a Scots name, a good Scots name. And I canna return to the land of my birth, to the hills that my baby eyes first saw."

There was a long silence in the clearing. Jack Smithson gazed thoughtfully at the burly Scotsman. Ludwig's head was bent in thought also, his mind busy.

"We are men," he said finally, quietly. "We live a hard life, but we are somewhat free. Perhaps that is all we can hope for in this world. Pride and a desire for money drive me out to the wilderness. An Indian might sink a tomahawk into my back. Nature herself is raw and harsh. I may die in the freezing lakes, and no man know my grave. Yet here in this new land, I am my own man as much as possible. I drive myself, I work for myself and my beloved wife and my new son."

"You have a son?" asked Blaise MacCameron with more interest.

"*Ja.* And when my Colin is a grown man, he shall not know the fetters which bound my childhood. He shall go to school," said Ludwig proudly, "and learn of the hardships there of Germany and of Hess. But he himself shall be surrounded with ease and pleasure, he shall wear good clothes, he shall choose what work he shall perform. My son shall be a free American!"

"Ah," said MacCameron. "And my son shall be a free Canadian."

"Or a Britisher?" snapped Ludwig.

"Paa! Man, let us not start another quarrel," and Mac-Cameron began to laugh, a merry rollicking laugh. "I think you have won this one, damn it! Come, let us sit down together, and eat and drink together, for one night at least! And maybe tomorrow I shall persuade you not to hunt in my forests any longer!"

"Your forests?" asked Ludwig, shaking his shaggy blond head. "I see we shall not cease to quarrel!" But he got up and took out his pack of supplies, a pan, plate and knife, a paper in which fresh bread was wrapped, and some cheese.

Pleased, the Canadians brought out raw meat, which two of them cooked over the fire, turning it on long whittled spits of wood. Smithson made the coffee in his much-loved and battered copper kettle, and they sat down to eat and drink together.

They remained together for several hours the next morning, before parting. The Canadians, more at ease, told the two

Americans stories of the wild west frontier of their land, of the Indians who were friendly and of those who fought with stealth and in the night.

Before they left, big Blaise MacCameron held out his bronzed paw to Ludwig, and the two men shook hands. "I warn you, stay out of my lands, and do not trade with our Indians," said MacCameron with a booming voice and an ominous scowl of his bearded red face. "I tell you as a friend, do not come here! It is our land, and these furs you hold here belong to us!"

"You have treated me with courtesy. I shall not forget it," said Ludwig. "But you must permit me the privilege of thinking with my own mind!"

The other men laughed and joked, shook hands, and strode away. Jack Smithson drew a long breath as Ludwig kicked out the large fire and poured water from the small stream over it.

"Whew, I thought it would come to battle last night! Yet we still have our furs."

"There is an honest man," Ludwig told him, indicating the departing MacCameron with a nod of his head. "But I will not willingly cross him. His temper is fierce."

"I think yours could be also," said Smithson with a grin.

Ludwig was quiet and thoughtful as they returned to the French farm, loaded up. He thanked the taciturn French couple for their aid, paid them in gold, and he and Smithson drove the two wagons loaded with furs and covered with canvas back to Pennsylvania, and to New York, and to the city.

It was summer, hot and humid that year, and the men sweated in the warehouse as they scraped the raw pelts, stretched them, hung them to dry in the clean air.

Ludwig had much to think about. Agatha was expecting another child, and the hot weather seemed to trouble her this time. Colin was running about like any two-year-old boy, full of mischief, a devil in him at times, bothering his mother until she fretted at him. They would need a larger house soon, and a maid to help with the work.

And should he return to Canada? Or should he make up a small party of men, himself, Smithson, two or three other experienced men, and go west of the Mississippi? There would be danger, for the Indians were more ferocious, and many trappers had lost their scalps. The Indians were not so interested in trading. They would buy what rifles and ammunition they wanted, and fight against each other readily.

Mr. Franklin Baines had another worry for Ludwig. He

waited a time, until the work let up, and they sat with pipes smoking comfortably in the warehouse. They sank back into their thick armchairs, and the blue smoke curled up to the rafters where the pelts were hanging.

"I sent four packs of furs to England while you were gone, Ludwig," Baines began abruptly. He reached out for his mug of strong coffee. His face was pale and more drawn than last winter, thought Ludwig.

"So?" asked Ludwig. "I saw the figures in the books. The pelts were not so good, *ja?*"

Baines shook his graying head very slowly. "The pelts were good, Ludwig. A man brought them in, an old hunter who no longer wished to handle his own goods. He will bring more to us. He is experienced in the West. A man named Billy, who would give no last name."

"So?"

"He is down on our books as Billy Montana, for he said he had gone so far as a place where the name was Montana. It is the Spanish word for mountain. I bought his furs and said we would buy all he had and give him an honest price. Ludwig, the furs were of prime quality."

Ludwig frowned slightly, watching the blue smoke of his pipe weave its way up to the pelts.

Mr. Baines added, "When the merchant returned, he claimed the pelts were not of first quality, so he did not get much money for them. I know he lied, Ludwig."

"Well," said Ludwig. That was the end of the matter for the time. They could no longer trust the merchants; everyone was out for his own greedy purposes. "We must find another way," he concluded.

He would do nothing until his child was born. He had vowed never to leave Agatha while she was with child. The woman was capable and sturdy, he thought. His woman, his wife. Yet when he returned from a long hard journey, how she ran to greet him! Her arms curled about his hard waist, and she put her head on his filthy dirty coat as though she did not notice the grime. She hugged him, and there were tears in her blue-green eyes, and she laughed and cried for joy.

When their first son had been born, her hand had gone out to his, clasping his fingers weakly. Her eyes had sought for his gaze when he came in from work. A blush came to her cheek at a caress from him. She leaned on him, not like some weak missish girl, but as a strong woman turned to a man she loved.

And Ludwig thought constantly while he was gone of his woman and his son. His family! They needed him, they depended on him. And he needed them, for his purpose in life. He did not want wealth for himself alone. He wanted it for them. He would build a larger house—for them. He would make a fortune—for them. Nothing mattered as much in the world to Ludwig as his wife and his son, and the child to come.

So he waited through the long summer, not venturing out to the forests again. Smithson worked in the warehouse, wandered the streets, lost all his money in games of chance, and laughed about it. He might never settle down, but he was a good worker when directed by another stronger man. He would go west when Ludwig said so.

In mid-September the trees began to turn to crimson and gold. Fallen brittle leaves scattered over the dirt roads of the city and the sidewalks, but Agatha did not go out to sweep them. Ludwig hired a lad to help with the outside work and a girl to help inside.

And soon Agatha was to bed with the child. It did not take so many hours this time, but it was long enough to make Ludwig walk up and down the hallway, clenching his fists in futile agony as the cries resounded from the bedchamber.

After about eleven hours his mother-in-law came down to him. Her face shone with sweat, but her eyes were serene and her mouth smiled. She put her hand to his and clasped the white-knuckled hard hands.

"You have a daughter, Ludwig. A most beautiful little flower of a girl, she is." And her eyes began to glow with tears.

He went upstairs, his heart full. And now a daughter he had! He looked into the little crumpled face, touched the wee fingers, and felt as though he had melted to honey inside. Such a beautiful little girl! All the women hung over her, and Agatha glowed with pride.

She was so lovely, his little princess, his Minna. Big blue eyes, blond tufts of hair on her well-shaped head, a round little face, the loveliest little girl he had ever seen.

Colin came running to see what the excitement was about. Agatha had been telling him that a child would be born, and one day he could play with her. But even the strong mischievous child knew that this dainty little doll was not to be played with. His hand touched the wee fingers and he kissed them impulsively.

"Who is this?" he asked, and they laughed with pride, and

93

told him. "My sister? What is sister? Minna? Hello, Minna!"

When visitors came, he spread out the little fingers on his brown hand and showed them, "Look at her little hand! Look at her little feet, how tiny they are!" And the baby gurgled and waved her arms when she saw him coming.

Ludwig could scarcely tear himself away from his small family that winter. But he had resolved he must go himself to England. He took the rich loads of furs with him, more then twenty-five packs of the most precious of mink, marten, blue and silver fox, land otter, and went to the best merchants with them.

The sums he received made him purse his lips in a whistle of amazement. He was a wealthy man now! He had hundreds of thousands of pounds, and he turned them into dollars as soon as he came home again. He received such high prices that he knew that the shipping merchants had been cheating him. He must go himself to deal on the furs from now on. More trouble, more work he must do himself.

On the ship home, in January, he pondered, leaning on the railing as the winds and waves lashed the small sailing vessel. His pipe puffed fiercely as he thought.

He had orders in his pockets for three times the furs he had brought this time. Three times! How could he get such furs? Where could he go? Must he go out to the untamed wilderness beyond the Mississippi? Or could he send men, such as Billy Montana or Smithson, or both together?

Or go up into Canada? Men like MacCameron would resent him the more fiercely, should he deliberately come again after their warnings.

Baines could handle the warehouse, with the clerk. But the man was visibly weakening. Never again could he travel on that troublesome tough road west, to buy furs. Ludwig must do it all himself, directing the men.

Success had brought more trouble with it. He pondered, watching the waves curl toward the ship, the green deep waves covered with the white spume.

Would it always be like this? Success brought more success, and more trouble. Money breeded money, and spawned more work, which brought more money—and more work. A never-ending spiral.

Chapter 9

Reluctantly Ludwig Gunther made up a company of reckless, experienced fur traders and led them west for the winter. He hated to leave his Agatha and the two children, but it must be. His fortune forced him into new paths. He could no longer go alone, and his days of total freedom in the wilderness were over.

The group traveled by horseback across the new lands of the Northwest Territory, and they kept guard every night. They saw new raw cabins rising in the wilderness of western Pennsylvania, along the Ohio River, beyond that into the new lands. Soldiers of the Revolution had been awarded some lands in lieu of money to pay for their fighting, and they had left the worn-out stony soil of Connecticut to go west in covered wagons, or horseback, or even on boats down the rivers to the Ohio River and on to the new, untried soils.

The Indians were fighting, Ludwig soon discovered. They had to beware of the Shawnee, the fierce Miami, the Wyandot who had been the Huron of the French north. Driven out of Canada, those who were left had come south into the lands below the Great Lakes. They stole horses, fought the new settlers, burned forts, watched sullenly as more and more whites came into their lands in the huge wagons covered with white canvas, carrying beds, chairs, all household goods. The whites with blue eyes were coming to remain, and the Indians feared and hated them.

The animals of the forest had fled before the white settlers. The fur traders had come early, taken most of the pelts, and gone further west, across the great river, the muddy winding wide Mississippi. So Ludwig went and his party also, traveling by day, cautiously, keeping more guard, making campfires in the lee of rocks, and putting out the fires at night.

They had left in September. It was November when they reached the lands they wished to find. There were some Indians who knew few whites. They had met fur traders, and roving bands would come and stop a night or two with them to trade the pelts for knives, coins, the copper kettles they enjoyed.

Finally the fur party came to some mountains covered with

snow. Billy Montana had taken over the guidance of the party, and he knew this land like the palm of his dirty bronzed hand.

"Here is good land, many animals here," he said. "I know the Indians. I can talk to them. We set up camp here, for the winter. They come to us."

Ludwig found that hard to believe. They had crossed a vast plain, the winter winds blew unceasingly. How would the Indians come to them? Did they not go south for the winter, or snuggle into cabins to rest? No, said Billy Montana, shaking his grizzled head.

"They hunt in the winter. They find the best furs then. You wait, you'll see."

Old Billy Montana chose the site for their winter quarters. He showed them how to build cabins of wood, felling trees, sharpening the points of each end, fitting them into notched slots so as to make the four corners of each cabin. They made roofs of more wood and interwove evergreen branches. In the lofts of the small cabins they set their supplies of dried meat, pemmican, which was pounded buffalo meat with berries, flour, salt, a little molasses, and the precious gunpowder and bullets.

They made three cabins and settled down to wait. And the Indians came. Warily, watchful, the men arrived first, then their women and children. They set up their tents of skins, squatted around fires to talk trade, and brought furs to the whites.

One group came for the winter. They simply settled down beside the same stream, set up their tents, and lived there, not moving away. Billy Montana went to talk to them and returned to report.

"One of the women is with child. She has lost two children, and they want to remain in one place and make sure she bears the child. She is wife to the chief, and has no other children. So it's important to them that the child comes alive."

Ludwig was curious about them. It seemed to be an extended family group. There was an old woman, white haired, who smoked a pipe. There were two older men, one the chief. And there were several children, ones the chief had adopted. Some were related to him, reported Billy.

Billy went over to talk to them sometimes. Ludwig came with him twice, and brought pemmican, flour, molasses. The old chief greeted him courteously, and the women were grateful for the food. They seemed hungry. Ludwig thought that the chief was probably too old for hunting.

The other man was crippled. Jack Smithson went with them and sat silently watching one of the young girls of the group. He said later, "They need a young man to hunt for them."

Ludwig was surprised at him. He had not thought Smithson would think about that, or care.

Ludwig liked to bathe more frequently than most of the fur hunters did. Not having a bathtub, he went to the river, cold as it was. He had found a sheltered place, and ducked into it, clothes and all, washing himself and his clothes, except for his boots.

That cold December day the sun was coming over the horizon in a crimson glory. He gazed up at it as he stripped off his heavy boots. He thought about home, and it seemed a long time away.

Then as he was about to slide into the cold icy waters, he heard a soft splashing. He froze, and he put his hand on his rifle. Would Indians come up by stream and attack them? It might be the quiet splash of a paddle in a war canoe.

He peered around the bushes, and then he did blink. A girl swam naked in the stream, her long black hair over her tanned shoulders, her breasts pink tipped, her long arms flashing as she soaped herself.

Ludwig stared, and in spite of his willpower he felt a strong erotic feeling in his loins. There was a girl to behold! Slim waisted, full breasted, yet young, doe-eyed, her black eyes soft as she gazed up at the trees. Her long black hair streamed wet, soft as silky cloth. And when she rose out of the water, and the river dripped from her, he saw her whole body, from the black hair to her slim waist and young firm breasts, down over her rounded loins, to her legs and well-turned ankles and feet. She scampered out of the cold water, shivering, laughing softly with pleasure.

Then she saw him, standing on the bank, boots off, staring at her. Her hands went to her breasts, then to her loins. She blushed with dismay and embarrassment. She froze there, unable to move.

Ludwig swallowed, took one step toward her, then paused. She was afraid, her eyes black and horrified. He shook his head and gestured slowly toward her clothing.

She watched him warily. He stepped back and turned from her, and waited. He heard her movements, and finally he turned back. He had thought she would dress in her brief skin garments, and run away. Instead she stood there, waiting, her red mouth soft, her black eyes waiting.

He stared again, at the water streaming from the black hair as her hands wrung and twisted the silky ropes. She watched him, and a smile began to curl her lips.

She wore only the slim slip of a skin which revealed every curve of her body. The blanket which she would have put about her shoulders still lay on the ground. Her legs were bare, since she had not put on the long tied skins which wound from feet to knees.

She stepped closer to him on slim bare feet. She smelled good, of the fresh water, and green leaves, and the crude soap they made of lye. She smelled like—a woman. She came up to Ludwig and put one hand on his chest.

"You—big," she said softly.

He licked his lips, she was looking at him as Agatha did. Agatha! Whatever was he thinking about?

The slim hand reached for his cheek; she touched him. He felt the strong reaction of a lusty man who had been without his woman for too long. The heat in his loins—the slimness and the smell of her—the body he had seen—

He reached out blindly and hauled her against himself. He put his mouth against her neck, that creamy golden neck, and felt her tremble. Her hand went to his thigh, and she pressed it deliberately. He lifted her head with his hand at her neck and put his mouth on the pink mouth. She seemed to sink against him. His lips were hungry, his body wanted hers, he wanted to throw her to the pine ground and crush her beneath himself.

A twig snapped, and he froze and pushed the girl from him. She tossed back her head and was away from him a dozen paces when Jack Smithson came from the bushes.

"Hello, there!" He looked young, eager, a little puzzled when he saw the two of them. He gazed hungrily at the girl. "Day Wind, you come to bathe?"

"I bathe," she said softly, slanting a look at him.

"Seems I chose the same place to get a bath," said Ludwig, his accent heavy. "You—come to bathe with the girl, Jack?"

"Well, sometimes we bathe here," said Jack, flushing, his gaze again on the girl. "You see, well, there ain't no men her age in the camp."

The girl slipped away in the trees. Jack looked disappointed. Ludwig shrugged and finished taking off his jacket and ducked down into the waters. He shivered and shuddered, but soon became accustomed to the cold river water. He bathed, swam a little, and came out, to strip off his clothes, and let the warm sun dry him and his clothes. Jack swam about, then did the same.

"She's a beauty, ain't she?" he asked dreamily. "I could make her my squaw, easy. They need a man in their family. The old chief likes me, he said so. They need a hunter for them."

Ludwig leaned back on his arm, watching Jack's expressions. The girl was looking for a "husband," a hunter for the tribe. Any big strong man would do, it seemed. He felt contemptuous of himself that he had almost fallen for her. Yet desire was hot in him when he thought of that creamy soft young skin.

He had wanted her, yes, he had wanted her, with a mindless, lusty desire that disregarded the fact she was an Indian. And he had felt contempt for Blaise MacCameron for taking a squaw! Men needed women, and in this wilderness there were no women but the Indian women.

And the girl was trying to help her tribe. The chief was old and slow and could no longer hunt the buffalo. He could trap and kill small animals, just enough to keep them from starving. Yet that was not enough. The little group needed a man.

Ludwig was not surprised when Jack Smithson left his cabin and settled down in a tent with the girl, Day Wind. He was happy, the girl bloomed and ceased to look at other men with a longing, slanting gaze.

The chief's wife had a son, and they all rejoiced. The baby was squalling and red faced when Ludwig came over with gifts for the wife and child. The chief was proud, his graying head erect, noble in his acceptance of the gifts. He thanked Ludwig for the presence of his men that winter, for their protection. It seemed another tribe was the enemy of his and had chased him from place to place.

The information gave Ludwig an idea. He talked to Jack about it. They agreed and set up a small trading post there, using the cabins. The Indian tribe would remain, and Billy Montana would be their contact. The white fur traders had hunted and trapped that winter, and there was plenty game, mostly beaver, fox, muskrat, along with a few bear that lived in the mountains.

By spring all was arranged. Ludwig had a trading post on the frontier. Jack Smithson would run the post and buy furs from fur traders and trappers who came by. Billy Montana and two others would come West each summer, collect the furs from them, and take them back East.

"I like it here. New York ain't good for me," said Jack Smithson simply as he came to say farewell. "I just drink and gamble there. Here's the place to live, under the big sky, with the white mountains protecting us. And Day Wind is a good woman. She's going to have my child, come autumn," and he smiled, the smile of a happy man. He was bearded, more mature, more settled now.

That was the answer for him, thought Ludwig as they turned homeward. By July they were back in New York with four wagons of furs and half a dozen trappers eager for the saloons and some good food. He dismissed them, paid them well, and told them to be ready to set out again next winter. Billy Montana would lead them to a new place, get more furs, and end up at Smithson's in the spring, to give them even more furs.

He had a whole company and felt weary and more responsible. It was so different from being a loner. But Ludwig was tough, and he soon adjusted to running a company from a New York post, and handling the selling end of the business on frequent trips to Europe, usually two or three trips a year.

The next years were ones of growing wealth and increasing hours of work. Ludwig found it more difficult to direct the work of others than to do everything himself. He had to control his impatience over trying to teach others to do the bookkeeping, to handle the furs properly.

Mr. Baines died one cold bitter winter; his heart gave out suddenly. Ludwig mourned him, surprised at himself that he missed the old man as though he had been his father. How good and wise he had been! How much Ludwig missed the long sessions working on the furs, the hours of talk, the quiet times of smoking their pipes and discussing the affairs of the world. No one could take the place of Franklin Baines. He had taught Ludwig much, and though his final years had been ones of pain, Ludwig quietly regretted that he had gone from him so soon. Yet he was now better off. The pains had gripped him so badly at times.

The house became too small for his growing family. Otto was born, and then William two years later. The instrument store was closed, regretfully, but no one had time to work with it. Ludwig decided to build a new home, but Agatha's mother did not wish to move from her little white house.

"*Nein, nein,* Ludwig, my son," she said gently. "You move with your big lovely family to a new place. However, allow me to remain where I had so many happy years with my husband and daughter. Let me live out my life here. Colin will come over and keep me company at times, and so will dear pretty Minna."

So it was settled, the old house was returned to its former state, that of a pretty little house in an aging neighborhood.

Agatha enjoyed the new house, with its many bedrooms, two parlors (one for everyday and one for formal company), the huge kitchen with its iron stove which gobbled up wood and coal. Her four children kept her happy and busy, and there was a good school nearby which the boys attended. She taught Minna at home, not only the sewing and music and drawing that girls were to be taught, but also how to keep books, how to read and understand a newspaper, the news of the world and finance in New York.

Ludwig was happy with his family, and as he grew older, he was happy to remain home with them instead of roaming the West for furs. He depended on Jack Smithson, Billy Montana and several other fur traders and trappers to gather up the furs and get them to him in New York.

Roderick Dindorf had continued to call upon them, since they were relatives after all. Ludwig kept a sharp eye on the handsome first mate, in his smart blue uniform, and managed to be home whenever he called on a Sunday afternoon during the times between his sea journeys.

The older cousin of Agatha had never married, and Ludwig suspected strongly that the sea rover still longed for lovely Agatha, plump and matronly that she was. Agatha greeted him with welcome. Often he stayed in the home of Agatha's mother, living there between voyages.

Colin would race over to his granny's house when Uncle Roderick came, and sit and listen, scarcely breathing, while the man told stories of his travels, the people he had met and their strange ways.

A warm winter came to the West. The furs that year were poor, and Ludwig could not fulfill his commissions to New York and to England.

He began to worry once more about plans for the future. In the various bank accounts he had around the city were hundreds of thousands of dollars, and he had invested a considerable sum in a choice piece of New York real estate. One day he would build a beautiful home there for his family, a wish he could never have realized in Germany. He did not invest in stock in another man's company. Why should he make money for other men? He invested in land he could own, and hold deeds in his hands.

But it was his old rival in love who gave him the idea for a new venture. Roderick Dindorf, older and angry, came home from a voyage. He had a private talk with Ludwig, for he was so angry and upset he did not wish to speak before Agatha.

He paced up and down in Ludwig's warehouse office as Ludwig watched him gravely. "Forty years old I am!" said Dindorf. "And always they promise me that 'next voyage' I shall be captain. That next voyage never comes. I am always the first mate, so I receive fewer profits, and a small share of the spoils! Yet time and again it is I who must say where the ships go! The last time out, we were a convoy of three ships, and I was in charge! I directed our course, I got us through the storms around Cape Horn! It was I who spoke German and translated when we met the Russians up in the far cold waters of the Pacific above the Sandwich Islands. It was I who bartered our trade goods for the seals and sea otters and made the huge profits in Canton!"

He paused for breath, and sank into a chair, glaring at Ludwig. "When we returned home," he said more quietly, "with three full ships of China ware, silks, teas, do you know how much the owners awarded me? Do you know what percentage I received, Ludwig?"

"You will tell me, Cousin," said Ludwig. He knew those Boston merchants, tight-fisted as their tight mouths.

"Five percent!" breathed Roderick incredulously. "After all their promises! Oh, they thought me a fool! I had signed no contract to spell it all out! Such a fool I am!" He pounded his fist vexedly on the table. "I will die a poor fool in some sailors' home, and not a cent on me!" And tears came to his brown eyes.

Ludwig leaned back in his chair thoughtfully, his big hands flat on his large thighs. He let the man rave on, but all the time he was thinking of the figures Roderick recited. So much for the sables and minks, so much for the sea otters and the sealskins, the high price for the prized white ermine, the thick beaver skins in China. And all the money in Boston for the China porcelain, the teas, silks, and bolts of taffeta, all fine, delicate fabrics.

He questioned Roderick about the voyage and shuddered a little inside at the terrors of Cape Horn. He had come to dislike ships himself, preferring the land under his sturdy boots. But Dindorf had sailed the seven seas again and again. He knew their ways, he knew his ships, he was careful in his choice of men. No wonder he was in demand as a first mate! But yes, he was a fool in trusting the merchants. Ludwig did not make that mistake any longer. Merchants were all out for themselves and reluctantly gave any part of their fortunes in payment.

"How much does a large ship cost to fit out?" asked Ludwig.

Roderick paused in his long enthusiastic tale of the merchants of Canton, how strange they were, their habits of living and eating. He stared at Ludwig in bewilderment.

"About one hundred thousand for a smaller ship; maybe two hundred thousand for a larger sturdy three-masted ship, counting the trade goods, copper pots, iron skillets, needles, cotton fabrics, and such like."

That was too vague for businesslike Ludwig, and he set about inquiring discreetly in New York for the cost of a vessel. Eventually he bought two ships and hired their captains to sail them. He bought trade goods in New York and in Boston, and sent Dindorf off on his commissions.

He told Dindorf, "We shall draw up a contract and be partners. You shall have twenty-five percent of all we make, and I shall have seventy-five percent. From my share I shall pay for all the trade goods, the wages of the captains and crew. No one gets a percentage. They are hired by me. Is that understood?"

He trusted Dindorf's sailing ability, not his business acumen. Roderick was ecstatic. He hired and interviewed more sailors, put together two crews, and examined the ships from one end to the other and top to bottom. For ballast they took goods the Russians could use in their primitive trading posts up near the Arctic, some sturdy oak and pine logs, oiled canvas, as well as the usual cotton fabrics, woolens, needles and thread, pins and nails, tools, knives, rifles, ammunition and gunpowder. They loaded the ships smartly, according to Dindorf's directions.

Ludwig left his wife Agatha in charge of the warehouse. She listened thoughtfully to his directions, her face paling. "But how long will you be gone, my dear husband?" she finally asked.

103

"It will probably be two years, my angel," he said, kissing her whitening cheeks. "You will be patient? My dove, it is necessary. I hate to leave you and the children. But if all goes well, I shall never need to make this journey again. We shall be wealthy beyond our dreams."

"I do not wish us to be wealthy, oh my Ludwig!" whispered Agatha. She burst into unaccustomed tears and wept against his chest. "Do not go, I fear for you."

He soothed her, gently, and loved her much those last few nights before he departed. There were trusted clerks in the warehouse, and he had given instructions to Agatha about the sales of furs to trusted dealers in New York. None were to go to England for the two years he was gone. He had better control over the New York markets than the English ones.

In September the two ships set out, with Dindorf as supercargo in one ship, in charge of everything, and with Ludwig Gunther himself in the other as supercargo. A supercargo had charge of the commercial interests of the voyage, and complete charge of where they would go and how they would sell. In this case Ludwig Gunther was also the master and owner, and had the owner's cabin on the one ship.

The voyage lived in his nightmares for years, though for Dindorf and the experienced sailors it was a normal journey. They set sail out of New York on a chilling September day and headed south, past the fragrant isles of the Caribees, down past the dark jungled lands of South America. Then they came to icy-cold waters, with white icebergs sticking from the freezing seas. The winds howled eternally, and ice formed an inch thick along the ropes leading to the masts.

Ludwig remained in his cabin much of that horrible time around the Horn. He had never been so cold in all his life. The wind seemed to creep under the tight-fitting doors and around the small-windowed portholes. He sat wrapped in furs and sables, even to his feet, and he tried to forget the blasts of rain and snow and ice that battered outside. He wrote a journal of the journey, read books he had not had time to read for years, and wrote letters to Agatha that might never get posted unless they found helpful messengers in the lands occupied by the Spaniards near the Northwest Coast.

They finally left those horrid lands of ice and snow and sailed north, while the sailors set to clearing the decks and repairing the ropes, singing about their tasks. The worst was over for a time. They went ever north, avoiding the shores, for the Indians there were said to be cruel and merciless.

They came to the Spanish lands and stopped a week at a Spanish mission. There they took on fresh fruit and cured some of the sick sailors of the scurvy by feeding them the oranges and limes that grew in fragrant valleys. Then after loading some more stores, dried beef, tins of fruit, barrels of apples and potatoes, bags of rice, they went north once more.

They sailed, and sailed, and to the seasick and weary Ludwig, longing for home and land, it seemed never to end. And this was only the first quarter of their journey!

They sailed ever north, avoiding the lands. Once in a while they would come into a neck of land, stop briefly, cut some wood for the cook's stores, and hastily sail on. During these land stops, a dozen sailors would stand guard over the wood choppers, with rifles loaded and ready, giving furtive looks about the thick dark green of the evergreen forests. How dense and untamed they looked! How the forests went on and on, and behind them tall mountains clad with snow even into March and April.

They sailed into one bay, and gazed in awe at the immense river of ice that stood like some horrid frozen statue before them. It was frozen solid, and in the dusky evening it looked vivid blue. When the sun shone the next day, they could see it was a dirty, gravel-covered huge ice chest, whose frozen breath they could feel though they were more than a mile from it.

"We do not sail closer," said Dindorf, rather pale. "When some ice breaks off, it falls with such a turmoil into the waters of the bay that a tidal wave could swamp a ship and turn it over, and all will be lost. Pray, do not linger here!"

They sailed on, out of the bay, but Ludwig did not soon forget that dread bay, with the immense frozen ice clinging to the barren scoured rocks and boulders. All the time they were there, they had heard sounds like thunder, as the ice cracked, and some of it would break off and fall with a great splash into the blue-green waters of the bay.

The two ships kept close together. They sailed on north and then turned west. Now curious sights could be seen. Seals lay sunning themselves on great chunks of white ice floating in the ocean. Great whales came up near the ship, gazing curiously toward them, then thumping down into the water, with a great splash of their immense tails. The men wanted to shoot one, but Dindorf forbade it.

"One whale alone would fill our ship!" he told them earnestly. "No, no, we do not want them! You do not know how large they are!"

They teased him, not believing any animal could be so large, but one day they were very close when a whale surfaced; he came so close he seemed to open his mouth as though to swallow up the ship. He stared at them, then dived under their ship, and the ship rocked until the sailors cried out in fear. After that, there was no talk of trying to kill or capture one of those immense creatures.

"Where are the Russians?" Ludwig wanted to know, as did the others. Dindorf reassured them.

"On some islands of ice and snow, out along beyond the mainland. There are Indians there called the Aleuts. Some are fierce, so we will keep our rifles at hand. The Russians make friends and workers of them, but I would not trust them an inch, much less a mile."

And one day they sighted on one island the small signs of human habitation: smoke wavering up into the blue sky of a sunny day. As they neared the shore, cautiously, for fear the smoke might come from hostile campfires, men came running to the shore, waving, crying out in strange tongues. They were bearded, and wearing furs, but they were not Indian.

Ludwig commanded that small boats be sent out to ask if they might land. The word came back that the men were eager but could not speak English.

Ludwig directed the ships into a small port, where anxious hands of the bearded men helped make them fast. He came ashore, and looked about, his blond bearded face reassuring to the others with thick black beards ashore.

A small nervous man came to him, thin-faced but commanding. They tried English, then Ludwig spoke in German. "Do you speak German?" he asked.

The bearded face lit up, and so did the sad dark eyes. *"Ach, ja, ja, Deutsch!"* said the man. They conversed slowly in German. They were eager for the trade goods.

Ludwig learned that no ship had come from Russia with goods for them for more than a year. They were hungry, weary, yet loyal to their great and good Queen Catherine, they said. They would remain forever, if that was her royal command. He felt pity for them, and relief that he himself had no such royal monarch over him.

Ludwig brought out some of the trade goods, a quarter of

106

them, at first. How they fell on them, hungrily, grabbing at the poles of wood, the canvas, the cottons and woolens.

They traded with such magnificent furs that Ludwig was amazed. The men were clever, as were their Aleut slaves. The Aleut Indians were sullen and unhappy and thin. Ludwig thought they were treated with meanness and cruelty. But it was not his business to interfere, though he felt pity for them.

The furs had been scraped clean and were in beautiful condition. Out came the great skins of seals, with a gloss and shine to them. Then the men showed them the skins of beaver, the beautiful pelts shining in the sunlight of that icy cold air. They brought then the sea-otter skins, piles and piles of them.

Ludwig bargained shrewdly. He had told Dindorf and the captains to leave all such matters to him. He bargained for all they had and asked for more. They hesitated, he brought out copper kettles, tins of dried beef, and then the fruit. They went crazy.

The Russians were so hungry for the fruit, the tea, the potatoes, the beef, they would give anything in exchange. Out from rich wooden storehouses came treasures in more sea-otter furs, carved ivory objects made by the Aleuts and other men further north. The leader of the Russians told them, "I wished to send these to our queen, but oh my God, how hungry we are for fruits!"

Ludwig commanded that they keep back only enough to get them to China, and to trade all the other foods and goods they had. They traded woolen blankets to the Russians for more furs. Every day the Russians sent out their Aleut slaves, who got more seals and dried the pelts, and scraped them clean for the Boston men, as they were called.

When all the trading was done, in about a month, the leader of the Russians said to Ludwig, "You will come again, my friend? We cannot always know—that our own ships will come to us."

Ludwig sensed the wistfulness, the loneliness, the fears. "Ja, ja, my ships will come again," he said. "Every year I will send one or more ships to you, and with someone aboard who speaks German. If I can find one, I will send a man who speaks your tongue, the Russian tongue."

"We will be most grateful," said the man more frankly. "We do not always—believe—that our ships will come. The winters are so long." He sighed, then straightened his lean shoulders. "I shall tell you. The next ship may not find us here.

Go first to the green-clad islands along the coast up from the Spanish lands. You know the bay of much ice?"

Ludwig nodded. "We came that way. You will settle there?"

"Nein, nein!" shuddered the man. "It is dangerous. No, we plan to settle further south, along the green shores. We shall build a town and bring out more settlers, and even our own priest! Our great Queen Catherine has promised this!"

Ludwig wanted to say he would not trust their great Queen Catherine for anything. But that would be a gross insult to them in their devotion to her. He nodded politely.

"I will direct our captains to look for you below the great bay of ice, above the lands of the Spaniards," he said. "You wish more fresh fruits? More dried beef? I will so instruct it. We can take all the furs you will trade. I hear that the Chinese desire the seals and the sea otters especially, and the white skins of the great bears of the north."

They shook hands in farewell. As the great sailing ships drew away, Ludwig watched, leaning on the railing, as the Russians gathered at the shore, and waved and waved.

Dindorf was on his ship with him. "Poor devils," he muttered. "They might not live another winter, if they don't receive their own ships. All the food we brought will not last them more than four months. And there are fewer there than the last time I came, two years ago. Many have died."

Ludwig nodded, his mouth compressed. So it was when men went out at the idle direction of some far-off monarch who cared nothing for their lives. He was glad he was his own master, who could go where he pleased!

And for now they were pleased to go to the Sandwich Islands, to cut down some sandalwood, barter a bit with the natives there, and then—on to Canton!

Chapter 10

Ludwig found the islands of the Sandwich group most fascinating. The natives were strong, bronzed, laughing like children. They wore little, only brightly colored cloths over their lean bodies. Even the women would go naked into the warm waters to swim.

The natives cut down sandalwood for them and traded willingly, with lighthearted ease. They were accustomed to the sailor men. They brought fresh fruit, and Ludwig and his men ate hungrily of the delicious strange foods. The men sang and danced for them, with strange motions of their hips and swaying of their hands. They told stories with their dances, stories of their long journeys on ships from lands far to the south.

Then the two sailing ships set off again. The natives hung around the necks of the departing sailors great wreaths of sweet-smelling flowers whose fragrance lingered about the ship for days.

It was summer in the Pacific Ocean. Some days the sea was calm and blue and as pacific as its name. Then other days it would swell up and grow gray with rage, and the huge waves threatened to swamp the small sailing vessels. They avoided land now. There were some that were hostile to white men. They did come close to the coast of China, and sailed down it, not setting ashore, much as they hungered to feel hard earth beneath their feet. The Chinese forbade any landing but at Canton.

Dindorf set guards on deck, the best men with the sharpest eyes, day and night. Pirates roamed these waters, Chinese pirates with cruel faces who had no pity on those they captured. They avoided every island, every spit of land, and watched sharply for strange vessels.

They saw odd ships, with crimson sails, and whole families aboard, women and children sitting in the shadows of the sails, while their men fished. Sometimes they stared curiously, sometimes they waved shyly, and as the ship passed, a sailor or two would throw into the small vessel a bit of food, dried meat, a bottle of fruit, a small bag of limes. The brown faces would beam, the children would wave more frantically.

Around the curves of land they went, until they came to

the island owned by the Portuguese, called Macao. Dindorf told Ludwig that the Portuguese had come first, successfully, and persuaded the reluctant Chinese to trade with them. The Chinese would trade, but only on their own terms.

They docked at Macao, and Dindorf found a house to rent for their headquarters. They set guards at the ships, and at the house, stout sailors, with rifles, and then unloaded the ship of all its furs, the sandalwood, what remained of the trade goods.

Then Ludwig and Dindorf and two tough sailors bought a small boat that could make its way up the channel to the port of Canton. Ludwig put in the boat one box of special importance, which he kept in his own charge. They took two packs of furs, one of sealskins, and one of sea otters. They took a pack apiece of their own clothing, in case they must remain more than a day or two.

In New York Ludwig had listened carefully, silently, to the many stories he had heard of the strange Orientals, the inscrutable Chinese with their odd ways. He had listened and thought for a long time about how he would proceed. He was a clever man, and he had traded for many years. And he was a proud man, he understood others who were proud of their freedom, their culture, their own ways.

They arrived at the wharf on which stood a number of bright fresh houses which were half-shop, half-apartments overhead. Over each hung the flag of a different nation, Dutch, Portuguese, British, Canadian, American. Ludwig looked thoughtfully at the American flag, but did not head for that.

He had heard about the spacious warehouses called "hongs." Chinese merchants, called mandarins, ran the hongs. Each mandarin was a member of the "cohong," a guild which had been authorized officially by the emperor. There were usually thirteen such mandarins, and they were in charge of all foreign trading.

Yet, not only were they in charge, but they were also responsible for the foreigners. If any sailor committed a crime, the mandarin or hong merchant was blamed for it. He must find the man—and punish him. If he did not, he would lose face, and probably his job, if not his head. Crime was strictly and instantly punished.

Merchants were of very low class, no matter what their intelligence or learning or wealth. In China, where the trading of goods was scorned, merchants were despised. The Chinese did not think they needed anything from the rest of the world.

110

They did, however, understand that the world wanted their own magnificent silks and porcelains; no one else had anything like the Chinese goods.

Since the West wanted their goods, and traders would pay in gold and silver, the hong merchants were allowed to carry on this work—so long as the foreign devils behaved.

Ludwig asked for a merchant of the hongs. The Chinese pretended not to understand him. He persisted and finally a man came, a short slim man in a blue silk robe. The man looked at the boat, the load of furs, and at Ludwig, curiously. Finally he nodded and beckoned.

He had several Chinese to pick up the loads of furs and bring them with him. Ludwig reluctantly entrusted the small box to one man, but stayed close to that man, to their curiosity.

The interpreter—for he spoke some English and some German—told them he was taking them to the hong merchant to whom they were assigned. They would deal with him, and him alone. They must not attempt to contact any other merchant, or they would be sent away immediately.

Dindorf said to Ludwig, "That is their way, Mr. Gunther." He was very respectful in front of the Chinese, showing that Ludwig was the leader.

The small procession wound through dirt streets, back into the town. The brisk Chinese who led them halted at the red-lacquer gates of a strange building, which had beautiful blue paint on it and gilding that dazzled the eyes. It had an odd shape. It wound around and around, the tiles of the roofs were green, and the house seemed to be in an odd pattern. The gatekeeper let them inside, into a courtyard lined with blue-green Portuguese tiles.

There was a long pause. Ludwig lounged in the shadows and pondered. It was very hot here, though it was September. The air was humid and scarcely a breeze stirred the air.

Dindorf grimaced a little at him. "They like to keep foreigners waiting. They think it shows their importance," he whispered.

Ludwig nodded. He took out his pipe, stuffed it with tobacco, in spite of the scowls of one guard. He lit up, and puffed away, found a seat on the ground in the shade, and sat down, in a leisurely way.

The thin interpreter finally reappeared, amazed to see Ludwig sitting down and smoking. He beckoned, shook his head at the pipe. Ludwig nodded amiably, finished his pipe for

111

several minutes, knocked it out, and put it in his pocket. Then he stood, yawned, stretched, and nodded graciously that he was ready. The thin Chinese watched him with expressionless black eyes, his yellow face crinkled with lines of age.

They were then shown into a large room. The two sailors were told by indications to remain outside. Ludwig and Roderick entered the room.

Roderick Dindorf knew the hong merchant. He waited respectfully to be recognized. The merchant was a huge man, seated on a lounge before a tapestry of precious silks, showing a simple scene of a crane in water. The colors were marvelous, and gold threads glimmered in the blue water scene.

Ludwig's attention went first to the merchant. They were introduced, formally, and a servant brought in a small black lacquer table. Another servant brought in small cups, which were filled from a china teapot. The tea was hot, green, fresh. It was refreshing, with a tingling taste of some kind of spice.

Ludwig drank three cups, then turned over his cup politely as Dindorf did, an indication he could drink no more. Then the merchant, one Mouqua, spoke. He indicated the furs.

"You have only these poor furs, and you come all the way to Canton, the middle of the earth?"

The interpreter translated, his eyes on the ground, where lay a precious rug of the softest colors of pinks, rose, green, blue, with a border of creamy brown.

"There is more at my house on Macao," said Ludwig.

"How much more?"

"More," said Ludwig impassively, shooting a frowning glance at Dindorf. Ludwig had a plan for trading in China, and he did not want any rash remarks from his friend to spoil it.

The hong merchant then indicated to his servants to open the two packs of fur. He could not prevent his black eyes from gleaming as he stared at the fine sea otters, the shining well-cared-for sealskins.

One was brought to him, the servant kneeling before him. Mouqua stroked it with his plump hand. He finally nodded. "We will take them all," he said indifferently.

Ludwig said slowly to the interpreter, "I wish many bolts of silk in exchange. I trust the fairness of the merchant Mouqua. I wish also the porcelain for which China is justly famous. I wish also some of this magnificent tea, to take back to my country, and show them how fine are the teas of China."

All this was translated solemnly. The hong merchant finally nodded, and said, "Tomorrow."

They were shown to rooms of marble floors, of beds hung with magnificent woven tapestries on posts of carved red woods. Servants brought them trays of food, much more than they could eat, more tea, in beautiful porcelain teapots, served with tiny cups rimmed with gold. The colors were never gaudy, Ludwig noted.

The porcelain he had seen in the stores of New York was often of very strong colors, featuring bright blue peacocks or imitations of American or English scenes, all in gaudy colors, brightly painted and fired. The pottery was thick, of a pasty white color.

These were different. Ludwig took a cup in his hand and held it to the candle. One could see the light flickering through the creamy thin white of the cup. The gold rim glimmered softly.

The servant watched him with alert eyes. Ludwig nodded in satisfaction. The servant bowed and took away the trays.

The next day silks were brought out, and Ludwig shook his head. "No, not fine enough."

Other silks were brought; he shook his head. Finally the hong merchant waved his hand, and servants took away those silks and brought in others.

Dindorf gasped in amazement as the bolts were shown with reverent care. There were saffron silks, of the most beautiful patterns. There were plain blues the color of the sky, and others with woven white patterns of the most delicate embroidery. There were violet silks, and green, and other colors, all so deliciously light that they floated on the bronzed hands of Ludwig. He nodded, and let himself smile in satisfaction.

"Ah, yes, yes, these are the famous silks of which I have heard!" he said. "The best only!"

The hong merchant got the message. Ludwig knew what he wanted, and he wanted only the best.

The same little drama was played out with the porcelain. The usual export porcelain was brought out, brightly colored with crudely drawn patterns. Ludwig shook his head.

A little better quality was brought. He shook his head and looked sad and displeased.

Then the servants brought a small black lacquer tray with only one tea service on it. It was similar to that with which

113

they had been served—pure creamy-white translucent porcelain with a simple rim of gold. No decoration. Ludwig nodded.

The silks and porcelain were packed into boxes before his eyes, and counted carefully. Then the merchant pointed to the box in the care of Ludwig.

"What is that?" asked the interpreter.

Ludwig opened the box with a small key from his pocket. He spread out a length of raw silk from the top of the box, and laid it on a table. Then he set out, gently, carefully, the long oddly shaped pieces inside the box. The Chinese hissed in surprise.

"Ginseng," said Ludwig.

"Ginseng," they whispered over and over. Their eyes glistened. Ginseng was much treasured in China, for it was a magical property. It was a good medicine, and more, it increased a man's virility to great extent! And this man had a whole box!

He waited until their excitement had calmed a little. The merchant then asked, "How much for ginseng?"

Ludwig pointed to the tapestry that hung behind the man's head. "Something like this most beautiful work of art," he said. "At my home in New York I will build a mansion for my good wife. She is the finest wife a man could have, and when I return, I shall build a magnificent house for her. Inside that house I shall place tapestries such as you have here, of the finest designs, of the most beautiful fabric. I wish for this box a tapestry for my good wife."

This was translated. The hong merchant stared for a long time at Ludwig, black eyes keen and sharp.

He shot the interpreter a question. The thin man bowed, and without lifting his eyes, he said, "Has your excellency many children of his great manhood?"

Ludwig did not blush, though he could have squirmed. "I have the great pleasure and delight of having one beautiful daughter and three fine sons," he said.

"Ah," breathed the hong merchant before the words could be translated. And Ludwig understood then that there was really no need of an interpreter. The man understood English, though he would not speak it to foreigners unless he wished! "You are a most fortunate man," he said more formally, through his interpreter.

Ludwig nodded. "My good wife is intelligent, faithful, a fine wife and mother. And she has given me four children as good and fine as herself. Indeed, the God I worship has been good to me."

Mouqua sat and thought. All were silent. Then he told Ludwig in Chinese, "When you return with more furs, I will have for you some tapestries of the finest quality. There will be other treasures for you to give to your good wife, for the mansion you will build for her. You may depart now."

He gave nothing for the ginseng, but Ludwig did not argue. He nodded and took his leave. Servants took him back to the boat with Dindorf and their two burly sailors. They left at once, to return to Macao.

Again Ludwig returned with Dindorf. The man was curious. "Aren't you going to take it all to him? We could hire a dozen boats," he asked.

"No. A bit at a time," grinned Ludwig. "Let him guess how much we have! I'm saving the best furs for the last!"

"We'll take the sandalwood today?"

"Right, half of it."

So again they made the long journey up the channel, to be received by the interpreter and taken to the house of Mouqua. It might have been coincidence, but quite a crowd was on the wharf watching them.

Again they were taken to the house of the red-lacquer gates, again received into the courtyard. But before Ludwig could light up his pipe, they were ordered brought into the house, into another room this time, with the burly sailors ordered to remain outside.

The room was larger, more impressive. On the floor were more carpets, probably from Persia or other places of the Near East, thought Ludwig. Such carpets he had seen only in the finest mansions, the best shops. And the pieces were immense. This man used them as though carelessly, one flung on another.

The hong merchant received them with cool courtesy. Tea was brought, the weather commented on. Then the two packs of furs were opened. These were some silver fox and blue fox, and two huge pelts of the white bear of the Arctic. Mouqua nodded and approved of them. Then, unable to contain his curiosity, he pointed to the box Ludwig carried.

"What is this?" he asked.

Ludwig solemnly opened the box, spread out the silk cloth, and took out—more ginseng. The merchant gasped, he stared at Ludwig.

"More ginseng?" he whispered.

"More on the ship, more at the house in Macao," said Ludwig. He had brought ten boxes of the herbal medicine with him, feeling foolish, but tipped off by a friend of his. The Chinese paid high for ginseng.

Mouqua gestured to his servants. This time there was no wasting of time with inferior silks. Magnificent bolts were brought out, and porcelain of the most beautiful quality. Mouqua murmured to one servant, he nodded, and returned with a black lacquer table which he set before Ludwig. He returned again, with a black lacquer box, into which had been packed some of the most beautiful porcelain Ludwig had ever seen.

The bowls were of a pale strange green, translucent, carved like jade. Dragons writhed around chrysanthemums, one bowl was immense, and all fitted into the black lacquer box.

"All for you," indicated the hong merchant.

"I have never in my life seen such beautiful work," said Ludwig. His words pleased the merchant. He seemed more relaxed today.

They bargained for the furs. The merchant would supply many packs of ordinary porcelain, to be used for ballast in the ship, and would bring good prices in New York and Boston. This was the painted and glazed porcelain which was the usual trade goods. Also the merchant would supply more silk and more taffetas.

Then he ordered his servant to bring forth tapestries. Ludwig showed his pleasure at them—five grand pieces that matched, showing scenes beside rivers and streams. Herons, mountains, pine trees twisted in the wind, all simple and beautiful, with delicate colors and magnificent work.

"You have more furs, more ginseng?" asked Mouqua.

"More," said Ludwig and returned to the house in Macao.

Roderick chuckled over and over as they came and went. "You are the cleverest fellow I ever met!" he exclaimed. "You make him wait, like a Chinese puzzle, to see how much and what goods you will bring!"

Ludwig brought to the merchant some of the carved ivory of the Alaska natives. He had kept back some for Agatha and the children. Mouqua was pleased and showed it.

The third box of ginseng was received in silence and awe. For it, Ludwig received four huge vases, more than three feet tall, of white translucent porcelain. On them were flower designs, of Chinese flowers and trailing vines.

"These will be for the huge magnificent house of my wife.

They will reward her for my absence of two years," said Ludwig, solemnly, formally.

Mouqua bowed his shaved head, the single pigtail bobbing. He wore saffron robes today, and ivory beads about his neck. His trousers were of purple satin, full to the ankles, and he wore purple velvet shoes with turned-up toes.

"More goods?" he inquired.

"More," said Ludwig.

The fourth trip, he brought more ginseng, more furs. The fifth trip, he brought out knives, copper kettles, some goods of Boston and, on the sixth trip, some of the best minks and a dozen white ermine furs, with bits of black on them.

Mouqua sighed, but his eyes shone. "You have more?" he asked after the trading was done. This time he had brought out more tapestries, of a kind that would sell very high in New York. He had brought out the finest bolts of silk. He had had ready crates of good porcelain, not the exquisite green, but a fine white quality with gold design.

'More," said Ludwig, and he allowed his eyes to show silent mirth, a little joke between them.

After the seventh, the eighth, and the ninth trips, Mouqua was wild with curiosity. Ludwig managed to surprise him every journey, bringing sandalwood, more ivory, herbs from New England and scrimshaw which the sailors had carved on the long journey. The intricately carved ivory made from the tusks of whales was graciously received.

On the ninth trip Ludwig said, "Next time is my last journey to your most beautiful home. I appreciate your hospitality, and it is with regret that I say this next journey will be my last to you. You have treated me with honor and graciousness. I shall not forget to send more furs to you in two years."

"Ah, the journey is almost over," sighed Mouqua. Sometimes he spoke English to Ludwig. "I will have a feast for you next time. I will say farewell with regret. You will return to Canton?"

Ludwig shook his head. "I have many duties at home. My supercargo, my trusted friend and relative, Mr. Roderick Dindorf, will return for me," and he indicated Roderick. "I have much work that only I can do at my home place."

The relationship of Dindorf was inquired into, politely, accepted with warmth. Relationships were very important to the Chinese, Ludwig realized.

"He will be accepted as you would be. It is to be hoped,

117

however, that one day Mr. Ludwig Gunther will return to us, to be received again," said Mouqua with regret. He had enjoyed the game they had played.

Ludwig brought on the tenth visit the rest of the ginseng, and the finest furs, the sea otters of the best quality. They were served a fine feast of about twenty courses, and Ludwig found it difficult to eat something of each serving. They ate egg soup, with odd herbs in it. They had veal, lamb, many vegetable courses, then sweets, so many he lost count. And always fresh cups of hot tea were served in tiny exquisite porcelain cups of white translucency and gold rims.

When the meal was ended, Mouqua gestured, and servants began to bring in items. To Ludwig's delight they brought a dozen excellent Persian carpets. Mouqua had shrewdly noted his pleasure in the carpets.

"And for your sons," said Mouqua. He had brought in a fine long bow and arrow for the eldest son. For the others, smaller bows and arrows. And for the beautiful daughter, an ivory ball about as large as an orange. It had been carved into patterns so fine it took a long time to see them. Farther and farther into the ball the patterns went. One could see a house, a bridge, tiny people, trees, flowers.

"My Minna will be most thrilled with this beautiful ball," said Ludwig, a smile softening his hard mouth. He turned it in his huge hands, gently, thinking of the pleasure of his small daughter.

For Agatha the Chinese hong merchant had more presents. He did not trade for these, he said. These were gifts for the good wife of his guest. A tapestry was spread out. It was of a simple scene, a house on a canal, a bridge, a willow sweeping into the water.

"She will enjoy this, and would wish me to thank you a thousand times," said Ludwig, pleased.

More silks were brought. The merchant had inquired respectfully as to the color of Agatha's hair and eyes and the silks were of odd blue greens, just the color of her eyes. And some were of creamy silk, like her hair. Some were violet blue, and others were of saffron yellow.

Ludwig had saved back one box. The merchant had kept eyeing it curiously, but this time he did not ask.

"I have brought one gift, a humble one, to present to Mouqua if he will permit such a gesture," said Ludwig.

He handed over the box to the interpreter, who in turn set

it on a table before the merchant. The key was set in his hand. He turned it, and opened the box, and his narrowed black eyes opened wide in amazement.

A cloth of velvet was hurriedly set beside the box. The merchant with his own long clever fingers drew out the silver chased set of teapot, sugar and creamer, spoons and knives and forks, which Ludwig had especially commissioned. The design was simple, elegant, and the silver shone in the candlelight.

Ludwig said quietly, "It is made of the best silver, by the finest craftsman I could find. I hope you will accept it, with my gratitude for dealing with this American."

Mouqua looked directly at him and bent his head. "You are most gracious, most generous. I have enjoyed our dealings, though trade is a poor thing for a man to engage in. It is men like you who make it a pleasure for the mind and the hands." He caressed the silver teapot and examined the elegant curves of the lines.

It was with real regret that the two men took leave of each other, and Ludwig and Roderick returned to Macao. They put all the heavy barrels of trade porcelain in the bottoms of the sailing vessels, for ballast, then distributed the other boxes and parcels about. The silks were put high above the waterline. Ludwig kept the best on shelves in boxes in his own cabin, and Roderick took care of more. The gifts for Agatha and the children were also in Ludwig's cabins, in trunks and boxes, some of the best black or red lacquer, which were treasure pieces of themselves.

They set sail for home. They had no difficulty at all in obtaining sailing papers, and everything was made smooth for them. Other captains exclaimed over that and teased Ludwig about his Chinese friends. "We sometimes have to wait for weeks for the permissions you received in three days!" one said.

It was late February. The winds blew in another direction. The smart thing to do, the captains and Dindorf advised, was to sail home by another route, around the Cape of Good Hope of Africa. So they set sail, and the winds took the sails, and blew them away from Canton, to the west.

They sailed through the Indian Ocean, and to the spicy scented islands. They paused to take on board some spices, cinnamon, the blackest peppers, fragrant cloves, saffron, and other rare and exotic ones. They also took on some monkeys, and the sailors cared for them so carefully that they remained alive and chattering through the whole voyage into New York.

It was not so difficult, this route, and Ludwig thought if it were not for having to go to the Northwest Coast of America for the furs, it would be good to be able to go directly from New York to Canton around Africa, and return. Many merchants did so, taking goods of America to trade directly with the Chinese. For silver and gold, they could also obtain much.

But it was furs that intrigued Ludwig and were making his fortune. So furs would remain his business.

They returned home safely, in the summer of 1799. Agatha was tearfully happy to greet him and wept as he told her of the long hard journey, the strange adventures. The children listened, wide-eyed, the youngest with thumb in his mouth. But not Colin. He sparkled with interest and begged to go on the next voyage. Ludwig said no, sternly. He would not risk such a child.

"Younger boys than I are midshipmen on vessels," stormed Colin and stamped off to beg Roderick to sponsor him. Roderick, laughing, refused, but soothed him with more stories of their adventures.

It was Roderick who told Agatha and the children of the little amusing game that Ludwig had played with the Chinese merchant, intriguing him into giving more and more. "He enjoyed it so much," said Roderick, "that he gave much more for the furs and ivory and sandalwood than he would have given if Ludwig had brought all at once. I shall use that trick, believe me!"

Colin sat at his feet and begged for more stories. Adventure ran in the veins of that lad, his father thought. Colin was the kind who would go out into the world before long, to take it all in with great gulps of excitement, reveling in trouble and danger.

Agatha could hardly manage him now, and he was but fourteen.

The mansion was built, on the land Ludwig had bought earlier. He himself supervised the building that winter, making sure the finest marble was used, granite from Vermont that gave a rosy sheen to the facade. And when the huge forty-room house was completed, and stables set behind it to house a dozen fine black horses and five carriages, he began to take the treasures of Mouqua from the warehouse.

In the giant hallway were placed the five tapestries in the

set. Before them now stood the tall porcelain jars, three feet high. All New York heard about them and longed for invitations to come see the Gunther mansion.

In Macao Ludwig had purchased more pieces of furniture, and one formal dining room was completely furnished with them. There was a couch of black mahogany, carved in intricate fashion, covered with dark rose silk. Matching chairs of four were set formally nearby. He had bought a huge table of mahogany, also carved, with some fine gilding of a hunting scene. The black and crimson lacquer boxes in which Mouqua had put some presents and some trade goods were set about, in designs that Agatha arranged. She could not be done touching the beautiful works.

Her own tapestry was set in the huge sitting room next to the master bedroom on the first floor above the ground floor. The ground floor contained several parlors, a small dining room, a huge dining room for guests, and a music room, with a library beside it.

On the first floor above, up a winding marble stairway, were the bedrooms of Ludwig and his wife, as well as a sitting room for her, furnished with silks and the beautiful special tapestry. Smaller vases of fine porcelain set about were kept filled with flowers summer and winter. Ludwig had his study up there, and his own treasures of ivory and porcelain, including the little minature tea set he had so enjoyed in Canton.

The floor above, the second floor, held the bedrooms of the children, and the nursery for the youngest, with his nanny. A large playroom was furnished with every toy a child could wish, though Colin was beginning to scorn them and begged to go to the warehouse and down to the wharves with Ludwig.

Agatha launched reluctantly into society. Her kind, gentle manner, along with her breeding and her good taste in music, stood her in good stead, and the other society women never knew of her lack of desire to mingle in their company. Now that her husband was home, she would have been more than content to spend every evening with him in the new house. Ludwig had also never cared for society, but he thought it necessary to deal with other wealthy New York families. Besides, he was proud of his wife. And he looked ahead, far ahead, to the marriages of his children. They should marry into the best, most wealthy, finest families he could find!

Roderick Dindorf never did marry. Though a handsome sea captain in his late forties, he no longer wished to wed. He came over often, between voyages. He kept on traveling for his German cousin by marriage. Ludwig had trusted him, and Roderick was turning into a shrewd trader.

The date changed to 1800, and the year marking the start of the new century did not seem so different from those that had preceeded it. But more changes were to come, inevitably. for Ludwig, and for the rest of the world in the new century.

PART II
1800–1820

Chapter 11

Ludwig looked proudly about the long table, covered with a pure lace cloth over pink silk, with pink candles shining at every one of the fifty-some places. His Agatha did him proud in the social events so new to her—a daughter of immigrants herself married to an immigrant.

Young Minna had come down for tea, and helped serve it, demurely beautiful in a new pale rose gown, with new silver earrings in her ears. Agatha was matronly, calmly lovely in one of the gowns made of the Chinese silk, the blue-green shimmering fabric over which the dressmakers had exclaimed with reverence. The women had made it up in a simple style, to show off the shimmering fabric so it glowed like the ocean seas on a calm day under a summer sun.

Minna had retired to her own rooms after tea, and the older ones had gone in to dinner. Young Minna had attracted many critical appraising looks from the other matrons there. She was only thirteen, but tall for her age, her curly blond hair reaching down to her waist, tied back with a rose ribbon. And such nice manners, and a lovely face. And nature to match, thought Ludwig proudly. Yes, he would marry her well, when she was of age.

Colin had not appeared. Even his beloved mother could not persuade him to come to tea fights, as he called them. He had probably gone off to talk to Billy Montana. At fifteen he was more and more eager for an exciting life, and controlling him was like trying to hold quicksilver in the palm of the hand.

He was so tall, so handsome, with such a fiery light in his blue eyes! Smart, knowing, he studied hard, played harder, and then was usually off to practice with his new rifle under the tutelage of Billy Montana or one of the idle trappers in town.

Yet as Ludwig sat at the table thinking, he had mainly Blaise MacCameron on his mind. He had had a letter from him that day, outlining how they could join together into a corporation. Blaise resented the way Ludwig's trappers kept coming up into his territory, yet Ludwig felt wary of a merger. Could the free-spirited fiery Americans, owing no master, work with the wild Canadians who went mad with their freedom in the wilderness, knowing little in Montreal and Quebec? And the way they acted with the Indians galled Ludwig.

Yet was it better to sleep with the Indian girls, and make friends of the chiefs—or was it better to keep them at a distance, use them as trading sources, and never friends? It was something which had troubled Ludwig for years. He had never been close enough to any Indian, man or woman, to learn how their minds worked, if they were so different from whites, or really the same after all.

There were more problems to consider as the next few years saw the vast enlarging of Ludwig's companies and work. And there were also more social events, especially in the wintertime in New York, dinners, balls, and operas, over which he and Colin privately groaned.

And as though business and social obligations were not enough, both Colin and Minna were going through difficult teen-age years. At least Agatha thought that was the trouble with them. Ludwig feared that it was more serious.

He had expected Colin to inherit his own restless adventurous nature. Not Minna! She was such a gentle sweet girl—until she got wind of the fact that Colin had a rifle, Colin was working in the warehouses when the ships came in and out, Colin was learning about the West.

She came to Ludwig's study, demure and only fourteen, in a blue gown that set off her blue eyes so like Ludwig's. But her chin was round and stubborn, the little notch in it was also just like Ludwig's. The stubborn notch, the willful one that some said "the devil puts in there for a warning. Beware!"

Minna stood before her father and opened the conversation. "Papa, Colin is going to the warehouse."

"Yes, my dear darling daughter. What would you like from Uncle Roderick's precious stores this time?" asked Ludwig indulgently. "A new silk dress? Some ivory, some emeralds? I'll have a necklace made—"

"Thank you, Papa, you are very good to me," she said in her deceptively amiable tones. "But, Papa, it is not enough! In the old days Mama says she helped you much. She worked on the furs; she ran the instrument shop. Why can't I do something too?"

Ludwig blinked and took another look at his sweet-faced daughter. How she reminded him of her mother! "But, my love, there is no need!" he remonstrated. "We have money

126

now. Your mama does not need to keep books, or scrape furs, no indeed! It was always my ambition to become wealthy, and make your mother so comfortable—"

The steady blue stare unnerved him. "Papa, a girl should learn to work also. Mama says so. One never knows what will happen in life, my governess says," and the blond head nodded wisely. "I want to come to the warehouse today and help check in the stores."

Faced with an ultimatum from his beloved daughter, Ludwig gave in. Besides, he thought, she would soon weary of the work. But she did not. She took quickly to the counting of stores, and the keeping of the accounts. As she sat on a high stool with her ankles curved around the posts, she endured the stares of the clerks, the bold amorous looks of the sailors, and sweetly went to work.

And she was so quick to learn! She had mathematics at her fingertips. She could read and write swiftly, and her script was so clear and bold and black that Ludwig soon had her under his chief clerk, making out final entries. And how she loved to roam the ships as they came in, her nose quivering to the scent of the cinnamon and nutmeg, the cloves and furs, the ivory and monkeys and lacquer boxes. She would dive into a cedar chest and bring out the contents, gloating over them like a sea pirate, as Ludwig teased her.

Colin teased her as well, in his careless affectionate manner. "Minna, you act like a sailor! You cannot go off to sea, like a boy! Calm down, you have to be a lady, and remember, you promised to serve tea for Mama today!"

She gave him that unnerving blue gaze. They had always been friends, playmates, close in the early years, much alike, as Ludwig realized now. "Yes, I shall, Colin. I shall go off one day, and nobody shall stop me! One day, I too shall travel and see the world!" And she gave a decided nod of her beautiful blond head.

Even Ludwig laughed, and Minna stormed off in an unusual temper. It took all of Agatha's power to calm her. But even her beloved mother would not still Minna's restless nature now.

The years went on. Ludwig took Colin with him on a trip West when the lad was sixteen, and again when he was eighteen, and now Minna did storm. She wanted to go also.

Ludwig refused, finally and completely. The girl had learned how to fire a rifle, secretly, against his orders. She

127

could handle a heavy pistol which would seem to break her sturdy young hands. She could mold bullets. She had begged the cook to teach her to make bread from yeast and to make pemmican. How Agatha worried over her young beautiful daughter! This was not training her for a life as a wife and mother!

"Let her play, she shall not go adventuring, I promise," Ludwig tried to reassure his wife. "It is that she is jealous of Colin. Wait until a young man attracts her attention. Then you will see a change in her! All ribbons and bows, then!"

In 1805 Ludwig received a disturbing letter from Blaise MacCameron. The man had received loans, and now he was having trouble paying them back. He had learned that he had signed papers which meant that his creditors might try to take over some of his furs in payment. "What shall I do?" asked the Scotsman plaintively. "I was working out West all winter. When I return, I find them in my own warehouse, ready to count *our* furs! I am half-mad with it."

Ludwig had never become partners with the man, but a reluctant friendship had grown up between them. They had met on three different occasions out in the open West, and had quarreled, laughed, made up, talked, compared their lives, and become more open with each other. Ludwig shook his head over the tangle of Blaise's finances. It was not like a Scotsman to be in such trouble, he thought, unless the fable of their tightness with money was just that, a fable.

He resolved to go to Montreal and discuss the matter with MacCameron. Maybe he could advise him and get him out of the difficulties. It might be that MacCameron was not too smart about finances, and some advice would put them straight.

At about the same time that Ludwig had heard from Blaise, Colin came home from college at the end of his second year. Summers made him restless. He studied hard, in all the subjects his tutors advised him to take—world politics, history, philosophy. But when summer came, he was like a wild creature, ready to run off where his nose might lead him.

"You're going to Montreal?" asked Colin eagerly of his father. He was tall now, lanky, filling out to the muscular strength of his father. He put his hand coaxingly on his father's hard shoulder, proud of the toughness of the "old man" of forty-three. In 1805 Colin was twenty, and he kept reminding Ludwig that he himself had left home when he was twenty-one.

"You do not have my permission," said Ludwig. "I waited until I was twenty-one and had my mother's goodwill, though Father did give his permission with reluctance."

"Now, Papa, I know he never did give permission!" Colin teased him impatiently. "I have heard the stories from Uncle Roderick!"

"Your uncle talks too much," grumbled Ludwig.

"You are just going to Montreal! Come along, Father, let me go! I long to talk to the French Canadians. I met some two summers ago, and we got along splendidly!"

His father glared at him and shook his head. "I do not like some of their habits," he said.

"Oh, they drink, and gamble, and tell stories, but, Father, all men do so!" said Colin, ready to beg if that would get him what he wanted.

Minna sat in the other chair opposite their father's desk in the huge mansion. She was eighteen now, and taller than most of the girls in her set. She had come out that winter, wearing a gown of white lace with an underdress of blue Chinese silk which the Chinese hong merchant Mouqua had sent especially to her. She played sometimes with the ivory ball, gently fingering the intricate carvings, adoring it. The ivory ball the size of an orange had always intrigued her. It meant much to her, this symbol of adventure and romance, of travel to faraway places.

Colin mistrusted the look in her blue eyes. When Ludwig had gone off to a bank, after telling them he could not come, he turned on Minna. "Minna, don't think you are going to mess this up for me!" he stormed at her. "If you make complaints, Father won't take me!"

"I will make a bargain with you," she said deliberately, the blue eyes beginning to glow. "I long to go to Montreal also. Colin, you have gone on travels twice with him, me never!"

"But you're a girl!" he cried. "Girls don't go on adventure!" He looked down at her from his six foot height, surprised to find that she already reached above his shoulder. "You're growing up, Minna," he said, more slowly, and put his arm about her. "Mama wants you to find a nice beau, and maybe get engaged."

A smile played about her beautifully carved pink lips. "The man I want isn't in New York," she said cryptically and changed the subject. "Colin, if you help me to go along to Montreal, I'll persuade Papa to take you with us. We'll work together. He cannot tug against us both."

"What will Mama say?"

"Nothing, if she doesn't find out until the last minute. And it is just for a month, Papa says. She cannot mind my meeting Montreal society for a month in the summer!"

"Hm . . . Montreal. You know, Minna, I think that isn't a bad idea. You have turned up your thin nose at all the men she has produced." He tickled the end of her nose and made her sneeze. He laughed. "Minna, tell her—after you have talked Papa into it—that you are bored with the society here! You find the men too involved in business. You want to meet different people and compare them. Maybe all men are like this!"

Minna reached up and kissed his scratchy cheek. "Colin, sometimes you can be very kind and understanding, and a dear brother. You help me, and I'll help you!"

Ludwig was helpless between them. Minna looked at him, coaxed, talked reasonably, coaxed again, and finally let tears come to her blue eyes. Colin had already won his point, with Minna's clever help.

"Colin needs to learn about men of business, Papa. After all, one doesn't learn everything in college. You certainly did not! You learned about men from dealing with them, seeing how they act and work. He needs to meet many men of different caliber, of strange natures, men of different countries. How best to learn, under you, dearest Papa!"

Ludwig sagged and gave in. Her words made sense. She had more trouble with Agatha, for the woman knew that there was more beyond the desire to travel than Minna said.

"But why must you go to Montreal to meet people? People are the same everywhere," moaned Agatha, brushing back her graying blond hair. She hugged her lovely tall daughter. "Do not think to go, I pray you, my love. I need your support here, with Papa gone so much."

"Very well, Mama, I shall never marry," said Minna sweetly, a dangerous fiery spark in her lovely eyes. "I shall stay here, while Papa and Colin roam the world. Never shall I leave you, not to marry or have grandchildren for you! You need me too much!"

"Naughty girl," said Agatha fondly, her smile coming back. "You think to tease me! Such a beautiful girl, you will not remain unmarried! What a pity your granny is gone, how proud she was of you. She would adore seeing you in your beautiful lilac dress with the amethysts which your papa gave you."

130

"Dear granny," said Minna and changed the subject to speak of the old days, and how Agatha had worked with Ludwig, and found such pleasure in being of help to him. "Men are not like that nowadays, Mama, are they? I have met no man who would marry me, and let me help him in his work." She shook her curly head. "No, no, they would all set me in the parlor to sew a fine seam. How I wish it was the old days, and I could find a man who truly loved and needed me, as Papa loved and needed you."

Agatha sighed and told of the old days, and talked and talked. "How I wish I could help him in the office now," she said. "Instead I plan dinner parties, and talk to the ladies, when I would hear what your papa and the men say when we have withdrawn to the parlor while they smoke and drink their port."

"No, no man needs me, not a girl like me," mourned Minna deliberately. She gave Colin a naughty wink over her mother's head, and he watched with amusement as she proceeded to win over her mother. "If I do not meet any men such as you did when you met Papa, I shall remain a spinster. They don't make men like that any longer."

"It is true, your papa is unique," agreed Agatha. "But the country was wild then, and needed strong and vital men, not these hothouse daisies such as that dandy last night. Ugh!" And she turned up her nose as she thought of the affected young man who had been a recent dinner guest.

"If I went to the frontier, I might find someone," said Minna. "But Papa would not let me travel to California on the ship with Uncle Roderick, I suppose. Still, I could ask Uncle—" Minna seemed to muse over that.

"No, no, my dearest Minna, never that! Not on those rough ships with crude sailors! You would not consider that!" implored Agatha in real alarm. Roderick Dindorf adored Minna, indulged her, brought her presents from all over the world. He could probably be coaxed into any mad scheme she wished!

"Probably not . . . but if I could but travel a little bit, with Papa—" sighed Minna.

She got her way, and triumphantly set out with Ludwig, Colin, and two trappers, on to Montreal in early June. They drove a huge barouche both for her comfort, and to carry the fancy trunks filled with fine clothes to make an impression on the society there. Ludwig grumbled privately to Colin.

"In the old days I set out on foot, or drove a wagon, or rode horseback! Look at us, like a king's procession through the countryside!" And he jerked a disgusted thumb at the huge lumbering barouche with Minna sitting like a queen in it, two trappers as outriders in their buckskins, Ludwig driving the light spring carriage they would need in Montreal, and Colin riding alongside. Two coachmen had also come to drive the huge barouche and help care for the horses.

"Are the old days gone forever?" asked Colin dreamily. "Perhaps out in the wilds of Canada they still remain, those days when a man could live and work alone, and lie under the stars, as you used to."

"Ah, yes, they still exist—hundreds and thousands of miles from here," sighed Ludwig. He glanced about the roadside, to the fine farms, the stone and wood houses, painted barns, clearings with acres laid in wheat and oats and corn. "All this was wild country when I first came, with but a few horses and farms. Now look at the apple orchards, the mills, the factories, vast farms even in the stony countryside."

They proceeded slowly to Montreal, and had to hire a ferry to get them across the St. Lawrence. As Ludwig grumbled under his breath, Colin exchanged a wink with his sister. Demure under her navy blue bonnet, her face was alive with delight. How she reveled in the campfires at night, drinking hot strong tea from a tin cup, helping cook the steaks and burying potatoes in the hot coals. She had exchanged her fancy cloak and dress the first traveling day for the dark denim skirt and jacket she had secretly made for herself.

It required two weeks to drive so slowly to Montreal. They arrived in the middle of June, and were glad to pull up at the house of Blaise MacCameron. Ludwig eyed it critically and whispered happily to Colin, "Not one fourth the size of mine!"

Colin laughed at him. "Snob, New York snob," he whispered back. "You once lived in such a small house, you could not fit all your growing family it it!"

Ludwig dug him in the ribs. "And was happy there, for all that," he said sharply, smiling at the same time. He enjoyed sharing a little joke with Colin, since the two were much alike.

MacCameron was sent for from his office as Mrs. MacCameron welcomed them with calm formality. Yolanda MacCameron was from an important French family of the community. Slim and dark, she had cool features and a length of black silky hair that wound about her patrician head in a smooth coil. She had little warmth in her eyes, eyes that were so dark as to seem black.

132

What a difference from MacCameron, Ludwig told his daughter Minna that night as they spoke briefly in her bedroom. He looked about the flowered room, the wide bed with the mosquito netting wound round the high posts, the smart gray-painted chest of drawers and matching wardrobe. "She looks a cold woman," he said. "Don't let her freeze you out."

"I think she is an unhappy woman," said Minna. "Is he a cruel man, Papa?" Her round sweet face was puzzled.

"Nein, nein," said Ludwig. "A careless laughing man, but not cruel, unless—" He scowled. "Unless—it is those Indian girls he has each winter. She knows of that, he told me, and seemed to think she did not care."

"Of course she must care, Papa, if all the world knows and she is shamed," said Minna. She cocked her head and studied the aging face of her father, the gray in his blond hair. "If you had done so, would Mama love you as she does? I do not see how. She knows she has all your love."

"And so she does, so she does, except for all that I would pour on you, my children," said Ludwig gruffly. He snorted at his own emotion and went off to his room.

Colin came to Minna's room before dinner. "What are you wearing, Sister? Do I look smart enough?" he asked anxiously.

Minna grinned at him. "Gamecock," she teased. "You know you look splendid! I like that blue-gray silk suit for you, and your white cravat is—no, I must retie it," she chided, and with deft fingers she formed a new design for him, pressing the cravat neatly against his sturdy chest and the white ruffled shirt. "How do I look?" she asked as she twirled around for him.

She wore a blue-lavender silk dress, ruffles about her slim white arms, ruffles about her throat, showing demurely the rounded bosom in girlish fashion. Ruffles finished the dress at the hem, in the latest New York fashions from London and Paris. Her hair she had swirled up in a coronet about her round face, a style which gave her even more height and dignity. She wore the amethysts her father had given her, earbobs and necklace, and slim bracelet.

Colin complimented her heartily, and took her arm as they walked down the stairs, where their hostess awaited them. Their host had come home also, and the tall Scotsman eyed the two tall grown children in amazement.

"All grown up. And what handsome children you have, Ludwig! My, my, I wish Etienne had come home. What can

133

be keeping the lad, out West so long? My other traders came home two, three weeks ago," he fretted.

"Etienne will come when he pleases," said his wife, a tinge of bitterness in her voice. She introduced the other guests, three couples of Montreal, who eyed the smartness of the American guests in unconcealed surprise.

"And I thought we had the latest French fashions," murmured one lady in a dove-gray gown with a single ruffle at her heels. Colin winked at his sister. Her eyes sparkled back at him. They were accepted in real grown-up company, as adults! And here there was no mother to hold them back, or to scold them afterward, if they drank a glass or two of wine. Their father never noticed. He was absorbed in business conversation already.

Ludwig and MacCameron went off to the office the next morning and were gone all the day. Colin disappeared on his own accounts, and came back about teatime, to appear in Minna's room, dirty, muddy, with blazing excitement in his blue eyes. "Minna—I have met some trappers! They go West soon, to be out there before the snows! They go West, out to the Rocky Mountains where the snows fall early. Oh, my God, Minna, how they talk! They ride in huge canoes, and each carries a pack—"

Minna listened in silence, rather worried. Colin was so excited, he reminded her of a dog she had had once, wild and loving, frantic with the desire to see the world, yet adoring his little mistress. One day he had snapped his leash, and was off, and never returned. How she had wept for her Fluffy.

This was more serious. She wondered if she should speak to their father, yet to do so would be a betrayal of all she and Colin were to each other. Much closer than Otto and William were to them, they shared secrets, helped each other, and were close in feeling and understanding.

"Be careful, Colin," she finally said lightly. "You'll get the trapping bug and be off. Remember you must be back in college before long! Just two more years, and you can join Papa in the firm. Hold on to that thought."

Colin sobered, kissed her cheek. "I must be off to change," he said absently. "Yes, yes, you are right—of course—"

The next day he took her about the city in the carriage and pointed out the sights, the houses, some rather crude, in lines along the river, the deep dense forests behind, and some small vegetable plots. Then they passed the riverbank, the immense wharves, the great canoes drawn up to various warehouses. Tall Indians with their savage heads in plumes walked about, blankets covering their dignified figures. The laughing, teasing French-Canadian voyageurs were striking, impressive even, in their winter-dirty buckskins, bright plaid jackets and red scarves, some with red cummerbunds about slim waists. Many a bold black eye followed the blond girl in the carriage.

The business talks went slowly. Sometimes Ludwig and Blaise MacCameron seemed to be angry with each other, scarcely speaking in the evening. But they kept their arguments to themselves, being always polite in the company Yolanda invited to meet the Americans.

Yolanda MacCameron was very polite and formal with Minna. She invited women and girls to tea and went out in Minna's carriage to shop with her at the few stores, but was cool about the goods. "We have little of value here," she said one day. "The only goods of importance come from London and Paris."

"Papa gets much beautiful silk and porcelain from China," said Minna, not meaning to sound impertinent. Yolanda stiffened.

"We do not trade there directly, only through London," her hostess said.

"I like to go down to the docks, when one or two of Papa's ships come in," said Minna, determined to be more friendly. "He lets me go on board with my uncle, Captain Dindorf, and see the first of the goods. Oh, the furs, and the spices, such smells—"

"Dreadful smells," said Yolanda MacCameron. "I refuse to allow the furs in the house until they have been treated properly, and are at least one year old."

"But the ivory, and the porcelain, surely you like those?"

The woman said stiffly, "I have seen little of such goods."

Minna persisted, and the woman finally managed to smile at her, and relax a little. But she seemed frozen inside, formal with everyone.

Colin returned to the MacCameron home early that afternoon. He had known Minna had an engagement with Mrs. MacCameron to go shopping, and his father never came home until time to change for dinner.

Rapidly he stuffed several woolen suits into his valise, then added some things he had purchased, two sharp knives, a copper kettle, cups. Into another pack he had bought he put a bright blue trade blanket, rolls of coins of silver and gold, extra wool shirts and underclothing. Then he dressed in his new outfit, and laughed softly, joyously at the image in the mirror.

He looked now like a French Canadian! He looked like a fur trapper! He wore new buckskins of cream color, a red cumberbund about his waist and a matching red scarf at his throat. On his head was a bright plaid cap. But for his blond hair and blue eyes he looked like a fur trapper, a Frenchman. And some of the Scots were blond men, much like him.

He wrote a note, hastily. "Papa, I have decided to go West this summer and gain some experience of my own. I have long dreamed of this. Do not try to pursue me. I must find my own life, and live it, as you did. My love to Mother. Tell her not to worry. Minna does not know. I shall return one day, and tell you of my joy in wandering. Your loving son, Colin."

He pinned the note to his pillow and slipped out of the house, two packs in hand, and made his way to the wharf where he had met the half dozen trappers. He had made friends with a fellow the very first day, and the young man of his own age had already spent four winters in the wilds! That had sent Colin blazing with excitement. He was twenty and had never spent a winter in the wilds.

The man knew how to trap and hunt, how to fish and live, and build a cabin, or live in a tent. Twice he had gone as far as the white peaks of the Rocky Mountains. He knew the land.

"Come along with us; we'll be setting out soon and get the jump on the lazy ones," urged the man.

Colin could not resist. And so he went.

They went that very night, not waiting for permission from the trading companies. They were loners, trappers and hunters, who returned with furs and sold them where they wished. They liked the strong courageous daring young man, who longed so intensely to live their life. They would take him and show him how to live, they said. They bought some food supplies for him with his coins, advised him what to get for himself, laughed and said they would share. Once West, they would get him started on a trapping line.

So when Ludwig Gunther returned to his host's home that night, he found his eldest son gone. The note sent him white and silent. He read it again and again, unbelieving. Minna was in tears.

136

"He went without me, he went without me," she was saying when Ludwig came back to his senses.

"Girl, what do you say?" he asked sternly. "Of course, I might have expected that one day he would do this! But to go behind my back. Why did he not ask my permission and consent?"

"You would not have given it, you would have thought of Mama and her grief," said Minna, calming herself, wiping her face. "Come, Papa, you knew that one day Colin would go. He is too much like yourself to remain in a city."

"But the boy is not experienced! He does not know—"

"Neither were you, when you came to America," said Minna.

She talked to him quietly, soothing him as Agatha would have done, with her arm about his bent shoulders. MacCameron was interested and amazed at what had happened. But his own son had gone off with his consent many years before, he said.

"Etienne—why he has gone trapping and hunting by himself or with friends for many years," he said.

"Yes, and almost forgets he has a family," flashed Yolanda, twisting her white lace handkerchief in her hands.

"But he does return to you, he does return, does he not?" begged Ludwig.

MacCameron patted his shoulder. "Of course he comes back. I expect him any day now, coming in with beautiful furs. He is a fine trapper, and knows the trade like any good man. I trained him myself," he said.

But Ludwig shook his head over the letter, mourning. "How can I tell Agatha? How can I tell my wife that our son has gone?"

Chapter 12

With Colin gone, the days dragged for Minna. Her hostess took her out two or three times a week, and often they had guests. However the young men were the type Minna most disliked, young green men who blushed and stammered and could not look her in the eye.

They thought of her fortune, and mentally counted the value of the pearls and amethysts she wore, and the diamond ring on her finger. They listened to her father, and said "Yes, sir, no, sir," until she could have screamed at them to voice some opinion of their own—if they had any!

She took to going out with just one of their coachman in the light spring carriage Ludwig had brought from New York. The coachman was young and strong, a sturdy farm lad with some sense, and Ludwig trusted him.

Minna would tell Duncan to drive her into town, and she would look about the little shops and wander about while he waited patiently for her. Or he would drive her along the streets, Minna in the back in a pretty dark blue suit with her pearls, and her blond hair mostly concealed in a shady dark blue hat with a curled brim. Or they would drive down to the wharves.

Minna loved the waterfront. If Colin had been with her, she could have walked from ship to ship, or to the huge canoes being drawn up to the warehouses on the banks. They would have walked along the wooden planks and sniffed at the strange sea-salted scents from the St. Lawrence River. They could have talked to the laughing French Canadians, the grave Indians, for Colin had the charm of one who could talk to anybody and not be rebuffed.

But she was alone, and a woman. Duncan watched carefully where he drove, and his young face was anxious as he drove about the more dangerous wharves. He adored his employer, would do anything for him, and being entrusted with Minna was a grave responsibility.

One sunny afternoon Minna was especially restless. Yolanda MacCameron had withdrawn to her room for two days with a migraine headache. Minna wondered if she really had a headache, or simply was bored, or if she might be anxious about the continuing absence of her son, Etienne. She had only one child. She seemed anxious about him, yet almost—almost contemptuous, thought Minna.

Was the son like the father? She herself liked MacCameron. He had a big hearty laugh, and was full of stories, and he patted her shoulder and told her she was a beauty, and that Ludwig was a very lucky man. But shrewd Minna noted how he ogled all the women. And everyone knew about the Indian girls he took into his tent or cabin in the winters. She had heard jokes behind his back.

This afternoon Minna had escaped from the dark house and the drawn curtains. Everything had been made dark, so the mistress would not be disturbed, and the servants tiptoed about and spoke only in whispers. Minna could not endure the strained atmosphere any longer.

So she and Duncan had ridden out, gladly. She had been about the town, and now she said, "Let's go down to the wharves. From the sounds, more canoes have come in. I long to see the furs; perhaps Papa will be at the MacCameron warehouse."

Duncan had turned the horse obediently in that direction and touched the pistol warily at his belt. His mistress was too beautiful and young not to attract attention. Today she wore gown of pale blue the color of her eyes, had pearls about her throat, and a light cream-colored cashmere scarf about her shoulders. She would attract the young men like bees about a honeypot.

He drove down the street to the wharf and was at once enveloped in a confusion of men and canoes, Indians and packs of furs, boxes of cedar and pine being carried this way and that. He finally pulled up the horse and carriage in the shadow of one warehouse, where Minna could watch the goings-on with fascinated eyes. She sat very still in the carriage, gazing this way and that with wide eyes.

There was a huge canoe pulling in, filled with some Indian trappers, wearing dirty worn buckskins, with ragged scarves about their throats. On their heads were more bright scarves, or sometimes plumes. Their dark glances at her made her quiver.

A bar was on the corner near the wharf. The Indians stood near the door, longingly, but did not go in. Out staggered some sailors, hanging onto each other's shoulders, and laughing.

Minna shrank back into the shadow of the fringed carriage. But the sailors went away, too drunk to notice her.

Another canoe came in, and another. Minna sat, enthralled, gazing with her wide blue eyes at everything. Huge packs of furs—she longed to open them and look at the fresh soft pelts. The odors did not offend her, and she had even helped scrape some in her father's warehouse. She wanted to learn all that her mother had done, and more.

The huge heavy packs of furs were carried into the nearby warehouse. Men came and went. Some sailors staggered into the bar and out again. She relaxed, and watched, in the warm afternoon sunlight. Her nose quivered with the odors as some sandalwood boxes were carried from one huge wagon into the warehouse. She smelled the sandalwood and knew the goods were from the Pacific. There must be herbs and spices in the shipments, as well as ivory, and maybe even silks.

If only she had been a man! She could have sailed before the mast. Or gone trapping in the wilds. Or sailed to the Orient with her father—or into the far Northwest with her uncle.

She was so rapt she did not see a huge man who came up to her carriage, and she started violently when he spoke to her.

"Well, little lady. Waiting for a real man?" he slurred the words and grabbed for her arm.

Duncan whirled about and slashed at the man with his whip. "You go off, there! She is a lady, and not for the likes of ye!"

The man turned on Duncan, yanked him off the seat, and with a blow of his burly fist knocked him against the warehouse. Duncan slumped down, blood on his head.

Minna had never screamed in her life. When the grinning man turned on her, she grabbed at the handle of the carriage, and with her free hand she hit at him with her heavy silken purse with coins in it. He did not flinch. He reached for her and lifted her out of the carriage, ignoring her blows as though they were fly swats.

"Come along, lady, you're just what I'm hungry for," he grunted. He was so huge she could not pull back from his iron grasp. She struggled and kicked out and yelled at him furiously.

"You let me go, you damn bully! You let me go! I'll tell my Papa. Duncan! Help me—help me—"

But Duncan lay still and quiet, slumped against the wall, out cold. The big man laughed, and tucking her over his shoulder, carried her off down the street toward the wharf. Then Minna did scream and kick at him.

A tall, red-haired French Canadian hesitated, then turned to watch them. He frowned and came after them. "Gentleman," he said politely. "Is the lady willing?"

"No!" yelled Minna. "He carried me off. I was just in my carriage. He is drunken! Make him put me down!"

A grin slashed the attractive mouth of the handsome young Canadian. He tapped the big man on the shoulder.

The drunk turned about, set Minna down with a thump on her plump behind, and fists whirled above her as she sat in the dirty street. The tall Canadian evaded one blow of the huge man and landed one on his chin.

The huge man lowered his bullet head, and lunged at the lithe young man, and butted him in the stomach. "Oof," said the Canadian, grunting, and backed off, and then headed more warily at him. Minna scrambled out of their path as long legs kicked at each other over her head.

She stared, wide-eyed, as they fought. Her brothers had fought, and she had separated them, but never had they fought like this. The tall young man could move like a whirlwind, his arms and legs slashing and punching. The big man would have been his match, but for the drink in him. He moved too slowly for the rescuer.

Thud after thud sounded, and the big man was down, blood streaming from his nose. He lay quite still, arms out, as though he were sleeping in the street.

The tall man wiped his face with his red kerchief from about his throat, settled it, and turned to Minna. "Now, little lady," he said and sat her up. "Good for you, you are not the screaming kind. I'll just set you in your carriage—" And he picked her up as though she were a child and set her there. Then he leaned over Duncan, shook his head, and picked him up, over his shoulder, and dumped him into the back on the floorboards at Minna's feet. Duncan sprawled there. The tall man climbed into the front seat and grinned around at Minna.

"I'd best take you home, miss. Where do you live?" His admiring eyes were so dark a blue that they seemed black in his bronzed face. He had reddish dark hair, and a reckless air to him. One of the voyageurs, she thought, but a kind man.

"The MacCameron home, sir. It is up the hill three streets and then to the right. I shall direct you. You are most kind," she added as the blue eyes stared at her.

"Ah—right, ma'am." As he turned around, she thought he seemed a little stunned.

He drove up the street, calling out cheerfully to the men or carriages in his way, handling the horse and whip expertly. She directed him, holding Duncan steady against her skirts, not regarding the blood that stained her blue silk gown.

141

He pulled into the lane and drove back to the carriage house. A couple of men ran up, and he shook his red head at them and handed over the reins.

One of the men took Duncan out, and said, "I'll care for him, miss. He's coming to. Did you have a time of it down on the waterfront?" The Englishman who had the care of the horses looked at her disapprovingly. He did not think it nice of her to go out driving alone.

"A drunken scoundrel," said Minna, preparing to get out. The tall Canadian came up to her and lifted her out by the waist. She glared at him, in spite of her gratitude. "I can get out myself!" she said.

"Yes, miss," he grinned down at her, his eyes frankly admiring.

She must put him in his place, kind though he had been. She didn't care for dirty trappers staring at her all up and down her neat, rounded body.

"I must reward you for your trouble," she said primly, though she was flushed and mussed. She reached for her beaded purse, heavy with coin, for her father was generous to her. She was about to open it, when he put his iron arm about her.

"Aye, that you will, miss," he said, and before she could cry out, he had put his hard warm sensuous mouth right on hers and pressed it there. He lifted his head. "Warm and sweeter than molasses," he said brazenly, grinning at her.

"You oaf!" she said coldly. "Let me go!" She gave him a good hard kick with her slippered foot, right on his shin.

"Ouch!" He hopped away from her, holding his leg and grimacing. The men in the stableyard stood staring, holding their breaths, but giving her no aid.

She glared at them all, and said, "Have a care for Duncan!" and sped into the big house by the back door. She went up to her room and took off the blue dress. She sponged cold water on the blue silk, and had the satisfaction of seeing the blood-stains come out. All the time she fumed about the brazen young man. Though he had rescued her, he must have thought her cheap.

The house seemed to be wakening from a long sleep. Voices were heard in the hallway, someone cried out. She wondered if the word of the attack had gotten to Mrs. MacCameron, and if she might soon expect a solicitous visit from her hostess. But no one came to her.

Masculine voices were sounding out, and someone laughed,

and a woman cried, weeping. Minna put on her robe and laid down. She was outside their affairs, she thought, and she was shaking with reaction. She could use a hot cup of tea—but nobody came, and she did not wish to ring for a maid if the household was in turmoil.

She slept a little, relaxing after the rather wild experience of the afternoon. She wakened to find blue dusk creeping into her pretty gray and pink room. She stretched and yawned, her young body refreshed. She got up, washed a little, and pondered what dress to wear.

They had not entertained for three days. She was not sure if any company came this evening. But from the sounds of it, the household was stirring, and excited. Best to be sure and wear something fine.

She found her white lace dress, and the underdress of blue. She put that on, along with a single strand of pearls, and wound up her blond hair into a coronet. Then, dissatisfied, she brushed it down again demurely, and tied it back with a blue butterfly bow at the back of her neck. There, that was younger and prettier.

The wide lace sleeves fell back when she lifted her arms. On one wrist she set a thin gold bracelet. On the other she set her favorite bracelet, of blue-rose amethysts. She put on pearl earbobs, and studied herself. Was it too much? No, she looked all right, by the standards of New York.

Her father had not knocked on her door. That was odd. She heard the clock chiming six thirty, and it was time to go down for sherry before dinner.

She went out to the stairs and blinked in surprise. All the oil lamps covered with mother-of-pearl shades were lit, up and down the stairs, and in the hallways. Candles on tall candelabra were in the downstairs hall. The house rang with the joyful sounds of talking and laughter.

What company had come?

She moved to the stairs and started down. A man came into the hallway from the huge living room, and stood in the doorway, watching her, a glass of sherry at his lips. He lowered it and stared at her unwaveringly as she moved down the stairs, her feet in the blue slippers hesitating on each step. Who was he? Strange to her—yet somehow—familiar—the way he stood, feet apart—red hair—

Anger flared through Minna. He had gotten dressed up in some borrowed formal suit of blue silk and white ruffled shirt, and dared to come around to claim acquaintance. She came up to him, and chin in air, she said, "You are very brazen, sir!"

He blinked down at her. "Brazen, miss?" he grinned, and the very white teeth seemed sharp against the bronze of his dark skin.

"Yes. To dare to come here!" She gritted her teeth at him. She had never been so furious. "Papa would reward you. You can go to the MacCameron warehouse tomorrow morning, and he will pay you some money! But to come here—"

Yolanda MacCameron slipped through the door and put her hand in the tall man's arm. "Etienne," she murmured. "Come back, I cannot believe you are home!" She was smiling, radiant, gowned tonight in red silk, so different that she seemed a new woman.

The man's mouth twisted, he gazed down significantly at Minna's red cheeks as she took in the strange information. Etienne! He must be the son of—

Yolanda MacCameron turned to her young guest. "Minna Gunther, this is my son, Etienne MacCameron! Just returned from the West!" she said proudly and her hand clung to the long arm in the blue silk. He held out his hand to Minna, his eyes daring her to blaze at him.

Her white hand slipped into his fingers and would have slipped right out again, but he held onto her fingers tightly and raised them to his lips. She felt the hard warm mouth on her fingers.

It took all her poise to remain cool with him that evening. He grinned at her across the beautifully set dining table, he hovered over her in the parlor as the MacCamerons and Ludwig talked animatedly. Etienne was begged to tell his adventures. He shrugged.

"Not this evening. It would bore our so charming guests from New York City," he demurred as he gave her a bold look.

"No, no, it would not," said Ludwig, oblivious to the communication between them. "Do tell me the conditions in the West. My son Colin has just gone out there—without my permission," and he sighed. Minna slipped her hand into her father's arm and squeezed it comfortingly, her face softening.

"Do not worry about Colin, dear Papa, he has trained for this, and longs for it," she murmured.

Etienne must have sharp ears, she thought, for he caught her remark and commented on it. "Trained for this? How can a man in New York train for the wilderness?" he asked.

144

Minna thought he sneered, and her toes curled up in her little slippers. How she longed to kick him!

Yolanda MacCameron changed the subject. "Do let us forget the wilderness for one evening," she said, her dark eyes flashing. "Minna, will you play for us? The harp has been tuned again. It will be most beautiful tonight, I assure you."

"I think the men would rather converse," murmured Minna.

"Shy?" muttered Etienne with a dark mischievous look in her direction. "You look very—poised, Miss Minna."

"Of course she is. She has played for many in New York," said her proud father. "Do play, dear Minna. And Mrs. MacCameron, I understand you have a fine talent with the piano. I am most fond of music myself."

Minna was forced to go to the harp, and with Mrs. MacCameron on the piano, played a duet. The long wide sleeves of the white lace dress had to be folded back to her elbow, then her long fingers moved gracefully on the harp strings. They played well together, having practiced a few hours in the days when Yolanda felt well enough.

"Now you must join us, Etienne, my son," urged Yolanda.

To Minna's horror the tall young man lounged forward, produced a flute, and stood himself at her elbow, peering over her shoulder to follow the music. Her fingers turned clumsy, and she had to exercise great will to make herself play the Scottish and German folk airs they played for the gentlemen.

As her long fingers rippled along the strings, the music relaxed the older gentlemen, and they lit up their cigars and leaned back contentedly to listen. Minna's nerves were so on edge, she could have screamed in fury when Etienne insisted on another tune, and another, and then some classic music of the Germans, especially of Johann Sebastian Bach.

They played quite two hours, and Minna had never seen Yolanda MacCameron so glowing and happy. When they finally stopped, and she could leave the harp and return to the couch beside her father, Etienne brought her a glass of nut-brown sherry.

"For your nerves," he whispered wickedly as he handed her the glass, bending much too close toward her.

She allowed herself a single fiery look at him. He chuckled, and bowed, as though she had said something witty to him.

"We must entertain, now that Etienne is home," said his mother happily. "So many have asked about you, my dearest son."

"I'll be bound," muttered Minna.

Etienne heard, and his dark blue eyes glowed at her, his mouth twitched. Minna thought, he is another like his father. I'll be bound he has more than one Indian maiden in thrall, to say nothing of the easy women of Montreal!

She vowed to herself to have nothing to do with him. She agreed amiably to accompany his mother shopping the next day, believing that the excursion would take her out of his company. To her fury Etienne came with them, driving the carriage.

He did whisper to her alone, "Your man Duncan is recovering. I said nothing to your father. He would be angry, yes?"

She had to be grateful. She nodded, her mouth tight. "I would never forgive myself if Duncan, or any of ours—"

"That is understood. And Papa shall not know of your escapades!"

In the days that followed Minna found this was typical behavior of Etienne. Considerate one moment, and teasing and wicked the next! He would assist her from the carriage, and manage to squeeze her hand devilishly. He would laugh from the sidelines when she was bored or when her feet were stepped on during a set at the home of friends. The next minute he would stroll to her rescue, take her away, get her some cool drink, and fan her with her white lace and ivory fan.

He could gravely compliment her on her dress for the evening. "Miss Minna, you look most lovely and girlish in your rose gown, and the jewelry sets off your eyes most admirably."

She would bow, distantly, frostily, while his mother smiled fondly at him, admiring his manners and address. At the door Etienne whispered, "I do not blame that drunk for trying to carry you off! Over the shoulder and down to my ship, and off we would go—to the far lands of ecstasy!"

Oh, how she could kick him!

They played well together, usually the harp and the flute, though sometimes Minna sat at the piano while Etienne played the violin almost as well as he did the flute. The parents would sit and admire them, the beauty of the music, as well as the sight of the tall blond girl in blue or rose or white and the red-haired Canadian, his face soulful as he played.

They played every evening, by request, when they were home. When guests were there, Minna and Etienne were asked to perform. When the families were alone, the older men called for their favorite numbers and often sang along with them.

Only Yolanda MacCameron, with her sharp black eyes, began to realize how often they were together, driving out, playing together, Etienne often escorting Minna to the wharves or to shops. Etienne was not usually so attentive.

Yolanda came up to Minna's room one afternoon, after all had returned from shopping. She tapped on the door. Minna, having changed to a cream silk robe in which to rest, went to the door and opened it. She was surprised to find the distant Yolanda there.

"May I talk with you?" asked the older woman abruptly.

"Of course. Pray, come in."

Yolanda came in, closed the door, looked about absently. "You are comfortable here?" she asked.

Minna indicated a chair and sat down also in the plump chintz-covered armchair that matched the colors of the room, a soft pink and gray. "Most comfortable, Mrs. MacCameron. I fear my father and I are imposing on your hospitality. I do not think he intended to remain all the summer." She sensed that this might be on the woman's mind, these guests who remained week after week.

"No, no. I am happy to have you here. Minna, you are a good and gentle girl," she said unexpectedly, her mouth turned down unhappily. "Your mother must be a good woman, a fine mother. She has raised you well."

"You are most kind, Mrs. MacCameron," said Minna, her face composed to hide her startled feelings. "I shall repeat your most flattering comments to my mother in my next letter. She is grateful to you for your kindness to me, I assure you."

"You are cheerful," added Yolanda absently as though she had scarcely listened to Minna. Her long artistic fingers twisted in the lap of her dark gray dress. The black eyes glanced at Minna, then away to the windows, to the dresser, anywhere. "You are pleasant in the house. I know you have prepared several fine dishes for us, for the desserts. Not many guests would trouble themselves to help out so, like a daughter."

The last words rang in Minna's ears. Surely the woman did not think Minna had designs on her son!

"I have never seen Etienne so attentive to one girl before, and such a very suitable one in every way," said Mrs. MacCameron. "May I speak—very frankly—to you, my dear?"

"Yes, of course," said Minna, sitting up straight and ready to argue that she cared not a fiddle for Etienne.

147

"Etienne is very like his father," said Yolanda. "When I met Blaise he was—a little *triste*—sad—subdued, because of the deaths of his wife and infant son. I was drawn to him, for many reasons. But the marriage was a mistake. He never forgot that wife and son. I never could take the place of the girl he had married in Scotland."

Minna caught her breath sharply. This was not what she had expected to hear. She stared, her blue eyes wide.

"We married, we were happy. I began a child. Blaise went West for a few months, for furs, trapping, though I begged him not to leave me in that time. He did not listen to me."

She paused, bit her lips savagely.

"The child came, a son. Blaise returned, he was most happy. He had a son. My father wished him named for him, and his father. Blaise was not here for the baptism, so I obeyed my father. Blaise was furious. I said, 'You were not here, what could I do?' So we quarreled, and it was the first of many quarrels. When I spoke French, he was angry. When I begged him to join the Hudson's Bay Company, he said he would do what he thought best, and stubbornly he went on trapping with his own men. I could do nothing right."

Minna finally interrupted, embarrassed beyond words by this frank disclosure from the older woman. "I pray you, *madame*, do not tell me this! You will be sorry, and berate yourself for disclosing to me—"

"No, no, it is—necessary. I see how Etienne looks at you," said Mrs. MacCameron with a sigh. "Listen. I soon learned that when Blaise went out to the frontier, he lived with an Indian girl. A different one each winter, so I was told, by the women who enjoyed telling me, then sobbing over me, as thought they cared how I was hurt!" she added savagely. "How they stared at me, how they gloated—my handsome husband, gone all the winter, living in the stink of an Indian tent, with a girl—one of those trollops that inhabit the Indian camps!"

Minna folded her hands tightly. This was nothing she should hear, but she could not stop the words from torrenting from Yolanda's red-bitten lips.

"Every winter, every winter," panted Yolanda, sitting very stiffly, "I had to live with the knowledge that out—there—he lived with another girl. Younger and younger. He bragged when he returned—fourteen-year-old girls! And I, older every year. I went alone to balls, to dinners, until I could not bear the loneliness. I made excuses, I was ill, my mother was ill, and she died, which sent me into mourning for a year. I welcomed it, my God, I welcomed the excuse not to go out alone, to endure their stares, their whispers, their snickers—over me!"

The thin hand went to her mouth, a small lace-edged white handkerchief wiped the spittle tremblingly from the tight red mouth. She visibly composed herself, and she became more calm and cold once more.

"I should ask you to excuse me for speaking in such a manner to you, my guest, and a young lovely girl," she said formally. "I would but warn you, as a substitute for your own mother. My son is like his father. I think every winter he goes West, not just for the hunting but for the women. He is very popular. He cannot avoid a pretty face. He loves to dance, to sing, to play music, to woo a girl with a glance and mischief and his caressing voice. Oh, I know him, he is even more of a flirt than his father! And I—I doubt—I doubt if—he would be faithful to you—even if he did—marry you. I beg you—avoid him, Minna. Avoid Etienne! He will hurt you again and again, even if he should be serious enough to wish to marry you!"

Minna swallowed. "Oh, *madame*, I am—so sorry," she gasped. "But surely you mistake him. Your son, Etienne, he is not serious about me! He merely flirts, and I—I avoid him while I can without offending you."

"I know. I know. You try. But the more you try to avoid him, the more he pursues you. I know my son. Whatever he does not achieve easily becomes all the more attractive to him."

Yolanda pressed her fingers fretfully to her drawn forehead. "I wish to say—to say, Minna, that if you wish to return home to New York, to be rid of this—this situation—I will arrange it. I will send my most trusted coachmen, and you will have yours also. They are all devoted to you. You will be safe."

Minna swallowed, again, with more difficulty. "You—wish me to leave, *madame*?"

Yolanda shook her head, and half a smile came to her lips. "No, I wish you would stay, and marry my son, and make him settle down," she said with cool precision and smiled more widely at the dazed stare of Minna. "No, you are just the one I should like for a daughter. Fine, good, a solid person, with maturity and goodness within you. Too good for him, for Etienne," she said sadly. "I would hate to see the marriage,

149

for one day you might turn on him and hate him—as I have come to hate my husband. Hate and love, both. It makes me ill, so ill at times—"

She rose and clung to the chair arm, as though dizzy. Minna sprang to her feet and moved to assist her. The thin hot hands clung to the young arms. Then the woman stood erect and nodded her thanks.

"I will leave you to think of this, Minna," she said. "Whatever you wish, I will do. I would be happy for your company this summer. But beware. And if you desire it, I shall send you home."

With a dignified nod she left the room, leaving Minna alone with whirling, bewildering thoughts.

Chapter 13

Etienne was a charming tease. Minna, staying in his home, could not avoid him. She tried, and his mother tried tactfully to aid her.

Minna did not want to return home. She was enjoying herself immensely. Her father and MacCameron quarreled, made up, talked about a merger, and drew back from it throughout the summer.

But in September, she thought, she and her father would return home, and her mother would want her to become serious about finding a husband. She shivered. No, she would not marry one of those society dandies, one of those who sought a fortune by marrying one. She wanted a man like her father, daring, courageous, adventurous!

Duncan recovered, and started taking her out again in the carriage. He was sheepish and ashamed that he had been felled so easily, and now he carried a long sharp knife as well as a pistol.

Minna had breakfast one morning with her hostess. Etienne, to her relief, had eaten earlier and gone out, Mrs. MacCameron said. Etienne had teased her so last evening, that Minna had become visibly enraged and refused to play the harp after an hour.

Yolanda, in a beautiful rose gown today, was in a much brighter mood now that Etienne had returned. She glowed with love for her son, though she knew him for what he was.

To Minna's discomfort she could not cease speaking of him. "How kind he can be," she mused. "How courageous he is, and yet gentle as a woman when I am ill. If only marriage would change him, I would encourage him to marry."

"And send him off in the other direction, *madame*," said Minna tartly. "He thrives on opposition!"

Yolanda laughed softly, her dark eyes sparkling. "How you understand him!" she said.

Minna grimaced but was too polite to be more frank. After finishing her coffee, she went to her room and put on a thin silk cloak, for the day was cooler and rain threatened. Then she stole out softly. She intended to go down to the warehouse and prowl about. Her father scarcely noted her there, since he

151

was accustomed to seeing her in such a setting. Today she would see her fill, for many more packs of furs had come in.

Down the back stairs she went to the carriage house. Duncan was waiting for her, the horse already harnessed to the carriage. "Oh, good, you are ready, Duncan," she said eagerly. "I am pleased. We shall be off early—"

"Ah, good morning, my dear Miss Minna!" a too familiar voice called out. And there stood Etienne, a devil in his dark blue eyes, smart in his buckskins and red cummerbund. "I shall accompany you and make sure you come to no harm!"

"You followed me, you bastard!" cried Minna, hands on her hips. How the stablemen stared and snickered behind their hands, except for Duncan, who stood troubled and silent.

"Tush, tush, such language for a lady! Permit me," and he picked her up bodily and dumped her into the back seat of the carriage. He followed her up, pushing her over to sit beside her in the narrow seat. "All right, Duncan, let's go!"

Duncan looked at Minna. She nodded to him, her mouth compressed. "I wish to go down to the wharves today, to the warehouse of your father," she said coldly. "You may be bored."

"I—bored—in your delectable company?" he laughed softly and touched her hair caressingly. "How pretty you look today!"

She was wearing a white silk gown with a narrow stripe of bright red in it, over it a red silk cloak. The hood of the cloak half-covered her golden hair. Her mouth was naturally a deep rose pink, but her cheeks glowed with temper, and her blue eyes flashed. Etienne gazed at her from head to heels, as though he longed to stroke her.

Minna held fast to her temper and leaned back in the carriage. She would bore him today, she vowed that! He did not know what she intended!

She half smiled with mischief, and he gazed at her in even more fascination. "Never have I ever met a girl like you, Minna," he said quietly, more seriously. "You are like no woman I know, with your intelligence, your serene competence, your beauty, and the mystery behind those beautiful eyes. When you play the harp, at times, you have a poetry about you that would make a poet weep that he could not express it in words."

Minna gazed from the carriage, at the houses passing by, as though indifferent. But she glowed inside at his compliments. She knew he meant to flatter her—yet—

152

He leaned closer. "Why do you not speak?"

"I was thinking what a glorious cool day it is, for August," she said demurely. "Do you have red and golden autumn leaves sooner than we do in New York?"

"Devil of a woman!" he growled in her ear and took a sharp nip at the small lobe. She jerked and glared at him. He laughed.

Duncan looked about nervously, but she shook her head at him. Etienne was lithe, powerful, and like a young ox, too tough even for the farmer lad. And he would lose his position, should he try to strike the son of the host of his employer.

Minna straightened her shoulders. "I am going to your father's warehouse. Do you think he will mind if I poke about?" she asked, turning charming and smiling. "I do adore looking about the warehouses, and I have not seen much of your father's!"

"I don't know why you should like to, but he will not mind. All the ladies come in when the furs arrive and choose the best for their winter cloaks," Etienne shrugged. "Should you like a mink cloak made up?"

"Thank you, no, sir," she said decisively. She did not add that she had a mink cloak, as well as one of ermine and one of silver fox, and so many coats she did not count them.

Etienne leaned back in the carriage and seemed serious for once. "Minna, what do you want? I have watched you with young men. You do not even bother to flirt with them, or wave your fan in silent signals. Don't you seek a husband?"

"Not yet," she said with a mischievous smile. "Not yet, or for a time, if I can help it! No, I want adventure," she said. "I think if a sailor came to me, a captain of a ship, and offered me a trip around the world—to China—I would go with him, married or not!"

He stared at her thoughtfully and did not rebuke her. Instead, he studied the poppy-red cheeks. "I believe you mean that," he said. "Is there adventure in you like that of your brother? And your father? Do you not want to marry and have children, and a place in society?"

"I have a place in society. It often bores me intensely," said Minna. "I have furs, jewels, and men swarming endlessly about. I wish I were a man!"

"I prefer it that you are a lovely girl," he said quietly.

She did blush then. She turned silent, as they continued down the cobblestoned streets to the wharf. Duncan drove in beside the MacCameron warehouse, and pulled up as two In-

153

dians strode past them, huge pelt bundles on their backs.

Etienne got down, and helped her down, gallantly, politely. Minna went with him into the warehouse, her red cloak attracting attention from dark-eyed Indians, bold-eyed French Canadian voyageurs, tradesmen, clerks—and Mr. Mac-Cameron.

"Ah, Minna, my dear. My son, Etienne," and he embraced his son extravagantly. "What can I do for your beautiful guest? Minna, my dear, do you wish to examine our new pelts?"

She smiled at him, the graying gallant red-haired Scotsman. "Yes, I should like it, sir. But do not let me disturb you. I know you have much work to do."

"Etienne will show you about," he said.

To her relief they left her alone. Etienne started to show her about, but his attention was called by the chief clerk, who needed some advice. Minna strolled about, looking the picture of idle loveliness, but her blue eyes were sharply intent on the warehouse.

They had many good pelts, and more were coming in. The free traders did well even in Montreal, she thought, in spite of the Hudson's Bay Company's efforts to take over. She lifted a few mink pelts and examined them. Some were fine, but some needed more work on them.

She moved on, watching all. From her experience in her father's warehouse, she knew this was not a successful operation. More casually than in her father's warehouse, the clerks dealt with the Indians, and MacCameron himself made a bargain with a laugh, and a shrug. Ludwig Gunther stood disapprovingly by as MacCameron evidently settled for a higher price when bargaining would have done better for the warehouse.

Minna strolled over to the side of the warehouse which was the store. She gazed idly at the blankets, scarlet, blue, gray and cream. The Indians passed them by, and were insisting on coins, silver or gold, for their pelts.

MacCameron paid them what they asked, and did not insist that they trade with him. Some did want knives, or copper kettles, or iron pots, and staggered out with the huge pots clanging on their bronzed shoulders. Others wanted only coins. MacCameron let them settle the matter themselves, or the clerks would do so.

He must lose much in his operations, thought Minna. He was careless, generous, idle. He beamed at everyone, seemingly in his element. He talked a long time to one trapper, ignoring the Indians who had brought in more pelts. They grunted at each other and turned and walked out. MacCameron had lost a good sale.

Etienne was unexpectedly busy. Minna watched him without his noticing it, flinging him a glance from time to time. He was busy bargaining, his gay bright face smiling, yet more keen than his father. He would shake his head over the pelts, and insist that the Indians settle with him. Several times Etienne went to a clerk and in a low tone informed him he was not asking enough. He picked up furs, studied them keenly, pointed to flaws, shook his head when the price was too high. His business acumen revealed another side of the French-Scottish young man. Minna found herself thoughtful.

It grew warm in the warehouse, causing the smell of furs and Indians and newly returned voyageurs to become overpowering. Minna retreated to the small office and smiled at Mr. MacCameron. "May I leave my cloak here while I examine the furs, sir?"

"Of course, of course, my dear girl!" Gallantly he helped her remove the cloak, then he laid it carefully across his own chair. She smiled at her father, and he beamed back at her, so proud of her.

She returned to the warehouse and looked about in earnest. She saw a table at the back, where the bought furs were being laid out. She went to examine them curiously. She had been idle for weeks. She looked at one mink, saw that it had not been scraped properly, and picked up a knife.

A clerk gasped, but she ignored him. She scraped carefully at the underside of the pelt, examined it, scraped again. Then she took a brush and began lovingly to brush it, for the mink was muddy and dirty. She shook it hard, then laid it down again, and brushed along the fine sleek lines. Now the true beauty of the fur was coming out.

Etienne came up beside her. "What in the name of heaven are you doing, Minna?" he asked, stunned.

"Brushing a fur. Look how much better it is already!" she exclaimed as she held up the shining satiny brown fur.

"What do you know of working with furs?" he asked bluntly.

She looked beyond him and saw both their fathers. "I have worked in father's warehouse since I was fourteen," she replied calmly.

"A girl?" muttered Etienne, seemingly shattered. "A girl, working in a warehouse, like this?"

Minna's smile curled her red lips. "Of course. My mother

155

helped my father with the furs for many years, didn't she, Papa?"

"No one could ask for better help than my Agatha," said Ludwig proudly. "She minded our store, bargained for furs when I was away, scraped and brushed and hung the furs—oh, she is a very treasure to me!"

These sentiments were obviously something new to the French and Scottish, and Minna heard mutterings. She paid no attention and went on working with the mink. She brushed lovingly at another fur, and also had it in beautiful condition when Etienne finally returned to her.

"It is noon. We shall close for two hours for lunch," he said. "Will you come out with me? There is a place where we might eat. You shall not be bothered."

His dark blue eyes glowed. She hesitated, then consented. "If I might wash my hands first," she said.

He took her back to the office, brought a bowl and pitcher of hot water, and left her alone. She washed, used the small outhouse, washed again, smoothed her hair, and noted her glowing eyes. What fun she had had this morning! She put on her scarlet cloak over the white and scarlet dress, picked up her little silk purse, and went out to join Etienne.

"I told your father I was taking you to a fine restaurant you will much enjoy," he said, his tone caressing.

He drew her hand into his arm, and they went out to the carriage. Duncan sprang to attention. Etienne gave him directions, and the man nodded.

They drove along the waterfront for about a mile, then Duncan drew up at a smart-looking yet informal restaurant, with gay red and white checked curtains at the windows. As Etienne escorted her inside, Minna looked about with interest. She had longed to come to some such place that served good seafood with Yolanda; but she had not dared to ask. Women never went out alone in Montreal, it seemed, nor did they often in New York.

With Etienne, all was easy. He seated her in a chair next to the window, so she could gaze her fill at the busy crowded wharves and watch the great canoes coming in with their heavy loads which made them sink almost to the level of the river. He showed her the menu written on a blackboard. They chose fresh seafood from their own waters. He suggested baked potatoes, bursting in their brown skins, with melted butter and green herbs. The waitress, plump and white-aproned, speaking rapid French to Etienne, brought plates of green salad with a delicious vinegar and oil and herb dressing spicing it. They ate it while they waited for their fish to be quick-fried in the kitchen behind the restaurant.

As they ate, they gazed out at the bustling scene, and talked and talked. Etienne had set aside his flirtatious manner and would talk as seriously or as gaily as Minna wished.

"What do you really wish from life, Minna?" he asked.

She dug into the potato, taking a buttery bite with much appetite. "Oh, I told you. Adventure, travel—I long to go out as Colin did! Just take a chance, and—and disappear for a year! I would travel the waterways, portage—"

"Minna, Minna, girls do not do this," he said gently. "You long in vain."

"I wish I were a man," and she set down her fork, and her mouth was rebellious and pouting. "Oh, how I have wished it. Father went to the Orient once, and how he spoke of the trip. Etienne, he went around Cape Horn, and there were icebergs floating in the waters, and the wind howled in the masts, and ice caked the sails—"

She went on breathlessly, glowing, cheeks burning hot, as she spoke of the travel to the Russian ports, the Sandwich Islanders, their songs and dances. "Then on to Canton," she said. "And he met there a kind Chinese gentleman with whom he traded. Mouqua still sends me gifts every voyage of my Uncle Roderick! How I treasure what he sends me. I sniff the sandalwood boxes, and the spices. And play with my ivory carved ball..."

For once Etienne spoke little. He ate, and studied her face, and listened to her. Whenever she would falter, he would urge her on, encouraging her to tell of her dreams, her wishes.

They talked long into the afternoon. The plump one-legged man who ran the restaurant did not trouble them but to bring more coffee, offer some wine, watch them indulgently. Young lovers, he thought, all too obviously.

Etienne had some gentle advice for her. "Do not dream of such wild places, Minna. Girls do not go there without much danger. I know Indian girls can endure it, but not a gently bred white girl."

"I could go, I could!" she said but turned her face away as he spoke of the Indian girls. She remembered his mother's bitter advice.

"Well, we must return home now. Or do you wish to return to the warehouse?"

She started. "Oh, your mother has invited a dozen women

157

for tea this afternoon!" she exclaimed ruefully. "I must go home, she will wonder—"

Etienne escorted her out to the carriage, and Duncan drove her home. She envied Etienne, striding along the port happily, back to his work, to talk to Indians, to work with the pelts, to speak to each man in his tongue, Scottish, French, English, or one of the Indian dialects. How she envied him! Her brother Colin would be well on his way West, digging his paddle into the deep waters of a blue lake somewhere, laughing as the wind blew his blond hair.

She returned to the MacCameron house, hastily washed and changed to demure blue, and went down to help entertain a dozen ladies. But her mind kept drifting off to faraway places.

There were other guests for dinner also, six couples of the best society. Yolanda entertained lavishly these days, her face visibly more joyous, her step light. Her son was home, and he remained there, with no talk of leaving for a time.

Minna remained home the next day. She had much to think about. She must return home to New York soon. That meant not seeing Etienne again, probably. Back to her mother's plans for her, back to the old round. Would her father let her continue to work in the warehouse? Or would she be more and more occupied with social duties, with being thrown at eligible young men?

To keep herself busy, she helped polish the silver for the evening. Yolanda had planned a gay occasion, a buffet dinner for forty guests. Minna had been asked to play the harp, and there would be dancing to the music of violins. She scrubbed away fiercely at a huge punch bowl of silver. Her visit was coming to an end. She wondered what her father had decided about the merger. He was more silent and thoughtful these days. Blaise watched him anxiously.

The dinner and ball were a great success. Minna played with demure grace, first the harp and then the piano. Etienne accompanied her several times on the flute or the violin. Minna had chosen to wear her favorite lace gown over blue silk, and she saw admiration in the eyes of many young men. But Etienne studied her gravely and did not pour compliments on her. He seemed rather quiet this evening.

Minna grew warm in the crowded lamp-lit rooms. When the guests finally began to drive away in their carriages, she drew a breath of relief. It was past midnight.

All her guests having left, Yolanda yawned her good nights

158

and moved slowly up the stairs. Ludwig and Blaise muttered to each other and went back to the Scottish trader's office.

Etienne watched Minna. She hesitated, then smiled slightly. "I am going out on the terrace for a breath of air, Etienne. Good night."

To her surprise, he said nothing. She slipped out the French doors and stood on the terrace overlooking the river. How the lights shone in the town! Lamps in windows, lights in the taverns, and rollicking laughter rolling up the hills toward her. Lights in giant canoes, as some of the men started out to their homes downriver.

Etienne came out and set a cloak about her shoulders. "It is chilly here, Minna," he said, and his hands lingered on the cloak.

"Thank you, Etienne."

"You will be—leaving soon. I think things do not go well between your father and mine. Both are too much loners, each wants to be the boss," he said whimsically. "You think so also?"

Minna nodded, her blond hair shining in the dim light from the emptied drawing rooms. "Yes, I'm afraid so. They could work together—but I fear they will each pull and tug in opposite directions."

"Our paths will part also," he said.

She turned and glanced up at him, surprised. "I was thinking that also. How we fought at first!" she remembered, and she gave a little laugh. She pressed her hand to her heart secretly under the cloak. It was thumping so hard she was afraid he would hear it.

"I do not want to say good-bye to you—ever," he whispered.

His hard arms went about her, swiftly. One hand went to her thick blond hair, where she let it stream over her shoulders and down her back. His fingers played in it for a moment, then his hand closed about her neck. He tilted her head up to his.

The warm, generous, laughing mouth came close to hers.

"Minna," he whispered. And the mouth came on hers. She shivered and stood silent in the embrace, not fighting him. She could not fight him tonight.

He drew her closer to his warm body, and under the cloak her body trembled like an aspen in the autumn breeze. "Etienne, Etienne—you should—not—"

"Should not? Ah, but I love the taste of your mouth—molasses—" he teased, yet there was a regretful, longing note

159

in his voice. His mouth closed over hers, and she answered the kiss with a movement of her own generous mouth. And they kissed, and held each other tightly together.

She saw the moon over his shoulder, a big bright full moon, dazzling through her bewildered eyes. She had never felt so—so dizzy and whirling and excited and shaken. His mouth sought her throat and brushed over the fragrant skin of her shoulders, her neck, up to her ear.

"Ah, my darling, my sweetest love," Etienne was whispering in French.

Minna finally drew away. His arms tightened, then he slowly let her go and stood to gaze down at her. She could see his face in the moonlight, his profile dark against the sky, his mouth stern, lips slightly parted, his eyes dark under dark brows.

"I must go in. Good night—Etienne."

"Good night, Minna, my lovely darling," he said quietly. He still stood there as she slipped in the French windows, and tiptoed up the stairs to her room.

She lay awake a long time, restless, still feeling his hard arms about her, his heated body against her own. And she remembered what his mother had said of him. If Etienne was serious, how would Minna handle it if after their marriage he turned to other women? Or was Etienne different from his father? Would he change, become loyal and faithful?

Ah, but she did dream, she thought wryly. He had said nothing of love or marriage. She turned again to her side and gazed out at the waning moon.

She slept late the next morning. She was surprised to find Etienne waiting in the hallway as she came downstairs, having had her late breakfast and tea on a tray in her bedroom.

He had her cloak with him. "Come out with me," he said. "We must talk today."

He was not smiling. His dark blue eyes were keen and sharp, their gaze turned to her pale face.

She nodded. "I will just tell your mother I am going out." However, she could not find Yolanda. She finally spoke to the maid.

"Madame remains in bed until afternoon," said the maid.

Minna went out then and found Etienne had the carriage himself. He lifted her to the seat beside her and smiled down at her. It was not his usual gay merry smile. His bronzed face was serious, and he seemed gentle with her.

"I should like to ride, just with you; perhaps to one of the parks overlooking the river," he said.

She nodded, her face shielded by the blue bonnet she had slipped on when she went upstairs in search of his mother. Her dress was bright blue, and over it she had set the scarlet cloak.

She did not try to speak as he drove. The traffic was heavy filled with carriages and barouches, horses and men walking every which way, up and down the streets, and around the wharves. It was a busy, gay scene. Her sharp gaze noted that some men were preparing to set out for the winter in the West, loading their huge canoes, carrying thick packs of supplies and trade goods. One man ran lightly down the cliff toward a huge canoe, carrying half a dozen long paddles.

The late August day was cool. The sun shone brightly, but the west wind was sharp in their faces. Etienne drove to a green park, lined with scarlet maples, and drew up near the edge of a cliff. He tied the horse, came back for her, and lifted her down.

Minna's scarlet cloak blew in the wind. Her bonnet was torn at by the wind, as though by impatient fingers.

Etienne had her hand in his arm and was drawing her close to him.

"My men grow impatient to leave," he said finally.

Her heart seemed to stop beating, then tumbled into a thumping heavy beat. She could not speak.

"I usually am gone by this time," he continued slowly. "The supplies are ready. You see, we must go so far west, to the Rocky Mountains, where we trap and remain in cabins for the winter. The snows come early there. If we do not leave soon, we will be trapped like panicky rabbits far from our cabins. The rivers and lakes will be frozen, we will not be able to get through."

"Yes—you must—leave soon," she finally said. Tears blurred her gaze, so the gay river scene below them was a riot of color, reds, creams, blues, without any object clear.

"Minna, would you marry me, and come with me?" said Etienne rapidly. His hand went to her waist, and he turned her to face him. His dark blue eyes were keen and stern. "I have thought long about this. The West is no place for a woman. Yet you long for adventure, to travel in a canoe. We would care for you, my men and I, as though you were a piece of rare porcelain! One winter in the snows, in a crude cabin. You would be gay with me, we will laugh and be happy. Oh, Minna, say you will come with me—"

It was like a dream come true. "Marry you? Come West

with you?" she whispered, staring up at him, her fingers clutching the buckskin arms.

He nodded. "Will you, Minna? And after that—would you be content to wait for me here, in Montreal—perhaps—with our children?" He asked it solemnly, with no trace of his mocking smile. "We could not risk it, not for you, not more than one year. But for one year, oh, Minna, a life like no other! The wild white wilderness, the traplines, seeing the great brown bears, the blue rivers, the white rapids. Traveling by our great canoes, the strange white wilderness after the snows. The evergreen trees smelling like heaven itself. You will like the Indians, you will make friends with everyone. The Crees are kind and friendly with us. Oh, Minna—come—come with me!"

She could not resist it. He offered everything she had wanted. A tough courageous man, gay and kind and laughing with her, he would allow her the adventure of travel in the wilderness for which she had long envied her father and uncle. Trapping! Living in a cabin! The snows closing them in, snug and cozy with their cookfire burning red hot. She making him comfortable, he providing for her—his wife!

She could not speak for a minute. He misunderstood. He closed his arms about her tightly.

"Minna, what do you want of me?" he cried brokenly. "I love you, I adore you. I want to give you everything in the world you want—you said you wished to travel—oh, God, my darling, what gift can I give you? How can I make you want me as I want you? I have longed for you, lain awake, feverish with desire! I have never thought of any woman as I do of you! I will love you all my days. I cannot endure the thought of life without you. Oh, my love—oh, Minna."

"Oh, yes, Etienne. Oh, yes," she whispered. "I—I love—you, Etienne." She said the words against his lips. He snatched the words from her greedily, his mouth pressed to hers, as her cloak swirled in a crimson flame about them.

She felt so wild, so crazy, she could have laughed aloud, could have wept. It was everything in the world she wanted: Etienne—her wicked teasing lover, and the wilderness she so longed to see for herself, and adventure! Adventure! What she had longed for all her life! She must marry him, she must go with him!

Chapter 14

Like two children, that evening, hand in hand, they stood before his parents and her father. Etienne glowed with excitement. Ludwig gazed up at them uneasily.

"I have proposed to Minna, and she has accepted me," Etienne said, concluding his little speech. His big bronzed hand closed more tightly on Minna's. "We love each other."

Blaise was staring, then he broke into a big pleased grin. "But this is good!" he cried, starting up. "We will celebrate with some good wine—your Minna and my Etienne, engaged! I am most happy!"

Ludwig got his breath. Minna stiffened as her father jumped up, his fists clenching. "Are you mad? Minna, what nonsense is this? Him? Etienne MacCameron, the image of his father?"

Blaise caught his breath as Etienne's head went back proudly, incredulously. Only Yolanda was quiet, gazing at the young couple with compassion, her dark eyes suffering for their suffering to come.

"We love each other, we wish your permission to marry," repeated Etienne, more strongly. His fingers hurt Minna's hand, he clenched it so tightly. "We wish to marry soon."

Ludwig did not allow the young man to finish. *"Nein, nein, nein!"* he shouted, his face turning red in rage. Then in a spate of German which only Minna fully understood, he yelled, "Not to one such as you, a bastard, a man with a weakness for all women! I have heard the stories of your father, and you are another one such as he—chasing the women, living with the Indian girls—"

"Father," said Minna in English as he panted for breath. "I love him. I love Etienne. We have talked and ridden together, we understand each other's hearts." She dared not speak of the trip West. For now she realized that her father despised the MacCameron men. Her heart was chilled.

Ludwig returned to English. Deliberately, insultingly, he said, "Never! Etienne has such a reputation with the women! Never would I allow a child of mine to marry him! He is too much like his father!"

Now Blaise did understand him. The older Scotsman flushed also, and turned on his guest. "How dare you insult my son in such a manner. And myself! I have a reputation for honesty and integrity in my dealings with all—"

"Except women," said Ludwig cruelly. "You have bragged to me of it. Even a fourteen-year-old Indian girl, you said to me. A different girl every winter! And even here in Montreal—practically under the nose of your long-suffering wife, you have an Indian squaw, and also a woman in the town of bad repute—"

Minna glanced uneasily at Yolanda MacCameron; however, except for a tightening of the slim hands, she showed no expression. She listened as calmly as though to a debate over legislation.

Blaise was uneasily trying to justify himself. "I do not speak of women. Those women are—are part of any man's life. I speak of honor, you say bad words about my honor."

"Business is one matter, I can deal with you there. But your way with women disgusts me!" said Ludwig forcibly. "I have been true to one woman all my days, and how she rewards me! She gives me comfort, encouragement, assistance in my work, advice, respect. Can you say the same of your—" Then he turned to Yolanda, and shook his head. "Forgive me. Madame, this is not your fault. I have seen what goes on. But I cannot endure to have my daughter, my precious Minna, marry your son."

"Have I nothing to say about this?" Etienne's bronzed face was haggard. "I love Minna, I respect her. She is different from other women. A man would be loyal all his days to this woman, this magnificent wife! She is intelligent, beautiful, fine—"

"So is your mother," said Ludwig. "*Nein, nein*, I have heard stories also of yourself, Etienne." He shook his graying blond head like a magnificent lion. "No, Etienne. My Minna is not for you. She will marry the finest man I can find for her. She deserves the best man in the world!"

The men argued and spoke violent, terrible words. Etienne finally turned to Minna, raised her hand to his lips and kissed it tenderly.

He smiled down into her white, strained face. "Go to bed, my adored. We will speak tomorrow. No good comes of arguing."

She nodded and shyly kissed his cheek. Ludwig watched them with a scowl. He said, "Tomorrow, Minna, you will begin to pack. Tell your maid to pack everything. We go home in a few days. This summer has been a waste of time! I must get back to serious work."

Minna went upstairs to bed and heard the deep angry voices of the two men for quite two hours. But she did not hear Yolanda's beautiful tones, nor did she hear Étienne's musical baritone, nor his laughter.

She heard the rustle of paper in the darkened room. She waited, then rose, and lit a lamp with shaking hands. She saw a slip of white paper under her door and went to take it. Was it Etienne's farewell? Had he grown impatient, and this was his leave-taking of her? Would he ask her to wait for him?

Her heart thumped heavily as she unfolded the paper and took it to the lamp to read it.

"My adored Minna. Do not despair! If you love me, come with me. Tomorrow I shall arrange our marriage and the packing of our canoes. Tomorrow night, dress in warm garments, and meet me at the stables just past midnight. Pack one small trunk, and two valises.

"Tomorrow afternoon I will have a man come at four for your trunk and two cases. I will not see you until midnight. Do not fail me, my love!

"I shall show you the West. We shall travel in the great canoes, we shall laugh, and be wild and merry. You shall have your great adventures, my darling girl! Come with me, and we shall be happy beyond our wildest dreams! Your Etienne."

She sat down on the bed with a thump and stared at the note.

Marriage—without her father and mother present? Marriage—to wild and laughing Etienne? Marriage—and off to adventure in the unknown.

She remembered Yolanda's sad warnings, but she thought also of Etienne's words, his hand clasp, his kisses, the warm light in his dark blue eyes. He loved her!

And the adventure of it! She, Minna Gunther, would go off like one of the voyageurs. She would travel, she would see the faraway places, with the most courageous, tempestuous, daring lover a girl ever had!

The next morning she rose early, had her breakfast on a tray, and began to pack. Her father came to her. His face softened as he saw her packing. He kissed her cheek.

"There are other, finer men, my Minna, you will not be sorry. I shall finish some business, and we shall depart in three days."

Her decision almost left her. Her heart quailed. Never had she deceived her father! Oh, she and Colin had played little coaxing tricks on him, to get their own way. But not lies—not deception—not an overwhelming deceit like this!

She put her arms about his neck and put her blond head on his strong chest. "Oh, Papa," she said, almost ready to confess.

"He is not worthy of you. He will run off and leave you for the West, for there is adventure in his blood, and I know he is already planning his next journey. Would you wait here all the winter for him to return to have a honeymoon?" Ludwig scoffed.

Minna raised her head, her resolve strengthened. No, she would go off herself—with Etienne, her lover!

She packed with the help of a maid, who saw no reason to be surprised that one trunk had heavy woolens in it, a blanket, and boots. Minna would not need those on the trip home, since it was but late August. And she packed the valises herself, quietly, after the maid had gone to do other work. She put in medicines, bandages, a couple of knives, a pistol and ammunition; and her own small neat rifle went into the trunk along with its bullets. She added scarves, practical bonnets that flattened to little bulk, and more stockings.

At four a man came up from the stables and took down her trunk and two valises. It was the hour when Yolanda rested, and the men were not yet home from the warehouse.

Conversation at dinner that evening was very stiff and formal. Etienne did not appear. "He is sulking," said Ludwig with disdain.

Yolanda's gaze rested thoughtfully on Minna's pale face. As the girl went up to bed, Yolanda went to her and kissed her cheek. "All will be well with you, my dear. You are strong," she said.

Minna did not know if the woman guessed what the two young people had planned, or if she was merely sorry for the scenes which had happened, and for her lost love for Blaise. She smiled weakly, kissed her hostess's cheek, and thought, she will be my new mother!

Would they welcome her and Etienne when they returned in the summer following? Or would his parents be as displeased as her own? But surely they would understand!

At midnight she stole quietly down the back stairs to the stables. She wore her gown of white with the red stripes on it, with the gay red silk coat. It was something for her wedding, and she had a tinge of regret for the lost, beautiful ceremony she would have had at home, in her own German Lutheran Church, and her own friends and family about her.

She had not thought further. Etienne met her, clasped her close, kissed her mouth exultantly. "You came!" he whispered and set her into the closed barouche. They drove out, his man driving them, and Etienne held her in his arms and kissed her as they went.

They drove at a merry pace along the quiet cobblestoned streets of Montreal, to the west, out of the city, along the riverbank.

"I have found an old man to marry us," murmured Etienne in her ear, kissing the lobe in a distracting fashion. "He is so old and foolish, he doesn't know night from day! He will not ask questions as to why we marry at such a time. Then we go down river, to a cabin. Some trapper friends of mine are loaning us the cabin for a few days, until the canoes are ready. Father will not find us there!"

Her mouth trembled. It was such a step she was taking! She wanted to shrink back, yet something in her was quivering in excitement, in ecstasy. Marriage to Etienne—and going with him West! Going as Colin had gone, and her father before her, and Billy Montana and all the wild free trappers she had met and envied.

They drove a long distance, rattling now over dusty dried trails. Finally the barouche pulled up with a jerk, and some laughing, calling bronzed men yanked open the door of the carriage.

"Etienne and his bride!" they cried in French. Bold hands helped her out, bold eyes went over her in the lamplight and the light of flares at the small log chapel.

They went inside, to kneel at an altar. The priest was in white robes, his white head balding, his face absent and benign. It was then Minna realized she was being married in a Catholic service!

The knowledge somehow shocked her. Etienne whispered his responses in Latin, and nudged her to say the same. She answered the words, spoke again—and put herself in Etienne's keeping, in a Roman Catholic service!

The service was brief, and Minna did not understand much of it. They stood, knelt, were prayed over. Then Etienne wanted her to sign some papers.

Her father had taught her to be suspicious of any documents.

She must read first anything she signed.

"What are these?" she asked, taking them over to the table and spreading them out under the lamp.

Her quick gaze went over the words. One was a marriage certificate, pure and simple. She signed it and gave the pen to Etienne to sign. Then she glanced over the next—and went cold.

It said that she promised to bring up their children in the Roman Catholic Church, to baptize them in the Roman Catholic religion!

"What are these, Etienne?" she asked lightly, masking her uncertainty.

"Only papers, dear Minna, hurry up and sign." He scrawled his name boldly across them and gave her the pen.

One of the trappers made a gay remark to him, and Etienne turned to laugh with him. Minna made a deliberately vague line across where her signature would be. Not her name, it was but an up and down line. She picked up the marriage certificate and slipped it folded into her small purse; then she gave the other papers back to the priest, who held them closely to his eyes and smiled and nodded vaguely.

"Good, good, he will register them in the parish after we have slipped away," said Etienne, a satisfied smile on his lips.

Minna drew a deep breath. Etienne would have fooled her. She felt cold and chilled for a moment. Then she smiled, her head up. She was a smart girl, she would not be fooled so easily!

They went away to the cabin of the trappers, accompanied by the gaily singing Frenchmen. Etienne was laughing and exuberant, singing with them as he leaned from the opened window of the barouche to answer their shouts and sallies.

The priest had a copy of their marriage certificate and would register that, she knew. But the other papers—when the parish record clerk saw them—she grimaced. Well, she and Etienne would be away some distance, and Etienne would not discover what Minna had done until they returned. And somehow Minna would have the courage to defy him. She would not bring up her children as Catholic! Not without much soul searching and thinking.

She had her father's distrust of Catholics, and the pope. She must wait and see. Perhaps the children could make their own decisions when they were of age.

But that was a long time away! She would relax and enjoy her wedding. However something inside Minna was hurt. She wished she had stayed, to argue gently with her father, to promise to wait for Etienne until he returned next summer. A year might have softened the matter, and all parents might have consented by that time. Too late now, and besides, she would have her adventure!

Ludwig would never have allowed his Minna to go West. Agatha had never gone. Minna's mother had said she was content to remain home, and to hear about everything on their return. But—had she been speaking the strict truth? Or was it convention that had made Agatha say that? Women did not travel boldly. Women were to remain home and take care of the house and the children. Minna had seen her mother take up a precious bit of porcelain and stroke it gently with her fingers. She had held the bits of mink, and brushed and brushed them, her gaze far away. She had opened the sandalwood or cedar boxes from China or Africa or India, and murmured as she took out the contents from the rice paper or cottons.

Had Agatha not longed at times to travel and see the strange and marvelous places of the world?

"What are you thinking, my darling?" Etienne's arm tightened around Minna.

"I was thinking—about my mother and father," said Minna.

"You were wishing they could have attended our wedding?" he said gently. "You know, we could have another wedding when we return, a big celebration with all our relatives. We will have a priest to bless us, a merry feast, much wine and singing. Would you like that, eh?"

Minna smiled and rubbed her cheek against his chest. She did not have his exuberant confidence that all would be forgiven when they returned. His father might, his mother—perhaps, if all worked out well. But her father and mother—they had another kind of nature, stern, strict, at times unforgiving.

Tears came to her eyes, but she blinked them away, and laughed as merrily as the men when they arrived at the little log cabin. Torches were lit, the men sang to them, and made so much noise once Minna and Etienne were alone inside that Etienne finally opened the door and shouted, "Go away! Go away, or I shall so pester you on your wedding days you will hate me forever! Go away, you monsters, and leave me alone with my beautiful bride!"

They laughed and went away. He slammed shut the door, shot the bolt on it, and turned to Minna, standing uncertainly in her scarlet silk cloak and white bonnet.

He turned sober, and came to her, gently removing her bonnet, then her cloak. "Minna, Minna, it is our wedding night. I can scarcely contain my joy!"

He kissed her deeply, and his fingers were slow and gentle, unfastening the long row of buttons on the dress, drawing off the numerous petticoats and undergarments.

He laid her on the crude fur bed in the corner. It had fresh sweet-smelling blankets on it, and she was grateful, for she was used to sheets and cleanliness. He drew a blanket over them, against the chill of the night air, and the fire crackled in the huge fireplace, sending up orange flames against her closed eyes.

Minna was confused and embarrassed at the strangeness she felt with his naked bronzed body against her shrinking rounded form. Etienne was unexpectedly patient and slow. Agatha had told Minna much more than mothers usually told their daughters, and from the time the girl was thirteen, Agatha had answered every question the shy girl had asked.

Etienne caressed her a long time, his lips against her throat, her breasts, her arms. He stroked over her with his long fingers, murmuring his adoration, his admiration. "How lovely you are, so soft, so silky, so sweet. How fortunate a man am I, to possess and worship such beauty. You attracted me from the first, the mischief in your smile, the twinkle in your eyes, the gravity behind the laughter. Minna, my love, do you love me?"

"Oh, I love you, Etienne," she whispered, and her hands began slowly to imitate his, stroking over the chest, the arms. She found thick hair on his chest, then down below his waist, and her fingers tangled in it. She pressed kisses on the bronzed throat so near hers now. She whispered love words in French, as he did.

They came closer, and his long legs entwined in hers. She felt his thigh pressing on her thighs, and something began to tingle and burn inside her. He rubbed his knee teasingly against hers, pressed that knee further up between her thighs, opening her to him. His fingers went down her waist, to her rounded belly, her hips. Then they slid slowly to her secret places. She murmured, tried to shut her legs against him. He kissed her lips closed with his.

170

He waited for her, though, not rushing her. When she felt burning hot, and wriggled with the strange feelings he was rousing in her, he came close to her and whispered what he would do.

"Did anyone tell you of this, my darling?"

"Yes, my mother. Etienne—oh—"

"My love, my adored, let me come in now."

He came into her slowly, carefully, hurting her a little, then making up for it with his gentle love play. He kissed and nibbled at her throat, teased her earlobes with his tongue, pressed kisses and caresses of his tongue down over her breasts. She almost forgot what his thighs were doing to her, until she felt the thick weight of him in her, and on her. And they were one person, holding together, clasped together, one marvelous, shaking, shivering person.

He drew out quickly, and she felt the moisture on her thighs. He gasped, and lay limply on her when it was over. She stroked the thick red hair tenderly as his head lay on her breasts.

They slept for a while, then Etienne wakened Minna again with his kisses. He was hungry for her once more, yet again he was gentle and sweet with her. How grateful she was, because of the strangeness and shyness she felt. How marvelous a lover he was, drawing her on to feel some of the ecstasy he knew. They lay long that night and the next day, and he had her a third time before they rose. The sun was up high in the sky, and Minna heard voices outside the cabin, men's voices.

Minna lay under the blanket and watched Etienne wash his naked bronzed body with water in the small bowl. How handsome he was, tall, lithe, lean as an arrow, like a young god he seemed to her, like a picture in one of the Greek books. He had strong wide shoulders, and his young throat rose above his torso proudly to the thick red hair. She marveled at his narrow waist and sturdy thighs, one with a long scar on it. His strong rounded legs ended in large sturdy feet. He was all grace and strength and young proud masculine aggressiveness.

He caught her watching him and gave her a wicked wink of his dark blue eyes. Minna blushed and shut her eyes. He came to her, bent down, kissed the closed eyelids.

"I go out now and work with the men to prepare the canoes. You can wash in peace, my Minna. We will probably not leave until tomorrow, so dress as you wish today."

He went out and shut the door after him. She got up, uneasily aware of her young body as never before, shot the bolt on the door, and had a good wash. There was some blood on her, though not much, and she did not feel bad. There was just a dull ache in her thighs, and some bruises on her back and arms where he had hugged her so tightly. She did not mind that.

She dressed, and brushed her hair, braiding it into a single long braid. That would be the most practical for traveling, she thought, surveying herself in a small mirror on the wall. She unbolted the door, then turned to seek something to eat for them.

As the strong good smell of hot coffee and frying pork drew him, Etienne returned to the cabin. He came in, laughing and rollicking. He teased Minna with kisses as she set the table, jumped up and kicked his heels for the fun of it.

"Imagine, Minna, what is going on! My men tell me that Father and your father are already out searching for us! They ask everywhere. One of my boys got the priest drunk, so he sleeps and cannot register the marriage yet!"

"Oh, Etienne." She paused in her work to stare at him, aghast. Her father and his were sick and worried about them, going about looking. "Could we not go back, now we are married, and tell them—reassure them—"

"Nonsense, Minna! Have courage! We cannot turn back now! Now it is too late. They would separate us, make you go home. Don't you want to come with me?"

He teased her, coaxed her, made her laugh. They sat down at the table for their first meal as man and wife. He ate hungrily of the pork and bread, hot coffee and molasses, and fried potatoes. Minna tried to smile, and she was excited. Yet— yet—she thought of her father searching for her, and she felt as if stung by nettles. She wanted to go on with Etienne, but— but she felt worried and sorry about her father. He had always been so good to her! She smiled over the hot coffee cup and swallowed down tears with the drink.

Ludwig raged about Montreal for a week, searching for his daughter. Blaise went with him sometimes, and other times went off in other directions, searching. Finally word came that the marriage had taken place in a small log chapel, by an elderly priest, who had finally ambled into town to register the marriage.

And someone had seen them set out in two huge canoes, laden with packs, to the West. Along the river, said the man. A trunk, many cases, many packs. "Gone for the winter," he told them.

Ludwig gave up. He was sick at heart and took out his grief

in rage heaped on his host's head.

"It is your fault. You have set such a poor example to your son that he dared to elope with my daughter! My God, to think of such a thing! Married to a Roman Catholic, and a man who never respects women. Whatever will become of her."

Blaise raged back at him. Only Yolanda was silent, enduring their arguments, their quarrels. There was no more talk of a merger now. That was over.

The final dinner came. Guests were invited, and Ludwig tried to be polite to them, for the sake of their reputations. But all of them were whispering about Etienne and Minna. Everybody knew about the elopement.

"A girl—to marry in such haste—there must be a reason," he heard the whispers and burned with hurt inside. They talked of his good Minna, his fine and upright and gentle Minna!

The next day the barouche was loaded with some furs and goods, and Ludwig was ready to go. Duncan would drive the empty carriage.

Yolanda had offered to pack Minna's clothes, but Ludwig shook his head. "You will—welcome her—when she returns," he suggested. His eyes were tormented.

She laid her slim hand on his arm. "Do not fear that. I shall treat her as my own daughter. My Etienne is a loving man, I have hopes for the marriage. She is a girl of courage, also."

"Yes, yes, Minna has courage," he said absently. "But why would she go West? Did I drive them to it?"

"Heaven only knows. I warned her," murmured Yolanda with a sigh. "But she is young, impulsive, and I left them too much together. She is so spirited. I thought she would reject Etienne. Instead that brought them together. He cannot resist a challenge. And Minna—she has something of you in her, I think."

"Something of me?" asked Ludwig in surprise. "What do you mean, madame?"

"Of your courage, your spirit of adventure, your longing for the far places of the earth."

"No, no, she is a girl!" protested Ludwig. "Colin, now, I could understand him running off. But not my gentle Minna! She is much like her mother."

Yolanda smiled and changed the subject. "Then I will keep her clothes here, her jewels, and be ready to welcome her when they return. God pray it will be soon. The winters out there are so difficult."

Ludwig fidgeted with his hat. "Madame, there is something

her mother will wish to know. Were they married in the Catholic faith?"

Yolanda nodded. "A priest married them, and the marriage certificate was registered in the parish records."

Ludwig shook his head slowly. "That I find hard to forgive. We brought her up to be a good German Lutheran. A good Protestant. And she married a papist!"

Yolanda stiffened. "Sir, you do not mean to insult us. But take care of your words. I myself will help Minna to learn of our religion. A woman must change for her husband."

"What if the husband is Protestant and the woman Catholic?" asked Ludwig shrewdly. "Then your tune would sing in the other key, madame!"

Her mouth went dry. "I do not doubt that, sir. However the Catholic faith is strong here. I brought up Etienne to be a good Roman Catholic. Of course, Blaise—well—"

"Umm, yes, madame. He converted?"

"Indifferently," she was forced to admit. "He goes through the forms, for my sake. But his heart—well, he has a good kind heart, I—I do not ask more."

Ludwig left the MacCameron residence with a heavy heart. Agatha would find it hard to forgive him, and Minna, for what the girl had done. And not only had she left her home and her family for the forsaken wilderness. She had left the faith of her family.

Ludwig's eyes were indifferent to the beauty of the river, the streams and the forest on the way home. He was thinking how he must tell Agatha what had happened. He knew that his good wife would weep over her lost and erring daughter.

He wanted to weep himself. His eyes stung. His lovely gracious good Minna! Whatever in the world had happened to her? How could she have done this? She must be deeply wildly in love with that young pup. Oh, God, he prayed silently. That she be not disappointed as Yolanda MacCameron had been. That might break her young strong spirit.

Chapter 15

The first winter, that of 1805–06, Colin Gunther lived with the French trappers. He enjoyed their company, since they were a rollicking singing happy lot. He learned much from them, especially how to lay a trapline and how to deal with the Cree Indians who lived all about them.

He scraped his own pelts, which he already knew how to do, and he brushed the furs to prime condition. By the end of the winter he had four packs of furs he had gathered himself. With the coins he had brought with him, he bought more furs from the Indians, and had another dozen packs.

The French were amazed at him. They worked half as hard; after all, one lived only one life, they said. There must be time for music, laughter, getting drunk. Most of them had half the amount of furs that he did.

They took their packs of furs to the nearest trade post to store them, and in the spring they started back to Montreal, gathering their great canoes, and stacking them full. Colin hesitated, but he had already really made up his mind. He was a Gunther, and his profits would go to the Gunthers, not to the Hudson's Bay Company or any other Canadian trading outfit.

He had found an elderly trapper who worked with him sometimes. The man was from the south and had wandered north this winter, further than he had planned. Colin took him in his tent with him and brought him food when the old man was too sick to go out to the fire.

Now Colin asked his aid. "I want to take my furs south to our own post," he said. "Will you drive one of the wagons?"

The old man agreed. "I been wanting to go back nearer my kinfolks," he confided. He was going home to die. Both of the men knew it.

Colin managed to hire two wagons and four horses, with the understanding if he did not return them, he would bring back money to pay for them. The trading post manager tried to persuade him to throw in his lot with their company, as he saw that the young blond man was bronzed, hardworking and tough, for all his youth. He was just the kind they wanted in the company. He might one day run a post of his own, said the manager.

Colin refused and in early spring started to head south for Smithson's post. He had not made up his mind whether to return home yet. If he did go back to New York, he was in for a scolding and a dozen lectures, his mother's weeping, and then for some job in the warehouse. No more wandering wild and free.

They drove south and made it through the Sioux territory by traveling nights and hiding out days. They reached Smithson's trading post by mid-June. There they were greeted heartily by Jack Smithson and his huge Indian family. After they were welcomed, and the furs counted, they were fed, and they finally collapsed in sleep.

Smithson said to Colin, "You want to go home? Your father will be sending out for our furs before long. Wait for them, and travel safe. The Indians are more stirred up than ever, so many whites coming out to the territory."

"No, I think I'll go back up to Canada for another winter," said Colin thoughtfully. "If I go home, Father will have plenty of work for me! I want to be free for a while. I like the trapping life."

Smithson winked at him. "So did I—so well I never left it. A man can be free out here, nobody to tell him what to do and where to go." He looked husky and contented, and he was plainly fond of his plump, still comely Indian wife.

And his sons and daughters! They were laughing, well clothed, clever with the rifle and knife. He had his two eldest sons working now in the trading post. He was so proud of them that Colin had to tease him a little.

The young man wrote a note to his parents to be taken with the fur packs when they were carried back East.

"Dear Mother and Father: I send you respectful greetings and hope you are very well. Forgive me for running off as I did. I could not help going. The wild life called to me.

"I send sixteen packs of furs, four of which are of my own taking. The French trappers taught me well, and I also remember the teachings of my father! I am happy in this life. I mean to remain another winter in the Canadian wilds.

"Do not worry about me. I have friends everywhere and have already learned some of the Cree tongue. I enjoy the snows and am wary of being frostbitten. I take every care, Mama. Do not fret.

"My love to dear Minna, my love to you all. I shall write again or come next summer. Your own Colin."

176

Smithson promised to send gifts to the family from Colin, and the note. He supplied Colin for the next winter, paid him for the furs as though he were a regular employed trapper of the company, and gave him credit for all the money he didn't wish to take with him. It would be put on his account in New York. Colin chuckled with delight at the idea of his having his own trapper account in his father's books!

The money would help set him up later, when he returned. Or he might buy a little house of his own, and be independent. He might buy fine clothes and swank around a little more. He could even take a journey to Europe! His father raved at times about the beauties of London, of Germany, of Amsterdam, and other places. Maybe he would earn enough one day to fit out a ship of his own to the Orient! He grew dreamy, his blue eyes sparkling with the hope of strong youth.

Colin filled the wagon with supplies, and by July 1, he set out for the north again. Traveling alone, he had to be more wary. He was glad to fall in with two trappers who wanted to go north. In exchange for some food and ammunition, they went with him through Sioux territory, and they came out safe the other side of it, in the land of the Crees.

They parted then, and cheerily Colin drove on. He had it in mind to go further north, not to meet with his French friends this time. He was hungry to see more of this wild, horrid country, as some called it. He drove toward the mountains, and along them to the far north.

Here it was colder, even in July. Yet one day, driving over a ridge, he dipped down into a valley and gasped. For it was warm and fertile there, and wild flowers grew in profusion.

He halted the wagon and got down to stare. Here was a beautiful blue stream wandering through a meadow of wild grass. Flowers grew so thickly that in one area was a red meadow, and in another the flowers were golden as the sun. Patches of small blue flowers drew him—they were as blue as his sister's eyes. "My God, how lovely a place," he murmured. It was a place to make a home.

He lifted his gaze upward. To the west were the high stern mountains, covered in snow so late they probably had snow on them year round. Yet here was this warm valley, sheltered from the winds by those very mountains.

He studied the lay of the land. From the smoke rising in the distance, and the little brown spots on the horizon, he figured there was an Indian tribe settled on the far side of the

177

valley. He gazed up again at the mountains. Was that a cabin up there?

He freed the horses of the wagon traces and staked them to the grassy plains. Then the next day he took his rifle and made his way up the mountain to the cabin. He found it deserted, the door sagging on its hinges, only a few stores remaining on the shelves. It was dusty, as though nobody had lived here for years.

He looked around, liked the place. It was up about two thousand feet, he figured, high above the valley. Since the land was snowy in patches above him, he knew he could run a good trapline.

His quick gaze caught glimpses of small animals, squirrels, marten, mink. And he saw larger ones as well, an elk standing far above him, the magnificent branching of his horns telling his advanced age.

He went down to the valley, brought up the horses and wagon and supplies and cleaned out the cabin well with water from the fresh-flowing stream which ran past the cabin down into the valley. He would have water at his doorstep without any trouble! He sang as he worked.

He heard a snuffing about the cabin the next morning as he lay abed. He became alert, took his rifle, and in bare feet went to the door and peered around the edge. He started. Was it a wolf that gazed at him with green eyes? Gray of fur, large of build, gaunt, the animal stared at him. Then it gave a wuff! Colin laughed, and said, "I do believe you are a dog! But you sure do look like a wolf, old boy!"

The animal stared at him, fascinated at the sound of his voice. Then the long plumy tale began to wag, harder and harder.

Colin dared to step outside. The dog backed off warily, but there was something in those green eyes. Colin went back in the cabin. The dog waited on its haunches.

Colin brought him a bone and tossed it. The dog went after it happily and crouched down to munch on it, keeping a green gaze on Colin.

"Well, I got me a pet, maybe," laughed Colin and went back to wash and dress himself. It was such a sunny day, he decided to wash all his blankets and clothes and peg them out to dry on the grassy slopes.

The dog watched his every move. When Colin fixed his meal, the animal came closer and began to whine. Colin tossed him a piece of raw meat. The animal pounced on it, and carried it a little distance away to gnaw on it. By the end of the day it started to creep closer to Colin.

By the second day it came close enough so that Colin could touch the thick fur of its head. He allowed Colin to pet him, then whined and wagged his plumy tail even faster. "You belong to some man, I'll be bound," said Colin. "You remember the smell of a man, the feel of his hand, and I think he was kind to you, because you aren't scared of me."

The dog barked, his clarion voice carrying over the valley.

The following day some Indians rode up about five hundred yards from the cabin, and stared at him for a while. Colin waved in a friendly gesture, but they wheeled their horses and rode away.

He hoped he would not have trouble with them.

He went out with his rifle, changed the horses to another location, and pegged them down securely. Then he went up into the mountains to explore while the weather was still nice. He found a field of berry bushes, and ate some hungrily, resolving to go back for a bucket and get a pack of them. He could put them up in jars for the winter, the way his mother used to do. She added a little molasses, he remembered, and boiled them in water, and put them in jars. He had some empty whiskey jugs. Those might do.

He was beginning to feel like a settled man! He got out his traps that night and sat by the small fire he had built a safe distance from the cabin. He kept his rifle by his side, and Wolf, as he had named the dog, crouched contentedly beside him, snoozing in the firelight. But the dog was alert. At the least sound of an animal or a crackle from the fire, his gray muzzle was up, sniffing the wind. He would get up, steal around quietly, then finally return to snuff at Colin's hand and settle down again. "Good dog," Colin praised him, patting his head. "Good, good dog. You'll be a fine watchdog for me."

Colin polished and sharpened his traps and put them away. It was nice to have a dog to talk to. He rather missed the trappers, with their rough humor and laughter.

The next day he took a bucket and started along the slopes to pick berries. The closer he came, the more curious he was. There seemed to be some small round black balls in the berry bushes.

Someone squealed. An Indian girl jumped up, stared with wide scared eyes, dropped her bucket, and ran down the slopes.

179

She was followed by another, and another. Finally only one girl was left, a tall slim girl who stared at him with a defiant gaze, her eyes black.

She was lovely, perhaps about sixteen, her eyes dark, her skin golden. She had long black straight hair worn in a plait down her back below her waist. Her deerskin outfit was neat, but shabby and worn.

Colin held up his hand in the peace signal and spoke slowly in the Cree tongue. "I come to pick berries. I will not hurt you."

She glared at him, said nothing, merely dropped down to her knees again to pick more berries, her slim fingers moving rapidly in the prickly bushes. She called out sharply in Cree, "Come back, foolish ones. Have you never seen a man before?"

The other girls returned, creeping back, casting uneasy looks at the tall blond-haired man. He grinned at them, then bent to pick berries.

They were all working so fast, giving him worried anxious looks. Suddenly he understood. They had come to pick the berries for their winter supply. They were afraid he would take so many that they would not have enough to feed their tribe. He had no idea how many were in the tribe, but he did know berries were used to make pemmican. They pounded buffalo meat with berries, to give flavor to the hard dry flesh, and smoked it for the winter.

He picked enough berries to look convincing, filling the bucket about one fourth full. Then he got up and left the berry patch, giving them a casual wave of his hand. A couple of the little girls waved back and giggled. The tallest girl eyed him soberly.

He went back to the cabin and thought. Best make friends of the tribe, and that meant meeting the men. He got out his trade goods, chose a scarlet blanket and a blue one of wool, then a large jug of molasses and a small one of honey. He set out that afternoon, riding one of the horses, wearing fresh buckskins and a woolen shirt. It was turning cool at nights, the chill wind sweeping down from over the mountains and from the north.

When he arrived at the Indian camp, he found he was expected. The chief, an old man, wore a bonnet with fine feathers on it, and some fine buckskins and boots. The younger men stood about, rifles in hand, not menacing, but warning quietly. The women were preparing kettles of food over several campfires. The camp contained probably a large family group, about a dozen men, a dozen women, and maybe twenty-five children of assorted sizes.

Colin held his rifle cradled in his left arm, and held up his right in greeting. The chief answered him solemnly, and then Colin slid down. He unfastened his gifts in the canvas pack and staked his horse with their quick ponies at the long rail near the campfire of the chief.

He strode to the fire. The chief sat quietly, his wizened face calm, black eyes watching intently. Colin stood about a dozen feet from him, lifted his hand again, and said, "I am a man from the south. My name is Colin Gunther. To whom do I have the honor of speaking?" He spoke slowly in Cree, choosing his words to make sure the man realized he spoke with respect.

The chief grunted his name and waved for Colin to sit down. They both smoked the pipe the chief held, then spoke again. Colin presented his gifts, the two blankets, the molasses and honey. The chief was curious about the honey, and Colin opened the jar. The chief smelled it, tasted it, and grunted his approval.

The men and women watched soberly. The children were quiet for a time, until the chief offered Colin some of their dinner. He ate with them, told them he lived in the cabin, which they knew, and told them he would live there for the winter and trap, which they had already guessed.

He ate with them, then departed at dusk, riding back to his lonely cabin. It had been rather nice to have someone to talk to, he thought. They lived in the valley all the year, the chief had said.

The weeks wore on, and the flowers bloomed lavishly. Then a frost came one night and turned everything brown. Colin picked a few more berries and smiled as the girls came to pick the rest from the bushes. The tall girl only stared coldly as he spoke to her. She did not speak to him.

She was pretty, with her dark eyes and her golden skin. She seemed to be in charge of the younger girls, but they treated her oddly, as thought she might be a servant. He wondered about that, wondered if she had an Indian fellow after her, wondered if she was about to marry one of them. She might even belong to one of them, but somehow she seemed free and alone.

She walked with a graceful step, carrying a small barrel of

181

berries on her head, swinging a bucket in her hand. How slim she was, and rounded, fully grown, yet innocent. She looked directly at him and was not coy or flirting with her eyes.

Colin got up very early one morning. He had not slept well. The dog had been whining all the night, starting up uneasily to sniff at the door. Colin went out and saw bear tracks around the cabin. "Uh oh, Wolf. We had a guest last night," he said, patting the dog's shaggy head. "We have to look out, don't we, boy? I'll carry the rifle all the time, and keep it loaded, until that old fellow goes to sleep for the winter."

He went out with a bucket to get water, the dog close at his heels. He strode over to the mountain stream and stopped short in surprise when he came near.

The tall Indian girl was there, washing her hair. She must have been bathing, and had come out to scrub her hair, and then duck down again into the cold waters. She gave a little scream of dismay. She was naked from her black streaming hair to her golden heels.

She ducked into the water, landing with a splash. Colin grinned down at her mischievously.

"Come on out," he said. "The water is very cold."

She glared at him furiously The water was so clear he could see every curve of her body. She hugged her arms about herself. "Go way, go way," she said in English.

He started. "Why go way?" he teased. He yanked off his boots and jumped in beside her. He grabbed at her, and she fought at him, splashing water in his face, kicking at him with her bare feet.

Colin had been lonely. He had been thinking about the girl. Now something exciting was rising in him, making him warm even in the cold water. He grabbed at her again, and caught her, his arms holding her tightly against him.

One fist struck at his cheek, glanced off. They were near the bank. The dog barked excitedly, thinking it was a game. Colin tossed the girl up on the bank, and before she could get off the grass, he had followed her up there.

He caught her about the waist and pushed her down on the grass again. "Hold still. I want to talk to you. What English do you know?" he panted.

She glared. "Let go, go way," she repeated furiously. She tried to kick at him again.

The rounded wet body in his arms was stirring Colin to a madness he had rarely known. He had had women, the cheap laughing perfumed women of the town that frequented the waterfront, but never anyone in his arms like this girl, young, soft, silky against him, struggling—

He caught her again, turned her, and lay her on the grass. He bent over her, held down her legs with his legs. He meant to talk to her, he thought, to tease her, to take a kiss or two. He put his mouth on the parted red lips and was lost.

He took another kiss, and another. She was struggling and squirming under him, panting when he let her mouth go for a moment. He yanked open his trousers. He had never had any but a cheap woman, he didn't know much about this kind of innocence.

She moaned when his hard instrument touched her thighs. "Hold still," he muttered. "Hold—still—I want—just let me— oh God, I have to have you—hold—"

His masculine energies were bursting in his young male body. The touch of her drove him out of his mind. He held her still under him, with his hard hands holding her waist, and her thigh, and he thrust himself at her furiously, the way he did the experienced women of the waterfront.

He buried himself in her, disregarding her cry. She was thrashing about under him, making the sensations in him all the more delicious. He closed his eyes, pressed his head against her rounded breasts, his mouth open against the nipple. Whenever she struggled again, it felt so good—so good—he groaned in delight at her movements.

He came with her, hard, bursting in her. He was shaking with ecstasy. He held her tightly, not letting her go, and his instrument got hard again almost at once.

He took her again, burning hot, thrusting back and forth without heeding her cries of anguish. Only when he had come a second time, did he draw out and look down at her. Colin stared, aghast, and shocked into sanity.

Blood stained her legs and thighs. She trembled with pain, and blood covered his instrument. He had taken a maiden.

Brutally, forcefully, he had taken a maiden.

"Oh my God," he whispered. "I am sorry—girl, I'm sorry—"

The tear-wet black eyes opened slowly in the golden face. She gazed up at him, her mouth red and trembling. He bent and kissed her gently.

"Sorry—understand? Sorry," he said.

She shook her head, and her wet hair blew about her face.

183

He took a wet strand and kissed it. She was so silky and soft, he wanted her again, but he forced himself to get up off her. She put her hand to her face, shamed.

He fastened his trousers, still gazing down at her rounded golden body, the long slim thighs with blood on them. He stared at her face, the slim hands and arms.

Finally she got up, watching him warily, and reached for her clothes. Her mouth compressed, she tugged at her deerskin dress and put it on. She pulled on her boots, then reached for the worn fragment of blanket to dry her hair.

Colin knelt beside her, not regarding how she shrank from him. He took the blanket from her and began to dry her hair for her. He loved the feel of the wet strands in his hands, and gently he rubbed each strand dry.

She took the blanket from him then and got up.

"I will see you again soon," said Colin definitely.

She had so excited him that he thought about having a woman for the winter. Blaise MacCameron took an Indian girl every winter. Colin's father thought it was terrible. Colin did not now. He wanted her again.

She gave him a dark sullen look, and shook her head, more in despair and sorrow than in defiance. She walked slowly away, her head down in shame.

Colin watched her go. He could go to the chief and offer more blankets for her, and maybe one of the horses. He had to have her. He wanted her badly. The first taste of love had been enough to waken him to his own masculine needs.

The girl did not come back the next day. There were more berries on the bushes, the last of the season. She would come again soon, he figured.

He waited one day, then two, then three. He polished and sharpened his traps, and began to plan where to lay them. Frost would come soon, and the pelts would be at their best then. Soon the snows would come also, and he would see the marks in the snow. He thought he could get beaver up here, he had seen tracks in the river, and they had lain a small dam across the river farther downstream.

The valley was large. The Indians would be trapping, but there would be enough for them all, especially if he went up in the mountains. He had heard these Indians didn't like going too far up, for fear of running into bear. And he had seen some wild fierce golden eagles up there. They could be mean if one came too near a nest.

He would trap, and skin his own furs, as well as buy the pelts of the Indians. If they didn't do a good job of skinning, he would show them how the traders wanted them. He could buy all they had, since he had plenty of coins and trade goods with him. Yes, that would do it. It would be a good winter. If he could just have the girl also.

The dog whined again all that night. Colin gave up and rose early. "Wolf, you're a nuisance!" he said. "I bet that old bear is around again, huh? All right, all right, let me get my pants on."

He got dressed, and taking up his rifle, checked the load and his ammunition. He had his skinning sharp knife in his belt also. Then he took a bucket and set out. Maybe the girl would come for water and a bath today, or berries.

As he set out, he saw a brown head bobbing in the berry bushes. He grinned—this was his lucky day! Softly he started out, scolding the dog as he started to whine.

"You shut up, Wolf! Be quiet. You want to give me away, huh? Spoil my courtship?"

The dog whined deep in his throat and hung back.

"Oh, come on, I don't mind if you help me court," said Colin. He snapped his fingers, and the dog came at his heels, but slowly.

Colin strode up to the berry bushes and got into the patch. The brown head seemed larger somehow—and not so shiny.

He frowned. He wished he knew her name. "Girl?" he said.

The head stopped moving. A large body swung up, and before Colin's popping eyes reared up a huge black bear.

The bear came up full on his back legs and roared. He was staring right at Colin, and he wasn't more than a few dozen feet away.

Colin dropped the bucket and ran! Damn it, there wasn't a tree nearer than a mile down in the valley! He ran down that slope so fast his feet slithered on the thick wet grass.

The bear was running after him. He could hear him snorting and puffing. He was fat and sassy, stuffing himself for the winter sleep, but he could still run.

Colin reached the cabin, turned around. The bear was right behind him. The dog Wolf had raced ahead and sat panting near the coals of the campfire, his eyes wide, giving short deep angry barks.

Colin, so well trained in shooting that he could act through his fear, lifted the rifle and fired. The black bear kept right on

185

coming. Colin jumped around the campfire, with its hot coals. The dog whined and leaped ahead of him, keeping out of the range of the bear.

Colin, almost hysterical, ran around and around the campfire. When he stopped to load the gun again, the bear gained on him. He couldn't get it loaded so he wildly reached for a stick from the fire, disregarding the burning, and thrust it right at the eyes of the bear. A great sharp paw swiped at him, and he felt the pain begin at his left cheek and go all the way down to his shoulder. He fell, rolled over the campfire, and out the other side.

Colin was now finally able to stuff another load into the gun. Blood was filling one eye. He blinked, but it did little good. He could scarcely see, and he felt faint with the pain of his face and shoulder.

Then he saw a flash of gray, and knew that Wolf had sprung to his defense. The bear growled and turned on the new enemy. Blood streamed from his chest where Colin's aim had gotten him, but the big old black bear wasn't finished. He swiped again and again at the dog jumping at him. One big paw finally got the dog, and slashed across its head. It opened the dog's skull, right to his brain. Wolf slumped across the fire, and it burned his rough coat.

The bear was weakening. Colin had gotten the rifle loaded once more, and fired at him, but he still came. Colin reached for his skinning knife, and as the bear reached him, he rolled over. He got up, on hands and knees, blinked at the streaming blood, and stabbed upward, right at the bear's throat.

The animal fell over, slowly, rolling over and over, and down the slope. Colin watched to see if he would get up again. He did not.

The last thing Colin remembered was the glaze in the eyes of Wolf, as the dog crept closer to him, whimpered a little, and sank down at his side. The green eyes closed slowly, in pain, and the great bloody head pushed against Colin for a moment, then the whole gray shaggy body went limp.

Chapter 16

Colin wakened slowly. He had had a nightmare, he thought. He had dreamed that a great black bear had chased him, and that he had smelled the fetid breath right on his face as a giant paw had scraped him. Now he stared into the heart of a campfire. He was so hot—so hot—

He groaned at the pain of his cheek and flung off the blanket. He was so hot—and the pain moved along his cheek down his chest.

A hand reached across him and drew the blanket about him once more. He gazed up into a beautiful golden-brown face, and dark, concerned eyes.

"What—where—" he muttered.

"The bear clawed you," said the voice softly in Cree. "Rest now. Sleep."

He closed his eyes. He sensed now he was inside the cabin, and that the girl was there. He heard voices, deep and growling, one of a man, and then a softer, higher voice, an older woman's. He slept.

When he wakened, light was streaming into the cabin through the open door. A cool breeze came in and fanned the sweat on his face. He was cold, no, he was hot—he shivered.

A hand put the blanket about his shoulder, then soothed his hot forehead with a cloth, gently moving over his face to wash it with cool water.

He opened his eyes. He thought he would see the girl, but instead a wizened face was there, with gray-white hair straggling about it. Alert black eyes stared down at him, and the mouth moved, grinned, showing half a dozen teeth remaining.

He did blink then. She put a small cup to his lips. It was hot meat broth, and he drank it slowly. She nodded, cackled, and said something. He could not understand, but a girl answered her.

"He will sleep again, Grandmother," said the girl.

Colin did sleep, off and on for a week or more. He could not count the days. Sometimes he wakened at night, sometimes in the day, but in his weakness they were both the same. The girl and the old woman were looking after him, it seemed.

187

Sometimes he heard a deeper voice, and once he thought he saw the old wise face of the chief.

Finally he began to wake up for longer times. He had had a fever, and felt very weak, but he managed to sit up one day, and that was a relief. He felt his face, and winced. There was a long stinging wound down his left cheek to his shoulder. It had begun to heal near the eye, but it still hurt. And on his chest it had not yet closed. The women had smeared it with a mixture that smelled strong and medicinal.

The old woman was sitting at the fireplace, stirring something in a small kettle. The girl brought him a cup of hot broth with some cornbread. Colin ate it, with appetite, and the girl nodded, satisfied.

As he lay back, she drew up the blanket to his chin.

"My dog?" he asked, stretching out his hand, glancing toward the doorway.

The girl shook her head. "No—he die."

"Oh." Colin turned his head, his breath caught. Dead. His dog, his one friend. "He was—good dog. Friend." He managed to say the words.

She was watching him gravely. Now she sat down beside him, smoothed her deerskin skirts about her knees. The dress came halfway to her ankles. She was so slim, so lovely.

"My grandmother tells me story," she said slowly, searching for the words. "She says—when a good friend die, he not go to dark ground. He live again, in bird, or flower, or star. Maybe your dog live again, come again. Yes?"

Colin thought about that. It was a nice philosophy. "Thank you," he whispered. "Where—did the dog—come from?"

"Man come, trap, last winter. Stay few days. Bear get. He had dog—dog stay. Not come to Indian camp. Come to you."

So the bear had killed before. Well, he was gone now, wasn't he?

"Bear—dead—killed?" Colin asked in Cree again.

The girl nodded her shining head. The hair was in a neat plait down her back once more. He liked it shining round her shoulders, loose and wet. He remembered how she felt in his arms.

The girl was saying, "Men skin bear. Him very big for black bear. Bad one, many fear. Now him bearskin!" And her dark eyes shone as her face crinkled up in a smile.

He smiled back at her weakly. "Good, good. Bear better as just bearskin!"

She laughed softly, and the old woman cackled. He had made a joke, so he must be better.

The Indian chief came the next day. He squatted down and gravely smoked his pipe as he studied Colin who was sitting up, feeling stronger already. Except for the pain in his cheek and shoulder, and some remnants of fever, he felt good once more.

"You stay winter?" asked the chief.

Colin nodded. "I wish to lay lines, and trap. Not where Indians trap. Up mountain, maybe?" he asked.

The chief nodded. "Yes, good. Beaver there, fox. You like Morning Star?"

His pipe indicated the tall girl standing at the fireplace.

Colin was flushed, not from fever. "Yes, I like—Morning Star." It was pretty name, suited her. She was shy, peeping softly from the morning sunlit clouds—he was getting poetical!

"She live with you here," said the chief. "And her grandmother, Wind in the Pines," he added, indicating the old woman.

Colin swallowed. He had not meant to adopt a whole family! But the old woman stared at him anxiously, and he nodded. "Yes, Morning Star and grandmother, Wind in the Pines. I take care of them, they care for me," he said and that seemed to please them. All the faces relaxed.

The old chief departed, having settled the two women. Colin was able to get up in a couple more days and began to move about outside the cabin, preparing his traps. He laid the first lines, and at once began to catch beaver, silver fox, blue fox, several fine muskrats, and even one beautiful huge mink!

Colin was jubilant. The coats were thick and furry. The animals ate well in this sheltered valley, and their coats were thick in preparation for the cold weather. He brought them back and began to skin them.

Morning Star shook her head and took the skinning knife from Colin. "Grandmother and Morning Star do this. Woman's work," she told him.

He was surprised, but watched them. He wanted it done just right. They worked beautifully, evidently used to this. They skinned the animals, scraped the skin, brushed the furs, hung them to dry, and cooked the meat for them all. Colin wasn't used to eating these animals, but he became accustomed to the taste.

Morning Star slept in the blankets with him, on top of

189

bearskins and blankets. When he felt able to do so, one night, he drew her to him and caressed her body.

She stiffened but yielded to him. He kissed her shoulders, her cheeks, her soft arms. She had lain down in her deerskin dress. Evidently she wore a dress night and day, and washed them in the streams.

He enjoyed caressing her, but somehow—his hand wandered again to her stomach and thighs. Was she larger than before? Had she been eating more?

He was puzzled. But she made no resistance when he lay over her and took her more gently. She seemed relieved at his care, and put her hands awkwardly on his chest, and patted him. He guided her fingers to caressing him, down his thighs, and over his back. She learned quickly.

He found her shy, but willing, soft-spoken, whispering in his ears. "You are good to Morning Star," she murmured.

"Morning Star is a most beautiful girl," he whispered back, and kissed her ears and chin. "Morning Star has lips like flowers, ears like little shells of beauty. Her voice is like the butterflies hovering with pleasure over the plains."

Her cheeks grew warm, and he could see her dark eyes sparkle in the firelight.

Remembering how brutal he had been the first time they made love, Colin was more careful now. He didn't want to hurt her, such a quiet, shy girl, serious and anxious to please. He wanted to give her pleasure.

He moved slowly with her, but his desires soon overcame him. He thrust more and more deeply, and came hard, lying over her with gasping breaths of delight. Oh, she held him so tightly—he came hard in her, and no sooner drew out than he wanted her once more.

Morning Star let him do as he pleased with her. He had her the next night, and the next. They lay together under the blankets, as the winds blew the message that winter was coming, causing the autumn trees to sing and rattle their branches.

The old grandmother approached him one day as he brought back half a dozen animals from the traps.

She looked worried and upset. "Colin, I wish to speak to you," she said slowly in the Cree tongue. Colin could easily understand her, since he had been learning more and more words from Morning Star. It was a pleasant way to learn a language, he had found, under the blankets with a pretty soft-skinned girl!

"Yes, Grandmother," he said, dumping down the animals. He squatted down to begin the skinning. She took her knife from her belt and began also.

"I am worry about Morning Star," she said slowly. The jet black eyes studied him, then flicked down to her task again.

Colin wondered if Morning Star did not really like him. Or if she did like him, but worried that he would leave after getting a few skins.

"I stay all winter," he reassured her. That meant he would feed them all this winter, relieving the Indians in the camp of that responsibility. "I bring food for all, I take gifts to the chief for Morning Star."

The anxious face was not relieved, though she nodded vigorously. "Morning Star—young girl," she said. "Morning Star—not with any other man," she added hopefully.

"She is innocent except with me," said Colin, flushing. He found the conversation difficult. Was she asking his intentions? Did she want him to marry the girl in a Christian ceremony? Colin was confused, not knowing what to do, or even what he wanted. Surely no man could ask for a sweeter wife than Morning Star. Could he marry her—and take her home to his family in the East? How would Morning Star react to that?

"Morning Star have baby," said the old woman abruptly.

Colin was rocked back on his heels. He stared, blinked. "Baby?" he asked in a hollow voice.

"From first time," said the old woman. "I see her come home, with blood on her legs. She tell only me, her granny. It was you. And soon she no more bleed. She have baby long spring."

There was a long silence. Colin stared into the distance. His heart was pounding. He was shocked, yet delighted! A baby, maybe a son! He would be twenty-one in November. It was time he married and had a child. His father had married about this age. But an Indian girl—

Well, why not? She was a lovely girl, intelligent, shy, sweet, and gentle. Everything a wife should be. And her child would be strong, healthy and well cared for.

He got up and went into the cabin. Morning Star was bending over the steaming kettle of meat and corn. She straightened and stood with her back to him, her head bent.

He went to her and put his arms about her.

"You will have my baby?" he whispered. She nodded, and a pink blush came into her golden cheeks.

191

"You—like?" she asked anxiously, her voice husky.

"It is—fine! Splendid! Maybe I have a son first time!" he burst out and laughed joyously. "Maybe a son, come spring!"

She turned in his arms and kissed his neck. She pressed her cheek against his. "I try to give you a son, fine and strong," she said quietly, her voice musical and happy.

"A daughter is fine too," he said hastily. "A daughter is fine, pretty like her mother. However, if son—that is great! He will be strong, straight, good." He held her and rocked her against himself. "A son, maybe a son!" he murmured in English, and she smiled against his chest, snuggling closer to him.

Somehow, everything was happier then. The cabin was a cozy place, ringing with Colin's laughter, Morning Star's singing, and the happy cackle of her grandmother. They worked together well through the days that grew shorter and shorter.

And at nights the fire blazed in the fireplace, and Colin lit his pipe and smoked his tobacco, a present from the chief. Morning Star and her grandmother told him stories of the Cree people, legends, folklore, stories about the stars, the animals and birds, even the flowers that grew in the valley.

He felt contented, even joyous. He now had a family of his own, and Morning Star expected his son! And he was truly part of a community, one based on family ties and mutual needs, not like New York society. When the snows were deep and they could travel on the rounded showshoes which Morning Star had made, they went over to the Indian camp for a day or two at a time, talked, ate together, and became more friendly.

Colin made a deal to buy all their furs from them. Though they were dubious at first, he told them he would give them the blankets he had, the trade goods, and some gold and silver coins. The chief nodded then, knowing that was a good deal, and they would not need to travel many hundreds of miles to the nearest fur trade post of the Canadians.

Some of the young men were even encouraged to go further north, to return after a month or two on each journey. They brought some of the most beautiful silver fox that Colin had ever seen, as well as mink and white polar-bear fur. Colin got so many furs he wondered if he could carry all of them in one wagon.

Yet in spite of how busy he was with his booming fur business, something had made him curious. He had had more chances now to see Indians living together. Their girls were treated well. The chief's own daughter was like a princess, haughty, waited on, spoiled with her own saddle and creamy pony. Yet his own wife, Morning Star, was talked to with thinly disguised contempt and the princess even turned her back on her one evening.

Colin finally ventured to ask his beloved woman about the treatment she received. It might pain her to discuss it, but he must know—did they despise her for living with a trapper?

He put the question bluntly to her one night. Morning Star hesitated, then looked at her grandmother. The old woman grunted and shrugged.

"They have always despised me," she said, her musical voice low.

"But why—always?" asked Colin, very surprised. She was lovely, intelligent, gracious.

"My father—white man. Trapper."

He stared at her, shocked to the core. She did not look very white to him, though now he stared, he could see she was lighter than the other girls. Her hair, though almost coal black, had reddish lights in it, while theirs was usually dark brown. Her eyes were black, like theirs.

"A trapper?" he asked. "You know your father?"

Her mother had died a long time ago. She rarely spoke of her.

Morning Star shook her head, mournfully. "Trapper live here one winter, then go 'way. Mother have her baby in the summer, very sad, very sad. Everyone mock her. Grandmother take care of her. And when she has a girl, even chief is mocking her. She not live very long. I am six years old when she fades like a flower and curls up and dies. She is buried on the plain."

Colin was silent for a time. It was a sad story, and his heart burned with indignation that a man could father a child and then walk away.

"Do you know the trapper's name?" he asked finally.

She nodded. "He is named MacCameron," she said.

Colin gasped. "MacCameron?" he repeated. Could he have been mistaken? "What MacCameron? What was his first name?"

Morning Star stared. "You know him?" she asked in excitement. "His name Blaise MacCameron." She had trouble with the first name, lisping it, having to repeat it several times before he was sure.

"Blaise MacCameron. I have met him. Is he tall, with bright red hair?"

She nodded, putting her hand to her head. "Hair—very red, bright red. Mother say he handsome man, very tall, very strong. He live one winter with her, only, then go home, to wife, he say. Mother weeps when she says this."

Colin no longer wondered why she was so sad at times. She thought he would treat her as her mother had been treated. What could he do? He had never planned to remain all his life in the West. Perhaps time would tell him what to do.

In May Morning Star was delivered of a child. She had had a difficult birth, and her grandmother was troubled over her. Other women came from the camp to help, not mocking her now, but soothing, helping. Finally the child came, after about thirty hours of labor.

He was such a big baby, that caused the long labor, according to the grandmother. He had strained her body, in coming out. Big, lusty, bawling, he had a head of thick black hair. His eyes were dark also, rounded and black like those of Morning Star. His face was like Colin's though, lighter skinned than his mother, with cheekbones and a chin like Colin's.

"What a boy he is, strong, strong," the chief kept repeating and seemed to approve of the child.

"What shall we name him?" Morning Star asked Colin timidly.

Colin had been thinking about a name, his father's name, as well as others of the family. "What would you like?" he asked.

Morning Star smiled fondly at the black head nuzzling into her breast as the boy sucked hungrily at her breast. "He is strong, husky. Maybe Wolf. That is a fortunate name."

Wolf. The name he had given his dog! Colin stared at the child. Had the boy come, because the dog had been taken from him? Was it possible for a good friendly animal like Wolf to come back in another form—even that of a human? "Yes," he said. "Wolf. Black Wolf, for his dark hair."

In June Colin gathered together his furs, made them into packs, bought the last of the furs from the Indians, and loaded the wagon. He still had the two horses, which he had carefully watched to make sure they did not stray. The wagon would be heavy and hard for one horse to pull.

194

Morning Star came out to watch, the baby in her arms. Her eyes were sad, her face somber.

"I will come back in two months," said Colin over and over.

She nodded, but he thought she did not believe him. Like her father, he might never return to her.

He set out reluctantly, asking the chief to take care of his wife, telling the others he would return. They nodded politely.

Colin had a hard time of it, traveling alone with the heavy load of furs. He had to hide out in the hills several days when some Sioux Indians camped below him to have a drunken party. They had evidently just killed some whites. They showed scalps to each other and sang joyously over their victory.

Colin did make it through to Smithson's, to find the man anxious over him. "Man, you made it!" said Jack Smithson fervently. "The Sioux are all stirred up bad. You'd best not go back."

"I must," said Colin. "I have a wife and child up there."

The man did stare then, and Colin briefly told him what had happened during his stay. But he did not tell him exactly where he lived.

Colin was pleased to find that there were letters for him. He turned over the wagon and furs to Smithson's son and sat down to read, not even stopping to wash and change into new clothes. He was hungry for news.

His father had written anxiously, "Come home, my boy, come home, your mother and I are so worried about you."

And then the news from his mother—"Minna eloped with young MacCameron. She and Etienne were married, and went West. We have had no word from them. Father is furious with Etienne and also with his father." His gentle mother was obviously grieved and upset over her only daughter.

Colin had thought to write them gleefully that he was married to the daughter of MacCameron. These revelations gave him pause. No, he would not tell them yet. This proof that MacCameron, the elder, had lived with Indian women would not be pleasing to the Gunther family. They would worry all the more about her.

So he wrote that he had an Indian wife who was beautiful and good. She had just given him a son, Black Wolf, who was a handsome young fellow. He had had a run-in with a bear, and now had a heavy scar down his left cheek, but he was growing a long beard to cover it. The blond beard was thick

195

already, covering the lower half of his scar. Above the beard, the scar reached to his left eye. Though the attack had almost killed him, he did not write that. He did inform them he had many furs, and that Smithson would send the account.

"I will stay another winter or two," he wrote. "Then I will come home with my wife and child. I hope you will welcome them. I shall set up my own house, and I am very happy. Morning Star is a lovely girl, and this winter I will teach her more English. She learns quickly. You should see my son! What a lusty strong boy he is!"

He put the letter in Smithson's care, to go back East with the furs. Then he had a long talk with Smithson regarding women, and with Smithson's wife. He had things to ask which embarrassed him, but he felt he must know more about women in order to treat Morning Star right.

Privately he resolved not to give her one child after another. He did not want her to work hard, and live as Smithson's wife did, with a dozen children and enough tasks to make her worn and gray before her years. Perhaps one in another two years, or three, and another later on. But not one a year!

Smithson sent two trappers back with him most of the way. Colin thanked them. The Indians were thick in the Black Hills, and he had worried about the journey. He bade his companions good-bye above the many rivers, and turned west and north, to his own valley. Autumn was coming, and the trees were turning crimson and yellow. The flowers would be thick in the valley.

When he drove the wagon above the ridge and looked down into the valley, his heart leaped for joy. The nights had grown cold, and he saw a thin line of white smoke rising from his cabin. Morning Star would be waiting for him, she and his son!

As he drove into the valley, the wagon rattled from emptiness. He had many blankets and trade goods, but they did not fill the wagon as the furs had done. He drove at a brisk pace down the hills and gazed with pleasure at the fields of crimson flowers, the streaks of golden flowers, the blue stream falling from the hills in one white waterfall. His valley, his home.

Indians on ponies were riding toward him, almost flying at a reckless pace. He wondered at once if something was wrong, but they lifted their arms and shouted their welcome! He yelled back at them, laughing. They surrounded the wagon, grinned at him, and asked if he had brought tobacco and more blankets.

"Yes, yes, and honey, much honey for the chief!" Colin laughed. "The chief will welcome me, yes?"

"Yes, yes, and more than the chief will welcome you!" they said.

He pulled up the wagon and halted it at the foot of the hills. The door of the cabin opened abruptly, and out dashed Morning Star. She came running down the hills, the two-thousand-foot slope, toward him. He lost his control and began to run up the hill toward her, as the grinning Indians laughed and shouted and teased them.

Morning Star must have been washing her hair, since Colin noticed that it streamed out behind her in the cool afternoon air, black silky smoke billowing about her laughing face. She ran, her skirts flying about her long slim legs, her arms held out wide.

Colin paused, panting, and extended his arms toward her. He watched her with pride, joy, and love. Yes, love. He loved his golden girl, his Morning Star. He held his arms wide, and she flew right into them.

"You—came—back—you—came—back—" she panted, and began to laugh and cry in his arms.

He lifted her chin with his fingers tenderly and said, "I told you I would come back. I come back to my Morning Star, my wife, and to Black Wolf my son. How is my son?"

She blinked back tears with her thick dark lashes. "He grows, he is so big and strong. You will be proud."

He held her tightly, and in front of the grinning Indians, he kissed her mouth hard, pressing his lips to her rosy ones. She was shy in front of the men and put her face against his chest. He caressed the wet hair, drawing the strands through his fingers.

The Indians were soon unfastening the horses, pegging them to the thick grass. They unloaded the wagon with many jokes, and rode their sleek swift ponies up the hill to the cabin, carrying the many loads of blankets, kettles, bolts of cloth, molasses, sugar and honey, salt and flour, stores enough for another winter.

He had bought more rifles, pistols, and ammunition, bullets and several kegs of gunpowder. The Indians fingered the rifles longingly, and savage looks came to them.

"The Sioux are making war in the mountains to the south,"

Colin told them quietly, his arm still about Morning Star as they walked up the hills. The men had clustered about them on the last part of the long walk up.

"Ah—bad," grunted one of them. "We tell chief. Maybe move north in spring. Sioux come up and make war. Bad."

"They would come up here?" asked Colin, startled.

"Yes. Come north, more far every year."

That was bad news. He had no wish to leave his valley. But perhaps in another few years he would take Morning Star and his son back East, home.

He picked up his son and admired him. The boy was four months old, and twice the size no, more than twice, than when Colin had left. He blinked up at his father, held securely in the buckskin-clad arms, and grinned, showing one small tooth. Colin laughed down at him with joy.

"What a son I have! What a wife I have!" He almost sang the words. And Morning Star beamed at him, softly, her eyes filled with wondering joy. Her man had come home.

Chapter 17

Even while Colin had not yet heard of their elopement, Minna and Etienne traveled many thousands of miles in the huge canoes. The French voyageurs paddled and sang to help pass the time, but the hours were long.

Each day they would start before dawn, eating hastily, loading up, drinking a sip of coffee, then beginning to travel further upstream into the heart of the vast wilderness. Minna looked around her in wonder as they continued onward. The cabins grew fewer in numbers, and sometimes days would pass and they would see none.

One day she realized she had seen no cabin and no other people but the trappers for a week. The river wound round hills, and at times it would cut such a wide curve that in order to save time and effort, the trappers would unload the two huge canoes, pack all on their backs, and make trip after trip over hills, sliding down slick wild grasses to the next point. She thought it would be simpler to paddle around that curve, until Etienne pointed for her, down from the hill.

"Look—the rapids," he said somberly. "Those can kill a man quickly. Even a strong man can drown in those cold waters. He freezes, he cannot move, and the rapids draw him under."

She shivered a little, even in her thick woolen dress and woolen plaid cape. Her first taste of the rawness of nature showed her that it would kill as well as delight and inspire.

She found more and more evidence of this new realization the further they traveled. Some of the men were older. Antoine, the eldest, was a grave man who did not speak much. François was young, wild and with a wicked twinkle in his eyes. But even he sobered as Antoine would tell stories of his youth, briefly, when the wilderness was first approached for furs.

They told of living near hostile Indians, one staying up all the night to guard, fearing that a bullet would bring them down, or an arrow. Once one was attacked by a grizzly bear and killed with one swipe of the massive paw, and they had seen trappers bitten by wild animals as they were caught in crude traps, causing fever, and sometimes death.

And some of the trappers carried such heavy packs, and in such cold snows, that they would fall down, and something broke inside them. One of Antoine's brothers had died so, bleeding from the mouth.

After enough of these horrifying tales had been told, Etienne would finally stop the talk around the campfire impatiently, authority in his tone. "No more such talk, you make my wife sad!" he said.

The men would then laugh and joke and sing songs, and Minna would feel better about it. But sometimes, tired as she was from the weight of the two valises she insisted on carrying herself, she would lie awake and remember the stories of the men who had traveled here, and who had fought, worked, and died alone. The wilderness was vast, and cruel, and impersonal. Deaths were absorbed into the cycle of the earth—birth, fighting for life, struggles, mating, and then death again.

They traveled more than eight weeks before they reached their destination, far into the Northwest. They came to a small fort surrounded by wooden palisades with a blockhouse at each of four corners. Inside was the tiny fur trade post of Mac-Cameron, with the proud banner of the MacCamerons flying from the center post.

There was one cabin filled with trade goods. The small building was about the size of Minna's first bedroom, she thought. At one side was a counter about a yard long. The trader kept the books, and every Indian for miles around had a page in his account book.

There was also a keg of gunpowder, and another of black bullets, along with a few rifles and pistols. These were not sold to Indians, Etienne told Minna. They might get drunk and make war on the whites.

On the shelves were the goods for the Indians, wool blankets in shades of crimson, blue, yellow. Shirts, warm undershirts, thick trousers and stockings, and boots for the wet wilderness of rain and snow made valuable trading commodities.

On the other side of the store was a small triangular ledge. Up there were kept precious stores such as coins, gold, more rifles, ammunition and the best furs. Other furs hung from the rafters, drying, to be scraped and brushed when ready. There was also a crude stove fueled by wood, and when Minna went into the cabin, some Indians were sitting by it. The trader pushed them out to make room for Etienne and Minna and a couple of Etienne's men. The Indians left gravely, wrapping their blankets about them, casting only a single dark look at the new people.

The party of Frenchmen remained at the post for several days to rest, stock up, and talk business. They also partied day and night, and Minna got rather tired of that. She was the only woman at the post, but Indian girls came in from the camps nearby and danced with the Frenchmen stoically, their stolid faces not showing a sign of pleasure. At midnight the music of the fiddle and pipe ceased abruptly, and everybody left.

Finally Etienne and the others were ready to leave. They traveled north, Minna on a horse, the others walking, through snow that was already thick. The ground, where bare in the hills, was like solid iron. There were few trees, and these low and stumpy. She saw no flowers, or signs of them. It was not the beautiful wilderness her father had described.

Yet, in spite of the harshness of the landscape, it had a fascination all its own. She would look upward and see the sharp jagged lines of mountains to the west. Though they were covered with snow, the touches of white did little to soften them. They seemed so aloof, so grand, rearing up against the vivid blue sky. As the party traveled north, it seemed to get colder every day, and the snow was thicker. Etienne kept watching the sky.

"We best get under cover before the snows come. We are late," he said one day.

"That is your fault. We should have started three weeks earlier," said François sharply, glancing at Minna in rebuke.

Etienne scowled, his dark blue eyes flashing, and he bawled out François in rapid French. Minna caught some words, though not all. Antoine finally soothed them both, and they traveled on.

They finally halted about two hundred miles north of the fur trade post, and the men quickly threw up two cabins about one hundred yards apart. One cabin was for Minna and Etienne, and the other would shelter the six men who had decided to hunt with them that winter. The rest of the men had traveled to other points to hunt and trap, a few by themselves. They would meet again at the fur trade post in the spring, and travel back to Montreal together.

Minna was glad to move into the cabin, and have some privacy with Etienne once more. He had not made love to her in the blankets on the trail. Etienne did make love to her now, and she enjoyed it, lying in the warm blankets with him on a bed of bearskin. She could hold him as she wished, closely, and his kisses were so sweet. While loving him, she could forget the hurt she had done to her family, the sorrow she felt that they had married and left as they had. All the pain would be worth it, to have this time in the wilds.

She was amazed to find a vast Indian encampment near them. She spotted it one day, out traveling on the snowshoes Etienne had brought to her. "Isn't it dangerous?" she asked Etienne that night when he came home from the trapline he was laying.

"Dangerous? No, they are friendly Indians," he laughed. "We know them. Don't be silly, Minna," he said in his teasing fashion. "Don't be scared!"

She was silent and a little hurt. He had always teased her. He enjoyed making her angry, then soothing her with kisses. But lately his teasing had begun to sting.

Etienne was visibly restless. He laid out his lines, and began to bring in mink, silver fox, and other beautiful animals. Minna worked with them, but Etienne was worried about that.

He would take her hands in his and study them. "They are getting red and rough, Minna. Put some bear grease on them. I wish you wouldn't work on the pelts. I can get some Indian women to work them," he told her, concern in his eyes.

And he would take the pelts away. But Minna insisted on working with the beautiful minks and making sure they were scraped properly. Etienne finally shrugged and gave in.

Then one day he said, "I'm going further out on the lines. I'll be gone a few days, Minna."

"Gone? At night?" she asked, trying to remain calm.

"Yes, of course, at night!" he answered her, laughing. "Minna, don't be nervous. I spoke to Antoine, and he will keep an eye on you."

She was silent. Not expecting that he would leave her, she had not told him that twice François had come to the cabin during the day, while Etienne was gone, to speak to her, to look at her with bold black eyes, to tease her, to ask her to go walking with him.

"I am busy, go away," she had responded, not angrily, but briskly.

He would remain awhile, trying to get her to talk with him. Then he would finally depart, gazing back over his shoulder at her. His visits made her uneasy. She was so alone in the cabin when Etienne was gone.

And now he would be gone several nights! Well, she would endure it. But privately she resolved not to be caught alone in the cabin with the door unbolted.

And sure enough, the first day, as she sat outside in the clearing, cleaning a pelt on the table Etienne had set up using boards, François came around. Minna saw him coming and touched the pistol at her foot lightly. She kept it loaded, dangerous as that was. She did not have Etienne's faith in the Indians, nor in some of the Frenchmen. Yes, even Etienne's own men had looked at her in a certain way. She recognized that look and was wary of it. She had walked the waterfront and seen the same hungry intensity in the eyes of the sailors coming off the ships as they gazed at her and the other women, the first they had seen in months or years. Minna was not stupid about life and men.

François came closer. "Good day to you, Minna!" he said boldly.

"Mrs. MacCameron to you," she told him curtly.

François laughed. "How haughty we are today! Are you expecting ladies to come to tea?" he mocked.

She kept on scraping the pelt, keeping a side glance for where he stood. If he came too close, he would be in for a surprise. She had the skinning knife and the loaded pistol at hand, and she knew how to use both.

"You'll be lonely tonight," he said boldly. "Etienne being gone all the night, and the next day too."

She shrugged. "I have work to do," she said indifferently.

"I'll come around tonight," he said.

At first she could not believe he had said that. She stared right at him. He had lost his smile and was staring right at her.

"The hell you will," said Minna bluntly. "You'll stay away from me!"

"Why should I? Your man is off with another woman!"

"You lie through your wicked teeth!"

"I do not lie. He went off to visit his Indian girl. He calls her Yvette."

Minna caught her breath. She felt as though he had punched her in the stomach, the way Otto had once when he was little and playing with her. He had knocked his little bullet head right into her stomach, pushing her down, and she had been so winded she could not breathe for a minute.

"You lie again," she said finally.

François shook his head, the handsome beaver hat covering

the thick black curly hair. He had a handsome young face, but she didn't like his eyes. They were too shrewd, too knowing, too—hungry.

"She is a girl of French and Indian parents. Her father was one of us, a trapper. But he left her mother when she got old and fat. Yvette is beautiful. She has black long hair and bright blue eyes. She lived with Etienne last winter."

François flung the words at Minna, watching her face keenly.

Minna kept her face lowered over her work. "So?" she asked. "That was last winter, wasn't it?"

"He cannot stay away from her, she is so beautiful!"

Minna did not answer. She lifted the pelt and studied it with unseeing gaze. François was goaded on by her indifference.

"You'll see! Smell his clothes when he comes back! She wears strong perfume he brings to her!"

"What is that to me?" asked Minna. "François—"

"Yes, Minna?"

"You stay away from me, or I'll shoot you," she said coldly, looking him right in the face.

He laughed, but he went away. She watched for him, and the others, and made sure the cabin was securely bolted, both door and window, whenever she was inside. And when she was outside, she kept the loaded pistol and the skinning knife with her.

She was intensely relieved when Etienne came home after three days and nights away. He brought but five pelts with him, and he smelled strongly of perfume.

Minna did not mention the girl to him then. She brought out a basin and pitcher, filled them with hot water from the huge iron kettle over the fire, and silently waited on him as he washed.

"Am I weary!" yawned Etienne. "Three hard days of work!"

Fury filled her. She said quietly, "François came around while you were gone."

Etienne frowned and looked up from scrubbing himself. "Oh, what did he want?"

"Me," said Minna. "I told him to stay away, or I would shoot him."

Etienne became furious at once. "That bastard! I'll tell him to remain away from you! He won't be my friend, if he hangs about you!"

The next day Etienne went out, and when he returned, his

nose was bloody and his face had heavy bruises on it. And when he stripped to wash, she saw bruises on his body. But he was cheerful.

"I told François to leave you alone," he said.

He made love tenderly to her that night, holding her closely. But Minna wondered why, when they were so close, he would suddenly jerk away from her, and she would feel his seed spraying on her thighs. Didn't he want to have a child of her?

She had thought she would be pregnant almost at once, Etienne having been so passionate at first. But she did not get pregnant that winter.

Etienne continued going off for several days at a time. He always returned with a few pelts, but she could smell the perfume on him. And he would be so weary that he would not want to make love to her.

Minna burned with rage and shame. Even with his wife here, Etienne could not stay away from the Indian girl! Why had he not married the woman? If she was so beautiful, why had he married Minna?

Then she remembered what his mother had said, that Etienne hated to be denied anything. When rebuffed, he only wanted something all the more. Minna had discouraged him, been cool to him, and he could not endure that. He had to win her, and the only way was to marry her.

She had long hours to contemplate what she had done. She was not sure if she regretted it completely. She began going out on the traplines that were close to the cabin, for she found that Etienne sometimes neglected them for days.

Minna often found little animals caught in the trap, whimpering or silently suffering, their paws caught, or their fur, not dying, but unable to get away. Her mouth tight, she would manage to kill them with a cord about the throat. Then they were safe to pick up and carry back to the cabin to skin and scrape and brush.

She was always cautious. She would come back when it was still light, watch the cabin for signs of life, hold her pistol in hand when she flung open the door, and wait. Only then she would step inside and bring in the pelts.

The days grew shorter. Etienne asked her if she wanted to go to the fur trade post over Christmas. She refused gently.

"No, it is far, Etienne. And the days grow so short. Let us have Christmas here."

He kissed her and made love to her. For Christmas he had

gifts for her, a bottle of the same strong perfume he gave to his mistress, a bright new blanket of blue, a coat made of furs by the Indian women. Etienne seemed pleased with her gifts, a plaid coat she had made from a blanket, and especially by a gold ring she had formed by taking apart the links of one of her bracelets, and melting it slowly and painfully over a candle.

In January he was gone again, for more than a week. Minna went out daily to the nearby traplines, but she worried about the more distant lines. She had not gone up into the mountains.

However, once when Etienne was gone for a long time, Minna decided to go. She had a small sled which slid over the ice and her showshoes. After making a pack of two blankets, ammunition, bread and dried meat, a cup and copper kettle for tea, she set out. She wondered whether to tell any of the French trappers she was going, but finally she set her mouth and said nothing. She was burning inside with rage against Etienne.

How flattering were his words, how empty his caresses! He kept going to his mistress. Well, Minna would go out also to her love, the wilderness. This was why she had married him, why she had come. She would not deny herself.

She had learned on her short journeys how to tell time by the sun, and how to find her direction by the shadows of the short stumpy trees. She set out, and the first night she camped out to the north, along Etienne's trapline. She saw nothing of him, and the second day she saw nobody at all, not even Indians or French trappers in the distance.

She lay out under the stars, wrapped in the blankets, her face chilled, but her eyes wondering as she gazed up at the heavens. She slept with one blanket pulled over her face, the pistol loaded at her side.

Small animals crept close. She often saw bright yellow eyes gazing at her from a distance, but the little fire kept them off. She sat at the fire, drinking her hot tea, and chewing on the meat, and spoke softly to them. "Are you of this wilderness?" she would ask. "Or do I dream I see you? Who are you? From where do you come? Are you the spirits of the dead, as some Indians say? Etienne says you are, but he laughs."

Thinking of Etienne made her sad, and she turned her thoughts deliberately from him. She gazed absently to the sky, to the north. Then she stood up, staring, gasping. It was late at night, or was it dawn? Had she lost track of time? What was that light?

Across the sky spread shades of green, yellow, and rose.

Lights flung across the whole heavens, like some great bolt of silk from China, soft as the silk, fiery as the colors. She clasped her hands to her breasts in wonder as the colors flared, died, and flared again, for hours.

Minna stared and finally sat down to watch those lights. She forgot the fire, and it died down. Little animals crept close to the warmth, and she welcomed them without words, without sound, and together they shared the night.

In the sky was such a wondrous show that she forgot all her own troubles. How glorious were the lights! Stars shone palely in the northern sky, more deeply in the south. And always those strange green lights streaked again and again across the north.

She felt the same wonder she had felt as a child looking at the Christmas tree and its candles, such an ecstasy and warmth that she felt close to God. She felt as though enveloped by the warmth of her family, only now her situation was different. Minna was alone in the wild, and she could hear the lone howling of a wolf. She was not afraid. She was with God, and nature, and the universe. The whole world and the heavens were spread before her. How could she fear?

She stirred up the fire at dawn, and the lights faded. She did not sleep, but went out to the traplines and rescued and killed some little animals. She mourned over them, as though they had been friends.

"I did not know trapping was like this, little brother," she whispered at the agony in the eyes of a mink. When he tried to bite her, she could not be upset. He wanted to live as much as she did.

She slept a little in the daytime, for the northern lights flared again and again at night, and she did not want to miss them. Daily she would go out to the trapline from her little camp, with its blankets and campfire, and return again by dusk. By the light of the fire she would skin the animals, and scrape them, burying the remains. She could not bring herself to eat them, not after she had killed them herself. Her mouth twisted in scorn of herself. Etienne would laugh at her!

She had a different feeling now about the wilds. She stayed out more than a week, marveling at the heavens, the gaunt line of the white-clad mountains against the vivid blue in the daytime. She counted the stars, finding patterns in them. She watched the little animals that crept to her fire and regarded her with wary bright eyes. She knew the mink now, and the fox, their sounds, the pattern of their paws in the snow. Wolves came one night and howled nearby, and then she did worry. But she threw a flaming brand at the eyes of one, and they all yowled and disappeared into the night. There was easier prey out there.

Now she knew why the wilderness drew men like her father. She had been wondering for so long what its attraction was. Now she knew. It was aloneness, but not loneliness. It was being one with the earth and the heavens, part of them, a small fragment of the earth, someone who was born, who lived and loved, and finally returned to the earth.

Minna found she was talking to herself out loud. She smiled, but she did not stop. "Why not, Minna?" she said aloud. "Talk, think, speak. The earth will listen. You know, I think I am not afraid to die now. It will be just returning to the earth, as the animals do. It is life and pain and the hurt of other people that hurts one. Dying hurts sometimes. But death—why that is only returning from whence I came."

She felt peace within herself when she finally packed up the blankets, loaded the sled, she set out. She was so confident that she only glanced from time to time at the shadows. She went straight south and at the end of the second day she came to the cabin. No smoke rose from it.

She left the sled at a distance and approached the cabin from the side. She flung open the door, and glanced inside. No one was there. After breathing a sigh of relief, she went back for her supplies and pelts.

She had a huge pack of pelts from the trip. She slept well that night, and the next day she took out the table and set it up and began to work on the furs.

François came over promptly, approaching her from a distance.

"Well, well, where have you been, Minna?"

"On the traplines," she said innocently, scraping away. "And you, do you ever work?"

He flushed at the sneer, for he was notorious for his idleness, and the men often teased him.

"Etienne will not like it, that you were gone so long," François finally went on, coming a little closer.

"That is close enough. No closer," said Minna as she put the loaded pistol beside her on the table.

"Etienne went up into the mountains with Yvette. She has

208

a pretty cabin up there," said François, laughing, watching her face sharply. "Gone nine days this time, isn't he? What a little beauty she is!"

Minna said nothing but continued to scrape away intently. No longer burning with rage, she felt some peace from her experience. Poor Etienne, unable to stay away from that girl. What would she do? She could divorce him, but did she want to? She still loved him, and she was having the adventure Etienne had promised her, though she knew he had not intended her to do this.

"You are more beautiful than she is, with your golden hair and blue eyes," said François, not moving from where he stood, his eyes hungry on her slim form in the dark blue woolen dress and plaid shawl. "You know Eteinne is a fool! He should not leave you like this. You are his wife!"

"I know it. It would do you good to remember it," said Minna.

"What about Etienne? He does not remember it!"

She ignored him for a time. François watched her, keeping his eyes on her until she could have screamed. He spoke again, "Minna? What if I come to the cabin tonight? Etienne will not care!"

Minna's hands paused in the working. He stared at her eagerly, his mouth working in his hunger, as though he could taste her.

She said, flatly, "I do not want you. Go away."

François stood there for a time, but when she did not speak to him again, he turned and left.

That night Minna heard sounds around the cabin. She stiffened, felt for her pistol, and relaxed. The fire was going low in the fireplace, but she did not rise to replace the wood. She wondered if there were cracks in the cabin walls where a man could peer inside. Probably so, since it was not well chinked. The men had done a hasty job in putting it up.

The next day she went around the cabin and looked. She found two places big enough to look inside, and went down to the stream that stood ice covered a hundred yards away. She broke the ice, got a bucket of water, and then took an ax to the clay around the waterhole and dug up a bucket full of clay.

Back at the cabin she stood the clay in water, and let it warm near the fire until it was summer consistency, thick and gooey. She plastered up the cracks, first the big two, and then

209

all the small ones she could find, from the inside of the cabin, and watched the clay harden in satisfaction. Now he could try staring at her!

Etienne had still not returned. She began to worry. It was almost two weeks. Didn't he care about her? She went out daily to the short traplines and took the animals. But she fretted about the far lines. Should she go out again?

That night, she half dreamed at the fire after dinner, drinking her tea. What should she say when Etienne returned? What would he say to her? Would he try to pretend he had been out at the far traplines? Should she accuse him?

Someone knocked at the cabin door. "Etienne!" she breathed, joy and relief welling in her. She started for the door, reached for the bolt that lay across the door, then paused. She went back for the pistol, loaded it, and went again to the door.

"Etienne?" she called.

"Yes, darling," said the deep French voice.

Minna frowned. Was he drunk? He did not sound like himself. Slowly, cautiously, she put down the bolt and jumped back as the door was pushed in.

François's grinning face was there, and he stepped inside. Smelling of drink, he reached for her with his long arms, his dirty hands.

Minna had the pistol trained on him. He did not seem to see it. He stepped toward her, one pace—

She fired. The pistol kicked in her hand. François stared at her blankly and fell at her feet, slowly, slowly.

Blood welled on his shirt, at the shoulder. He lay limply. Minna waited, then loaded the pistol again. She felt cold, empty of emotion. When François did not move, Minna stepped around him, and went outside, glancing about. She saw the trappers shooting out of their cabin, and run to stare across at her, peering into the darkness.

She called at them. "Come and get François! I have shot him!"

Antoine and another man came across and awkwardly came into the cabin. She kept the pistol in her hand, steadily. Antoine bent over François's still body.

"Is he dead?" she asked curiously.

"No. Knocked unconscious. I'll take him down to the Indian camp. The women can take care of him." Antoine looked up at her, his face wondering. "You—shot him?"

"Yes, I shot him. I told him I would if he came around me. He knows Etienne is—away."

Antoine nodded, and he and the other man carried François to the camp. Minna watched them go, and it was only as she saw the blood staining the snow that she began to feel sick. She went into the cabin, threw the bolt hastily, and dashed over to the basin. She was sick violently, losing all her dinner.

She sat still for a long time, rocking back and forth, her arms cradling her chilled body. She had shot a man! He might die! He had asked for the treatment, but she, she had never shot a person before. His grinning face, those knowing black eyes, his pestering presence—

Minna could not sleep that night. She lay in bed, huddled under more blankets, but could not get warm. Her eyes were burning with unshed tears. She hugged herself and wondered if she would be sick again.

"Oh, Etienne, Etienne," she murmured once. Why had he left her so long? What could she do about him? Was it her fault?

She should never have married him. But stubbornly she told herself, she was glad she had. She would never have seen the wild beauty of the mountains, the stark grandeur of miles of dazzling blue-white snow. She would not have seen the strange glory of the northern lights. She would never have sat alone at a campfire of her own building and gazed into the darkness, at one with the big and the little animals. Alone, yet not alone.

"I cannot be sorry," she said aloud. "I cannot be sorry. I shall have no regrets. No matter what happens, I shall have no regrets."

Dawn came late, but she was already up and heating water for her tea. She opened the door cautiously and peered out to see the trappers starting out on their rounds. She would go out also today and take care of Etienne's traps. In the clean snow, alone, working with her hands, she would forget the incident of last night. She would be strong, she would have courage. She would be strong as any man.

Chapter 18

Etienne finally returned after an absence of fifteen days. He strode in, flung down a few pelts and a load of thick, dirty clothes.

"Well, glad to see me, Minna?" he asked, laughing, but his eyes flinched from her steady gaze. He bent and kissed her cheek, briefly. She smelled the strong perfume on him.

"Welcome back, Etienne," she said steadily.

"Well, well, well, have I had a bad time of it," he began, moving about the cabin uneasily. "Few pelts, a storm came up. Out on the trapline it got very bad. Have you had storms here?"

"A few, short ones, usually at night," she said.

He saw the pelts piled in stacks in the corner of the cabin. His gaze widened, the dark blue eyes she had adored.

"Where did those come from? Did Antoine go out on the traps for you?"

"No, I ask no one to do my work for me," she said, her voice determinedly cheerful. "I went out myself."

He went over to the furs, examined them. "But these are splendid! White fox! And ermine! These are from the near traps?"

"Not the ermine. I got that when I was out on the far traps. I went about one hundred miles north," said Minna.

He stared, laughed, got red, then angry. "Don't try to tease me like that! And don't lie to me, Minna! These are from the near traps or else you paid Antoine to go out for you. Or some Indians."

"I went out myself," said Minna, stirring the stew in the iron kettle without watching his face. "I was out about ten days. It was marvelous, I enjoyed it."

Etienne stamped around, fumed at her for teasing him, calmed down, ate supper, searched for some clean clothes. He had a bath and went to bed early, snoring before she had even undressed. She watched him sadly. He had not even asked how she had been.

Minna rose early the next morning, went down to the river, and brought back several buckets of water. She filled the huge iron kettle over the outdoor fire and began to boil Etienne's filthy clothes. Yvette must be a poor housewife, thought Minna, or else they had not bothered much with clothes. Still, these were covered with mud. Had they lain in the mud?

Etienne came out about noon, raging hungry. She put his food before him, silently. He grew cheerful as he ate and told stories about the trapline. The wolverine had been after his animals, he said, the same one that had pestered them in the fall. "I'll go out hunting him soon, can't afford to let him have my pelts," said Etienne.

Her husband was smoking his pipe as Minna stood outside pegging his clothes, when Antoine strode up from the trappers' cabin.

Etienne greeted him cheerfully. "Hello there, here is Antoine. Antoine, I have to thank you for looking after my traps while I was gone!"

"Not I," said Antoine. "I have my own work to do!" His wise black gaze went to Minna shrewdly. "Your wife went out on the hundred-mile traps. The old chief was worried about her."

"How did he know I was out?" asked Minna curiously, while Etienne stared at her openmouthed. She wrung out a shirt, finally cleaned, and hung it on the boards.

"Two of his Indians were out, up on the trail. They saw the white woman with hair like gold, alone on the trail, and thought she was lost. They watched her for two days," said Antoine solemnly, but there was a twinkle in his eyes. "They said to the chief, it seemed the woman with gold hair knew as much as a trapper about the furs, and she kept her fires going well. So they came on back. The chief was upset. He told them if the woman did not come back, he would send them again and ask them to bring you back safely. I sent word down to the camp when you got back, Mrs. MacCameron."

Etienne had jumped up, his fists balled. The pipe fell unnoticed to the ground. "You did go out on the line?" he asked sharply, his face reddened. "You went out—there? You could have died on the snows. It is dangerous!"

Minna wrung out another shirt and pegged it carefully. She didn't know what to say. Etienne had claimed to be out on the lines, and both knew he had not been.

Antoine said, "Not so dangerous as when she returned. She had to shoot François."

Etienne looked as though he would burst. Minna sent a

sideways look at grave Antoine, who was enjoying himself immensely.

"Shoot François! You shot François! But he is my friend! What did he do, for pity's sake?" yelled Etienne.

"He came to the cabin often," said Minna. "He offered to remain at the cabin with me during your long absence with Yvette. I refused him, said I would shoot him if he came at night. He did come, pretending to be you. I opened the door, but I had the pistol loaded and ready. I told him, I warned him—but he would come." She picked up the thick trousers and began to wring them out.

Her hands were cold and red. Etienne did not seem to notice them any longer. He was staring at her aghast.

"You—killed—François?" he whispered.

"No, no," said Antoine. "Just shot him in the shoulder. I think he will not come around again. He recovers in the Indian village where he has a pretty girl to wait on him."

"And what did you say about—about Yvette?" asked Etienne of Minna, ominously.

"I must go now," said Antoine hastily. "Etienne, the wolverine is at our traps again. We go out tomorrow. You come with us?"

Etienne nodded. Antoine went away. Etienne went up to Minna, took the trousers out of her hands, and flung them back in the hot water. She faced him, her hands on her hips, her blue eyes flashing.

"You said—about Yvette?" he asked.

"I know where you went. And you have gone to her often, Etienne," she said, quietly furious. "What do you want? A divorce? She is a sluttish housewife, that is certain! Not even to wash your clothes! I hope she is good in bed for you. Certainly she is not worth much else!"

Etienne went red again and began to shout at her. "You speak vile words, Minna MacCameron! How can you speak so? Women who are good do not think such things! They do not speak of it—"

"What do they do, endure it?" she spat at him, her eyes blazing blue fire. "No, when I get back to Montreal, I shall divorce you! Shaming me before everyone! All the trappers know about you and your Yvette! They taunt me with it! Well, I shall tell the chief she is a poor example of the Indians! They are usually clean!" And with that she picked up the dripping trousers and thrust them into his face.

"She is a fine woman!" said Etienne furiously. "She is warm and good for me! A man needs such! It is not for a real man to cleave to one woman alone! One woman is not enough for a man who is strong and tough!" And his chest swelled out.

Minna calmed. She gave him a pitying look and began to wring out the trousers once more. "Your father's example," she nodded. "Well, your mother warned me. When you saw how your father was with women, especially the Indian girls, I suppose you thought it was the way of all men. Well, let me tell you, my father is not like that! He has no need to prove he is a man by lusting after every girl around! No, he works hard, he is loyal to my mother, he is good—"

"Your father! You fling your father in my face! So he has made much money and spoiled you with jewels and fine gowns!" roared Etienne, furious again.

"Yes, he spoiled me, but with love and attention, courtesy and goodness. I am most spoiled. I work hard, and expect to earn thanks. Instead I am told I am lying and blamed for not welcoming François to the cabin in your absence!"

Etienne cooled abruptly. He rubbed his chin, rubbed his red hair. He looked troubled. "Minna, did François really come chasing you?"

"Whenever you were gone, even for a day," she nodded. Her eyes stung with tears, suddenly, when he was kind. She blinked in the wind of the cold February day.

"I must find out about this," muttered Etienne and went off to the trappers' cabin. When he returned, he was very quiet, frowning, puffing at his pipe fiercely all the evening.

Etienne went out early the next day, to help hunt the cunning tricky wolverine with the other trappers. Minna worried for the safety of all the men, since her father had spoken of these animals, which were as large as small bears and very fierce. She remembered that as a small girl she could hardly believe his description. She knew that the animal could range up to fifty miles for its kill. If it could take smaller animals from traps, for its own young to feed on, it would do so, for they all needed much food. Bold, and very cunning, it would sometimes follow a hunter and watch where the traps were put, then go back and boldly steal all it wished. It would feed off a trapped animal, leaving the pelt in rags. When a wolverine was about, the trappers had no rest until they had killed it, and its young as well. But it was difficult to kill them since they were so wary of men, and so sly and intelligent.

215

Etienne returned in three days, with the tired satisfaction of a man who had succeeded. "We got him finally, mean brute," he said. "He got five animals from Antoine's traps, and six from Henri's. Now we should be safe from him for a time, until his, or rather her, cubs are grown. A female can be worse than a male," he said absently, taking out his pipe.

"Thank you," said Minna dryly. She had regained her sense of humor and her calm and was ready to fight as cunningly as a wolverine! Harsh words would drive Etienne from her back to Yvette, rather than draw him. More flies were caught with honey than with vinegar, she reminded herself.

"Now, Minna! You know I didn't mean women as females!"

"Did you not?" she teased and laughed. "Now I have you! What a statement to make about a woman!"

He teased her back, and by the time they went to bed, he was ready to take her. He wanted her, and she had been a long time without her man. She deliberately put Yvette from her mind and welcomed Etienne to her arms.

He watched her undress, and she left only the cotton night-dress on her body as she slid under the blankets and onto the thick fur bed. She had hung out the furs while he was gone, leaving them in the cold air until they smelled fresh again. And she had washed the blankets and all his clothes, so he had all clean garments once more. She had resolved to keep him well clothed, well fed, and satisfied. Perhaps he would not go again to his mistress.

He took her in his arms and began to stroke her silken skin. "All but your hands," he mourned. "Your hands are so rough, my darling. I should never have brought you to this wilderness."

"I am enjoying it," she said calmly. "Etienne, while I was out on the trail, at nights I saw strange lights. They were so beautiful, green, rose, golden—"

"Ah, you saw them? How marvelous, my Minna! You are a strange woman, different from the rest! What woman would go out on the trail as you did! But truly, I am disturbed. You should never have gone out so far. What if you had been lost in the snows?"

She smiled secretly against his bare chest and kissed him on the shoulder. "Do not worry, I was not lost, my darling. I am liking these experiences, and I never tire of gazing at the white mountains."

"When spring comes, I shall take you home to Montreal,"

said Etienne firmly and began to kiss her neck and throat. "I shall miss you in the winters, but this is no place for a woman."

The Indian women remained, she thought, but did not say it. Her hands stroked over his hairy chest, and she kissed him more boldly, and pleased him with her caresses on his thighs. He soon wanted her, needed her. He moved on top of her, and came fiercely to her body. She held him to her, her fingers fierce and scraping on his hips, ·as they writhed in the final embrace.

This time she held him tightly, and he came in her. But he was so excited, he did not really notice, she thought. He lay on her, and she held his hard body to her softness, and let him roll on her, until he wanted her again.

She forgot everything, and everyone, as they embraced. A skillful lover, Etienne knew how to kiss her throat, her neck, her ears, biting in little nibbling kisses down over her breasts, under her arms, over her waist and thighs. Under the blankets, he pressed kisses over her silky young body, down to her feet, and up again to her thighs. When he kissed her in intimate places, she writhed with pleasure, uttering little incoherent cries.

"Oh, you are so very sweet, my Minna," he groaned as he came up to lay fully on her body. "Do I hurt you?"

"No, no, I adore you," she panted. She felt quite savage as she tugged him closer to her. "Oh, Etienne, hold me tighter—hold me—that way—oh, yes—oh, love, kiss me again."

He kissed her roughly, pleased with her wild responses. They rolled back and forth on the furs, until the blankets fell off. Laughing, Etienne tugged them back and went under them to kiss her all over the body again. She reached boldly for him, pulled him by the arms strongly to lie on her once more. When he hung back, Minna reached under the blankets to his thighs and began to fondle him.

"Oh, my God—oh Minna—love—don't—you drive me out of my mind." He was muttering in French.

Minna smiled against his shoulder and squeezed firmly once more on his thigh. He came to her and thrust against her. She opened wide for him, her legs up around his body. He came inside her, and she closed her legs about him and held him tightly.

This time she seemed to drain him. He came hard, and the seed spurted inside her body. Minna was wild with ecstasy at

217

the pleasure of him, but alert enough to know what he did. It would be a completion of their marriage. And children settled a man, she thought, as well as a woman.

Etienne fell asleep on her body, rolling half off, still connected to her with their bodies together. She held him on her breast, stroking her hand over his thick red hair, and thinking how she loved him, in spite of all he did.

He could be bad and wicked, he could tease her to fury, but still she loved him! It was something beyond her power to stop. He was her man, he was her lover.

They lay often together at nights that February, and March, and April. Etienne stayed near the cabin, taking care of the traps that belonged to him and to Antoine. Antoine went far out for them both, remaining for two weeks, to return and divide carefully the pelts for them both. Etienne had quarreled with François, and they no longer spoke to each other.

Many a time Etienne fell asleep on Minna's breast, and she had the satisfaction of knowing she pleased him mightily. As he roused from sleep, often she stirred him to take her again, knowing that in the first rousing from sleep, he would not be so alert. He came again and again in her, and she longed the more for signs that she had a child.

By May she knew that she had succeeded. The blood had ceased to flow. Minna hummed about her work, the cleaning of the cabin, the cooking, the washing. Etienne had the Indian women clean most of the pelts, though Minna still did the minks and the ermine. He began to talk about going home, and about the fortune they would have from the pelts.

By June Minna was often sick in the mornings. She concealed it from Etienne for a time, by drinking hot tea and eating a biscuit before he wakened. Then he began to pack up the furs, talk about moving via canoes, trekking to the fur post and so on.

Minna finally stopped him one evening. "Etienne, if you go back east this summer, I cannot go with you. You must go alone."

His jaw fairly dropped. "Now, Minna! What are you talking about? Are you angry with your parents, or shamed, that you eloped with me?" And a twinkle came in his eyes.

She shook her head and smiled. "Nothing so simple, my dear. I am going to have a child, and I do not want to risk losing it."

He sat still, his spoon poised over the thick meat stew she

had prepared. He seemed to turn green under his heavy tan.

"What?" he finally whispered.

"I am going to have a child, Etienne. Your child."

"I cannot believe it is my child!" he blurted out hastily. "The child—it cannot be—"

Minna dropped her spoon. She gazed at him incredulously. "What did you say, Etienne?" she asked ominously. "Do you believe—do you dare to say—I played you false? How can you!"

"Now—wait a moment, Minna, wait a moment," he said hastily as her rare anger flared up. He held up his hand placatingly. "I was hasty, forgive me. But I cannot believe—I was so careful—"

Her mouth compressed. "No, you were not," she said flatly.

"I always have been. Any woman—I mean—I have never had a child."

"How do you know?" she flashed. "How many Indian women might have had a child by you, and you never knowing? Your father the same! You would leave the woman in the spring, and go back east. Is Yvette the only woman you ever had? I think not! There may be red-haired Indian children all over the West!"

He leaped up, knocking over the table, spilling the wooden bowls. He yelled, "How dare you speak of my father like that? And you malign me! I do not have women everywhere. Neither did my father."

"That is not how he bragged, and you also, Etienne!"

Minna got up, picked up their bowls, and set them on the heavy ledge. She got out the bowl of water to wash them. Etienne sank down on the crude chair again, rubbing his head.

"It cannot be true—it cannot be true," he kept whispering. "I was always so careful."

Minna felt such fury that she could not speak to him. Etienne went out, and stamped around in the snow, and went over to talk to Antoine and the other trappers. He did not return until midnight, and then he was drunk. What a welcome for her news, thought Minna, pretending to be asleep when he fell down beside her.

She had proof now that he did not want a child. He just wanted to play around, with one woman and another, and evade the responsibility that went with being a husband.

Etienne said little the next few days. Though he went out each day, Minna never asked where.

Finally after almost a week he spoke, gloomily. "I think we had best not return to Montreal this summer. Antoine will take my furs, and a letter to my father."

Minna felt an intense relief. She had worried about her child and wondered if she might stay the summer without Etienne, here in this cabin, with only Indians nearby. If anything went wrong, could she trust the Indians to help her?

Minna spoke carefully. "The child will be best for not having to travel about so. I do not wish to lose him."

"Yes. A child," brooded Etienne. "I wish you had waited until we returned to Montreal to start a child, Minna!"

"I did not do it alone," she said, and a dimple and smile appeared in spite of her anger.

"Oh, well, well," said Etienne and came and hugged her to him. He buried his bearded face in her thick blond hair. "A child, oh, Minna! I did not think to be delighted, but one day—a child, perhaps a son! Yes, I think I should like a son."

"If I give you a daughter, you'll have to be delighted as well, my husband!" said Minna and pulled his hair with mock anger. "Girls can be very sweet!"

"Hah! Until one married a girl!" he joked, and she shrieked and pounded his chest, until they fell down laughing on the furs.

Etienne arranged with Antoine to carry his furs back for him and take them to his father. Then he and Minna together wrote a letter to Mr. MacCameron. They told him about the coming child and said they wished to return in the following year, if he would allow them to return home. Minna sent a special note to Yolanda about the child.

"I am delighted about the baby," she wrote. "I expect the child about the end of January, or early February. The Indian women will help me with the birthing, they have promised. I am happy here out in the wilderness, for all the storms and snow and cold. It is an exciting world.

"However, I look forward to returning to Montreal, with the child. I hope you are not angry with us for what we did. Have you heard anything from my parents? I wish for their forgiveness and understanding as well."

She signed the letter and sealed the envelope with a sigh. It would be at least a year before they heard from home. She longed for news from her own family, wondering how they fared. Would they allow her to come home for a visit? Or was what she and Etienne had done beyond their forgiveness? Her mother was a good woman, but stern of morals, and always thinking of the right thing to do. And to marry a Roman Catholic—her mother would have been very angry about that.

After the fur traders had departed for the East, it seemed very quiet there at the camp. Summer had come, and Minna had little work to do, for they left the cabin door open for airing, and there was not a bit of trapping to do. The pelts would not be good.

Etienne mended his lines, worked on cleaning his traps, and took Minna at times down to the Indian camp to make friends with the women. She saw Yvette from a distance. She knew her by her scowl and sullen dislike, and her beauty, her long black hair and slim rounded form. The women whispered and giggled behind their hands, and treated Minna with courtesy, more out of spite for Yvette, thought Minna.

However the summer was pleasant. Flowers bloomed richly in the valley, summer flowers of golden colors, and pink and blue. Then the autumn flowers began to come, and at nights the wind over the mountains was cold.

She and Etienne took food to the meadows at times, and ate there as the bees hummed over the flowers, and small animals wandered with their young, unafraid, down to the streams. She went up the mountains a short distance alone, at times, and bathed in the cold mountain waterfall, shivering at the chill but delighting in the freshness and sweet-smelling odors of the spruce and pine. She gathered flowers every day for the cabin, and the two pottery vases an Indian woman had given her were always full of wild flowers of all colors.

By September Minna was heavy and wary of walking around alone. She stayed nearer to the cabin. Etienne was growing restless. By this time he had missed the annual trek back to Montreal, the quick visit in civilization, the roistering and bragging, the visit with his parents.

"I did not know I would miss them so much, Minna," he said wistfully. He seemed older somehow that summer, as though he had matured. "I think Mother will not be angry with me. She never is angry for long. And Father—well, he will be delighted to have a grandchild."

"I hope so," said Minna. "I think it will be best, once I have the child, for me to remain in Montreal."

Etienne sat up abruptly from his restful posture in the green meadow. He had been chewing lazily on a flower stem. He flung it away. "I should think you would stay in Montreal!"

he said vigorously, his eyes alarmed. "I would never risk you again on such a trip as this! I must have been mad to bring you out West! A white woman cannot endure this life!"

"Nonsense, Etienne, I have endured it very well," said Minna calmly. "I would not have missed it for the world. Only once I have a child, it will be well for the child's sake to remain in Montreal. Of course I will want to keep busy. Probably I can work in your father's warehouse."

Her serene words brought out a new storm from Etienne. Indeed no woman worked in his father's warehouse! A woman's place was in the home! No woman of standing worked! His mother did not work, she directed the servants! That was quite enough! Minna must make friends in Montreal, invite them for tea—

And so on and so on. She endured some long lectures from Etienne about how a woman of Montreal lived in society. She must do this, she must remember that. She must buy some fine clothes for by the time they returned, her other dresses would be out of fashion. He had money, so she must look well and do him proud.

"And you, Etienne?" she asked dryly once. "What will you do? You will escort me to the tea drinking and the concerts?"

"I? Of course not, I shall be out here earning our living," replied Etienne, managing to look injured and displeased.

She did not bring up the topic again, but Etienne did. He had much advice on how Minna should live. She listened in silence. She had other plans.

The trappers returned in late October, and with them was Blaise MacCameron! The older man was visibly weary, but satisfied that he had endured the long trip and carried his share of the packs. He embraced Minna tenderly.

"How could you doubt that we would welcome you?" he scolded her gently. "Yolanda and I have long waited for your return. When your letters came, we wept together, and I resolved to come out here and help you in the return. Meantime I shall help with the trapping this winter." He had been horrified when Antoine had told him that Minna had gone out alone to trap.

"You should never have done that! You might have been lost forever!"

Blaise moved into the second cabin with Antoine and two other French trappers. He came over often to help Minna with the work, or to bring an Indian woman to clean the cabin and do the cooking.

Etienne went out on the far traplines and brought back mink, ermine, silver fox, blue fox, and even a wolverine which had been scavanging their traps. He was working hard, and even though he was gone for two weeks at a time, Minna was satisfied that he was not with Yvette.

Then she heard from one of the Indian women that Yvette was also expecting a child. Minna's heart sank, for Etienne had said not a word about it. She did not bring up the subject, but she felt bitter about it. Two children for him this winter!

They spent a quiet Christmas, with Blaise to add to their pleasure. He had brought practical gifts from home, blankets soft and thin for the new baby, little garments that Yolanda had sent, a silver spoon and cup, even a small rattle. The letter from Yolanda was warm and affectionate and anxious, and Minna took it out and read it over and over, as her time grew near. The older woman had words of advice and warning for her.

In late January a storm came up. Minna heard the wind rising and felt almost at once an answering pressure inside her body. Through the snow trudged two older Indian women, to sit stolidly near the fireplace.

"Snow comes, heavy storm, wind," said one when Etienne questioned them. "Baby come sure."

And their wisdom was right. Minna was brought to bed with her child during the height of the storm. The women were helpful, knowing from experience just what to do. The child came, and it was a boy. Etienne and Blaise celebrated with drinks, while Minna was satisfied to lie there drinking herbal tea, smiling and smiling with the joy of her baby.

The women washed him, covered him with grease, laid him in a warm little blanket, and set him beside her. He cuddled against her limp, still aching body, and Minna was happy. She touched the tiny sleeping face, looked long at the lashes, the wee nose and mouth, the perfect little ears. His thin spikes of hair stood up and were red-gold in the firelight. His eyes were blue now, and she hoped they would remain that color, though a baby's eyes often changed in a few months.

Then she remembered something. She glanced at Etienne and Blaise, sleeping in the far corner on some furs, drunk and snoring. Neither had thought about this—not yet.

She motioned to one of the older woman and asked for a cup of water. The woman brought it, held it to her lips. Minna shook her head.

Taking a few drops on her hand, she touched the baby's head and murmured the words.

"Stephen Ludwig MacCameron, I baptize you in the name of the Father, and the Son, and the Holy Spirit, in the German Lutheran faith," she whispered.

She lay back, satisfied. The woman grinned through her remaining teeth, pleased. She knew the Christian ceremony.

But Minna lay there, half asleep, knowing that when Etienne found what she had done, he would be furious.

However Minna had determined this long ago. She was a Lutheran, a Protestant. She would bring up her child, and other children, as a good Protestant should. If Etienne wanted them Roman Catholic, he would have to convert them! And she had a strong feeling that he would not be home often enough to have much influence on them. While Etienne wandered, Minna would raise the children as she thought best. And he would just have to endure it!

Chapter 19

Spring came, and they set out for home. The men had never traveled such short distances each day as they did with Minna and the baby. By midsummer they had returned to Montreal, after a difficult journey, for Minna was to be coddled, though she protested. Yet it was better so, for by their anxious care her stream of milk for baby Stephen continued.

It took three months for the trip, and she heard some of the French trappers grumble a little among themselves. Yet never a one said a word directly to her, and they were always ready to hold the little baby, play with him, find fresh young meat for him, and cook it over the fire a long time.

But Minna was relieved to be back in Montreal, in civilization. It was one thing to take care of herself in the wilderness. It was quite another to take care of herself and a small child, even though Stephen was a good baby, and a strong one, rarely crying, gurgling away to himself, waving his little fist to the Frenchmen cooing over him. Pleased at all the attention, he pulled at Etienne's red beard, tried to sing when Etienne sang French songs to him, and slept well at night, and also in the canoe at times during the day.

Stephen's eyes remained blue, and his hair grew longer, shining bright red gold in the sunlight. He was the image of Etienne, said Blaise proudly, but Minna thought that around the chin and eyes he had the look of her own father. She said nothing about that resemblance, but resolved that Stephen should not be raised with the same beliefs of Etienne, that a man was all toughness and masculinity, for she wanted Stephen to respect women more than the two MacCamerons did.

She had been thinking long and hard about her own future. Yvette had also had a son before they left the wilderness, and the Indian woman had pranced around proudly with him, showing him off. Etienne would be returning to the same place next winter. And even if he went elsewhere, he would probably find a girl there as well. Minna doubted if he would give up his wild free life for many years. She knew that Blaise had been reluctant to give up his—even now he talked at times of returning to trapping, though he was over fifty years of age. Many of the Frenchmen trapped until they keeled over in death.

However he did have the warehouse to work with, and the store. Minna had offered quietly to help him there, but Blaise had only stared incredulously, then roared with laughter.

"A woman? In my store? Never! No women work for me! No, you stay home and enjoy yourself, my dear Minna! Your child and your social life will keep you occupied, as they do my dear Yolanda!"

Not a good judge of character, little did Blaise realize the effect of his words. Nothing he could have said would have more persuaded her of the rightness of the course she was considering!

Yolanda welcomed them joyously, with tears for the little squirming baby in her arms. "How lovely a child! How like Etienne at his age! And you, Minna, my darling, you are well? How tanned you are, though. We must get some lemon juice for your complexion," she added, worried.

Minna shook her head. "It will wear off in the winter, when I am not so much in the sunlight."

She had never felt so well, strong, sturdy, slimmed down again after the child. She had gone out quietly to the near traplines when Etienne wandered about. She had worked on the cabin, refusing the aid of the Indian women. She had washed clothes, cooked for the two men and her baby, and cared for the child herself. She felt wonderful.

However now that she was in a city, she must be pampered! She inwardly raged when Etienne refused to let her go down to the store "just to look at the furs."

"No, my dear," he said soothingly. "Tell me what you want and I will get it for you."

Already he was preparing to set out again, since they had been so late returning. But now that he was finally back in Montreal after a long absence, he felt obliged to make up for lost time, and was rarely home. She and the baby had their own large bedroom. Etienne often slept in one of the guest rooms, after returning late from a drunken party with his friends.

His behavior was known to all, though it seemed to affect his sad-eyed mother most.

"I had hoped he would settle down," said his mother.

Yolanda did not have the same strength of character as her hardworking daughter-in-law.

"So do I, and I think he will one day," said Minna with more confidence than she felt.

Etienne had rarely been with her at night since the baby. He was wary of starting another child, she thought. Why did he feel so? Did he think to divorce her and keep one child? Or did he spend his time with Indian girls, even here in Montreal.

At any rate he left cheerfully in the autumn, and the house was quiet. Blaise spent most of his time at the warehouse or with his friends.

Yolanda had guests in for tea when she felt like it or went out to the home of her special friends. Minna knew no one special, and Yolanda tried to encourage her to make friends of her age.

"Yes, yes, I will sometime. But I have something else on my mind," said Minna. She and Yolanda were dining alone that evening, as often happened. Blaise would dutifully appear if they had special guests. Usually, however, he would go his own way, to come home cheerfully drunk and often loudly singing in the wee hours of the morning.

"What is it? Do you wish to go to your parents for a visit?" asked Yolanda gently.

Minna had written to her parents promptly on returning to Montreal. She had told them about Stephen and a little of her life in the wilderness. She had closed with a plea for forgiveness for her hasty actions.

A letter had come back promptly from her mother. Agatha Gunther had written formally, coolly, in such a way that Minna knew she had hurt her mother deeply. It ended, "We shall welcome you, of course, should you ever come to New York."

Minna sighed. "No, I shall continue to write to them from time to time, but not go there. Not yet. One day I should like to go for a good long visit. But I shall wait, until the marriage has proved itself."

Yolanda looked troubled and touched her mouth with trembling fingers. "Not—not divorce, Minna? You do not consider it?"

Etienne had complained furiously about the baptism, and even more when he had learned about Minna's action regarding the church paper. She thought that was one reason he had not been with her, a reason he might not wish another child. If she raised them in the Lutheran faith, they would not be truly his, he had fumed.

Minna had found an Episcopal church in Montreal and was attending that, though she had not joined it. Yolanda had asked her gently to come with her to Catholic mass, and Minna had gone with her a couple of times. But for now, she would wait.

"I think you know how Etienne continues to act, *Maman*," said Minna. "I do not think seriously about divorce. However I do think about work. I think I should learn to support myself, in case—well, if anything happens. I do not wish to be totally dependent on Etienne. Besides, I like to work. I enjoy working in a store."

"You like to keep busy," said Yolanda, relieved. "Well, why do you not ask Blaise for some work there? With your experience, you could help with the bookkeeping and the clerical work."

"He has refused me, though I expected that," Minna informed her mother-in-law, and grinned impishly, the dimple that Colin would have recognized deepening. He would have known that his sister was planning something. "No, *Maman*, I think I know what I shall do. If I can raise some money, I shall start a warehouse and a store of my own!"

Yolanda looked stunned, but instead of objecting, she began to take an interest in the project. The two women developed their idea to the point where they knew they must take it to Blaise for his support. Yet Blaise refused flatly to fund it, and, adding insult to injury, laughed at them. Aroused, they determined to figure out what to do.

Yolanda brought a beautiful inlaid lacquer box to Minna, and recklessly spilled the contents over the dressing table. The younger woman gasped.

"Look, Minna. These are jewels which Blaise gave to me over the years." She touched a fine set of rubies, which she often wore. "These he gave me shortly after the birth of Etienne. I shall keep them, and the pearls—I enjoy those. But these diamonds, no. I think they are ugly, yet they cost much. And these sapphires do not suit me, nor would they suit you, they are so heavy and badly shaped."

"What do you mean to do, *Maman*?" asked Minna, touching the many jewels wonderingly. She herself had some fine pearls, as well as her amethysts and some sapphires, yet this was a wealth she had not seen before. There must be almost half a million dollars in gems here.

"I shall sell these and give you the money to start your warehouse!" said Yolanda triumphantly. Twin spots of color rouged her cheeks becomingly, and her black eyes snapped. "Minna, will you let me go into your project with you?"

"Do you mean it?" Minna questioned, excitement in her voice.

At Yolanda's nod, Minna jumped up and hugged her. All of a sudden, however, she calmed herself. A thought had just entered her mind.

"But Blaise will be so furious with you!" Minna recalled.

"Let him!" said Yolanda firmly, seeming younger than she ever had since Minna had first known her. "If we work quietly, we should be too far along for him to stop us when he does find out," and Yolanda laughed wickedly, joyously, like a young girl.

They did not need to sell all the gems so valuable were they individually. Minna went to a banker, and a jeweler, and sold those gems they had decided to discard, the heavy sapphires, the diamonds. With those, they had a goodly amount.

Minna, who had been looking about town for a suitable building from the moment she thought of her plan, had found a warehouse down by the waterfront run by an elderly gentleman wishing to retire. A courteous Frenchman, he listened to her with interest, scandalized yet intrigued by this lively lady with blond hair and snapping blue eyes. Quiet Yolanda sat beside her in her best black silk dress, looking the picture of a lady. And these two ladies wished to work!

"Well, well, why not?" he finally said, his palms out in a shrug, beaming with good humor. "You shall buy my business, and I shall remain for a time to aid you. The signs will be changed when you are ready for it. MacCameron?" he chuckled. "Ah, he has defeated me many a time, I shall have a good time with this! He can do nothing to me!"

The bank handled everything, including the legal work. Though the officers were rather shocked at Minna, they were not about to turn down a deal with a good commission. The warehouse was quietly transferred to the ownership of Mrs. Minna MacCameron at Yolanda's suggestion. "Put it in your name alone, Minna, I will be a silent partner," she urged, her face alive with the new interest. "Then Blaise and Etienne cannot stop you! And they cannot work on my fondness and foolishness with them. You are stronger than I am. You are like your father, I think. Be strong, Minna. Be a little hard. You will have a better life that way!"

Yolanda was hugged for her advice, and Minna resolved to follow the older woman's counsel. The two women went down to the warehouse daily, and Minna set up a store in the front. The furs and fur press were in the back and in addition to directing the treatment of the pelts, Minna supervised the clerks also and the buying of furs. After a few Indians wandered in and found that she would pay them in gold and silver, they sold to her though more out of curiosity than from a wish to deal with someone other than MacCameron or the company stores.

"But we will build up the business," said Minna confidently to Yolanda. "I mean to make a different store. Not just a store for trade goods, blankets and all that. No, I mean to bring in goods from far places. I mean to attract society in Montreal! You shall see."

She wrote to Roderick Dindorf, who got her letter that winter on his return to port. Intrigued, he packed up some trunks and boxes, and hired a barouche to take him to Montreal. He remained for two months, much amused by his young "niece," and her project.

A genial man, he was now an older handsome bachelor, and they had a happy time of it. Yolanda entertained frequently and Blaise suspected nothing. And every day Roderick came to the store with Minna, and they talked and planned.

He had brought a wealth of Chinese goods with him. Unscrupulously he had raided his own ship to bring her what she had requested. Yolanda exclaimed again and again, reverently, as she helped unpack and display the beautiful objects.

There was carved ivory, in boxes and beautiful round balls, chopsticks, images, little garden scenes and gods. The women gasped as Roderick showed them the finest thin exquisite colored silks, of crimson, golden, azure blue, silk-screened patterns of willow leaves, poppies, and crysanthemums. There were boxes of fine porcelain, vases and plates, and cups and saucers, full tea sets. These went first, for as soon as the Montreal ladies heard about them, they raced each other to Minna's store to buy them. The ladies were the first to realize who owned the store and ran it.

Soon the sign went up, a beautifully lettered sign in black lettering on pine boards: "Minna MacCameron, Prop. Trade Goods, fine Oriental goods, furs, bought and sold."

The Oriental goods sold out so fast that Roderick chuckled and told the ladies, "I'll go right back to the Orient for you!"

"Uncle Roderick, pray, go only back to New York, and bring or send me more goods from the ships!" begged Minna. "I need more at once, I cannot wait for that two-year voyage," and they all sat down and laughed and teased each other over the hot cups of Oriental tea.

Blaise heard, of course, and raged, incredulously, about Minna's project. He had enjoyed Captain Dindorf, without realizing he was harboring a snake in his bosom, as he grandly called it. Minna laughed to herself in her room as she thought how Yolanda and her uncle had handled that. They had soothed him, said he must not be troubled or disturbed in his own work. The ladies had a nice little project going to keep them busy this winter!

Blaise allowed himself to be soothed but said darkly that Etienne would have something to say when he returned! He had not yet fully realized that Yolanda, his own wife, was so involved in the project.

Christmas came and went. Roderick remained for the holidays, and they were joyous ones for Minna. Stephen was sitting up, crawling about, trying to walk, altogether an adorable age, and a great source of joy to his young mother. She wept a little at night, missing Etienne. Yet the holidays were happy ones for her despite her husband's absence. She went to midnight mass with Yolanda and to her own church the following morning.

Minna did miss the wilderness. Some evenings, playing the harp as Yolanda played the piano, she would have a flash of remembrance of the long cold winter evenings out West, of herself sewing or cooking over the open hearth. She recalled the mournful sound of the wolves howling in the distance, and the almost religious sense of wonder she felt while watching the great flashing northern lights, strange, romantic, and deeply mystical. She remembered fondly the Indians who kept a distant, watchful eye on her as she went out on her own, and the French trappers, kindly but for François. Though alone, she was not lonely, and she matured quickly as she faced who she was and what she had done to herself when she chose to elope with Etienne.

She told Yolanda a little about her experiences. The older woman listened thoughtfully. "You are a strong woman, Minna," she said. "And your life in the wild has made you even more confident of yourself. You are one who survives."

Minna often thought of that remark. Yolanda was much happier now that she had useful work to do. Eagerly she offered to learn the clerical tasks in the warehouse and the store. No good at bargaining for furs, she left that to Minna and the clerk they hired. However she quickly learned the bookkeeping, and soon had entire control of that phase of the work. Also she had a great deal of skill in selling the Oriental goods. She evidently loved each piece and parted reluctantly with it.

Now back in New York Roderick Dindorf hastened to send more goods to them by faithful men. Minna in return sent furs to him, and soon they had a profitable trade going illegally across the Canadian-American border. Much in the same spirit as her father, Minna paid no heed to the unfair laws restricting trade between the two neighboring New World countries. She had at first sold the furs she had bought and brushed to good condition to any dealer in town. She had no contacts to send them to Europe. Dealing with her uncle solved the problem, and soon she and Dindorf had a regular wagon going back and forth, evading the customs men who would have impounded the furs, if not the Oriental goods.

When a ship came, Dindorf was always first on the dock, and he knew all the captains. He wrote to Minna that he would send a wagonload every two months, and that he had bought a warehouse full of goods for her! He sent the Chinese porcelain well crated in boxes and barrels. Bolts of China silk came with them, wrapped around beautifully carved ivory, necklaces and earbobs of dark green jade, along with statues and figurines of white and cream jade.

Minna and Yolanda unwrapped the goods as they came in, purely for the pleasure of seeing the beautiful objects. They had no fear that certain items would be missing, items marked on Roderick's invoices. They knew they could trust the men he sent, since he inspired loyalty, and while Minna unwrapped the goods they brought, the two men would finish up the packing of the furs to be taken south.

Minna had a collapsible mold to hold the furs. The men folded the furs and put them inside, pressing them down with weights. When eighty pounds were reached, the furs were packed in bulk into a powerful, homemade fur press, and forced into a solid pack. Then they were bound with cord, covered with burlap, and marked ready to be put in the wagons.

As the winter wore on, the Montreal ladies became aware of this new entrancing shop that carried items they could not find elsewhere. As they came in, they swept the wooden floor with their long silk dresses and fur capes. Eagerly they asked to see all the Oriental marvels. Minna and Yolanda waited on them, bringing special trinkets from the back where they were just being unpacked. They sold item after item of the stunning merchandise.

It was a novelty to the ladies to be waited on by women like themselves. Minna began to make lists of the names of their regular customers, and to note what each wanted. She would then write to Roderick, and he would be sure to send her just such a set of porcelain as she requested, or matching huge vases, or special ivory necklaces.

The venture was running smoothly, until one day when a man came in, an older man, one who smiled too much. Minna distrusted him.

"My dear lady, what splendid goods! Where do you get them?"

"From the Orient, sir."

Yolanda, in the back room, could hear every word. She peered around the post, amused and tickled at Minna's gravity.

"I know that, dear lady. But how do you get them from the Orient? What dealer do you use?"

"Oh, many dealers, sir, I buy where I can. Gentlemen know my needs, and kindly send me little trinkets for my store. I am so glad you like them. Should you like to inspect the porcelain?"

She evaded his questions with a neatness that told of native cunning. He went away unanswered.

By April Minna had earned enough at the store to pay Yolanda back. Yolanda begged her not to do this. She wanted to have a share in the store. They kept their accounts in a bank that was not the same as the one Blaise and Etienne patronized. By law the men could get hold of their funds, but the ladies hoped to keep their earnings separate, one way or another.

"After all, Minna, you worked two winters in the wilderness, and earned not a penny from the furs you took from the traps yourself and scraped and brushed," said Yolanda. "Had Etienne paid you for your furs, or had my own husband, you would have this money."

"Men do not see things that way," said Minna. However, if Etienne tried to take her funds from her, he would have a fight on his hands!

Etienne returned in late June, early for him. Minna saw that he must have started early. Pleased with Stephen's progress, he also bragged about the many furs he had brought back, and offered Minna some ermine for a cloak which she accepted. Then he found out about her warehouse and store.

233

He roared with fury, like a wounded bear! How could Minna have done such an unladylike thing? All Montreal must be laughing at him behind his back! To allow his wife to work!

"I worked with you in the West," protested Minna, not losing her temper. She knew that this was to be only the first of many arguments.

Etienne tried to force Minna by anger, then by pleading, to sell the warehouse and store. She refused. Then he went to the bank and tried to get her money turned over to him.

The young banker, rather pleased at being part of a scheme to outwit the haughty young MacCameron, said gravely that Etienne would have to hire a lawyer and go to court in order to take the funds from his wife. He then looked at the red-faced man with some cool curiosity and added that the public sympathy might turn against him should he do so. "For you have much money of your own, sir," he had said.

Etienne came home, so fuming with anger that the very house seemed to smoke! He accused his father of having funded the women. Blaise denied it.

Minna got Etienne to come down to the store and see how nicely it was arranged. He demanded to know where the Oriental goods came from. She just told him "from contacts," and no more.

Then to find that his mother worked in the store! He again went up in smoke, roaring around like a bull. He raged at Blaise for permitting it. The father, like the son, was angry, but raised his palms outward, in hopelessness.

"What can I do with Yolanda? She goes her own way. She keeps my home comfortable, she does not interfere with my ways. What would you have me do, leave her?"

Etienne fumed and fussed, and got nowhere. It was a matter of weeks before he must go West again, should he go; and he was visibly mulling over his decision.

Should he remain home, stand guard over his wife, force her back into society, refuse her permission to work? That would deny himself the wild freedom of the wilderness, the life he loved and wanted.

Or should he go out to the wilderness, leaving all Montreal to continue to laugh at a man who could not control his wife? Leave the wife who did what she chose behind his back, worked, earned much money, dealt with many men with the ease of a born merchant?

Or was there some other course? Etienne was visibly thinking hard. Minna watched him warily.

Days they argued, except when she got out of his path and locked herself in her office to work on the books.

Nights she lay in his arms and enjoyed his caresses. Etienne grew more ardent as the summer wore on and autumn approached. And then she discovered his strategy.

She was pregnant again. Angrily she confronted him. "I thought you wanted no more children!"

Etienne grinned, smirking. "With a pregnant woman, there is but one course. She must rest, or the child may be damaged or lost. I know you, Minna, you love your son, and you will love the next child also. *Now* you will stay home and settle down, like a lady! Let my father sell the warehouse for you, or manage it for all of us."

"Never," said Minna grimly. "It is my store. I shall not give it up."

He laughed and teased her, confident he had found a solution. "You cannot work and bear children also. Why, you will not go out on the street when you increase! No, Minna, I shall return in the spring to find you with our new child."

He kissed her tenderly, and she forgave him. She did want the child, and Etienne was a fine lover. She enjoyed him, up till the day he departed, for he was more often home with her.

He left for the West in September. Minna told Yolanda what had happened, and her mother-in-law was unexpectedly helpful.

"We will hire a nurse for the children, and another clerk for the store," she said after a silence. "I do not wish to give up the work, do you, Minna?"

"No, I do not," said Minna, much relieved. And she was the more grateful as Yolanda went down to the store early in the morning on the days that Minna was sick. She hired another clerk, a nurse, and another maid. Thankfully, these were expenses they could well afford.

The shipments came regularly from Roderick Dindorf. And now Minna was able to buy more furs, for more Indians came to her, liking the gold and silver coins she paid them. She always had good blankets for them, sturdy iron and copper pots from the States. She never cheated them, and though she did not pay high, she paid fair. Word went around, and more furs came in. Roderick began to send two wagons of goods at á time to her, and she sent back loads of furs for him to sell to ship captains to take to England. Their four-way trade was working beautifully.

The winter of 1808–09 was better than ever for Minna. Heavy though she was, she went daily to the warehouse, except on the days of the worst ice. She was able to continue work in her store. A seamstress came to her and fashioned clever dresses that concealed her growing pregnancy with full-mannered gowns that flowed about her, instead of the tight gowns then in style. She also started to favor darker clothes, which made her look more slim.

And as no one said anything, she continued to work past Christmas, into the New Year and beyond. She worked back in the office, coming out only to bargain for furs, for no one did this as well as Minna MacCameron, the daughter of Ludwig Gunther, and of his shrewd wife Agatha. She also talked to ladies who wished to request special goods from the Orient, which Minna usually managed to get within two months, to the customers' amazement and to the frustration of other merchants, who could not get many Oriental goods at all.

They did not know Roderick Dindorf kept a warehouse of China goods and was able to buy anything else from the New York merchants! Work went so well, and his profits were so fine, that Roderick considered giving up the uncertainties of sailing ships. He had found a young captain he trusted, one who had been mate on his ships, and sent him out the next journey to China, with messages for Mouqua. He told the Chinese merchant that his favorite unseen friend, Minna MacCameron of the golden hair, was now in trade and wished much beautiful goods from her friend Mouqua. The Chinese merchant promptly responded with a wealth of silks, ivory, porcelain, lacquer ware, inlaid wood boxes, jewelry set in gold and silver, and jade that rivaled any Roderick had ever seen. As Roderick had been shrewd enough to send ermine, mink, beaver, and sea-otter furs to China for him, the trade was excellent, and all sides were pleased; the business prospered.

In May Minna had another son and baptized him Kendall. A smaller baby than Stephen had been, she worried secretly that she had damaged him by working so hard while he was on the way. However the baby was of good disposition, smiled much and wept little. He was a lovable child, and when Etienne came home, he marveled over the new boy.

He was a sweet, spirited lovable baby, good as gold, as his

236

grandfather proudly proclaimed. Young Stephen was always getting into mischief. However Kendall was not so lively, not so set on his own way. His smile was sweet as the dawn, said Minna, murmuring to him. "Sweet as molasses, my lovely! Beautiful as the sky in the wilderness, with the marvelous lights." As she rocked him and fed him from her full breasts, she sang to him, with Stephen standing at her knee, watching them both.

He was an independent child, as was Stephen, strong and husky. Yet every now and then he came to Minna and demanded, "Hug me."

And Minna would pick him up, heavy though he had become, and hug and kiss him, and tell him what a good boy he was.

Etienne had expected that Minna would have given up the warehouse and store. When he found she had managed to keep on with them, and have a healthy child also, he shook his head in wonder.

Minna was surprised at her husband's reactions.

He was more mature this year, she thought. He was as loving and teasing as ever, yet he talked more seriously with his father. He came to the store, looked over the books, and talked with Minna about getting more furs for her.

Etienne took her more seriously, she thought. Yes, that was it. Etienne realized she meant what she said! Their relationship that summer was better and sweeter, and she bade him good-bye that autumn with regret. He held her close the last night and whispered, "One day I shall not be able to leave you, my sweetest!"

"You must do what you wish, my darling," said Minna and held him to her and stroked his thick red hair. "I would not make you less free than you are, my wild eagle."

So they understood each other the more, and it was good. She had no more thoughts of leaving him and settled down for the winter's work with a feeling of happiness and deep contentment.

Chapter 20

Colin Gunther lay propped on his elbow on the thick fur bed and watched Morning Star brush her long black hair. He loved to watch her, so graceful was she, her face so absorbed in her task, her beautiful arms up and brushing at the thick crinkly locks.

After brushing it till it shone like ebony, she would then lay down the brush and deftly begin to plait it in one or two long plaits. Loose, it reached below her slim waist.

With a sideways glance of her dark eyes, she caught him watching her, and she gave him a shy sweet smile.

They lived alone now, but for three-year-old Wolf. A lively, yet silent lad, he was learning quickly how to talk, how to fish, swim. He was a sturdy walker, and Colin, when he had a short day, would take him along on the trapline.

"Morning Star," said Colin tenderly. "I have been thinking about going back East."

She dropped the brush and her head drooped. "Back—East," she said dully.

"Not alone, my love. I wish you to come with me, and the boy. You are my wife, and he is my son. My family will welcome you."

Her grandmother, Wind in the Pines, had died a year ago. Her tribe had moved further north, uneasy because of the advance and some battles with the fierce Sioux. Colin had decided to go further south, past the land of the Sioux, into the land where Smithson had his trade post. He had packed them up, moved them all, his wife and son and goods, and gone south.

Now they were settled in a land of sweet-running streams, white-tipped mountains, and green meadows. The summers were longer, yet the winters were cold enough to yield good furs. The only problem was the land was more overrun with trappers and Indian tribes, and some white settlers had come with land grants, and cattle.

Yet it was a good life, one Colin hated to leave. However he felt uneasy. The trappers were not always good men, generous of heart or courteous to women. The lot that had camped near him recently troubled him. The men would stare at Morning Star and make sly remarks in her hearing.

"I think it is time to go back home," he said thoughtfully. "It has been five years—yes, five—it was 1805 when I left my father in Montreal. Now it is 1810, and I wish to see my family. I wish you to meet them. We will make a house of our own. You shall live as you wish."

"In a city," she whispered, for he had told her from time to time what the life was like. "In a house, not a cabin. And they may laugh at me as the trappers do, and make remarks."

"You are a beautiful woman, they will welcome you," said Colin dryly. He got up and stretched and saw himself in her small mirror.

Tall, with a blond beard that half hid the long scar down his left cheek, he had blue eyes that shone like the cold wintry sky. Sure of himself now, he was mature, a man, with a wife and child.

He bent and kissed her head. "Do not worry, my lovely. You shall be at home there soon. And it will be good for Wolf. He needs to be near other children. He grows arrogant and willful. One day he must go to school."

"It will be as you wish," she murmured obediently. They ate breakfast in silence: Wolf was playing around and came back to eat only when Colin ordered him sternly.

Wolf pouted, then at a glance from Colin he sat down, grumbling under his breath. "Not hungry, hunger comes later."

"You eat now, when I tell you," said Colin. "Or you do not go out on the trapline with me today!"

Wolf straightened up, and began to eat, stuffing the food into his mouth with both hands. Colin watched him grimly. He hated to spank the boy, since he adored him so. But something must be done. Wolf defied both his parents. He took a spanking with set mouth, refusing to cry, then would run off and hide the rest of the day.

Colin packed up and was ready to set off. He kissed Morning Star, and she smiled up at him, her dark eyes soft. "You will be careful, Colin?" she asked as she always did.

"Yes, and you will have a care? Lock the cabin when you are inside," he said. He glanced across the meadow to where a campfire smoked. He did not like the trappers there. They had come about February, and they lingered. It was now April. Well, with the summer they would leave, and so would Colin and his family.

One named Jake Huster had come around pestering Morning Star. The others had come also but had taken her refusal politely. Yet they treated her like a cheap Indian girl they could easily have. They called her "squaw" and even "slut," and Colin had told them furiously to stay away from his *wife*.

"Wife? Huh, just an Injun slut," grunted Huster and laughed, evil in his dark eyes. He was a tall, thin, nervous man, his hand always reaching for the pistol in his belt or playing with his skinning knife.

Colin had knocked him down, and left him, furiously. But Huster and some other men were his chief reasons for wanting to take Morning Star back East with him. Most of the trappers he had met up north had been courteous, leaving his wife alone since she was his woman. Down here, it was different. The men were hungry for women and treated them rottenly.

His pleasure in the wilderness was marred by these men. Colin lifted his eyes to the heavens as he and Wolf started out. The spring was here. It was time to leave, he thought. In the North he had not left until June, but these woods and forests were different. The leaves shone softly green today, and fruit trees showed tiny pink buds. Flowers dotted the thick green grass, wild flowers of cream and gold, pink and rose, blue and violet.

It was a beautiful world, until some men ruined it with their lust and filthy minds, their greed and callousness. No, it was time to take his family East. He wanted the family to meet Morning Star, to understand what a fine beautiful woman she was. He wanted to show off his son, as well as tame him a bit and get him used to a civilized life. The lad should not grow up wild in the West.

Colin took the last of the small animals from the traps. The furs were thin from the harsh winter. The traps were picked up. Wolf helped him carry the smaller ones, eagerly. This was what he liked, to trudge along with his father, to listen for the little animals, to hear the birdsong. He walked like an Indian, without a sound, picking up and setting down his moccasin-clad feet as his father did, and his mother.

Colin and Wolf returned early, in midafternoon. Wolf was growing weary, though manfully he fought not to show it.

"Yes, we go back now, my son," said Colin, smiling a little as the boy straightened his shoulder and threw up his black head. "We go home early. I think we begin to pack today."

"Pack? Why pack? We go to Uncle Jack's place?" asked

Wolf eagerly. He had enjoyed Smithson's, and all the many boys and girls to play with.

"Yes, go to Uncle Jack's place, then back East. Home," said Colin.

"Where home?" asked Wolf, frowning, so his definite black brows almost met. "Home with Mama?"

"Yes, home with Mama, and with my mama, your granny."

"Granny is in the sky, in heaven!" Wolf was quick to point out, nodding to the sky.

Colin's face softened. Morning Star had explained to her son the death of his grandmother, by explaining that she had gone to heaven to become a star.

"You have another granny, my mother," he said. He left Wolf to think about that, and they strode on, back to the cabin.

As they came closer, Colin knew something was wrong. His step quickened, and he left Wolf behind, in spite of the boy's plaintive cry, "Wait for Wolf! Wait for Wolf!"

No smoke came from the chimney, no smoke came from a campfire. There was silence about the cabin, and the door hung open, loosely sagging on one hinge. Colin stiffened, his blue gaze swept the scene.

Then he saw her. He dropped the traps and began to run, his long strides eating up the green earth. She was lying before the cabin, limply, in a strange, crumpled position. He dropped to his knees beside her.

"Morning Star—My Star." He bent and touched the bloody face, the limp blood-covered hand.

She was cold. It was done. She was dead.

Her garments had been half-torn from her. Her neat white deerskin trousers had been ripped from her, and she was bloody from waist to knee. But more had been done than rape. Her blouse had been torn from her shoulders, and his hand trembled as he put his hand to her breast. A clot of blood, and under it the open wound—of a knife.

"Oh—God," he whispered. "God, say it did not happen—say I dream and will wake."

Wolf had panted up to him. "Mama? Mama? Why does she sleep? Mama?" He knelt beside her, bewildered, and touched her face. "Mama? She is cold! Papa, she is cold!"

Colin stood up slowly and gazed down at his dead wife. A fierce cold rage came into him, an anger such as he had never known before. One of those damned men—one of those filthy, cursed men—

241

Colin went over to the cabin door and examined it. The bolt had been shot off, the door ripped half off its hinges. The leather upper hinge had been shot off as well.

He put the pieces of the story together. As soon as he had left, the trapper must have come. Morning Star had fled inside the cabin, bolted the door, and waited, her heart beating in fear. Colin would be too far away to hear her scream. She knew how to shoot, and the pistol had been loaded. But it was one shot, and the trapper had his rifle, his pistol and his knife.

He had gotten inside. Colin saw the mussed fur robe, the bloodstains on it. He had used their own bed!

Then he had dragged her along the floor. Pieces of hair were on the side of the chair. Then outside, for blood stained the cabin dirt floor, all along from the bed to the door. And outside—to strike the final blow of the knife, into her beautiful breasts—

Rape—and murder—and still the birds sang overhead, a sleepy night song to the darkening sky.

Wolf came to him, and pressed his face against Colin's thigh. He said nothing, but his small hand went to Colin's, and the little fist was cold and shaking. Colin closed his hand over the little one.

He must take Wolf with him to the camp. He could not leave him here, frightened, with his dead mother. Colin loaded his rifle and his pistol, touched the knife in his belt, and said, "Come, Wolf."

He strode down the hill, the child just behind him. Wolf obeyed him in silence, as Colin gestured for him to stay back.

The men lounged around the campfire. Suspicious eyes were on him as he strode closer. He glanced around. Huster was not there. He looked deliberately at each man in turn. They looked at him, then away. But none sprang up.

"Where is Jake Huster?"

His low voice throbbed though the thick silence.

One man stirred, an older one. "Take it easy, Gunther. He had your girl, so what? She is just an Injun girl."

"He killed her. She lies dead."

Two of the men sat up slowly, stared, and a low murmur ran round the campfire.

"Where is he?" asked Colin flatly. "Does he hide from me?"

"He run," said the older man. He stood up. "We didn't

242

know that, Gunther, that he killed her. Are you sure she is dead?"

"Cold, with the blood on her. And a knife wound in her breast."

"Aw, God," breathed the man. He was silent. Then he told him, "Jake Huster went south. He packed up, quick, got his horse, and went south. About noontime, and he had blood on him."

"Just south? You know where he would go?"

Another short silence. They did not like to tell on a companion. But another man finally said, reluctantly, "I know Huster got friends near the Navajos. He'll go down there to hide out. Near the country where the big canyons are. Straight south. But, mister, them canyons are full of caves and such. You'll never find him."

"I'll find him, and kill him," said Colin. He nodded curtly and left them.

He fed Wolf, and put him to bed in the open, on a fur, with a blanket on him. Then he dug a grave for Morning Star, wrapped her in a blanket, and lowered her into the shallow dirt, and covered her with a green grassy blanket with flowers in it. He said some words.

"God, take care of her. She was so young, she was sweet and gentle. Make her into a star, God, like she said."

He had not wept. Fury burned in him, like a brand in the hot fire of the camp. He would not rest until he had killed the man who had done this horrible thing. To such a gentle girl! To one who had never harmed anyone. He thought of her soft smile on him, the gentleness of her hands, the shyness of her look. All were gone.

He spent the night packing the wagon and hitching up the horses. He took a few traps and the furs that were ready. Then he left the cabin as it was and roused Wolf.

He gave the boy food to eat, and mechanically he himself ate something. He must have strength. Wolf was rubbing his eyes.

He asked his father solemnly, "Where is Mama?" He was looking at the bloody spot before the cabin.

It was early morning. Colin pointed to the sky, where the light sparkling morning star hung. "Up there, Wolf. Mother is up there. She is the morning star."

Wolf stared up at the star, and his lips moved. He said no

243

more aloud for a long time. He kept gazing at the star, until it had faded in the morning sunshine.

Colin picked up Wolf and set him on the wagon seat. He leaped up himself and took the reins, and they set forth. He did not look back at the cabin he had built with his own hands, at the low grassy mound that held all that remained of his wife.

They drove all that day, and all the next. He slept little at night, restless, on guard. This was Indian territory, and the tribes were stirring in the spring. So many crimes had been done against them. Colin mused about it, but he could not think much now. His mind was intent on following the man he hated, the man he would kill.

They came to Smithson's, and the man came out to greet him, a broad grin on his face. It faded when he saw that Morning Star was not there and that Colin was looking cold and grim.

Colin told him briefly what had happened. Jack put his hand on Colin's shoulder, then said, "What can I do to help, man?"

"I need a strong horse. Dried food, bullets and gunpowder. And will you take care of Wolf until I return?"

"Of course, Colin. And then?"

"I'll take him back East with me." Colin hesitated, waited until one of Smithson's daughters had taken Wolf away with her for a bath and food. "If I don't come back, send Wolf to my home in New York with someone you can trust. Send a message, and ask my family to care for him as they have for me."

Jack's hand closed more tightly on his shoulder, then released him. "I'll take him myself, come autumn, if you don't come back. Now for the horse—"

Colin left that night, not waiting for rest. He could eat in the saddle, and even sleep there if necessary. He had lost five days getting to Smithson's, but he would not risk Wolf's life. Now he could concentrate on finding Jake Huster.

He rode straight south, following the path of the sun, and in two weeks he caught up with sign of Jake. The man had paused long enough to earn some money working for a Spanish rancher.

The Spaniard studied Colin's hard bearded face. "Why do you wish to find the man?" he asked.

"He killed my wife."

"Ah." The Spaniard pulled at his white pointed beard, then nodded. "Yes. I see. He worked but a week here and made

244

so much trouble with the ladies I asked him to leave. He snarled at me and stole one of my best horses. He went south. He asked one of my Indians about the trails south, and through Spanish Pass."

The Spaniard drew Colin a rough map, apologized for its crudeness, and gave him food to take with him. Colin thanked him and went on.

Always Jake was ahead of him, but Colin got word of him. The man was surly and a troublemaker. When Colin told why he hunted him, the taciturn ranchers, trappers, mountainmen would each in turn tell him where the man had gone.

He came to the wild canyon lands, but had no appreciation for the depths of the rusty red cliffs and valleys. He skirted them, as Jake would have done, and headed on south. He camped one night, as the cliffs were too dangerous to try to pass in darkness. He watched the sun setting over the canyon walls and noted how the shadows changed the colors as the sun moved in the sky. Rose, crimson, orange, blue rose, and purple played across the desert until the sun had gone down, and the sky was purple black.

He had made a small fire of pine cones, and the scent of them was pleasant. He had caught a large rabbit and made that his supper and the cold remains his breakfast. Then he rode on.

He spotted deer in the pine and cedar trees. They stared at him, flicked their white tails, and were gone. A beautiful land, he thought. He might have brought Morning Star here, instead of that wild country where the Indians and white men fought each other, and she had been—

He crushed down all emotion. He must put it all away. She was gone. And he would avenge her or die in the attempt.

He caught the trail of Huster again. He had been seen in a small Spanish town. He thanked the men and rode on.

Two days south he came upon a campfire, with several men around it. From their looks, they were no good, he thought. Wild, crafty, sullen, they could spare no wave of the hand for a stranger.

He saw Huster with them, halted, and stared down at the men.

"I'm looking for Jake Huster," said Colin.

They stared, shrugged.

Colin pointed at the man. "He killed my wife. I came to kill him."

245

The men fell away, leaving Huster across the campfire, his pistol at hand.

Both men fired at once. Colin's bullet hit him across the shoulder. Jake cursed and flung the pistol from him. Colin's hit the ground as he swung down from the horse. Colin ran for him. Jake hesitated, then fled into the darkness.

Catcalls followed him, curses. "Stand up to him, Huster! Damn you for a coward! Blast you, man, come on back! I ain't seen a good fight—not for months."

The calls followed the two men into the darkness. Colin slowed, waited to get his eyes adjusted to the dimness. He heard a branch crack just ahead of him, and tensed. He slid forward as the Indians move in the forest, barely lifting his feet, so nothing would tell where he walked.

He saw the dim form before him, waiting, knife in hand. He circled him, warily, the man was leaning foward, listening, tensely, confidently, knife held high.

"Here I am," said Colin behind him.

The man whirled about. Colin struck him in the neck, just about where the man had hit Morning Star.

Huster choked. The knife came forward, glinting palely. The knife skimmed Colin's face. Colin lifted his own knife, and struck again, again. The man fell down, choking out curses.

"Damn you for an Injun—damn you—following me—she wasn't nothing but—" He fell over, and his voice ceased.

Colin waited, then bent and felt the pulse of the neck. He touched slippery blood, but there was no beat. He picked up the man's legs by the booted feet and dragged him back to the campfire. The men glanced at the body, then scowled at Colin.

"Dead, huh? Why didn't you leave him out there?"

"He's your friend, not mine," said Colin. "I'll take his horse, considering he stole it."

The Spaniard had described the cream-colored, fast-running mare. Colin picked out the horse from the hitching post they had set up from a deadwood log. From the absence of protests, he guessed he had the right one.

The men were talking low. "You can stay the night, stranger!" one of them called to him. Someone laughed. Colin figured he would be as safe as a rabbit in a snake hole.

"Thanks, I'll be getting back," he said dryly, and went on, after picking up his pistol. He felt empty inside. He had killed

246

Huster, he had his revenge—but his actions did not bring back Morning Star.

He rode back the same way he had come. He stopped by the Spaniard's ranch and returned the mare. Profuse in his gratitude, the man begged him to remain and work for him.

"No, thanks, I'm going back East. For a time, anyway," Colin replied. He now knew he must leave this land, which was wild and beautiful, and, at times, unbearably cruel.

He did remain for the night and slept deeply in the elegant large room they gave to him. He wakened, and at first could not remember where he was, his gaze going around the carved wood of the room, the beautiful bed with mosquito netting hanging like lace from the tall carved posts, the heavy silk draperies at the windows.

And on the night table was a low bowl filled with gold coins. He wondered at that and finally asked his host.

The older man smiled gently. "That is for any guest, should he need it. It saves the asking for charity," he said simply.

Colin rode on, wondering. He had heard that Spaniards were cold, brutal, very tough *hombres*. But this was not so. He shook his head.

He arrived back at Smithson's by August, in time to meet with some traders returning East, one of the last parties. He collected Wolf, and his gear, loaded a wagon with packs of furs, and thanked the Smithsons.

"Did you bring back Mama?" was Wolf's first question.

Colin shook his head in silence. How did you explain to a three-year-old that his mother was gone forever? He did not understand it himself.

One day in time, perhaps one hour—and she was gone from him. It had taken but one cruel act, one horrible moment for her, and his life seemed empty, never to be the same again.

It was an evening in late September when the little train rode into New York City. Men stared curiously at the small procession, the bearded men, the wagons loaded with packs, the weary horses with lowered heads, the small black-haired boy in deerskins.

Colin took his son right to his home. The trappers would take care of the wagons and furs. Wolf rode in front of him on the handsome stallion. He looked up at the huge mansion, and his childish eyes grew big.

"This is your cabin?" he whispered.

"Right you are," said Colin. He pulled up at the stable and swung down as a man came to take the horse. The man stared at him. "I'm Colin Gunther," he said curtly. The man was new.

Others came out, recognized him, welcomed him. He nodded wearily and took Wolf's hand to lead him into the house, by the side door.

Maids were scurrying about in white aprons, carrying bowls of food. They stopped to stare, half scared, as the bearded dirty dusty man strode in, holding the Indian-clad boy by the hand. One of the older ones knew him at last. "Is it Mr. Colin, then!" she exclaimed, beaming. "I'll tell your mother, she'll be right glad!"

Agatha Gunther came from the drawing room, clad in purple silk, with pearls at her throat. She gazed at him, then held out her arms. "Colin, you came home! Oh, my lad, my lad!"

Ludwig came after her and could not believe his eyes as he saw Agatha hugging and kissing the tall bearded man. And the boy—wild and defiant—gazing about him like a trapped animal.

They had guests. Colin said, "I'll take Wolf upstairs. I'll look after him, don't worry. Could we have a tray in the room?"

"Yes, yes, whatever you want." Agatha was half crying, half wondering, wishing she could forget her guests. But they had half a hundred of some of New York's top society, and she could not. Questions must wait until tomorrow.

Colin trimmed his beard, but did not shave it off since it helped to hide part of the scar from the bear. He had changed in more ways, his family found, as he slowly spoke of the events. He was hard, tough, seemingly indifferent to everyone but his son.

Agatha took charge of the boy after she found him urinating into one of her precious porcelain vases in the downstairs hall. Someone had to civilize him! He was disobedient, listening only to his father, who was gone most of they day. He defied everyone, hid from them in the attic rooms, stole a horse and rode it for blocks before he was caught. "I want to go home," he kept screaming when he was brought back.

Colin, who was himself finding it strange to live in a house again, did not blame his belligerent son. The room was hot and stuffy, and the bed was too soft. He could not sleep nights

248

for lack of air, for the windows were shut tight against the dangerous night winds.

And the work—to be in a warehouse once more, instead of out on the trail, gazing at the open sky, smelling the cedar and pine scents. To eat at a dining table, instead of lounging on his elbow beside a campfire, watching Morning Star as she dipped out their meat stew into bowls from the iron pot. To speak to people of life, and work and prices, instead of talking to his wife about spirits and animals and stars.

Sometimes he missed her so unbearably that pain seemed to knife through his belly. He would turn over in bed and bury his face in the pillow, to stifle his groans. He would get up and pace the floor, slowly, back and forth, back and forth, half the night. Would the pain never end? Would he never forget?

He rose early one morning, and went outside, in just shirt and trousers, in the snow. He looked up at the eastern sky, and finally glimpsed the pale sparkle of the morning star. It was so dim here, he could scarcely see it. She was so far away.

Chapter 21

While Colin had been gone, living in the wilderness, Ludwig had set up a fur trade base on the northwest coast. He sent ships there, regularly, to pick up the packs of furs, to take out more trade goods, and restock the post. The men there were tough and experienced, yet Ludwig was worried about them.

"The Indians there are different from the Canadian ones," Ludwig explained as Colin leaned back in his chair and puffed at his pipe. "They've been treated badly by the Spaniards, I think. Can be a cruel lot. So the Indians too are tough and cruel. They'll trade, yes, and demand a good price. But you dare not turn your back on them a minute."

Colin had been working in the warehouse all the winter, and all the next year. He studied the reports, made out records, helped with the clerical work, and best of all for him he helped with the final preparation of the furs. He enjoyed working again with the pelts, scraping them, brushing them, shaking them out, packing them for shipment to England or to China.

Roderick Dindorf asked for some help at times. He was buying China trade goods for Minna MacCameron up in Montreal, and Ludwig was furious about the business arrangement between his wife's cousin and his own errant daughter, whom he still deeply loved.

"Why didn't she ask me?" he questioned Colin furiously, stamping back and forth across the wooden floor. "She could have asked me, her own father!"

"Do you write to Minna?" asked Colin. "Why don't you go up there for a visit?"

Ludwig looked sheepish and pulled his big thick moustache. He had turned gray, and the moustache was a faded yellow. "Oh, the marriage made us so angry. And she was gone two years out in that damn wilderness! I couldn't forgive Etienne for taking her out there, to suffer and all."

"Mama says she enjoyed it. Said she wrote and said how much she had liked the snow and the fur trapping, and seeing the sky at night." Colin watched his father from half-shut eyes. He meant to reconcile them to Minna. He had always loved his sister, who was so bright and brave and smart.

"Yes. But—well—I was so angry, and Mama was upset about the church, you know. And her defying us all...to marry that—that French dandy, after all the women...We thought she would leave him and come home."

"That would not be Minna," said Colin. He knocked out his pipe against the edge of the desk. "When she takes a path, she sticks to it. Maybe we could all go up there sometime."

Ludwig frowned and seemed anxious. "Not your mama, she is not so well," he said abruptly. "Her knees are so stiff, she can scarcely walk some days. And she has pains in her chest."

Colin nodded. "I should not ask her to care for Wolf. Yet she is good for him. I'm so grateful that she has calmed him much."

Agatha was very fond of her little quarter-Indian grandson. He was wild, but good-hearted. He was loving and sweet, and she could not even bring herself to spank him when he pulled up all the blossoms in a bed of spring flowers and brought them to her, beaming.

But while the Gunthers' lives were becoming more peaceful at home, the problems of their young, growing nation were soon to affect them strongly.

In June, 1812, the President of the United States asked Congress to declare war on Great Britain. The border with Canada was closed, and Britain sent ships to blockade the Atlantic ports. Ludwig was furiously angry, for the military action would interfere with trade. Yet he had had many a sailor impressed from his ships to serve on those of the British, and he knew why the troubles had come about.

They at first hoped to wait out the blockade, but by 1813 they figured the war would last a lot longer than the few weeks that had been predicted. Colin agreed that he should go to the northwest coast fur trade post and remain there for a year. Much needed to be decided about the future of the Gunther family business. The furs from that post were excellent, but there were problems. The long trip, the bitter cold of Cape Horn, and the ravages of the Indian tribes, all made it so much more difficult to work with that post.

Colin determined to go out there, study the situation, and make a decision as to whether to continue operating the post, or to close it. He set out, with Wolf's screaming following him, "Take me along, Papa! Take me along! Do not leave me! I want my mama! I want my mama!"

It rent Colin's heart that even after three years, his son had still not forgotten his beloved, gentle-voiced mother. Colin's eyes stung for a time as he drove away, down the coast, to where the huge sailing vessel, prepared for the long voyage, lay hidden in an obscure port against the blockade of the British.

The captain was used to this journey and knew every port where he could hide, and the mists that could conceal them and enable them to slip past the British ships. Still it was a dangerous journey, and Colin did not breathe freely until they were in the waters of the Caribbean islands, and then past them. Sometimes British ships rested there, in the bright sunlit islands, to take on fruits and vegetables and dried meat.

Around the South American continent, and through the icy hell of Cape Horn they sailed, and up again along the coasts. Colin's blond beard grew long, and his hair straggled about his shoulders, until they reached warmer lands. Then he became so hot that he clipped his hair and beard very short again.

They arrived at the Gunther fur trade post the following spring, that of 1814. Colin disliked the post from the first week. It rained constantly, in a cold miserable drizzle or a full soaking downpour, and the mists rose from the bushes and trees, making one wet from morning to night.

The Modoc Indians were sullen and treacherous. They brought in rich furs, but traded in rude style, shaking their fists in the traders' faces until they got what they wanted. They then furiously accepted the trade goods and stalked off in a temper.

The Arikara were worse, hiding in the trees to pick off the men as they walked about, stealing from others' traps, attacking anyone foolish enough to go out alone from the walled fort where the post was located.

The terrible weather combined with the dangers outside gave Colin much time to think that year. In fact he stayed indoors so much he grew pale. He sat by the fire in the huge fireplace, sticking his feet in thick stockings almost into the fire in an attempt to warm them.

He thought about Wolf, screaming and crying after him. His boy needed a mother. He needed brothers and sisters as well, if he were ever to learn how to behave around others. Otto and William had left home after college, and moved into their own homes. They had gone into real estate, taking no interest in the fur trade. They lived the lives of gay bachelors. One day they might marry, said Otto with a wink and a finger at the side of his nose, but for now they wanted fun and pretty girls!

So the big house seemed empty, even with Wolf yelling around, riding down the beautiful cherry banisters, sitting on the kitchen floor to eat the cream cake he had snatched. Yes, he needed a mother. But Colin thought he would never love a woman again. Still—one did not necessarily need to love in order to marry. A comfortable, pleasant wife could be a consolation.

In late summer Colin heard that some British trappers had come to the British post just fifty miles north. Their presence was another problem to consider. The British had their post close to them and seemed about to come further south in order to claim more land for Britain. They meant to push the Spaniards south, or even out of the land.

The Russians were much further to the north, up along the icy mountains and lakes, where the rivers were frozen blue and hung along the sides of the cliffs. The pelts in that area were good, and Colin's ships still went up there to trade. However the Gunthers had no intention of setting up posts there. It would be too cold there and too difficult, with the Tlingit Indians even worse than the ones to the south.

The Russians had Aleut slaves who did much of the work for them. Colin had shuddered when he heard the stories of how they were treated.

Colin decided to go visit the British post and talk with them; though their countries were at war, traders and trappers always had something in common, and these men were far from the scenes of battle. Besides, they might have recent news, perhaps even that the war might be over.

He took three of the men with him, men he could trust to fight alongside him should worse come to worst with Indians or British. They made a quick journey in the marshy land and the rivers, carrying one small canoe, using it when they could to glide swiftly over the waters of lakes.

When they reached the British post, Colin read the name on the brave sign swinging on the two posts of the fort entrance. He smiled wryly—"MacCameron, fur post—furs bought and goods supplied. Blaise MacCameron, Prop."

This northern establishment was larger and more magnificent than the Gunther post, thought Colin. Yet the guard was careless, merely peering at them and nodding to the open gate. Indians came and went, striding along with their rifles, their arms full of furs or goods.

Colin went in to the main office of the post. They had nice cabins for the men, and a long warehouse along one side. A

253

man came for their horses, and promising they would be cared for, took them back to the stable area.

Colin stepped in, and recognized Blaise MacCameron at once, though it had been nine years since they had met, and MacCameron had gone partly white of hair and beard. The man did not know him at first.

"Colin Gunther," said Colin briefly, and stuck out his hand, his curious gaze on the man.

"Colin? The boy? No, no, it cannot be—" Blaise shook his hand, clasping it tightly. "Minna's brother? The young lad who laughed all the time and teased us all?"

Colin smiled reluctantly. "I think I have changed somewhat," he said.

The blue gaze lingered on the long red scar half hidden by the blond beard. "Aye, that ye have changed," said Blaise. "Well, well, ye must stay for dinner and some days of chatting, eh? It's been a long, long time, laddie!"

They had dinner, and Blaise gave him news of Minna and Etienne. "Three fine lads they have already," the grandfather beamed. "Stephen is the eldest, and a fine strong boy! Born in the wilderness, he was. Ye'll have heard of him."

"Yes, the same age as my son Wolf," said Colin quietly.

"Um, yes. Ye had an Indian girl, I heard?"

Colin nodded. It still pained him to speak of Morning Star. Yet he would tell the man soon that he was the father of Colin's wife.

"And there's Kendall, a fine quiet lad, and sweet tempered. And then little Henri—ah, what a babe he is! Sings in his bath. He'll make much music, I warrant! Trying to play the piano already, picking out the tunes," grinned Blaise. "Takes after his mother. She plays the harp and piano so fine."

Blaise chatted the entire evening about family. He told about Minna's warehouse and store, reluctantly proud of her efforts. He said that Etienne had kept on trapping for years until the war. "Then the wild lad said he must join up. Now he's down guarding the lakes, all in a fine uniform, and Minna worrying night and day about him." Blaise shook his head. "It's a bad thing, this war. Stupid to fight between ourselves."

Colin agreed. "Wars are bad for trade," he said with a slight smile.

Blaise stared, then burst out laughing. "There, now, I heard your father in that! I'll warrant that is what Ludwig Gunther says of it, eh? Wars are bad for trade," and he slapped his knee and laughed and laughed.

The next day as they talked about business, Blaise Mac-Cameron told Colin he had come to close the post.

"We have lost many a good man from Indian attacks," he informed the younger man soberly. "Wild, they are, and cruel. Much bad has been done to them, I admit. But we can't change what has been done. The Indians don't forget, and it makes for bad feelings. Then with the war, and maybe if the Americans win, they'll take all this area. Nay, we're closing, and going back up north."

"How far north?" asked Colin.

Blaise shrugged. "Some of the furs here are thinner and we don't get so many any longer," he said. "I figure the area's been trapped too much. The pelts are so few. Should let the animals alone for a few years. We'll go up to the north, to the ice country, where the ermine and polar bear range. Can get some fine furs there, and not get the American competition, I'm hoping," he added with a grimace.

"I doubt if we'll go north, not that far," said Colin. "The Canadians are there, and I think one day there will be a line drawn between our countries. We'll stick to the mountain lands, and the plains."

"Well, I'll confess you can have the land and welcome," said Blaise, shaking his shaggy reddish–gray head. "The Indians here ain't like the Cree, good-hearted and gentle. Hard-working and faithful, they are. I'll be glad to get back to them, I'll tell ye."

Colin looked at him thoughtfully. "Now is the best time to tell you, probably," he said quietly. "I married a daughter of yours, Mr. MacCameron."

The man blanched. He stared, pipe forgotten in his hand. "What did ye say?" he whispered.

"You will recall maybe," said Colin dryly, "an Indian girl, a Cree girl, by the name of Rippling Waters. Her mother was Wind in the Pines."

Blaise thought, his thick eyebrows meeting over his big nose. "Aye, aye, I do remember. Pretty girl, long black hair, sweet smile, young, aye, she was young," and he sighed in nostalgia.

"Well, she had a daughter by you, and named her Morning Star. She became my wife, and we had a son, named Black Wolf. Your grandson," added Colin.

Blaise could not take it all in at first. He made Colin repeat all the names, and tell him all about the girl. He listened as to a strange tale, as Colin told of his wife, and how she had

255

lived and died. Tears tricked down unnoticed onto his moustache and beard.

"Aye, aye, aye, a daughter and I never knew her!" he mourned. "She sounded a sweet girl, like her mama. Why didn't the girl tell me? I would ha' left her some money, more than I did."

Colin sighed. The man did not understand yet. He might have left children all over the West. "She did not know she was pregnant until after you had left her," he said.

"Oh, aye, that would have been it, and I never went back to the same place twice," said Blaise, nodding. "And ye have a son, do ye? Indian boy?"

"One-quarter Indian," corrected Colin. "Wild, though, and hard to tame. Don't know what to do with him."

"Take him back to his people," advised Blaise, and the thoughtless remark made Colin so furious inside that he had to get up abruptly and go outside to stalk about for a time.

But the man was good-hearted, though callous about the children he had left here and there. Colin returned and changed the topic to the business here. Blaise was already directing his men, packing up the goods, buying the last of the furs, and telling the Indians that he would be gone soon.

"For I'll not leave the post to my men. They be good men and smart. Too many murders about here," said Blaise. "It ain't worth the lives. We'll go back north."

After a week Colin was ready to return to the Gunther post, his own decision made. They also would close up and leave. He told Blaise, and they parted with a hearty handshake. Colin found that he could not dislike the big hearty Scotsman.

"Tell Minna we miss her, and that we want to see her before long."

"Oh, aye," said Blaise but shook his head. "With Etienne afighting against ye, I don't know what to think. Hope the war is over before I get back. Damn silly thing, wars."

Colin agreed. He and his men departed and returned through the woods. The ground had gone solid and icy hard for the winter. But still an unpleasant mist hung over everything. Sometimes it would start to rain, a heavy, bitter rain with snow mixed in it.

They were glad to get back inside the fort. Colin resolved to close the post and depart with the men as soon as the next ship came. He told the others. Most were pleased with the decision, but some of the tough trappers were angry.

"Why should we leave? We can handle them damn Injuns!" said one tough character belligerently. He liked the wild free coast life, where he could catch his own game for a meal any day of the year.

Colin shrugged. By the time the ship came, they would all be heartily sick of the place and each other, and glad to go, he hoped.

But no ship came. They waited through the winter and bought furs as usual, paying for the later ones in gold and silver coins. Their supplies were running out. The Indians wanted the gold, but grumbled loudly that there were no more blankets, no more iron pots and copper kettles, no more tobacco. One threatened Colin with a knife, and the blond man had to throw him bodily out of the fort.

The Indian left, swearing in English and in his native tongue.

Three days later a band of Indians attacked the fort. Dogs had given tongue, warning them, and the trappers fled into the fort. Colin gave them rifles, bullets, and gunpowder, opening a fresh barrel. He had refused to trade the weapons and gunpowder and bullets to the Indians, fearing it would be used against them.

He had been right. The Indians fired on the fort until they ran out of ammunition. Then they used their more deadly arrows, of which they had an endless supply.

Colin told his men to go ahead and fire on them. He hated giving that order. He kept thinking of the Cree Indians and the others he had known, of Morning Star, of his own son. Yet he knew that his men would not get out alive if he got soft.

Bullets resounded against the trees, and the Indians were darting in and out, their thin bronzed bodies dressed in dark deerskins, hard to see in the mist, that damned cold mist, which hid all except for a glimpse now and then. Rain did not stop the attack. Arrows banged against the walled fort, and some penetrated inside through slits and a half-opened window. Two trappers were wounded.

The attack continued for three days and nights. Though it was spring, not a flower could be seen. The rain had drowned everything, the trees turning a dark green, moisture dripping from them continually. It was the most miserable time in a forest that Colin had ever endured.

The trappers were getting angry, and reckless. Some fired leaning out of the windows, and four got arrows in their arms or shoulders. Colin soon had quite a hospital going, being forced to pull out the ends of arrows after breaking them off. One wound festered, and the young man had an anxious time of it, using ointment such as Morning Star had used. She had taught Colin much about the salves and herbs to be made from bushes and grasses.

Finally the firing ceased. After it had been quiet for a day, Colin ventured out alone, forbidding anyone to follow him. He crept about, silent as an Indian, and found that all the living Indians had departed. Only their dead remained behind, limp, bloody, lifeless. One young fellow had long black hair. When Colin found him, crouched and curled up, he was still alive. He lifted his face and held out his bloody hand in pleading. For a moment he looked like Morning Star. When he fell over, gasping out his last breaths, Colin felt sick at his stomach. The boy died, his face to the ground, looking like Morning Star with long hair streaming to his shoulders—

Colin went back to the fort after several hours of creeping about. In his face, which was as cold as stone, only his blue eyes burned like fire.

"They have gone," he quietly informed the men. "The others are dead. We'll bury them."

"Hell, let them rot! We're pulling out anyway," said one burly trapper nastily.

Colin put him to grave digging.

No ship came that spring, none that summer. Colin was becoming worried. He knew his father; Ludwig would have sent a ship, and at least two or three in this time. What had happened? Had the British made a deeper blockade?

When a ship finally arrived, it was one of theirs that had made the China run, to the northwest fort, up to the Russian fort, over to the Sandwich Islands, to Canton, and back to the northwest fort. They had no news of the East Coast or Britain.

Colin loaded the ship with the furs and the last of the stores. When a few of the trappers still protested, he stared them down. "We are going, the fort is closing," was all he said.

He tore down the sign bearing his family's name. Let the place rot, with the bodies of the Indians buried around the fort, he thought. He was sick of the killing, the bloodshed, the ferocity of the Indians. Only a few had come to the post after the attack, demanding guns for their furs. Colin had refused and sent them away.

Finally, on a day late in August, the ship was ready to sail. Colin ordered all the employees of Gunthers on board. Several of the traders defied him and slipped away into the forest.

"We got to go after them," one young man exclaimed. "We cannot leave them here! The Indians will kill them!"

"They had their choice," said Colin with no emotion. "We sail today."

And he gave the order for them to lift sail and depart. As the ship pulled away slowly from the misty island, the fog lifted briefly. Colin and the men on deck saw what the mist had hidden. A band of Indians stood on the wharf.

They had guns and bows and arrows. And one carried a bloody scalp. He lifted it and shook it at them, shouting over the waters. "You go way, white eyes! Damn you all to hell! This our land!"

That was their farewell. Colin shivered in the fog and went back into the cabin of the captain to write out reports.

The journey back East was long and hard. The captain hated the trip around Cape Horn. His men complained aloud about the cold, the ice that clung to the ropes and bit their red hands, the snow on the slippery decks. They preferred the Sandwich Islands, the warm climate of south China.

They met no ships until they reached the eastern coast of South America. It was there that they finally encountered another ship, and it was American.

They both stopped, sheltered in a cove for a day, and exchanged news.

"The war with Britain is over," were the first glad tidings. "They signed a peace treaty in December of 1814. However a battle was fought in New Orleans in January of this past year, 1815, before the news of the treaty reached them."

Colin told them in turn about the conditions on the Northwest Coast, how he had closed his post and the British had closed theirs. The Indian wars were too bitter right now, and even the Spanish had drawn back from the Northwest area.

"Hmm," the captain frowned. "I think I'll trade with them Spanish then, and go on north, avoid the coves, and go up to the Russians. They're always glad to get Boston goods. Then we can take the furs to Canton. Good trading there, yet?"

"Yes, they want the furs. The market is never ending."

They thanked each other for the hospitality each had given, parted politely, and went on their way. Colin felt more relaxed than he had for a long time, knowing they would not have to sail cautiously to avoid a British blockade. All the ports would be open.

The Gunther ship arrived in the port of New York in the

spring of 1816. Colin had been gone almost three years, and he went eagerly to his home. Wolf would be so grown up. He longed for the boy. Nine years old now, he would be taller, and, Colin prayed, happier in his life with the family of his father.

Gunther men were at the wharf to greet them. One loaned Colin his carriage. "Your folks will be anxious to see you, Mr. Colin!" he called out, greeting the blond man with a hearty handshake.

He took with him gifts for his mother and his son. As the carriage rattled along the wharf, then up the streets to the north where the mansion was set on the fine streets of the gentry, he noted the changes that had taken place in his absence—more houses, more stores, more carriages crowding the dirt roads.

When the carriage finally pulled up in front of the Gunther home, out from the big doors darted a tall, black-haired boy. "Father—Father!" Wolf screamed. Colin jumped out of the carriage to hug him. The boy's head came to his chest.

"Can this be my Wolf, my little lad?" he asked, hugging him fiercely.

"Oh, Papa, you came home. Father, my Father." Wolf held him. "I thought you had gone to the stars also!"

Colin pressed his cheek against the boy's head. "Not yet, lad, not yet." He said it softly.

Ludwig came bursting through the doorway. "Colin, lad!" He grasped his hand, beaming at him. Colin half smiled. "Was it a good trip? What happened?" the older man asked.

"Had to close the fort, Father. I'll tell you later. But we have rich furs from the place, three years' worth. And I met Blaise MacCameron. We had a good visit."

Ludwig's face darkened in anger. "I suppose he'll take all the furs now! The old scoundrel!"

"No, he closed their fort first. Too much killing going on. He is moving further north, he said."

That reconciled Ludwig. He hated to be beaten by anyone, but especially by MacCameron.

Colin glanced at the doorway. His mother was there, smiling, holding to the doorframe. He let Wolf go and bounded up the steps and led her indoors before hugging her and letting her kiss his bearded face.

She felt more thin and frail, and she seemed to be limping heavily. But her smile was sweet as ever, and her hair still had some blond strands in the gray. "Oh, Colin, you came home.

260

How anxious we have been. Wolf asked often for you," she told her son, her eyes shining with joy.

Wolf had come up and pushed at Colin's thigh as he had as a small boy. But he came up to Colin's armpit now. Colin smiled at him and ruffled the dark hair. How like his mother he looked, the great dark somber eyes, the sideways glance, the shape of his mouth.

"Take me with you next time!" urged Wolf. He spoke better English, and his hands were clean. Colin noted the improvements with amusement, touched at his mother's hard work on the lad.

"I shan't be going out again for a time, boy."

"When you go, take me along!"

"I'll be working here, in New York. You can come to the warehouse with me tomorrow and help unload the furs."

Wolf relaxed and beamed up at him.

"He will miss school," said Agatha.

"One day won't hurt him. Tomorrow is Friday, isn't it? I lost track of the days and weeks."

He came into the house, and was at home. Fortunately there were no guests for dinner, and they could talk comfortably. Wolf was allowed to remain up for the meal, late though it was, and listened silently, intently, to all his father's words and stories.

He needed a mother, someone to belong closely to him, thought Colin uneasily. He himself felt no need for a wife—though if he could have Morning Star again—

That was impossible. He sighed and blocked out that thought. "Yes, Father, about a thousand packs of furs," he replied to a question posed by Ludwig. "We have collected them for these three years..."

The talk had turned again to business.

Chapter 22

After the loneliness and silence of the wilderness Colin was amazed anew at the noise and gaiety and parties in New York City. It seemed to him that his parents entertained constantly. When he mentioned this to his mother, who had herself never liked entertaining, Agatha said, "No, this is less than most people, dear Colin."

But Colin became suspicious when he realized that at almost every gathering a girl would appear, one who was lovely, young, rather wealthy, well dressed, and hopeful. Blond, brunette, even redheaded, they came and went that winter.

Otto or William would often bring their latest girls but were not possessive of them. Did they do this on their own, or at his mother's request?

Colin was furious at first, then amused, then indifferent, as the girls came and went. The only one who really attracted his attention was a lovely blond girl named Odette Raoult.

She had a quiet musical voice, she smiled often, and she was restrained, ladylike, cool of manner. She enjoyed opera and musical concerts, and Colin took her to several events in the company of her mother. The one point in her favor, so far as he was concerned, was that she was so different from Morning Star. When he was with her, he could forget the pain of his loss.

She spoke well on many subjects, she knew French and German, she played the harp a little, the piano less. Well bred and intelligent, she was an only child. And her father was anxious for her to marry and have grandchildren to inherit his dress goods shop. Without a male heir, he longed for grandsons.

Colin introduced her to Wolf. The boy took an instant, suspicious dislike to the young woman. "I don't like her," he said flatly to his father. "You ain't gonna marry her, are you, like Susie said?"

Susie was his governess and had a difficult time with him. He had been put in school now, but Susie was kept on, and still put him to bed, sang to him, told him stories, and saw he was clean when he started out to school. His state when he returned was a different story. A sturdy girl of farm stock, she was good-hearted and blunt.

"Don't listen to gossip, Wolf," said Colin, half smiling.

"How am I gonna hear what's happening?" demanded Wolf.

Colin sighed. He was rough of manner, his wild boy, and demanding constantly to go with Colin on his next trip. He hungered for the wilderness, as Colin often did, and the spirit of adventure was strong in him. He had run away from home a number of times while Colin was gone, always trying to find his way out of the city maze into the country and go West, like his father.

Worried about how Odette would react to his son if they were to wed, Colin asked her, with seeming casualness, "What do you think of my wild boy, Odette?"

They were waiting for the start of a musical number in the home of mutual friends. Odette was sparkling in a gown of pale blue embroidered with pearls, her blond hair was dressed high on her aristocratic head.

Odette turned serious. "He misses the influence of a mother, I believe, Colin," she said confidingly. "I know your mother has done her best, but she is older, and Wolf is too quick for her. Perhaps a good school with strong discipline? I have heard of such—"

So had Colin and did not like what he heard. He shook his head, and the music started. He glanced at Odette with cool speculation. He did not love her, but he liked her. She had many domestic talents, she had been trained well by her mother to entertain guests, direct the servants and keep the household accounts. He pictured himself in his own home, with Odette as his wife, taking care of Wolf, smiling a farewell as Colin went on a journey, welcoming him home to a beautiful house filled with warmth.

On the way home in the carriage he ventured to kiss her as the coachman drove on the icy streets. Odette stiffened at once, and pushed him away with a rebuke.

"None of that, Colin!" she said rather sharply. "Mother trusted you to take me to our hosts, and home again, because she was ill and we had promised to attend. She would be horrified if she knew I had allowed any liberties!"

She was quite serious. Colin drew back with a slight smile. He thought she was shy, in addition to having delicate manners. It also pleased him that she was virginal and did not allow men to tease her and flirt with her. Some women friends of Otto and William were not so delicate, or particular.

Odette was watching him anxiously. She found him different from the usual men she met, she had told him frankly. He was brooding, handsome in spite of his scar, tough, and was often silent for an hour in her company. She wondered what was behind his quiet air, and it rather pleased her that he did not talk and brag and laugh loudly as other men did to attract her attention.

He took her hand and pressed it lightly. She did not pull back, but she did keep her hand still, not returning the squeeze.

"Odette, if I should go to your father and ask for your hand in marriage, should you be pleased or no?" he asked abruptly.

Her greenish-gray eyes widened. "Marriage?" she whispered.

"Yes. I need a wife, and my son needs a mother. And I think I could make you happy, Odette. You please my eyes and my ears," he said with that odd half smile of his, as though he would never laugh aloud yet matters amused him in a cynical manner.

Her gaze turned away, her hand was limp in his. Yet she finally said in a low voice, "I think I should advise you to speak to my father, Colin."

It was her way of agreeing. Colin nodded and the next day called upon her father formally. The man had evidently been warned by his daughter, for he was ready with beaming cordiality and a bottle of excellent brandy. Odette and her mother were called in, Odette blushing and unable to meet Colin's gaze.

He was permitted to kiss her cheek, and they spoke of setting a day. Colin was all for having the wedding at once, but Odette and her mother refused, and they set the date for June.

It was all one to Colin. He looked idly about for a house, but none especially pleased him. One was too big, another too small. He decided to wait, and live in his same suite in his parents' home. Odette had no objections to living with them for a time, until they could decide on a home. Perhaps they would build one further north in New York, where the gentry were moving in increasing numbers. Colin's younger brothers were full of suggestions. Otto was eager to arrange a land deal, but William interrupted that he had better lands, and better prices.

Ludwig was heartily relieved that Colin was to be married.

Odette was a pretty girl, and Colin needed the steadying influence of a good woman. After a dinner party celebrating the engagement, he patted her shoulder and gave her a set of emeralds to match her eyes, he said. They did not, for her eyes could be a sort of wintry green, gray-green, rather than the pure green flame of the gems. But she was most pleased and condescended to kiss his whiskery cheek.

Agatha was not so pleased. She was silent and troubled, though unwilling to make difficulties. But the cool grace of Odette did not please Colin's mother, nor did her manner with Wolf. She was always uneasy when the boy was around, for he stared at her with his coal-black eyes and wore a typically belligerent expression.

Agatha ventured to speak to her son. "I am disturbed about this marriage, Colin. I fear your heart is not in it. Do you love the girl?" she asked bravely.

Her face showed her shock as Colin shook his head. "No, Mother, I cannot love anyone as I loved my Morning Star," he said quietly.

"But, Colin! This girl—" Agatha paused helplessly. "She—she is expecting—I mean—"

"She shall have my loyalty, my respect. I shall have a home, a mother for Wolf, and hopefully more children. I love my Wolf, as I shall love my other children. And perhaps one day I shall come to love my wife. We have not spoken of this."

"You have not spoken of this to her? Does she wish a marriage of convenience, like the society folks?" asked Agatha in gentle despair. She had longed for more for her eldest son.

"We do not speak of it. She blushes when I speak of marriage and will not discuss anything at all." Colin grinned slightly and shrugged. "I think she is very shy."

Agatha said no more. The marriage plans went forward. Only Wolf dared to speak out passionately against it. "She is not my mother, she is not my mother! How can you do this, Papa?"

The boy was only ten and did not understand anything, Colin thought. He told the lad firmly that he was to accept Odette as his mother from now on.

"I never will," said Wolf.

"You will learn to do so," said Colin firmly.

Wolf glared, and on the wedding day he had disappeared completely. "Let him go, he will come back," said Colin on hearing the news.

The lad was gone for a week, but finally returned, muddy,

skinny, and with a haunted look in his sullen eyes.

Colin rather looked forward to his wedding night. He had had only casual affairs since his return from the West. He sought out bawdy women when he had a need. His life would be different now. He felt an urgent need to marry and be able to turn to one woman for security and comfort, as well as for his masculine needs.

The bride was gloriously beautiful on her wedding day. And to oblige her beauty, the June morning was sunny, with blue skies, and a slight breeze blowing to lift the veil and swirl her white satin skirts to show the little white satin slippers on her narrow feet. Society had turned out for the fashionable affair, and the church was crowded with guests. Outside, women waited curiously to see the gentry, and the gowns of the wedding party, and shouted when they came out, and threw flowers at them.

Odette was pleased and smiled graciously at the crowd as she was escorted to the carriage. Colin laughed, and waved at them, recognizing some faces in the throng, their servants, some trappers, some woodsmen, men from the warehouse, and sailors from the ships he and his father owned and ran.

They called their rough good wishes, and Colin heard them above the laughter and the sounds of the dozens of carriages thronging the streets. "Best to you, Colin Gunther! Best of luck, good hunting! Wishes on your head, me lad!"

They drove to the reception, held in a fashionable hotel. Two hundred guests made short work of the tables of food, platters of glazed hams, pheasant, chicken, and turkey. All imaginable foods were being served: potatoes both sweet and Irish, green beans and corn, cheese dishes, and many fancy trifles of chocolate and vanilla and coffee flavor.

Besides the immense white seven-tiered wedding cake, there were plates of chocolate cakes, mocha cakes, cream-filled pastries, ices and the fashionable ice cream in strawberry and blueberry flavors.

The festival went on most of the day. It was late afternoon before the couple could get away in their carriage for a brief journey up the wide Fifth Avenue to the mansion offered to them for their wedding night and several days to follow. They had a suite to themselves in the wing overlooking the East River.

A maid brought up a tray of coffee and tea, undressed Odette and put her in her bridal night outfit of white chiffon and lace, and departed with a smile and knowing look.

Then they were alone, finally. Colin began to undress. Odette turned her face away and sat down on a sofa. "You should go into the bedroom to undress," she said sharply.

Colin raised his eyebrows, but she was shy, he thought. He departed for the bedroom, to return rather sheepishly in his long white nightshirt of linen and lace.

He found Odette sipping tea with lemon and eating a slice of fruit. She was as calm and placid as though they were dining at a restaurant following the opera.

He stared, then said, "I think we shall go to bed now, Odette. It is past ten o'clock."

She laid down the fruit, wiped her fingers, said, "Yes Colin, of course," and went calmly to the bedroom. She removed her chiffon negligee, revealing a short-sleeved white lace gown that showed her slim rounded form, the small high breasts. She was tall, rather stately, and slim in the fashionable way.

Colin had emptied his mind of his first wife, or so he had thought. Yet, lying down beside this form, so stiff and straight beside him, he could not but think with longing of Morning Star, small and brown, curling up to him on a wintry night, giggling and responding to his kisses.

He put his arms about Odette. She did not move. Her eyes were shut tight. He remembered her shyness and was gentle with her. He kissed her mouth softly. She did not answer his kisses.

He could not bring any response at all. He kissed her shoulders and her mouth, then fondled her breasts. She shivered, convulsively, once, then lay stiffly again. He was growing eager. She was after all, an attractive girl, and very much a virgin. He wanted her and felt desire strongly in him. His body was growing hot with hunger for her.

He finally lay over her and took her. She cried out, and wept for a time. Her reaction quenched his desire, and he lay back, cursing himself. He had been too rough. He apologized to her.

"I was too abrupt. Forgive me, Odette. Next time I shall try to be more gentle."

She sniffed, wiping her eyes with a handkerchief she brought from under the pillow. "It is all right, Colin. My mother told me what to expect," came the unexpected cool voice, quite composed. "I shall always do my duty."

Well! That was designed to throw cold water on any man's

ardor. Odette composed herself for sleep a good foot away from Colin's body, and he watched her sleeping, snoring a little as she lay on her back.

He could not sleep, so finally he got up and went quietly to the dressing room and lay on the rough couch. He managed to sleep toward morning.

The next day was better. Odette spoke of the house she would want eventually. He suggested building one, and they drew out some rough plans. She was eager about this project, and her cheeks grew pink with excitement.

"I want a house as big as Mama's, or bigger," she said. Her green-gray eyes snapped. "Father could afford one only that large, but you are wealthier than my parents are, Colin," she added complacently.

He looked at her reflectively and wondered if the glow in her cheeks came from the excitement of a child wanting a prettier toy than her friend? Or was it—something else?

The "honeymoon" dragged on. Colin went to his bride at night, but he could not stir up much desire for her after the first disappointing night. He hoped that after she was more accustomed to marriage, it might go more easily.

They returned to the Gunther house, and Colin and his wife kept to their suite much of the time. At least Odette did, busily planning "our own house," and Colin spent the days and early evenings at the warehouse.

Ludwig was now preoccupied by the fur posts near the Rockies. He had sent a man out there but was bothered by the fact that he received few reports, and by the low returns of furs.

"I wonder if I can trust the man, now that he is working alone. I pride myself on knowledge of human nature, but he baffles me. Perhaps he smiles too much," reflected Ludwig.

Colin listened idly, thinking of Odette. She smiled quite a lot in company, with a very charming smile. She also spoke well, listened even more beautifully, and was able to enchant many people by her gentle breeding and good manners.

But was there anything lovely behind that smile? Colin made himself go to her nights, several times, when she did not have to attend dinner parties, concerts, or other events. She always submitted with docility, was visibly relieved when he rolled on his back, and composed herself readily for sleep at a good distance from her husband.

He was finally forced to order that his study be turned into a bedroom by the addition of a narrow long bed, and he usually slept there, after working late at his desk. The servants whispered and Agatha was troubled, but separate sleeping quarters were now best for him.

In early September Mrs. Raoult asked for an appointment with Colin at his office in the warehouse. Puzzled, he sent back a note that he would be in all the afternoon, waiting her pleasure.

She appeared promptly at three o'clock, a fashionable hour for calling. One of the clerks showed her in and shut the door after her.

Colin showed her to a seat, and the prim woman sat down on the edge of it, her nostrils quivering in distaste at the smell of furs and dust.

"Is anything troubling you, Mrs. Raoult?" he asked, as she seemed to have difficulty in finding words to begin. He had attempted to call her Mother or Mama, but she disliked the familiarity so much that he had reverted to more formal address.

"Not trouble, no. I have a message from Odette for you," she said with a rush, her cheeks growing pink under her graying blond hair.

"A message from Odette?" he asked blankly. "I saw her this morning before I departed." For a wild moment he thought she was leaving him.

"Yes, yes, she is well, no fear of that, my Odette is rarely ill. I tell her it is all in the *mind*. If one thinks oneself in perfect health, one will be so."

Colin, further puzzled by the course their conversation was taking, fingered his scar gravely. He thought of that attack by the black bear, the fever—"A fine notion, Mrs. Raoult," he told her.

She shifted on the edge of the chair and drew her navy blue gown stiffly about her. "My daughter wished me to inform you that she is—ah—increasing."

Colin stared. "I beg your pardon? You said—"

She gave him an impatient look, biting her lips. They were thin and pale, he noted, like Odette's in shape but without her pink bloom. When Odette was older, would she look like that, with tight thin lips, a haughty nose—

"I said," she repeated with an obvious air of embarrassment and exasperation, "Odette is increasing."

"What does that mean?" he asked bluntly, unfamiliar with such delicacies of expression. "She is gaining weight?"

269

"Yes."

He puzzled over that. "What does she want me to do about it?"

"Mr. Gunther! Really. You have done enough!"

Now she was flushing and looking distressed. Suddenly he realized what she was trying to say. "Do you mean she is going to have a baby?"

She moaned, her hand on her heart. "Pray, do not be vulgar! Mr. Gunther, I beg you, we are of an old and revered family. We do not use current coarse expressions."

"Having a baby is coarse?" he asked with detached interest.

"Speaking aloud of the matter is, Mr. Gunther," she said frigidly. She rose. "Well, I have informed you of the matter."

"Where is my wife?" Colin rose, also, automatically.

"Where?"

"Yes, is she home, lying down, with the curtains drawn?"

"No, of course not! I told you, she is very healthy. She is outside in the carriage."

Colin began to smile. "And does she wish me to go out into the dusty street and call up to her in the carriage, that I am most pleased at the news she is—ah—increasing?"

"Mr. Gunther! Must you shock me again and again?" Her hand moved over her heart once more.

"I would think it would be less—vulgar—if my wife had informed me of the fact of our coming child in our bedroom, or drawing room at home." He said it distinctly, politely.

Mrs. Raoult glanced at him uneasily. He had not received the news with the elation and polite consideration she had expected. "My daughter is very aware of the niceties. Besides, she wished me to inform you—ah—that it is no longer necessary for you to—ah—sleep in the same bed with her."

"She told you—*that*?" Colin was incredulous now. "Odette said for you to inform her *husband* that he was not to come to *her* bed?"

"Yes. She does not wish to discuss the matter, naturally. Her delicacy of manner—" The woman was permitted to say no more. Colin showed her out. Then he sat down and thought, shaking his head. He could scarcely believe what had just taken place. And when he went home that evening, Odette had a calm complacent manner. He did not discuss the matter.

He waited for two weeks, then three. She still did not speak to him about the coming child, but she was definitely relieved that he did not come to her bed. She spoke happily about some social events that she might now attend up until Christmas.

One evening Colin finally said, "Well, my dear. I have some news for you. I am going West for my father and will be gone for a period of six months to a year."

Odette stared at him in surprise and growing alarm. "What? Colin, you will not! What need is there for you to travel and do that sort of thing?"

"Why not? It is my life, my work," he said. "Can you think of any reason I should not be gone?"

She swallowed. He watched the movement of her smooth white throat with amused interest. "But, Colin—Mr. Gunther—"

"You may call me Colin," he invited. "We were married in June, as you may recall."

Sarcasm flew past her beautiful head like a gnat which she brushed aside.

"Did not my mother speak to you?"

"Speak to me? Mrs. Raoult always speaks to me. She has exquisite manners."

"But about—about—"

He waited, politely. She swallowed, convulsively.

"About—the—child," she said faintly and put her handkerchief to her lips.

"Oh—that. Yes."

She waited, appeal in her greenish-gray eyes. He studied the fire intently. "Well you surely must see the need to remain home with me—in my need."

"Do you have a need?" he asked.

She turned cool and remote. "Of course men are different, they do not comprehend the agonies of a woman! *They* are distant from the events that make up a woman's life! I am expecting your—child," she managed to pronounce the words more neatly this time. "It may be your first son, your heir! Surely that does matter to you?"

"I have a first son and heir. Wolf," he said.

She did not speak to him for days, except for politenesses. She knew how to freeze a man, with distant cool words, with an icy manner. Colin was learning how to combat it. After all, he did not love her, and he was now beginning to think that he did not even like her much.

Colin continued with his preparations to go West. Wolf had been sent away to school, where he rebelled, yet sometimes enjoyed the rough comradeship of others like himself. The

271

boys, impossible to handle, often were of good families, and their teachers and tutors were employed to deal with them as skillfully and diplomatically as possible.

Colin spoke to his mother. She was shocked at the news that he was leaving and that his wife expected a child. "But when, Colin? When is she going to have the baby?"

"Mrs. Gunther has not informed me of the date," he answered. "She is too delicate to speak of the matter. You might ask Mrs. Raoult, who considers the matter too vulgar for speech, or at least for speech uttered in my presence."

"Colin, really!" exclaimed Agatha. "I am serious!"

So am I, said Colin to himself. He sighed, and added, "I am worried about Wolf. When he comes home, and finds me gone, you may have a tantrum on your hands. Console him, and tell him when he is grown, I promise that he shall go with me. Keep him apart from Odette. They dislike each other."

"She has tried to dismiss Susie," said Agatha slowly.

"Keep her. Wolf depends on her when you are not there. And she will be needed later in the nursery. She is a good sensible woman with a warm heart." And after having his mother promise that she would insure Susie's remaining with them, Colin was able to begin his preparations for leaving.

Colin left on a cold morning in early October. It amused him not to say farewell to Odette. Let her find him departed! He cared not a whit.

He enjoyed the trip West, especially after enduring the confines of the city. He lingered in the wild country, helped with the traps, and shrewdly watched the man his father had appointed commander of the post. He went over the books and finally located a clumsy attempt at embezzlement. He fired the man, with relief, and took over the post.

The winter was a cold, snowy one. He happily tramped around in the snow and ice, climbed the nearest mountain and laid traps there, dealt with the growing antagonism of the Indians, sent messages and furs East, and regretted the fact that he would eventually have to leave.

It was so calm here, so peaceful. Far from the so-called civilized world, there was no whining, no polite nagging, no coldness when one did not get his way. Out here, once a disagreement arose, it was settled after a fight, or by kicking a man out the door. Much more intriguing than society events were the exchange of furs with goods, the shrewd haggling

272

over a campfire, the need for constant wariness, the feeling at the back of the neck when danger was near.

That was his world. He relaxed in it, and grew tougher and leaner with the passing months. He found a trapper who had been injured in a wolf trap, his leg now crippled. Knowing that the man would be grateful, and therefore, he hoped, honest, if provided with a job that would enable him in remain in the wild, Colin taught him how to keep the books. He had some learning and could read and write and do sums, and he readily learned all he needed to know.

April came, and still Colin did not leave. He went out for the last of the traps, remembered Morning Star, and looked up often to the heavens in the early morning when the sky was turning a paler blue and the other stars blinked out. How long ago it was, how distant, yet his own star blazed white fire.

May came, and June. Colin knew that he must leave soon. The furs were packed, and the last of the trappers was soon to come in from the north. Then he must go—but he was reluctant to leave.

Chapter 23

Colin Gunther returned home in September. He was heavily bearded, dirty, and tired when he walked into the house of his father.

Agatha greeted him with tears and laughter, much the same way she had welcomed the returning Ludwig years before, hugging him in spite of his filth. Wolf ran down the stairs, sprang at him, hugged him and accused, "You went without telling me! Oh, Papa, Papa, you are finally home!"

Colin's face softened a little, and he hugged his son fiercely. He could not speak for a minute as his face pressed to the soft dark hair that reminded him so keenly of Morning Star.

He ruffled up the boy's hair and gazed down into his deep black eyes. "You have grown another two inches, my son," he commented, amazed and moved by how quickly he was becoming a man.

Wolf smiled radiantly up at him. "I'll soon be all grown up. Then I can go with you!"

"Yes, when you are grown up," said Colin. The two went upstairs to Colin's room. He glanced about, surprised by the silence there. "Where is Odette?" he asked absently. "Did she have the baby? Boy or girl?"

Wolf's face turned sullen. "She left, Papa. Don't speak of her, I hate her!" And he would say no more of the woman. Instead he pressed his father for the gift he had promised him. "What did you bring me? A pistol? May I have a pistol now?"

With half his attention turned to his son, Colin glanced about the suite. The rooms seemed strangely empty. Had Odette gone to her mother's for a time?

The little powder boxes were gone from the dresser, along with the mother-of-pearl shell cases she adored, the jewel boxes, the dresses from the wardrobe, and the white ermine cape he had given her. Colin grew thoughtful.

He bathed, as Wolf shot questions at him faster than he could answer. He cut his beard a little, just enough to trim it, resolving to see the barber soon or use his father's valet. He dressed again in a suit, amused to find it was now big on him. He had grown leaner in the year he had been gone.

When Colin came downstairs, dinner was ready, though the hour was early. Ludwig had come home, and he hugged his son affectionately. He studied his son's face as though to read the story of the year.

They sat down together. Colin looked about again and asked, "Where is Odette?"

Agatha and Ludwig exchanged looks. Wolf glared sullenly, glowering in his chair beside his father.

"Forget her. She is gone!" said Wolf arrogantly. "Father, did you shoot any bears this year?"

Ignoring the attempts of his son to win his attention, Colin turned to Agatha. "Mother, where is Odette?" he asked again.

"She went home—to her parents—soon after you left, Colin," said Agatha with evident effort. She glanced at Wolf and added, "She—thought she would remain through the birth of her child."

"I put a frog in her bed," said Wolf, and laughed, his mouth mocking, his voice harsh. "How she jumped and screamed! She yelled for an hour!"

"Wolf, that was very naughty!" Colin rebuked sharply. "I hope you were well spanked for that!"

"I didn't care! She left the next day!" said Wolf.

"I did spank him," said Ludwig apologetically. "However Odette was hysterical, and insisted on leaving, as Wolf said he would do it again, only not a frog the next time!"

"She called me an Indian bastard," said Wolf complacently.

Colin and Agatha jumped. Ludwig put his napkin to his mouth.

"She was very upset," said Agatha with resignation. "She did not mean to use such words, Wolf."

"Yes, she did. She called me bastard before. Several times. So I called her a cold bitch."

Colin put his hand to his head. "Enough! Enough! I will go to Odette tomorrow—was my child a boy or girl?"

"A boy," said Ludwig. "A fine child. Blond hair. Quiet. She had him baptized. We attended the ceremony."

"What name?"

Agatha and Ludwig exchanged another look. "She named him Gerald, after her father," said Agatha.

Colin went to the warehouse the next day to supervise the unpacking of the furs. He had some fine ermine and mink he wanted to handle himself, and then turn it over to the right man to work on.

It was two days before he went to the Raoult home. Odette came down from her suite wearing a blue afternoon gown of velvet. Her mouth was sulky.

"I was just going out to tea," she said, standing in the doorway.

"A fine welcome for your husband," remarked Colin ironically.

"Well, what about you?" The frightening thing was that she was not angry, just cold and sullen. "You arrived here two days ago. All New York told me about it! What snickers last night when mother and I went out to dinner! Asking if I had seen my husband yet!"

"If you had remained in our home, you would have seen me," said Colin. "However, go on out to your tea. I came to see the boy. Gerald, I believe is his name?"

She hesitated, then nodded. "Yes, go ahead. The nurse will show him to you. But don't disturb his nap." To his amazement she left the room with that admonishment, and he heard her say, "Colin is here, Mother. You will wish to greet him. The carriage is ready, however. Do be quick."

Colin went into the hallway, and under the impassive stare of the butler he greeted his mother-in-law. She was, as he would expect, frosty. He went on upstairs, then, hearing the carriage roll away.

He found the nursery up on the third floor. It was cool in that part of the house, and the wind got under the cracks in the door. Small Gerald lay kicking in his basket. The nurse got up from her rocking chair in a start when the bearded man came in.

"What are you doing here, sir?" she asked with alarm.

"I am the baby's father," said Colin simply.

A footman had followed him in. "Yes, Miss Nancy, he is the lady's husband," he confirmed and stood waiting, hands behind his back, respectfully, while Colin looked down at the boy.

The eyes opened. Blue green like those of his mother, they stared up at him without curiosity. The baby yawned. Colin wondered if it was an omen—Odette was bored by her husband, and the baby appeared to be bored by his father.

He remained only for a little while. He picked up the baby and held him, rocking him in spite of the nurse's protests. "He is not accustomed to this attention, sir. We never rock him except when he needs to give up his air!" she cried.

"Too bad," responded Colin. As he went on rocking him,

the baby relaxed in his arms and drifted off to sleep, his little pink mouth burbling little milky bubbles. Five months old, and already full of composure, noted Colin with a grimace.

After he returned the small form to the crib, Colin went down the grand stairway to the main floor. He remained in the drawing room until his father-in-law returned from his office. The ladies themselves came back about half an hour later. Mr. Raoult was visibly embarrassed about the situation. The ladies, as usual, were chilly.

Colin spoke to Odette after managing to get her alone in the drawing room. "When do you plan to return to my home, Odette?" he asked.

"When you have a home for us alone," she said calmly. "You may build one this winter. I think I should prefer something quite large, for entertaining."

"And until then?"

"I shall remain with my mother. After all, I have given you a son, an heir," she pointed out, visibly content. "We shall not need to—ah—sleep in the same bed—any longer."

"Is that your view of marriage, Odette?" Colin asked quietly. "For you to live in one house and me in another? Not to live together, not to sleep together?"

She looked surprised. "Why—my parents do not sleep together. It is not necessary any longer," she said. "One sleeps better alone. It is more healthy."

"That is a peculiar view of matrimony," said Colin. He leaned back in the large chair. She was attractive, and especially cool and pretty in the violet gown. She had changed on returning home. He thought the gown was new. A gift from her parents?

Saying nothing, she studied her long, elegant fingers. She wore bright rings on her hands, and only one was from him.

"You make me wonder," he finally said. "Have you, in my absence, taken a lover?"

She started violently and gave him an intensely shocked look. "Taken a—a lover!" she gasped. "Good heavens! I should never be so—so vulgar! It is very indecent even to speak of such a matter!"

"Then why do you wish to live apart from me, if not to receive your lovers?"

"Really, Colin! You are very suspicious and speak in such a dreadful manner! I shall call my mother if you persist in this."

Colin thumped his fist on the table beside him. She flinched and shuddered. "You are my wife!" he said. "You will come home with me now! The rest of your goods may be moved in time. But for tonight, you come home. Don't you realize all New York is gossiping about us?" He thought that shot might go home.

She tightened her mouth to a thin stubborn line. "New York gossiped when you left me to go West for a year, just after our marriage! I am accustomed to it. They understand I am the injured party. You refused to remain with me."

Realizing that it would be useless to continue the discussion, Colin departed. She wanted a big mansion, did she? Well, he was not prepared to build one, nor to waste money on her. She was evidently content to remain a pampered doll in her father's house.

They quarreled several times, she in a cool manner which exasperated him. And the fact that all New York society was talking about them, and that he was laughed about, displeased him. He cared little for her, but she was a lovely woman who still attracted him physically, and he was concerned as well for the feelings of his mother, who had to deal with society.

His wife remained in her father's home. Colin deliberately packed up some of his clothing and moved into the suite there with her. Odette was angry, though she still expressed her anger coldly.

"There is no need for this," she said, alarmed upon discovering him in her bedroom. "I shall return to you when you have built me a suitable house. I shall not go back to your father's house, with that dreadful Indian child running about."

"He is my first-born son," said Colin, knowing how she despised the fact. "You will learn to accept him. He needs a mother."

Odette shuddered delicately. "That Indian bastard? He needs a wigwam and bow and arrow! Why don't you send him back to his tribe? That is, if you know who they are!"

Colin eyed her gravely. In his view he and Morning Star had been married by the chief. Their union was not legal in American courts. But to him she was his first wife, and Wolf was his beloved legitimate son, and not a bastard child.

"Some years ago, when I went West for an indefinite time," said Colin finally, "I made out a will and left everything to my legal son, Wolf. He is mine in the eyes of the courts. I have arranged it all. And I never changed my will."

Odette went quite pale and sat down heavily on a chair.

"You did—what? But you must change it. I am your wife! Gerald is your son and heir!"

"He will have to prove himself," said Colin. "And so will you, my dear wife. If you go gadding about New York, continue to live apart from me, and receive your men friends as well as women, then I shall have no choice but to divorce you. What good is a wife to me, if she does not provide me comfort, warmth in bed, and the satisfaction of my masculine desires?"

"You—you are crude, vicious, and have no regard for me!" complained Odette, a flush coming to her cheeks. "I have submitted to you, I have done my duty to you, and provided a son and heir—much more suitable than your bastard Indian child—and you can say that to me!"

Colin lost his temper. He flung her on the bed and made love to her savagely. He tore her dress off and got some pleasure from making her lose her calm complacency. She cried out against him, fought him, and, to his amazement, he found satisfaction in having sexual relations with her while she fought. This sort of thing had never happened with Morning Star, who had always welcomed his caresses. Yet it was better than having Odette lie there, enduring his ardor with closed eyes.

He lay on her heavily, having stripped her of all her garments. She had a beautiful body, he thought, if all it did encase was a frigid heart. He stroked his hands over the small high breasts, as small as when he had married her. She did not breast-feed the baby. She had refused to do so, saying that it would not be healthy for her. She had hired a wet nurse.

Reflecting on that, he took a small pink nipple in his lips. Odette tried to push him off. "Stop that! It is dreadful!" she told him. "What are you doing? Colin—this is horrible—what do you think I am, a woman of the streets?"

"Oh, never that, my dear. They have some warmth," he said, mocking her until she lost some of her composure. She found it difficult to be calm, under his assault. She struggled against him, striking her small fist against his chest.

He rolled over on her, delighting in finally finding some emotion in her. Maybe there was hope for her yet. He kissed her mouth, until she gasped, then he thrust his tongue inside the lips. He kissed her deeply, until she lay quiet, breathless.

His free hand went over and over her, caressing the small high breasts, small neat wiast, and the long thighs, then moving up to her soft silky thatch of hair. He pulled at it, teasingly, and caressed her with his fingers. She cringed from him, embarrassed, rebuking him in agonized tone. "Colin, you are shocking me—Colin, no decent man does this—pray, do not!"

He did succeed in getting some physical response from her. He felt the gush of warmth from her, and thrust into her, finding her soft and wet for him. He enjoyed her that night, thrusting back and forth in her, kissing her breasts, taking her passionately. And he slept in her arms, wakening to find she had moved herself the accustomed one foot away from him.

Colin moved over to her, wakened her against her protests, and made love to her once more. Odette was upset. "I shall not get my proper sleep, Colin. I pray you, remove to the other room."

"Like hell," was all he said.

He insisted on making love to her other nights, usually against her wishes. If he could make her angry, he found she showed some semblance of passion, enough for them to unite passionately, which gave him some pleasure. But Odette hated it, and she let him know it.

"I have given you one child, that is enough! I do not wish to ruin my body with more. Only peasants have more than one or two children."

"Are you calling my mother a peasant?" Colin asked, lounging in the armchair in his wife's bedroom. They had returned late from a concert and dinner with some friends of Odette. The conversation, in fact the entire evening, had bored him intensely.

The thin mouth compressed in displeasure. "Of course not! I never insult your mother. However she did work in a shop, did she not?"

Colin surveyed her and saw through this time to the petty little soul she possessed. How could he have brought himself to marry such a little bit of tinsel? She had no warmth, no heart. Raised by a cold-blooded and foolishly prim mother, she seemed to have ice water in her veins in place of blood. Why, she was not shy! She was merely proud of her "virtue," of shrinking from any real emotion.

"You don't care for sex, do you, Odette?" he asked. "You've never gotten used to it, you don't enjoy it at all. Don't you realize that it is basic to our natures? How do you think human beings can create more human beings, so the world will continue?"

"I wanted a dog once," said Odette, gazing down. "My mother told me—what they did. It was so cheap, so dirty, I have never been able to like animals. I cannot even pet a cat belonging to a friend of mine. I think of how they go into alleys—you know."

Vague as her remarks were, this exchange was the closest to an intimate conversation they had ever had. Colin said gently, "Human beings are not animals, my dear. And even so, to create new life is not dirty, it is not horrible."

"Yes, it is," countered Odette. "I feel dirty after you—you know—are in bed with me," she said primly. She shook her blond curls and looked like a beautiful porcelain doll, sitting there on the vanity bench with the brush in her hand, the white chiffon negligee falling about her slim body. "I feel as though I must take a bath! And soap well. It is such a filthy sticky thing—you know."

Colin was appalled. She did not enjoy his lovemaking. She thought only of taking a bath! Would she never get over this emotion? Would she ever be able to live a normal life, to be a warm-hearted woman?

He tried making love to her that night but kept remembering she would want to take a thorough bath afterward. She remained stiff and unyielding, and after a time he got up and left her.

He never slept with her again. He returned to his father's house and absorbed himself in work. When he wanted a woman, he went to a certain house where the madam was shrewd and kept her girls clean. He even had a special girl there, one who was bawdy and kind, and made him laugh.

Christmas came, and he sent some presents over for Odette and his son Gerald. He did not even bother to call. Once he saw Odette during the New Year, at an opera, and bowed to her. She bowed back. New York watched them, tittering behind their hands, and gossiped about them. Their speculations no longer troubled Colin, and he thought Odette was too relieved of his presence to mind.

He began to consider a divorce. If he wanted to marry again, and live with a warm-hearted woman, he might as well get one and be done with it. Odette would never be the woman he wanted.

He made an appointment with her father and went to see him at his office over the department store. Mr. Raoult was a quiet, diffident man, and he stood to receive Colin.

281

In the office Colin said abruptly, "I came to see you because things are at a difficult point with me and Odette."

"I know," sighed Mr. Raoult, shaking his graying head. "She has been very upset—"

Colin doubted that. Nothing upset Odette except noise—and frogs in her bed. He interrupted his father-in-law.

"I have decided to ask for a divorce. Odette is not a woman for marriage. I disturb her, she prefers her teas—what have I said?" he finished abruptly as Mr. Raoult gulped and gazed at him in shock. "Divorce is not common, yet it seems the only solution."

"I thought so also—yet—" He bit his lips, his hands were still on the desk. "Colin, my lad, has she not told you?"

"Told me what?"

"She is to have another child of yours. She is angry, weeping, saying she does not want another child. Childbirth was very anguishing for her. So much blood, you know—"

"Oh, my God," said Colin. "Another child? And she hates the very idea."

He put his head in his hands, propping his elbows on the desk. Another Gerald, so unusually quiet a baby, so docile, so—so cold. And Odette—whining, and pitying herself.

"Yes, I fear so. Nevertheless it is done."

"When did she tell you?"

"Her mother informed me just after Christmas."

"And the child—?"

"Due about July."

Colin was silent, weary to the heart. He could not divorce her now. She would need support. And the child was his, no doubt of that. She hated sex so much, she would never in the world take a lover.

"Well, we must remain together for a time," he said somberly.

Mr. Raoult looked relieved. "Yes, I think so, my lad. I will inform her mother, and she will inform Odette. I think after the child comes, you might apply for a divorce, if you wish to. However, two children—with no father—"

"Yes. I see. I see." He had some responsibility to them. Poor children, growing up with a cold mother and an absent father. He would have to take some care of them, but he could not endure living with Odette.

Two days later, Colin paid a call on Odette, after sending a polite note to be sure she would be home that afternoon. He

282

found her sitting on the couch, resigned, her mouth bitter.

"I understand you are to have my child in July." He told her abruptly, weary of skimming around the subject. "I came to discuss some settlement with you."

"Settlement?"

"Yes. I do not wish to live with you any more than you desire my company. I shall contribute to the upkeep of you and the children here, if your family does not object. I should like to see the children from time to time and make sure they know who their father is," he added dryly.

She looked happier already. "Of course, Colin," she said graciously. "And you will settle sums on each of them. Gerald is your heir, after all."

He let that remark pass, as they had quarreled enough over Wolf. "I will make sure they are both well dowered. I think an amiable separate existence is best, do you not?"

"Of course I think so, Colin. I am glad you are so sensible about it. People will talk, but Mama explains so well about my delicate nerves, your exciting life and many travels."

"Is that how she explains it?" he asked. "Well, well, I expect so. You will notify me if you need anything. And I should like to be near when the child is due. In July?"

She agreed, flushing at the mention of the event. She did take leave of him graciously. "You must come and see Gerald when you wish. I will leave instructions with his nurse to admit you. Except when he is sleeping or colicky, naturally."

"Thank you. May I see him now?"

He had thought she might go upstairs with him. She merely nodded, rang for a footman, and then held out her hand. "Thank you, Colin, you are most understanding and gracious. I shall probably not see you—before July. I am not well and will remain quietly these months." She looked quite satisfied with that prospect.

"I wish you good health," he said and went upstairs.

Gerald was sitting up. He looked pale and wan, but Colin thought that perhaps it was his natural coloring. The nurse said she took him out in good weather. "However it has not been nice outside since October," she added.

"Fresh air would be good for him," commented Colin.

She sniffed audibly. "Not this cold bitter air!"

Poor mite, thought Colin on leaving. He strode down the street, having dismissed his carriage. He was disturbed about the arrangement. Growing up in that household could not be good for his children. They would be stifled, forced into the same prim mold as Odette. But what could he do? Take them away from her? It might come to that. He would wait to see what kind of natures they had.

The baby was born in July, a small mite with thin blond hair and wide blue eyes. A real beauty, the girl had Odette's heart-shaped face and little dimpled chin. Odette demurely consulted with Colin about her name, and they decided on Juliette for Odette's great-aunt who was a spinster and had money to leave. Since the name was pretty, he did not object.

He had called on Odette properly once a month, to make sure she was well and that all was going fine. After consulting with Mr. Raoult about financial arrangements, he contributed a monthly sum to the upkeep of his home, though Mr. Raoult was a little distressed about this. "After all, she is my daughter," he said.

"And she is my wife," interjected Colin. "No matter. I wish to be informed if anything is wrong with the children, and you may depend on my aid in any matters."

Odette recovered her health following the childbirth, and went out again beginning in September. She enjoyed her concerts, her teas, and began little musicals on Sundays beginning in October. They became popular with the smart set, and Odette glowed. Colin, entering the house through the side door on Sunday afternoons, would hear the tinkle of the pianoforte, the hum of the harp and scrape of the fiddle, and sigh for the days of Minna and their family musicals. But he had no desire to join Odette's parties. He would slip upstairs to see the children, then quietly depart.

Gerald had no desire to be picked up by this big strange bearded man, and would back off, glaring with gray-green eyes like Odette's. Little Juliette was different. She would coo at him and hold out her arms, and cry when he put her down. The nurse thought he spoiled her when he held her and rocked her, and sang French voyageur songs to her.

The little girl would laugh as he sang, and kick her heels, and wave her small arms wildly. He enjoyed her, and came more often, slipping in the side door and stealing up to her room. He longed for her at times, and wished he could take her home with him. Odette would not endure it. She was possessive. She had not wanted the child, but she had gone through the agonies of childbirth, and Juliette was "hers," not his.

Not that she spent much time with the children. "Half an hour in the mornings," she said, when Colin once asked her casually. "Every morning without fail. I want to oversee their training and make sure they are always kept clean. That is important to their health." And with that remark she lifted a fine China cup to her lips and regarded the man she had wed with her icy eyes.

PART III
1820–1830

Chapter 24

Minna folded the note thoughtfully. She had been wild with excitement when she first received it. She had thought to rush off to the hotel at once.

But Etienne—she bit her lips. He had been so coldly furious after he had returned home from the wars. He hated the Americans then, the depth of his emotion revealed in his voice as he told of his comrades who had died. Etienne had railed against the boldness, the arrogance of the Americans, who dared to come north for their furs, invading his country!

When Minna had suggested traveling to New York City to heal the breach between herself and her family, Etienne had been furious. "What? Do you still think of them as your family? They discarded you long ago! They think we are backwoodsmen! Peasants! I wonder at you, Minna. Are you not satisfied with us, that you must run to your parents? You think of them as your mentors, and you even put their faith above ours!"

Minna's refusal to take instruction and join the Roman Catholic church had been a sore point all the years of her marriage. Etienne said the children were brought up as heathens, and he tried to force them to go to instruction. In the early years it had not been difficult for Minna to evade his wishes. Etienne was gone nine months of the year.

Then—the accident. Minna sighed, her chin propped in her hands, as she gazed absently from the upstairs study window where she had been going over her accounts. Etienne was at his father's store. He went there every day now, and worked faithfully, for he felt he must "earn his keep," as he said with resignation.

Three years before, Etienne had been on one of his fur trade journeys. He had returned, literally carried by his voyageurs. There had been a mishap in carrying one of the canoes over rough terrain. A man fell to his death from an icy cliff, Etienne had tried to grab hold of him, only to fall himself. The others found him at the foot of the cliff, mercifully unconscious, both legs broken.

They had at least been able to set the legs, which healed crookedly on the slow, painful trip home. The doctors could do nothing. Etienne had lain in pain on a hard-mattressed bed for six months. Then he had declared, "This does no good. I shall be up and about. Get me two canes, Minna."

Minna had never admired her husband so much as during those months when he forced himself to walk again, and the years since, when he set his teeth and made himself go out daily to work. She had loved him even in the years when they fought, made up, quarreled again, parted in anger, met in love. But now, when he was in constant pain, yet made himself work for their living, she finally admired and respected him. Etienne was a complete man at last, loving and compassionate, strong even in his weakness, and perhaps because of it.

Etienne never complained. He sometimes sent Stephen on errands, which the boy did promptly and intelligently. No other concession was made to the crippled legs. Etienne knew the difficulties the family company faced. His father, now growing old, had never been shrewd. He had lost many of his voyageurs to other companies, and now the Hudson's Bay Company was trying to gather all the fur companies into their fold. They would crush him, force him out, or buy him out; it was all one to them. Though they were gentlemen all, trade was trade.

Blaise and Etienne were fighting for the company's life.

The struggle had cost them dearly. Blaise had had to dismiss half of his clerks, while Yolanda had quietly cut her household costs. She gave few dinners and did not replace servants who died, except for one much-needed coachman. And Minna had insisted on her finally taking pay for her work in the younger woman's warehouse and store. Yolanda reaped the benefits of her wisdom in not becoming a legal partner in Minna's business. If she had, it could be taken by a bank for Blaise's debts.

For the same reason Etienne and Blaise had agreed that he should not be a partner in his father's firm. When Blaise died, and Etienne inherited the firm, only then Minna would be responsible for Etienne's debts, and he of hers. That they would face later. But the company was in a poor way, and Etienne worried.

Minna heard the carriage returning at six o'clock and closed her books. She went downstairs to greet her husband and with a pang watched him come in heavily on the two canes. Stephen, a sturdy thirteen-year-old boy, stood watchfully at his side, moving as he moved, halting when he halted. What a mature lad he was, thought Minna. Always watchful of the other younger children, serious minded, and afraid of nothing, he had seemed to grow up in months during his father's illness.

The two came in, smiled identical smiles as they saw her waiting there. "Well, Minna, my dear, more beautiful than ever," teased Etienne, his blue eyes brightening.

Ever since a wistful beau of Minna's had addressed her so, on entering the house, Etienne, at first jealous, then laughing, had said that to her on occasion.

She gave him a kiss on his lean cheek and put her arm about Stephen as he gave her a quick hug. "My dears, what a beautiful day it is. Did you enjoy the carriage ride? Is the wharf all activity today?"

Etienne grimaced. "Aye, wish I could be off with them in a big canoe! Many came in with fine pelts, and we bought at a good price. The harvest is splendid this year."

"Oh, Mother," said Stephen, his intense blue eyes glowing, his tanned face bright, "I can scarcely wait until I may go off on a journey! Jacques came in today, with such fine animals! He has gone to the far north, and seen ice cakes floating on blue cold waters, and a white polar bear sitting on one! And the seals, and the sea otters! I may go when I am eighteen!"

Adventure sang in his veins, as it had in Minna's, and in Etienne's. How could she deny him? She had known the same bright driving urge to go to the unknown and learn from it, to see the brilliant blue skies, the white snows, the silence and beauty of the outdoors where no white man had been. The jagged line of the mountains, the playful activities of the otters as they made slides for themsleves beside the stream on a snowbank were like nothing to be seen in a civilized land. She sighed, and smiled, and patted his arm.

"I hope only to keep you until that time. What would we do without you, my dear Stephen?"

At dinner she kept the conversation pleasant but told Etienne quietly that she would talk with him. After dinner they went to the drawing room. The younger children were in bed, and Stephen wandered in the garden, near enough to be called and curious at the privacy of Minna's conversation.

"Well, my dearest." Etienne lowered himself slowly into the armchair. His face showed his pain for a moment, then he schooled it to reflect calm as he settled into the chair. "What has made you so bright with excitement?"

He knew her so well now, she thought and patted his thin hand. Pain kept him awake nights, and he was as thin as a rail in spite of her efforts to tempt his appetite.

"I have had a message from the warehouse," she said. "A clerk brought it. Etienne, Father is in town. He has asked to see us. They are at a hotel—"

"Your father! After all these years!"

"Yes. Colin and his son are with him. Etienne, must we remain strangers?" she asked wistfully. "I have not been able to take time to go to New York." She avoided his reproachful look and went on rapidly. "Now they are here, in Montreal, and we could go over for a visit. Perhaps they would come to our home. I long to show them how well we live. In a mansion, as fine as theirs," she exaggerated.

Etienne had a thin frown line between his reddish-brown brows. He gazed at the fire. "It had been so many years," he said in a low tone.

"Yes, much has happened since the time you persuaded me to elope with you, my impetuous one," she teased, hoping to win him with humor.

His mouth twisted in a reluctant wry smile. "Yes, many years, my darling. Happy ones?"

She jumped up and bent to kiss his cheek. "Such happy ones, my darling. What times we have had! And will continue to have with our beautiful family. I wrote them about our babies, and how they grow, but can you imagine it when Father sees Therese, and baby Michel? And he will admire Stephen as we do, such a grand lad! And my dearest Kendall, how sweet is his nature, and dear Henri, already trying to play the piano and the flute."

"Trying? He does play it, my darling Minna! He will be a magnificent musician. No one has such a talent as he does!"

"Yes, a startling, amazing talent," agreed Minna, a little troubled for her dreamy difficult Henri. He would neglect everything, even his meals, his schooling, his play outdoors, to spend hours at the piano, not just practicing, but composing music. How could they train him, how could they manage his genius? One day soon they must come to some decision about a teacher suited to his fine talents.

Etienne was silent for a time, then he patted her hand. "Well, well, they are here in Montreal, and we shall visit them. No sense in holding grudges against the Americans! They will trample over us all, no matter what we do."

"Now, Etienne." she chided, patting his arm. "You will not bring up politics with my father? I think he longs only to see us again, and to—to know my children."

Minna happily sent off a note that night to her father, saying they wished to call upon him the following afternoon. The next morning, a clerk came over very early, with the message, "We await you eagerly, my dearest Minna. You will bring the children?"

She laughed ruefully. "All five of them!" she said to Etienne. "We shall be so deafened by their chatter, we will not be able to speak!"

She flew about, deciding first on one gown and then another. The children clamored to go with her. "But I shall certainly go, for I am the eldest," said Stephen firmly. "I should meet my grandfather on my mother's side."

Minna finally decided to take only Stephen, but to invite her father to come to her home. She hoped he would agree, so he might meet the whole family. She sent off a note to Yolanda, to ask her to come to dinner the following night with Blaise, and had a prompt answer by the footman. They would be delighted to come. Minna felt a deep sense of relief, having feared that her beloved mother-in-law would hold a grudge against Ludwig because of his cruel remarks, uttered years earlier, when she and Etienne first wished to wed.

She wore her blue silk gown, with a little cape of mink over it, as the afternoon was sufficiently cool to permit that vanity. She wanted to show her father, subtly, that Etienne provided well for her. Though much of their money came from the warehouse and shop that she owned and ran, she would downplay that for Etienne's pride.

When they came into the hallway of the hotel rooms, she saw her father standing in the doorway, waiting. He was so much older in appearance that it shocked her. He was grayed, his face lined, though he was as bronzed and sturdy as ever.

He held out his arms in silence. Minna flew into them, and he held her close, his face in her thick blond hair.

"Oh, my father," she said, choking. "Father." His arms were tightly about her, and he held her close. She remembered the warmth and security of those arms from her childhood. "Father, Father, it is so good—so good to see you."

He drew her into the room. A tall bearded blond man stood to greet them, a deep red scar down his cheek. She gazed at him blankly, until he smiled, a slow world-weary smile, yet one filled with affection.

"Colin?" she whispered, shocked. Her gown rustled as she moved quickly across the thick rug to him. He held out his arms, and she moved into them. "Oh, my dearest, dearest, best brother." Her eyes filled with tears as she pressed her face to his. He was so changed from the merry, bright-eyed, laughing boy he had once been.

"Minna, let me see you." He held her off, gazed at her as she blinked, sparkling-eyed, a tear rolling down her cheek. "You are more beautiful than you ever were," he declared. "You have grown into a very lovely woman, my dearest Minna. I cannot believe you have five children, as you claim. You should be worn and weary."

His voice had a deep drawl, and his tone was cynical yet calmly affectionate. "My dear Colin, I have the best husband in the world, and my children are an aid and comfort, rather than any burden," she declared in a spirited tone. "Come, meet my Etienne again after all these years."

She drew him to where Etienne stood aloof, leaning on his two canes. Their hands met, awkwardly. Stephen helped his father into a deep armchair, frowning at their stares. They soon averted their looks. Ludwig came to shake hands with Etienne and then with Stephen.

"So, this is your eldest lad! He looks the image of Etienne," said Ludwig, comparing them. "The same color hair, the same eyes—and does he long for adventure also?"

"I fear so!" Minna laughed. "He cannot wait to go West with the voyageurs. But he must remain here until he is eighteen. Meantime he helps his father in the warehouse and learns his lessons quickly in order to go off and practice shooting. He has his own rifle. He received it for his twelfth birthday," she added proudly, anxiously glancing to see if Stephen would be on his best behavior.

Then she noted the boy standing in the corner, glowering at them, a dark, Indian-looking lad. She held out her hand to him. "You must be Colin's son," she said and smiled, inviting him to her. "Come, kiss me, Wolf. You are the same age as my Stephen, are you not?"

"Come, shake hands, Wolf," Colin commanded as the boy did not stir from his corner. Reluctantly he then came forward, touched the tips of her fingers, and retreated. "She is your Aunt Minna," said Colin.

"Aunt Minna," muttered the boy.

Stephen came forward to be introduced. He had very polite manners, almost French, she thought, for Yolanda had taught him well the manners that would please the ladies. He bowed formally, then shook the hand of Ludwig first, and then Colin. The two boys exchanged glances. Stephen nodded to him as Wolf glowered.

"Well," said Minna brightly, seating herself on the couch. "Colin, do come and sit by me. Tell me the news. Is Mama well?"

Her voice went up a pitch in her excitement and wistful need to be one of the family again.

"She is not well," said Colin. "She is much troubled by pain in her arms and legs. She sent affectionate messages, and a letter for you, and wishes that you will come to New York to see her soon. She longs to see your children also, but a trip here would be her death, I fear."

Minna glanced at Etienne. He nodded to her gently. She sank back, reassured. "I hope to come soon, Colin. I should not have waited so long. But my duties held me, and my love here. How I long to see Mama again. And what about William and Otto? They are well? And Otto's wife—what is she like? Eleanor is her name?"

They chatted. Minna went on and on, bubbling happily as she talked with her father and Colin. It had been so many years—fifteen years—since she had spoken with them. There was so much to say, so much to tell them, to hear from them. She asked after friends, scarcely waiting to hear their replies before telling them something of her life.

Ludwig shook his head affectionately over her warehouse. He said to Etienne, "And what did you think of that, my lad?"

Etienne grimaced. "I growled and fussed at her, but she paid no attention. Then I left her alone, thinking she would make a failure of it. Instead she and her project are an immense success! So what can I say?"

They all laughed, Ludwig in some relief, his brow clearing. "Aye, I taught my daughter well, *ja, ja*, she knows how to work, that girl. Her mother was the same, a smart woman, *ja, ja*. My Minna inherited some of my business ability, and that of her mother. You'll never find her sitting at home and receiving the ladies at tea, I fear."

"My mother finds the same of Minna," said Etienne. "So, instead, she joined Minna in the venture. They are indeed a marvel, Father Ludwig," he said, rather naturally. "My mother enjoys the shop, and she loves to handle the Oriental vases, the ivory and jade. Indeed she wept when she sold one pale blue vase, she had wanted it so much herself. I said, 'Why didn't you tell me, I would have given it to you.' She snapped at me, 'What, and lose the sale?' How can I please my mother and my wife?"

Ludwig laughed loudly at that, and Colin gave his wry smile. Ludwig slapped his knee, and Wolf jumped at the sound.

"Well, well, we must meet Blaise and Mrs. MacCameron again. How shall we meet? Shall you come to the hotel for dinner?"

Minna told him of the invitation for the next evening. "I wish you would come early, and let us have a good long visit first."

"That I will! I'll come as early as you please. I'll come all the day! I long to hold your children in my arms," he said so simply and wistfully that Minna jumped up to go to him and kiss his forehead.

"Oh, Papa, you shall. Come for breakfast, you and Colin and Wolf. We shall talk all the day, and you shall see my beautiful children. And Henri shall play for you."

The next day was pure joy for Minna. She was up early and ready for her guests when they came. Etienne remained home from work, since he also wanted to talk and listen. Minna had sent a message to Yolanda, and she and Blaise came early in the afternoon. The housekeeper took care of the meals, and the nurse and governess cared for the children, though much of the time they were with the adults.

Minna's children were excited at the prospect of meeting their American relatives. Eleven-year-old Kendall came first, to bow and greet them. He was a sweet-tempered boy, full of gaiety, with no meanness in him. He submitted to a big hug from his newly discovered grandfather and beamed up at him shyly.

Eight-year-old Henri was more shy. He stood stiffly, bowed, and looked hunted when he was stared at.

"Later he shall play for you," said Minna firmly. Henri gasped and retreated behind the curtains, jumping when he found Wolf there.

Wolf stared at him glumly. This was the most miserable visit of his life. He had begged to go with his father, thinking he would shoot, hunt, trap. Instead he was in stuffy houses, meeting more relatives! How horribly grim and boring.

Stephen came in, holding small Therese by the hand. The only girl should have been spoiled with all her attention, but she was so lovely and gentle of nature, with reddish-gold hair and wide blue eyes. Now five, she was conscious of her new blue dress and white sash, and black sandals with straps. She curtsied prettily, then came forward and submitted to the hug from her grandfather.

"What a charming girl! Minna, she is just like you, except for the touch of red in her curls. Lovely girl, will you sit on my lap?" She sat, obediently, her dimples coming out at his teasing praise.

Kendall brought in little Michel, now two and a half. He could just walk well, and he was cheerful and straight of back, giggling self-consciously when his head was patted. He stared at all the visitors and went to hang on his mother's knee, his finger in his mouth, studying them soberly.

And how they talked, those adults! There was so much to say, words tumbling over each other. They talked of the family, and they talked as well about the fur trade.

"You have joined in a larger company, Etienne and Blaise?" asked Ludwig.

A shadow came over their faces. "Yes, it was necessary for the life of our company," said Etienne. "Hudson's Bay Company wanted to gather all the companies together. We are banded together to remain alive, in a loose confederation. We make policy, set prices, consult each other. But always the Hudson's Bay Company offers higher and higher prices to buy us out. They say we may retain our posts, but they will have their name on it. Ha! How much authority will that be? In two years we would be swallowed up."

Presently Minna showed her father and Colin over the house. She was proud of it, this house she had built near her mother-in-law's home. She had planned it and supervised the builders while Etienne was off in the West.

There were three floors and a basement where the cool kept the foods in good condition during the summer and winter. On the ground floor were the drawing room, a formal parlor, and a beautiful little back parlor which Minna used for a study. She kept her desk there, and Etienne kept his also, and they often worked there of an evening. With the large dining room, there was also a smaller family dining room, and the two could be combined for a large group of fifty or sixty guests. The kitchen in the back was large and well arranged, with a pantry and stairs leading to the basement.

They had their own well, with spring water. And the garden was full of summer flowers, bright roses, petunias, phlox fragrant in rose and blue and mauve, and borders of fragrant green hedges.

On the second floor were the immense bedrooms, as well as another small study for Minna. She disliked small rooms which gave no air. The windows were large, and she often kept them open all the day. She and Etienne had two rooms since his injury, for he did not sleep well, and he hated to disturb her. She was close enough to hear him should he be in pain in the night, however, and she often went to him and put hot compresses on his legs.

The children's rooms were comfortable, with bare floors, good-sized beds, and space for their toys and games. Stephen and Kendall shared a room, and Henri had one of his own. Therese had a feminine room of ruffles and bows, with a shelf lined with dolls. Michel would graduate soon from the nursery to share Henri's room, if Henri approved.

The top floor held the nursery, with the nurse's room next to that. The governess had a room to herself. Two maids shared a room, and the cook had one to herself, and also the house-keeper.

The other servants had rooms over the stables, except for several footmen who came from town each day. They kept two carriages and a barouche, with coachman, and stable hands, to care for the five horses.

"This is very comfortable and pretty," Ludwig approved. His keen gaze and nose would report to Agatha that all was clean and well kept, informing her that her daughter, like herself, was an excellent housekeeper. "I like the colors, so bright and gay," he remarked.

She had made much use of crimson, blue, and yellow, for she was fond of bright colors. She beamed at his praise. Colin was strolling about, hands behind his back, his face revealing no expression.

Presently Minna tucked her hand in his arm and said, "Do let me show you the garden, Colin."

Ludwig returned to the drawing room, tactfully, while the brother and sister strolled together. Minna said gently, "Colin, you have changed much. Dare I ask you—Mama said you and your wife live apart—" She hesitated to finish.

Colin shrugged. "All the world knows we live apart," he said dryly.

"You are—not happy then? I am so sorry," she said simply, giving his arm a squeeze. "Etienne and I have made a happy

298

marriage of it, in spite of some quarreling and differences. We both have tempers, yet we always made up. Could you not—"

"No, my dear," he said quietly. "There is no quarrel to make up. You see, my wife has a strong distaste for anything so gross and vulgar as married life. She prefers to live with her parents and pretend she is still a child, playing with a tea set. I would get a divorce, but I think that out of spite she would deny me access to the children."

Minna caught her breath. It was worse than she had thought. And Colin was so grave, so unlike his old happy teasing self. Life had knocked the gaiety and joy out of him. She hated that. It was as though something vital in him had died.

"No more of that," said Colin. "Do come to New York, Minna. Mother so longs to see you. She almost came with us, but the doctor forbade it. Could you not come, and make up the quarrel? She no longer cares about the religion. She only longs to see you before she dies."

"Oh, Colin, is she—surely she is not—"

"We never know how long we have," he said. "No, she is not dying. But it has been fifteen years. She cannot very well last another fifteen."

Minna was silent for a time, strolling with her dear brother along the garden paths. She remembered the old days, how she and Colin and sometimes Otto had giggled and conspired to get their way with their father. The days in the warehouse, the smell of furs and spices in her nostrils. Sitting on a high stool, her feet unable to reach the wooden bars, she dangled her toes while she filled in careful entries. Running with Colin along the waterfront in an unladylike manner, she would race with him to be first to reach a ship coming in. Digging into the barrels and boxes and trunks, she sniffed with pleasure at the exotic smells, and had cooed over the silks slipping through her fingers. She remembered smoothing the jade figures, and marveling at the huge porcelain jars and vases.

For birthdays there were always huge cakes and some expensive ice cream packed in ice. After Christmas the house smelled for weeks of mincemeat and cloves and nutmeg and cinnamon. The pine tree, brought in from the nearest forests, was decorated by Minna and her mother in the way it was done in Germany, with ginger-cake figures, tiny porcelain angels, cranberries strung on a chain, and candles to be lit the eve of Christmas. She had missed that tree and had a small one each year for her own family. The Roman Catholics had other customs, and she enjoyed them. She felt that Stephen might become Catholic. He went often to the service with his father. Well, she had said when they were grown, they might choose.

"Why don't you come home with us, Minna? You and the children," said Colin at last, breaking into her thoughts.

"Come—home?" she asked, startled.

"Yes, for a long visit with mother, and the boys. I'll bring you back, safe and sound," he added with a half smile. "She would enjoy it so much. Let us not wait longer, Minna. Come back with us."

"Yes, yes, yes," said Minna, lighting up like one of the Christmas trees, joyfully, lights in her eyes. "Oh, yes, Colin, I will! I shall ask Etienne, he will agree, I am sure. He must agree. I long to see Mama again. And Yolanda will care for the shop for me."

"Good," said Colin, and he squeezed her waist, then kissed her cheek.

Wolf had been watching and listening from behind a tree, pretending he was a hunter. He rather thought he might like Aunt Minna. She was jolly and laughing, with a bright face, and when he had come today, she had caught him at the door, and kissed him before he could stop her. She was not cold, aloof, glaring at him behind his father's back. She was blond, but she was not like That One, who had tried to take his father away.

Satisfied that this visit might not be so bad, he ran off into the far garden and eventually wandered off. He was playing that he was an Indian in the forest, sneaking from one tree to the other, sighting for animals.

He was sighting from one tree, peering about it, when he became aware he was not alone. He stiffened and pressed against the tree, listening.

"Ha! I am a mighty hunter," said a small voice. "Bang! Bang! You are dead! I am an Indian of the Cree tribe. You are my brother. Turn your head for I must kill you."

Wolf was stiff, absolutely fascinated. Cautiously he peered around the large tree trunk, into the next garden. There ran a small black-haired girl, with a band around her forehead, a feather stuck rakishly in it. She wore a deerskin dress, small tan moccasins, and red paint streaked on her cheeks.

As she aimed her small bow and arrow, Wolf stepped around the tree. The arrow sped from her hand and hit him on the chest. It made him stagger, and even knocked him over, and he fell on the grass.

The girl gasped, and the bow fell from her hand. She hesitated, then ran to him where he struggled up, embarrassed.

"I killed you!" she gasped, eyes dark and wide and scared. "I—killed you! I'm sorry! I didn't mean—"

"You are a stupid girl!" snapped Wolf, enraged that he had fallen over. He got up, breathing heavily. The arrow had struck him full in the chest, and the force of it had taken his breath for a moment. "I'm not killed. I fell down because I wanted to! You are a silly girl. You're not an Indian. I'm an Indian!"

She stared at him. "I am so an Indian! My mother is Cree. My father is French. I am Eugenia Chantal, and I am an Indian!"

Wolf did gaze at her. He knew no other Indians in New York. No one claimed to be an Indian. It seemed it was something to be ashamed of. That was why he boasted of it, to defy the world. She did have black hair, and very dark brown eyes.

"My mother was Cree," said Wolf.

She said something rapidly. "There, that is the Cree tongue! What did I say?"

"I don't know. Speak slowly."

Something in the sound of the words had been familiar. Beads of sweat came out on Wolf's cheeks. She had sounded—like the sounds his mother had made, some words—

She spoke again, more slowly, glaring at him, a little uncertainly. She said, in Cree, "I am the Morning Wind. I sing to the heavens. I speak to the animals and the birds."

Wolf repeated the words slowly. He added, "My mother is beautiful, I love my mother." He had remembered those words, they came back to him.

Eugenia Chantal smiled at him in approval. She nodded. "There, you are Cree. At least you can talk it," she said in English. "But in school I have to talk English! Not French, and not Cree," she said sorrowfully.

"You go to school? I have to also. I hate it!"

"I don't mind," she said with composure. "I go with Kendall next door. Do you know Kendall? He is nice. He never pulls my braids."

"He is my cousin," said Wolf.

"Oh, is he? You are visiting him then?"

Wolf nodded. It was pleasant, to say he was visiting his cousins.

A woman's voice called, in Cree, from the nearby door. "Child? Heart of my heart? Come home now!"

The words echoed in Wolf's ears. The low melodious happy sounds of those words, spoken just as Morning Star had called to him, aroused memories of years hopelessly past.

"I have to go home now," said Eugenia Chantal. "What is your name?"

"Wolf—Gunther," said Wolf and waved briefly, shyly, as she ran off. She waved, and laughed, and he remembered that sound of laughter as he ran back to the MacCameron house.

Stephen was coming to find him. He stopped and let Wolf come up to him. "We have to wash up for lunch now," he said. "Did you enjoy the garden?"

Wolf nodded, speechless.

Stephen took him in, to his own room, and waited for him while he washed up. Then he took him downstairs, to the smaller dining room set for the children. Wolf was seated beside Stephen and Kendall, and they quietly saw to it that he received the food he wished and plenty of milk.

They talked among themselves. He might join in as he wished. Finally he said, "I like your garden. I like your house. It is a happy house, with music in it."

He had heard the sounds of Henri's playing. The eight-year-old boy stared at him seriously. "Do you like music?" he asked.

Wolf nodded. "Grandfather plays the flute sometimes."

"I can play the flute. I will play for you," announced Henri.

Stephen looked approvingly on his smaller brothers and his sister. "As soon as everyone has enough dessert," he said in grown-up fashion, "we will go up to my room, and Henri can play for us, and I will play my flute also, though I am not so good at it as Henri. Do you play anything, Wolf?"

"I played the flute a few times. And the drums."

"We have drums," said Henri. "We could have an orchestra!"

The children played for several hours in Stephen's room. They had an orchestra and Stephen directed. His cousin bossed them all, thought Wolf, yet he was good about it, not nasty. He even brought in small Michel and sat him on a rug while they played and taught Michel how to clap to the music.

They went downstairs for tea, and Wolf retreated to the corner to have his milk-weakened tea, and cakes, and to listen. He felt happier now. He knew everybody in the room, and they did not stare at him. And wonder of wonders, he had met an Indian girl, and she was friendly and nice to him.

It had been an amazing day for Wolf. He felt that he belonged to this warm, happy, laughing family. Even his father

302

smiled more today and presently Wolf crawled over the rug to Colin. He curled up beside the armchair where his father sat, and absently Colin put his hand on Wolf's head and kept it there. Wolf held his breath, then let it out slowly, basking in the protection of his father's strong gentle hand. He belonged to his father—and to these people.

Chapter 25

The months and years go quickly when one is busy, happy in his work, and matters go pleasantly, thought Colin as he brushed his hair and combed out his beard. There were traces of gray in the gold now. He plucked out one gray hair, but sighed—and grimaced at himself.

It was 1827. He had been very busy these past years. He now went West every summer, since he and Ludwig had decided to set up two more forts with their trading posts. As more settlers came West, the Indians became more alarmed and resentful. It was necessary to build large posts and have them well guarded. The army could not guard them all, and many Indian attacks had wiped out some of the smaller posts.

Yet the fur trade went well. The Indians wanted the blankets, iron kettles and copper pots, the flour and salt, that the traders would give in return for the furs. And few went North to trade with the Hudson's Bay Company men. It was too far. Why should they go north, when they could trade their furs in their own plains or Rocky Mountains?

Colin had cautioned his traders to treat the Indians well. "They will remember that long," he said. "Poor manners, contempt, and cheating will be rewarded with attacks on the post. Treat them fairly, and they will continue to trade with us, in peace."

Wolf had gone with him the past four summers. Wild with delight, he had traveled on horseback the whole time, getting more bronzed and wild looking, his hair as long and straggling as an Indian's. He found New York almost unbearable when he returned, and Colin had permitted him to go up to Montreal to work there for months at a time. He had gone again this autumn.

Minna and her children had come faithfully each summer, about the time Colin returned from the West. They always had a good long visit. Returning, they took Wolf with them, and left Henri. The serious, musically inclined boy was taking lessons from two of New York's best teachers. Colin would then take him back to Montreal and come home with Wolf.

Now Wolf had gone again. He was talking of going out to western Canada with Stephen who had begun to make fur journeys. Stephen was mature, but he was also a MacCameron, wild and adventurous, mischief sparkling in his eyes. Colin had worried about that team, Wolf and Stephen. Agatha had shaken her head.

Colin had said, "I remember when Stephen was young. No matter what he wanted to do, he was careful of the younger children, always responsible where they were concerned. I think Wolf will do well, if he listens to Stephen."

"If he listens—" murmured Agatha.

"He did not like New York, Mother," said Colin as he sat down to breakfast with his parents. How quiet the house was, now that Wolf, Minna, and the others had left. Only the three of them remained now, and he too was old, he thought. Old. "Wolf would never be satisfied to live here. He longs for the West. I think he will try to find his Cree people. He talked to the Indians at our posts, but none of them were Cree. He kept saying, 'They are not my people. I want to find my own people.' I was surprised when he said he could speak Cree."

"I think that is the girl, Eugenia Chantal, in Montreal," said Agatha thoughtfully. "He told me about her and her mother. He talked more about her than of Stephen and the others."

"Oh?" Colin wondered. Wolf had taken no interest in white girls. Perhaps Eugenia would encourage him to think of marriage, though Colin doubted it. He found nothing of domestic inclinations in his wild boy. He could not blame him, for he was restless himself.

Agatha's fading blue eyes twinkled a moment. "You do not set him a good example, Colin," she teased. "Always avoiding parties. Why, we could scarcely get you to attend William's wedding, and Lillian is such a nice girl. I am glad for him. I thought he would never marry. And now, how settled he is, with two girls of his own."

"Lillian Mauriac is from a good family," said Ludwig firmly. They had all been vastly relieved when William finally married, as well as Otto. The boys had gone with such wild women for a time, such fast women.

"Speaking of William and Lillian," said Agatha as she glanced mischievously at Colin. "They are having a literary tea this afternoon. Do go, Colin, it would be good for you to have some amusement. You work too hard."

He grimaced. "I would be amused, all right," he said grimly. "Literary, indeed. William would not know a classic unless it hit him on the nose."

"Lillian sent a message yesterday, asking Ludwig and me to come. But your father absolutely refused. Do go, Colin, and represent the family. I think sometimes we neglect Lillian and Eleanor. They are dear girls, and it is too bad of us to keep refusing their kind invitations. They move in different circles, with their teas and dinners and smart friends. Yet they continue to include us, which is most kind of them."

Colin frowned, but finally that afternoon he dressed up in a formal blue suit and tie, brushed his hair and beard, and sallied forth in his shiny black carriage to the event. He enjoyed the drive. It was a crisp late September day, and New York was looking beautiful with some of the trees just turning crimson and yellow.

William and Lillian had a smart gray stone mansion in the upper part of Fifth Avenue, where the wealthy were moving in increasing numbers. Colin drove his carriage to the large stable area and turned over his horse to the grooms.

To his surprise there was a goodly crowd there. They must expect excellent drinks, he thought cynically as he looked over the group. He knew some of the men well enough to know their wives could not have dragged them to such an event without the promise of good liquor.

Once inside, he made his way quickly to his brother William and shook his hand. William was perspiring in a thick gray suit, but he beamed and thanked Colin for coming.

"Lillian will be pleased. She ain't got you to any event since last Christmas," he whispered loudly.

Lillian came over to them. Thin, a brown wisp of a girl, she wore her hair in curls over her high forehead to disguise its height. She was not beautiful, but she was good-hearted. Her wealth had not spoiled her, and she was, said William, good fun. She smiled up at Colin, a little fearful of him, as most women were, afraid, yet fascinated. He was like Lord Byron, said one of the women, and the phrase was caught up. Such handsome gloom, combined with the scar on his cheek, his silence, his dignity, his crisp wry speech added up to a traditionally romantic hero.

"Dear Colin," she said, squeezing his hands nervously. "So good of you to come. Let me see, who will you know? I must introduce you."

"I think the reading is beginning," he said quickly. "Do not trouble, dear Sister. I shall find a place for myself."

He slid neatly away from them, to stand in a corner and listen. A thin young man was standing near the piano, and a girl seated herself at it with a ruffling of her white skirts and rippled her hands along the keys. The man began to recite to the music, a sort of poem, thought Colin.

Someone next to Colin muttered, "I think I'm going to be sick!"

Colin peered down at the dark brown short hair, the sallow face. "You can't, Jacquetta," he whispered.

"Why not?" The impish intelligent face turned up to his. "That poem, ugh. Listen to the words. Nonsense, sheer nonsense!"

"But all New York would talk," he said in a prim tone.

She chuckled, like a hoarse robin, and disguised the sound in her handkerchief as a cough. Colin took her arm and pushed them both farther toward the doorway.

They listened, politely, to the end of the song-poem, as it was described. Lillian was standing near them, flushed and happy. They could not escape and were forced to remain through a rather long dreary "excerpt from a new novel," read by a self-conscious young lady.

After that refreshments were served. Colin forced his way to the long buffet table, got a plate and two cups of Scotch, and returned to Jacquetta, now seated in the second drawing room. She glanced at the one plate he put in her hands.

"None for you, Colin?"

"I don't want to be poisoned. Look at those black eggs," he said.

"Caviar, dear boy. You must like it, it is all the fashion," she said, her eyes bright with amusement, and she put a bit in her mouth and made a face.

"Speaking of fashion, I like your gown, and that color. Coral, is it?" he asked.

"Thank you. Good guess. Coral silk with decoration of brown silk and matching brown pumps," she told him, and she thrust out her slim narrow feet for his inspection.

"Good-looking ankles, too," he said and laughed as she flushed. "Are you going to stay the pace?"

"Have to. I came with the girl who played the piano. Her father is calling with the carriage at six."

He pulled out his gold turnip watch and glanced at it before shoving it back into the watch pocket. "Four fifteen," he said.

"I guess I'll live," she said gloomily though obviously with doubt.

Colin smiled a little. He enjoyed this sharp-tongued, witty cousin of Lillian. They had met at the wedding five years ago, and at family events since. He never had much of a chance to talk long to her, and she seemed absorbed in her work as a novelist. She had had two novels published, with critical success and little money, as she put it bluntly. Good thing she was wealthy in her own right, reflected Colin.

Families always knew all the intimate facts about each other. Colin knew she was over twenty-six, many years younger than he was, but she had always spoken to him in such a mature manner.

"I hear you have a house of your own. Father approve?"

"Are you teasing me? Never. He had a heart attack on the spot. But I have my house, and may entertain my artistic friends and party until midnight without having Father come down in his gown and slippers demanding when those youngsters will be gone and he can get some sleep. Seriously I know I did disturb them. They think a girl should marry at twenty, produce six children in the next twelve years, and get plump and hearty. I could not endure such a life," she added simply.

"Your sister seems to thrive on it."

"Oh, yes, she is different. I am a writer," said Jacquetta.

"That is different? Cannot you do both, to marry and to write?"

He was leaning against the wall near her chair. She glanced up at him and shook her head. "A husband and children take up much time and energy. No woman can write well without great distress in such circumstances. I require long hours of solitude, of thought, before I can write a single page. Can you imagine—several hours of quiet, then as I begin to write, the youngest comes in requiring a fresh nappy? And the husband returns home from a hard day at the office, wanting a drink and an audience for his griefs? Never."

He half smiled at her vehemence. It offended him a little that a woman should speak so frankly and with such distaste about marriage. Yet, if women were honest, did they not, many of them, feel the same? Look at Minna, how happy she was in her work, running the warehouse and store. She managed her children and household competently, but her husband had been gone nine months out of twelve of the year. Could she have done that in the early years, with Etienne always about, demanding attention, giving her even more children, and frowning on her work?

"Well, I'm off, before they start again," he said, noting a general move to return to the music room. As she stood, he said, "May I offer you a ride home? Or do you prefer to remain?"

"Really, would you? Accepted. I'll just speak to Angela,"

she replied, and she was off. Back again in three minutes, she picked up a small beaver jacket as she came from the attendant footman.

"What excuse did you make?" asked Colin as they went out the side door toward the stables to get his carriage.

"Oh, I'm weak and feverish, feel a chill coming on," said Jacquetta. "What use to be a creative writer, if I cannot make up my own excellent excuses?"

They both began to laugh and continued all the way to the stables. Colin was not sure why he laughed, except that he felt stirred, amused by this cheeky robin in coral gown, and he felt more lively than he had in a long time.

They chatted as he drove to her house some blocks away. He enjoyed listening to her, and made an occasional comment. She was working on a new novel, about abused children, and had some lively remarks to make about that. She was spirited, biting in wit, yet he discovered a tenderness beneath her remarks. She was so indignant about the children.

At the house she briskly invited him inside to admire her new home. She showed him the small cheerful parlor with the crimson draperies, the fireplace and the shelves of books behind the two scarlet couches. A larger drawing room across the narrow hall held a piano, a harp, and more bookcases filled with leather-bound volumes, large folios of art plates, and some paintings of outdoor scenes which Colin stood before.

"He has captured the feel of the West," he said in front of one painting of the white-tipped mountains, a meadow of wild flowers, and a single horse grazing. Jacquetta came to stand beside him, head tipped to one side.

"Yes, I like that one. I wander the shops looking for art. I shall fill the house with what I like. Father is inclined to *natura morte* scenes, you know, dead rabbits and birds hanging head down with blood dripping. They gave me nightmares as a child. He thinks they are wonderful."

"I know the sort. Horrible," agreed Colin.

She took him about unselfconsciously. She showed him the pretty dining room with a large table for twelve set with silver. "I do love to entertain my friends," she said, smiling.

Flower vases were set everywhere. He noted them in the hall, in the upstairs hall, in the drawing room, in the bedrooms. She had four bedrooms on the first floor above the ground floor. Her own was trimmed in her favorite color, coral, with brown rugs and simple brown furniture. The bed was a large four-poster, with a coral canopy trimmed in brown flame stitch.

There were two guest rooms, and a room for her companion, an elderly placid woman, a distant cousin whom Jacquetta liked for her wit and wisdom, she said. She was out for the afternoon, "free to come and go, as I am," said Jacquetta. "She satisfies the proprieties for me, and I give her the freedom to come and go as she always wished. She is one of those poor but kind relatives that lives in other people's houses. I would hate that, being obliged to people."

"If you didn't have money, you might have to," said Colin bluntly. "What would you do then?"

Jacquetta shook her head. "Never do that," she said as briskly. "I'd get a position and earn money. Support myself. I will never be dependent on anyone."

Colin was a little amused at her, so brisk and sure of herself. "And what about a man, a husband, marriage? What then? Do you think he would allow you to gad about?"

"Of course not! That is why I shall never marry. A husband bosses one about, even when one is much more intelligent that he is. 'Yes, sir, no, sir, may I go out, sir?'" she mimicked and grimaced. "Not for me!"

"What if you fall in love, and cannot help yourself?" It tickled him to taunt her a little.

"Oh, I shall not fall in love."

"Indeed. Very strong willed of you."

They had come back to the front hallway. He looked down at her thin lively face. She was not beautiful, but she was somehow attractive.

He took her face in both hands, held her still for a moment, then bent his head and set his mouth on her lips. He found the lips warm and startled and enjoyed taking another kiss from them. He raised his head. She was staring at him, brown eyes wide and shocked.

"Well, good-bye, Jacquetta. Good luck to your ventures," said Colin gravely and departed. She had not said another word.

He was still smiling when he reached home and drove the carriage back to the stables. He swung down and gave the reins to the coachman standing there. "Here you are, Duncan. Wipe him down good, it's a chilly evening."

"Yes, Mr. Colin," replied the man.

From the shadows of the bushes nearby, a small voice came. "Papa, Papa—here I am."

He swung around, startled. "Juliette? What the devil are you doing out here?" She was hobbling toward him, shivering in her thin coat. He picked her up and tried to see her face in the dim lamplight.

She was shuddering great long shivers all down her tiny young frame. He held her more closely. "I'll get you in the house. What in the world are you up to?"

She was such a gentle obedient girl. He was concerned by her presence there.

"I am dying, Papa. I am dying," she choked and began to cry.

"Dying? Nonsense. What happened?"

"Gerald—was teasing me—he put a snake to—my face—it was horrible, Papa—horrible—I put up my—arm—and—tried to stop him—he made the snake—bite my arm—and I'm going to die—" Tears spilled down her cheeks, sobs shook her.

A chill went over Colin. He said curtly to Duncan, "Go for Dr. Von Oldt at once, take this carriage. Bring him right back with you."

"Yes, Mr. Colin!" Duncan swung into the carriage and turned the horse about.

Colin carried Juliette into the house. In the parlor Ludwig and Agatha started up at the sight.

"There she is! Odette came by a couple hours ago and demanded to know if she was here—" began Ludwig.

Colin was removing her coat. She held her arm out as though it was no longer a part of her.

"Gerald had a snake, Father," said Colin, pushing back her dress sleeve to look at the bite. "He made it bite her. I don't think it was poisonous." He examined the bite anxiously. It was red and puffed, and the teeth marks were plain. His mouth set. "If it had been poisonous, Juliette," he said quietly to his shaking daughter, "you would be dead now. No, I think Gerald had a garter snake, probably. My God, I'll beat that boy! He is all malice."

Such a thin little arm she had. And her face was all eyes and terror. Though she wore a thin muslin dress of rose pink and her hair was curled tight in ringlets, she was not cared for, he thought savagely. She was neglected. Gerald, his mother's pet, could do no wrong. And this little thin thing, his daughter, looked as though she did not eat more than birdseed.

"I'll go over and wring the truth out of Gerald," said Ludwig in grim anger. "I must find out what kind of snake it was. Unless you will go, Colin?"

"No, I depend on you. I'll remain with Juliette," said Colin. "Tell Odette the girl stays here. I will not have her treated so."

Colin sat down in a big chair and drew Juliette onto his lap. As he examined the bitten arm, her free arm curled up timidly about his neck. She put her face down against his shoulder with a tired sigh. She was still shivering with both cold and fear.

"Mother, a blanket. And would you have a room prepared for Juliette? One near me, if you will," Colin requested.

"Yes, yes, she shall have Minna's room," said Agatha, and she went off to give directions. A maid came in with a blanket, her look sympathetic. She offered tea, but Colin shook his head.

"No, nothing until the doctor approves." He knew the poison might be sent all through her system with liquids.

He stroked Juliette's soft head. She was curled silently against him, her long thin legs stuck over the arm of the chair.

"My poor baby," he whispered into her hair. "My poor darling; I should never have left you with her."

"Do I have to go back?" asked Juliette. "She hates me, and Gerald hates me. And Grandma hates me too. Only Grandpa holds me and kisses me. And Grandma doesn't like that."

"You shall stay with me, and my mother and dad, Juliette," he said decisively, his face grim.

The doctor came, examined the bite, and cleansed it. Juliette did not even moan as he poured fiery medicine on it. She just buried her head against Colin and held her arm still.

The doctor was bandaging the arm when Ludwig returned, his face red with fury. "It was a grass snake, Colin," he said. "I made him bring it down to the parlor. Odette screamed at the sight of it and called him a naughty boy. But she didn't care a whit that Juliette had been bitten. Damn woman! Cold-blooded as hell."

The doctor was listening gravely. Colin turned to him. "Dr. Von Oldt, will you be a witness? I want you to hear Juliette's story."

The doctor nodded. Colin asked Juliette to repeat her story. She did and whispered, "And I'm afraid of Gerald. He puts—things—in my food—I am afraid to eat."

"What things, Juliette?" Colin asked gently.

"Grasshoppers, and ants, and all kinds of horrible things. He shows them to me, and makes me watch him grind them under his foot. Then he—sprinkles them—on my food—when Nanny is not looking—and she tries to make me eat the food—and I throw up—and Mama gets so angry."

The weary little voice ceased.

"I walloped Gerald," said Ludwig. "I should have done it even harder, the little vicious beast." He was so angry he kept striding about the parlor, shaking his head, his fists tight.

"I shall go see Odette tomorrow," said Colin. "I'll get Juliette's clothes and things and tell Odette she is not returning there. Juliette shall stay with us."

The thin arm tightened about his neck, almost choking him. The thin face raised to his, and a radiant smile came into her pale face. "Really, Papa, forever?" she whispered. "Really, forever?"

"Forever, my dear." He kissed her forehead tenderly.

The doctor departed, and Colin carried Juliette up to her room. She could not eat, being half sick with fear and excitement. She drank a little hot tea and went to sleep holding his hand.

He watched her somberly. He felt guilty, having neglected the little girl all these years. He had tried to go over to see her, but Odette had put up obstacles. And when he saw her, she was pale, composed, clinging to his hand, but saying little. And all the time, this torment—

"My poor baby," he whispered. He kissed her thin hand softly, so as not to wake her. "My poor little darling. You shall not go back to that house."

He had a fight with Odette and threatened to take her to court. He had Dr. Von Oldt write down his testimony and kept it with his lawyer, just in case. Odette had her Gerald, however, and the boy satisfied her. They were much alike. Juliette remained with Colin.

Colin found himself telling Jacquetta about her one day soon after. "You see, it is not only the children of the poor, the orphans and the hungry, who are the abused. Even Juliette, my poor baby, in a wealthy home, with all the clothes and luxuries one could desire, was abused by a vicious brother and neglected by an indifferent mother."

Jacquetta had listened in intent silence to the whole story. She put her hand on his clenched fist. "I'm sorry, Colin, I had no idea. New York society had it that she was a gentle wife, too delicate for this world and your rough ways. This is a different side to her. And so she thought it was terrible to have a snake in the house, but not that Juliette was bitten by Gerald's doing!"

"Yes, that sums it up." He got up, to stride about the small parlor. "I shall have to watch what I do. If she finds aught

313

about me to take to court, and she is angry enough to do so, she will drag our name in the mud. The fact that Juliette now lives in my home may make people wonder about her stories."

"Um. That rather ruins my plans," said Jacquetta, a slight smile curling her pink mouth. She again wore her favorite coral today, this time with a trim of black velvet. She was sitting on the couch, like a bright bird on its perch, her legs curled under her.

"What plans?" asked Colin warily.

"I was going to ask you to be my lover," said Jacquetta, sounding practical. However her cheeks were turning pink, and she could not look in his eyes.

"That sounds—interesting," Colin told her in a strangled voice. "Why?"

"For my novels," said Jacquetta. "I need experience, you see, and I do like you. I should not mind getting experience with you. I don't find you—repulsive."

"Thank you." Colin stood up and came over to her. He gently moved her over, then sat down, pulling her into his arms. "And you don't mind if I kiss you, take you up to bed, make love to you wildly, passionately, like Lord Byron?"

She went scarlet. "I didn't know you had heard about that nickname," she gasped. "He wouldn't be so—so brutally frank and bludgeoning about it!"

Colin laughed aloud. He bent and kissed her cheek, turned her face to his, and pressed his mouth to hers. She put one arm about him, timidly. He unfastened the front of the coral dress and kissed down to the warm hollow between her breasts.

"Colin," she breathed. "What are—you doing?"

"Making love," he said solemnly. He reached into the dress, under the soft chemise, and found a delicate breast. She was so slim she had small breasts, high and taut. He fondled her, watching her face with amusement. She was trying to appear as though she were accustomed to this, but she was quivering.

"Don't undress me here," she whispered. "Colin, let us go up to my bedroom—please?"

Now it was Colin who was shocked. Did she mean it? Had she taken lovers before? He had meant to tease her, kiss her, and then leave. He studied her face warily, what he could see of it.

"You want to, Jacquetta?"

She nodded, her short dark hair flying about her face.

They went upstairs to her bright bedroom and shut the door.

She locked it with a click. She had gone pale. He helped her undress, removing the coral frock, the white chemise, the little undergarments, and stockings and shoes. She lay down on the bed, stiffly, watching him with wide curious dark eyes as he quickly undressed himself, ripping off the tight pantaloons, the stiff shirt and collar. He lay down with her, then, and put his arm across her.

"Sure you want to? If we don't stop now, we won't," he said quietly.

She nodded. "I want—you to," she said faintly and turned to bury her face against his chest. Her hand went to his shoulder, down it, and over his arm, slowly.

He kissed her, then, finding her thin but soft skinned, fragrant with some faint perfume, lilac or lavender, he thought. Her shoulders were hollowed near the neck, and he buried his face against her throat. He stroked over her arm, and then her breasts, finding them touchingly small and high, perfect in their shape, with little pink tips.

They kissed. Her lips were strangely innocent, learning to shape to his. He kept on stroking her, down over the slim thighs, her almost boyish legs. His hand went to the area between her thighs, and he began to caress her more ardently. She caught her breath. If he wanted to stop, she was damn well out of luck, thought Colin.

He rolled over on her, holding himself up with his knees and elbows. Her eyes were shut, and he feathered a kiss across her forehead and winged eyebrows. He found her mouth again and held it with his lips. She was soft and moist now, moving slowly under him. Was she experienced?

She must be—the approach—living alone in this house— her boldness, daring, frankness—

He pressed himself to her, smothering her gasp with his kisses. He held high, pressed again, and went in. She had stiffened in shock, but he held her closely, and kept on kissing her, as he moved slowly back and forth. He did not go in far. He had guessed the truth now.

He came to a climax, withdrawing quickly just before it came. He could not help the spurt of seed that gushed over her thighs. He lay back, breathing hard. She moved at last, to lie against him, her face concealed against his chest. He moved his hand slowly over the short dark hair, feeling the silk of it in his fingers.

"A virgin, Jacquetta? Why me, to give you this experience?"

Her muffled voice finally came from near his heart. "I wanted you, Colin. I can't bear anybody else—to touch me. Repulsive," she said with her old vigor.

He smiled, a curiously gentle smile. He kept on stroking her hair. "I cannot marry you," he said. "Not unless I get a divorce."

"Oh, I don't want to get married," said Jacquetta, and sat up, looking like a thin imp beside him on the bed. Her dark eyes were sparkling. She put her hand tentatively on his hairy chest and pulled teasingly at one curly hair. She stroked it down again, gazing over him with frank, though shy, approval. "I wanted a lover. To see how it was, you know. I wanted my book to be true, you see. And you're the only man whose kisses I liked. The others, they were all swarmy and wet, and one even dribbled on me!"

He laughed at her expression, the grimace on her elfin face. He reached up and stroked her cheek. "I promise not to dribble on you," he said. "Jacquetta—I'll try to be careful. But you must tell me at once if you—start a child."

"Get pregnant, you mean?" Her face was thoughtful. "I think I'd like your child, if I had one," she said finally. "But I don't mean to, really, Colin. I want to be a writer, that's all I want in the world. To write really well, and make them say, she is a fine writer, even though she is a woman."

He nodded. He did not understand her fiery ambition for writing. But he could learn, he thought, what she was and how she wished to live.

"All right, my dear. May I come again soon? I enjoyed this."

"Oh, did you really? I'm glad. I would hate for you to do it just because I asked you," she said naïvely.

"Oh, I enjoy it also," he said and pulled her down to him.

Chapter 26

Wolf leaned back in the oversized chair and listened contentedly as Henri played the piano. He enjoyed the MacCameron family immensely. Somehow he felt as comfortable with them as with his own family and grandparents.

Minna always made him welcome in such a calm, happy fashion. The boys took him about as though he were their brother. Therese confided in him, her round pretty face shining. At eight, she gave more than a little promise of becoming a beauty, with reddish-gold hair and the blue eyes of her mother.

Eugenia Chantal and her parents had come for the evening. His gaze lingered on her. She was now seventeen, and more mature, but her black eyes promised mischief as in his previous visits. What good times they always had. Her lively mind kept him hopping, and she could get into trouble faster than Stephen, Minna declared in amazement. She stole out at night, to run the streets with Wolf and Stephen, giggling at their antics. Once they had joined a wedding party and serenaded a bride, and another time they stole down to the waterfront, took a canoe, and pretended to be voyageurs. How the owner had scolded them when they returned at midnight!

Tonight she looked like a demure young lady, but Wolf was not deceived. Under that white muslin gown, behind the smooth olive cheeks and lowered eyelashes, her brain would be busily concocting trouble. Not malicious trouble, but fun trouble, as she called it. She had grown up beautiful like her mother, with glossy black hair, rosy cheeks, laughing black eyes, a slim but rounded figure, neat ankles, and a brain as sharp as a knife, thought Wolf. She was scathing about the young men who hung about her because her father had acquired money in his clothing store. She was his only child.

"They have trouble forgetting I am half-Indian," she had told Wolf in a biting tone. "But I remind them by slipping into the Cree tongue, messing up my grammar before their mothers, pretending I don't know what to do with my teacup!" She had giggled, but he saw the burning heat of her eyes and knew she was as hurt as he often was.

"Indian bastard!" He could hear his stepmother's acid voice now. "Son of a slut! If your Indian mother could see you now, how proud she would be of your muddy feet and filthy hands! Go and wash at once, and try to control your savage feelings!"

He had hated Odette with cold passion. But he could not hate her daughter, Juliette. He had been shocked when his father had first brought her home, but he soon came to pity, then to love the shy child. Poor girl. How she must have hated living in that horrible cold house.

Colin had written this week that he was keeping Juliette. He said little, but indignation burned between the lines. Evidently she had had a bad time at her mother's. Well, Colin would take care of her, thought Wolf.

The piece finished, Henri stood up and smiled quietly at their applause. His face glowed with a creative fire.

"That is very good, my dear, very good," said Etienne from his special chair, where he could sit without too much pain in his legs. Stephen had cut the chair legs down, and Etienne could stretch out his feet comfortably. "What a talent you have!"

"Thank you, Father."

Stephen spoke next. "You must play that for your recital, Henri. It is as good as any Bach or Beethoven or Haydn. You should show your talents as a composer."

Henri grimaced. "I can imagine what the reviewers would say at my daring to show off my own talents as composer! They would rip me to pieces."

"Now if I am there, with my rifle and my skinning knife," grinned Stephen, who then laughed at his mother's expression. He went over to kiss her hair. "Now, *Maman*, you really think I meant it?"

"Yes, my dear," said Minna with a twinkle, and they all roared at the pair. "My son is capable of doing that!" she said above the laughter.

"So is his mother," contributed Etienne unexpectedly. "She is capable of protecting herself and her own!"

Etienne smiled significantly at her, and Minna grinned back at him, her blue eyes sparkling. Wolf was curious. They referred to something definite, he thought, but they rarely spoke of their early days. In that household the present was so full and lively, they had little time to brood about the past or worry about the future. It was a warm household, and one he enjoyed.

Blaise and Yolanda MacCameron were there that evening. Wolf wondered about them. They seemed placid and contented, yet rivers of contention sometimes ran between them. And he had caught Blaise gazing at himself, Wolf, so strangely at times. Did he resent it that Minna's nephew was an Indian? Could be. Blaise could work with the Indians, trade with them, but he would not want to be related to one! He was polite. Wolf could not fault his Montreal French manners, and the Scottish bluntness was never turned against himself. Yet—

"So—you wish to go with my son to the West," said Etienne, turning to Wolf as though reading his mind. Henri was seated again at the piano, but playing lightly, tentatively, as though listening to music from the heavens. The others turned to Wolf curiously. "You have made trips with your father. But the Canadian West is different. You know that."

"I know. That is why I wish to go. I want to find my people, the Cree," said Wolf.

A silence stole through the room, lightened only by the few notes from the piano as Henri bent his head over the keys. Eugenia was gazing at Wolf with wide eyes, the smile gone from her face.

"Why do you wish that, Wolf?" asked Etienne. His face seemed to sag into tired lines. "That past is past, your mother is gone. Your father has raised you well. Do you think to turn Indian now?"

"I am an Indian," said Wolf. "In New York, they call me the wild Indian."

"And you are proud of it?" flashed Blaise angrily. "No, you should forget it, you are only one-quarter Indian. Do not wear your hair in that way, calm yourself, be a man! You should forget the past—"

"How can I forget the past until I know what it contains?" asked Wolf. "My mother died when I was three, and I never knew my grandfather, nor any uncles or cousins out there. What kind of people were they? Are there any left? I want to find my tribe and know from where I came. Then perhaps I shall know who I am and why I am."

The outburst embarrassed him. These were his private thoughts, not meant for others. He ducked his head and scowled at his shiny black shoes. He deliberately wore his hair long to his shoulders, to remind himself and others that he was Indian. He would have worn buckskins, if his father had not drawn the line at that, sternly. No, his son would wear neat suits and clean white shirts with ruffles while he worked with him. Only on a fur trip could he wear the rough clothing of his people and his trade.

Stephen spoke into the silence. "He can come with me and my men, Grandfather," he said thoughtfully. "I have made two

319

summer journeys and two winter ones. I know the lands now, and my men are seasoned. He will come to little harm with us, I promise you."

"But this is a foolish enterprise," said Blaise, his mouth tight. "To search for his people! Oh, well, he may do well with the furs, that is all right. But if he wastes his time searching for men who are long gone—"

"I do not know they are long gone. I have the names of my mother, her mother and grandmother. Those names would be known and not forgotten," said Wolf with dignity. "Indians do not forget so easily."

The conversation was finally changed by Minna, troubled over the situation. She asked Stephen when he would depart.

"In another month, Mother, to get a good start," he said. He grinned, his eyes flashing. "I can scarcely wait! To be free again, to sing the songs, to strain my muscles in the canoes. And then the snowy wilderness, the quiet, the comradeship of my voyageurs." He seemed to lapse into dreams, his eyes shining at thought of the adventures before him.

Minna pressed his shoulder as he lounged at her feet in the drawing room. "I understand, my son. To see the blue of the sky at midday, and then the purple at night in the long nights. And the northern lights, flashing their blues and greens and golds, and the crimson as the sun sets after its brief fling in the sky. The vivid stars, never so bright as when one is alone over his own campfire."

He reached up and touched her hand as it rested on his shoulder. His tanned face was upturned to hers, and he looked warmly at her dreamy face.

"You have never forgotten," he said.

"How could I? The happiest days and nights—and you, my son, were born there, in a cabin, with the wolves howling, and Indian women to attend me. So kind, they were, so good and kind."

"I was there also, my love," protested Etienne. "Father and I both helped."

"Aye, helped kill the bottle of Scotch when it was over," she said dryly. Blaise burst out laughing at Etienne's wry look.

"Yes, that was true enough! What a head I had the next day! And how we celebrated!"

On that joyful note the family group broke up, to go upstairs to prepare for bed.

Wolf escorted Eugenia and her parents to their house next door and lingered on the porch with her to talk when her parents went indoors into the candle-lit house. He could just see her oval face, thoughtful in the moonlight, and the dim candlelight from the house.

"Eugenia?"

"Yes, Wolf."

"I wish—I was wondering—if you would wait for me," he blurted out. He was flushed and hot, and he captured her slim warm hand in his big one.

"Wait for you?"

"I mean—" He was desperate. He had been nerving himself for this moment. For years he had thought about it, even when they were both still children. Now he was twenty, and she was seventeen, and a beauty, and all the men were after her, clustering about her. "Eugenia, you like me, don't you?"

"Oh, yes," she said.

Her reply was too offhand to suit him. He put his free hand on her waist and drew her closer. "More than like me?" he breathed, hopefully.

She leaned against his shoulder. "Wolf, you are going with Stephen in a month?" she asked.

He blinked. Was this a refusal, her change of subject? "Yes, I will go. But I wish you to wait for me, Eugenia. You have so many admirers. Do not let your father promise you to anyone until I return next summer. Promise?"

"Why should I wait? For what?" she teased, her voice more lively. He knew the mischief in her voice and drew her closer and dared to touch her cheeks with his lips.

"You know—that I—love you," he dared to say.

"How would I know that? You have never said," Eugenia murmured wickedly.

"Eugenia? I do love you—and I think—you like me some."

"Oh, I like you some," she said.

He could have blown up with impatience and desire. He drew her even closer, and she did not pull away. "We are much alike, we have many interests in common. We have always played well together. Your parents like me, and I think they approve of me. My father will dower us, and I think I could arrange to build a house in Montreal." He paused, peering to try to see her face. All he could see was the cloud of dusky black hair.

"Um," said Eugenia. "What would you do with a house in Montreal? You would never be here. You would be out West with your Indian people. You said so."

"I did not say so! I said I wanted to meet them, to know

321

who I am, of what people I come," he said desperately. "We have spoken of this, you approved. You understood! You said, yes, you should know your uncles and your cousins."

"Yes, that would be good."

"Then—will you wait for me? When I return, next summer, I will ask your father for your hand in marriage. I will look about for a house for us, or plan to build one. You shall choose what you want, I will give it to you. I love you. Father has told me I shall have wealth when I am twenty-one. He trusts me, we shall go into partnership with him. Eugenia, you will wait for me?"

"No," she said. "I will not wait for you."

He gasped, and his grip on her loosened. He felt as though she had pitched him from a warm cozy nest of certainty onto an icy river of denial.

"You—do not—like me," he said, low. He stiffened—an Indian took grief with stoicism.

"Yes, I love you," said Eugenia, the mischief back in her tone. "But I will not wait for you."

He grabbed her tightly and yanked her around to face him. He put one hand on her neck, and held her so her face must be upturned to his. Yet he could not see her expression.

"What do you mean? Do you torture me? Would you accept another man even though you love me?" he cried.

"I mean—I will not *wait*! I will not sit here meekly rocking on the porch and wonder what you are doing out West! I too wish to meet my people, I know their names. They are Cree. It may even be that we are related. I wish to find my people and come to know them."

"Oh, my God in heaven," said Wolf, crudely and forcefully. "You want to come with me! Oh, my God."

She laughed, a low rich laugh that stirred desire in his loins. As her slim body leaned against his, he felt the warmth of her breast and thighs. She was driving him crazy, turning to put her arms about his body and lean against him once more strongly, pressing to him.

Her face was turned up alluringly to his. Her full mouth was just below his. She was a tall girl, and with his head bent, their lips were so close. He leaned closer yet, and his mouth pressed hotly on hers. Oh, she was so delicious, her mouth was so rich and ripe with promise. She answered his kiss, and in surprise he kept his mouth there. The kiss was long, growing hotter, taking his breath.

She twisted away. "You are very daring and bold, *mon-*

sieur," she said mock demurely.

"Oh, God, Eugenia, don't taunt me! Tell me you love me. Oh, I love you, as I never loved anyone but my mother. Eugenia—love me. Love me!"

He pulled her tightly to him, and his mouth found hers again. Their lips clung, and her hands were fastened behind his back as his chest pressed against her rounded breasts. His hand went up and down her spine, urgently learning her curves, then resting on her thighs.

"Eugenia? You must come inside now!" It was her father's voice, stern, yet understanding. His voice came closer to the front door. "Eugenia? Why do you remain outdoors? Come inside!"

"Tomorrow," whispered Eugenia and drew away from him. "I'll meet you down near your uncle's store on the waterfront. I need new ribbons!" She giggled and moved inside. Her graceful form was lit briefly by the candles, and she seemed to be outlined in flame.

Wolf went back to the MacCameron's house in a daze. Did she love him, or not? He could not take Eugenia with him! But what would she do if he left without her? He knew her strong will, her firmness of mind. If she had made up her mind to go West—and he refused her—would she persuade some daring voyageur to take her as his wife? And Wolf would lose her, the one girl he could talk to freely, the one girl he adored, the only girl he could laugh with and tell his secret thoughts, and know she understood even when he could not speak.

He tossed and turned that night in his soft bed in the guest room at the MacCamerons. He could not sleep. What could he do? He was not even of age, and he had no money of his own except what his father gave him. And Eugenia was but seventeen! Girls married early, but she was her parents' pride and joy, their only child.

Wolf rose early, found a piece of bread and some coffee in the kitchen, and departed. He walked down to the waterfront, needing to think. He felt so confused. He strode along the wharves, ignoring the curious stares. The others were probably wondering if he was an Indian or a white man, he thought fiercely. Well, he was Indian, and one day he would show them he was.

Near the MacCameron store, he paused. He wondered when Eugenia would come, what he would say to her. He was terribly afraid of losing her. He knew she had a quick temper.

Would she listen to reason?

323

She was so young, so lovely, soft and silky and warm in his arms.

"Hello, there, young Wolf," said a Scottish burred voice. He turned around to find Blaise coming up behind him.

"Good morning, Mr. MacCameron."

"You're up early this bright day."

"Yes, sir."

Blaise MacCameron hesitated, then indicated a bench in the sunlight near the store. "Come, I want to talk to you, Wolf," he said and started for the bench. Wolf finally followed him reluctantly. What would he do if Eugenia came while they were talking? Then he realized that this was his chance to ask someone older and wiser his advice.

"I have wanted to talk to you—or someone, Mr. Mac-Cameron," said Wolf, slowly, as they sat down.

"Oh, yes?"

"You see, I spoke to Eugenia Chantal last night. I asked her to wait for me—until I returned from the journey, you know. She said she would not wait. She wishes to go West with me! For a woman, delicately brought up, but I love her—and she is so pleading in her ways. What shall I do?"

Blaise did not look surprised, he nodded slowly, and took out his pipe. "Aye, she is a spirited girl—like Minna," he said. "You know Minna went out with Etienne? She enjoyed her two years there, and I think she would have gone again but for the children."

"And you—would approve of that?" asked Wolf. This was not the advice he had expected.

"For you and for Eugenia, I think it may be the answer. You have always been close friends, aye? She feels as lost in our society at times as you do. One day you may feel you fit in, but not until you have learned, as you said, who you are. She feels the same. Attractive to men—yet whispers about her under their breath, the young scoundrels!"

"I would knock them down," said Wolf fiercely.

"Aye, and get a bloody head for it. But I know how you feel." Blaise puffed hard at his pipe, then removed it again from his mouth. "Something I must tell you, lad, though you may hate me for it."

Wolf was thinking about Eugenia, so he scarcely paid attention to the first words of the older man. Then he sat up and stared incredulously at the wrinkled face of bronze, the hand that gestured.

"Lad, many years ago, I was out West and met a lovely

Indian girl. I was wild as they came, and thoughtless to boot. I took the girl and kept her the winter. I thought I was careful in our relations, and it was years before I discovered that I was wild and—yes, brutally indifferent to what might happen to the girls I took so lightly." He drew a deep breath, gazing sightlessly out over the bright waters of the St. Lawrence River.

"You—had Indian girls—and treated them—so?" breathed Wolf. His fists clenched. So had his mother been treated, so was she the forgotten child of some trapper.

"Yes, lad. Many of us did and tried to be kind to the girls. We gave them gifts, left money for them—and forgot them. Then years later—" Blaise turned abruptly to Wolf. "Lad, I did not know until your father, Colin Gunther, told me. Your mother, Morning Star, was my daughter."

Wolf was left speechless, feeling as though he had been thumped hard in the chest or stomach, left without breath, shocked to the heels.

Blaise's burred voice went on, his accent so thick Wolf in his dazed condition could scarcely understand him. "I have worried long about telling you. I thought the truth could be hidden. I was a coward. Now you are going out West, and I know your people are in the Red River valley, near or in the post I myself own. Stephen told me the names of some Indians who come in, including their chief. He is a cousin of your mother, and he knows of her and of you. Morning Star's mother—whom I—knew—was named Rippling Waters. Her mother was Wind in the Pines. The cousin, who is chief, is named Strong Wind."

As Wolf tried to take this in, his hand went through his thick black hair. "Stephen knows about this? My birth? My mother?"

"He guessed, and he spoke to me. Stephen is discreet. He knew my wife Yolanda would be hurt. She knew I was unfaithful to her, but she does not guess about you." The pained voice ceased, and Blaise puffed fiercely at his pipe.

Wolf shook his head, dazed, feeling drunk with pain and shock. He had liked this old man. He had never dreamed that he was his own grandfather. He was doubly related, then, to Stephen and the others. Etienne and his own mother, Morning Star, were half brother and sister!

There was a long silence as they sat on the bench, gazing at the blinding sunlight on the river. They seemed to be removed from the busy scene, the French voyageurs in their colorful dress as they went about preparing for the autumn journey, Indians coming and going with silent padding step in tan moccasins and deerskin garb, drunken trappers quarreling and fighting, then laughing together, arms about each other as they staggered down the wharf. The canoes pulled up to the wharves, huge packs being taken to them. Their load of furs had been unloaded months before, now new supplies were being prepared. Soon they would paddle away, singing and shouting, off to the new year and hopes of rich pelts.

"Do you hate me, lad?" asked Blaise quietly. "Try not to, for I find I love you, my grandson. I have been proud of you as you grew and matured, and overcame the difficulties of your birth and appearance. You will be a man soon, and hold your head proudly. However, men will take you as you think you are, my lad. Be proud of yourself, live as you will, and make them accept what you are."

"What am I? Part Indian, less white," muttered Wolf. He rubbed his hand over his face. "What am I? Where do I go? What am I in this world? In school the boys spit at me and called me names. My father's wife, Odette, called me cruel names. I hated them at times, I longed to go back to my people—but am I one of them?"

"You may find that you are," said Blaise. "But you and Eugenia have idealized the Indians. You have not lived as they do, in filth, in tents, in rough cabins. Both of you have been groomed in luxury, been educated. You read and write, you attend concerts, you listen to works of Shakespeare and Milton. Can you adapt to their Indian life? You can hunt, but do you know with eyes closed when a wolf comes? Do you pray as you kill? Do you call to the Great Spirit? Do you know the lore of herbs, and can you accept the insults of thoughtless white men? I think you have not begun to know how the Indian lives and will live."

Wolf gripped his knees in pain, bending over. "What can I do? Where can I go? I am a stranger to my parents, I belong nowhere! I do not want to live in the city, I have thought only of returning to my people, the Cree. And now you blast that for me!"

"Lad, I do not blast it. I think you should go, and Eugenia too, if her parents will it," said Blaise very gently. "But you must discover truth for yourself, all men must. No one can tell you, go, and you will go, or stay, and you will stay. You must find your own path, and then you will be happy. You will find where you belong, and be content. And if you win Eugenia for your wife, I think your future will be joyous, for she is a good girl, spirited, yet gentle, beautiful, yet not vain. And I think she comes now."

Wolf raised his gaze in his misery and confusion. He saw Eugenia Chantal stepping down from a carriage, helped by Stephen. A man came forward to take the horse for them, and Stephen nodded toward the bench where Blaise and Wolf sat.

Wolf rose and walked blindly toward them. Eugenia was watching his face with a smile, and yet an anxious look. She left Stephen and walked toward him, along the dusty street. They met in the middle, and he held out his hands to her. She put hers in them, and they turned, and walked down toward the river. They gazed out over the canoes, walked among the Indians and voyageurs, yet did not seem to see them. His hand was holding her arm now, and his head was bent as he talked earnestly to her.

She was lovely in the sunlight, in a pale yellow muslin gown and matching wide-brimmed hat with a yellow rose on it.

Stephen waited for his grandfather to come. Together they went to the opened door of the warehouse. "You told him, Grandfather?" asked Stephen.

Blaise nodded. "I had to, my lad. I had to. He was so shocked. My God, will he hate me?"

"I think not. I think he is more concerned with whether his girl loves him. She does," added Stephen with a reckless grin and a laugh that rollicked along the waterfront. "Ah, they make a pretty pair, do they not?"

Blaise gazed at the young couple as they paused near the pier and turned to face each other. Wolf, so tall and dark, so bronzed and strong. Eugenia, tall, slim, golden, with her cloud of black hair peeping from under the yellow muslin hat. She carried a matching yellow sunshade, and her purse was a bit of muslin over her arm.

"Can you see them in an Indian camp?" asked Blaise gloomily. "Eugenia cooking over a campfire, stirring an iron pot hot as blazes? Wolf hunting in *their* fashion? If I had only known about his mother—"

"One cannot change the past, Grandfather, only one's view of it," said Stephen, then chuckled. "You are as worried as a hen with one chick. Come in, and help me mark the stores I am planning to take."

A friendly hand pushed the old trapper inside the door, and they went together to the back where the desks were covered with pages of paper and samples of goods.

Chapter 27

A messenger was sent to New York, and he returned with Colin Gunther, who was dazed at the suddenness of it all. His Wolf—to marry! And but twenty! Yet he knew and admired the Chantal family, and young Eugenia was a radiant bride.

At the wedding feast Colin observed the guests alertly. Something was bothering him, and he finally focused on the two guests who seemed so out of place in the happy family group. The older of the two men, Patrice Scudery, was graying, and shrewd, a Frenchman in a new fur conglomerate named Canada West. His younger associate was Leonard Richier, red-faced, jovial, and stocky. His humor rang false to Colin. What were they doing at this essentially family affair?

It was a Protestant affair, yet the men were French Catholics. The Chantals were indifferent Protestants, and Wolf refused to be married in a Catholic ceremony. The MacCamerons were divided, and accustomed to it by now.

The ceremony itself was beautiful. Eugenia wore a favorite yellow silk gown, with a headdress of bright golden color that set off her glossy black curly hair. Her black eyes sparkled with love for Wolf, and mischief for all who would tease her about her "wild honeymoon" in a canoe trip West.

Stephen had jollied Wolf into trimming his hair for the occasion. They were fast friends, and Stephen could talk Wolf into things the others could not. Wolf looked gravely handsome and suddenly much more mature to his father in his blue silk suit and frilled white lawn shirt.

After the religious ceremony the reception was held in the large MacCameron house, the guests spilling out onto the lawns that joined the MacCameron home and that of the Chantals next door. There was much laughter, toasts in fiery liquor, teasing jokes, and music from Henri and his friends. Dancing went on into the night, and it was well past midnight before the wedding couple could retire to Wolf's room.

Finally alone with this woman of his people, Wolf undressed his bride reverently. How beautiful she was, how he adored her. In bed they lay quietly, both weary from the days of preparation for the wedding and the thought of the journey ahead of them. Stephen was anxious to leave within a week, before the autumn turned cold and rainy.

His arm about Eugenia, Wolf found it hard to think of such seemingly distant things as journeys and his Indian people. "You are so beautiful, my love," he whispered. She turned into his arms.

Her voice quivered a little. "Are you sorry, Wolf?"

"Sorry?" He felt shocked. "For what?"

"That I—bargained with you. But I was so anxious to see my people, the Cree, you know—how I feel."

"I know how you feel, because I feel the same," he said tenderly, curling his arms more closely about her round form. "Our minds are much alike, my darling. I felt it from the first, did you not also?"

She nodded, and her thick loosened hair brushed against his bare shoulder. He turned and pressed his lips to her throat, to the cheek, to the little nervous place beneath her ear. She trembled, and her hands went to his chest, not pushing him away, but stroking softly. They were both novices at this, but their love made them curious, full of desire and longing.

Wolf managed to rouse her to burning desire as he felt for her, and soon they came together. At her gasp he knew he had hurt her. He whispered an apology. "Don't you mind, dearest Wolf," she said. "I love you, I love you. I have wanted to belong to you—to feel your body next to mine, to become one with you. Do you believe that in spirit we are truly one?"

He nodded, humbled that she could say the words he only felt so deeply. Her hands moved through his thick hair as he kissed her from throat to thigh, adoring her with his hands. When they slept, it was with a new sense that they had become one being, a spiritual unit that nothing could break.

Wolf wakened late in the morning while his bride still slept. He gazed at her with solemn awe. She was so lovely, so sweet, and her face was pure in the sunlight. Such a fine oval of a face, set off by the shine of her glossy hair as it spilled over his arm. The soft rise and fall of her round breasts gave him a deep sense of peace. He bent and placed his lips against the whiteness of her.

She yawned, opened her eyes, and smiled up at him. After they kissed for a time, she whispered, "Do we have to go down to breakfast?"

"No. I am not hungry for anything but you."

She drew him closer.

Downstairs the others were talking in the drawing room. Colin, who had risen early, paced the garden, worried. He must say what he had come to say, he had promised his father. Ludwig Gunther had not grown less smart in his age, in spite of the pangs of arthritis and a gouty foot.

The family breakfasted together. Even Etienne had come down to be with them. Minna joined them in the drawing room, her strong sympathy with her older brother warning her of the importance of the coming speech.

Stephen sat near to her. They were close in spirit, much alike, and Colin studied them, his dear sister and her son. He did not want to hurt them, but he must warn them all.

He began abruptly, since polite speech was alien to him and used only when necessary. "Father gave me a warning for you, Blaise. Much as you have quarreled at times in the past, he respects your honesty and integrity."

Blaise scowled. "That sounds like you are leading to an unpleasant matter," he said.

"I am. Those men last night—Patrice Scudery and Leonard Richier—what is your association with them? Do they not run the Canada West Company?"

Blaise sat up quickly, and then rubbed his achy legs. "Aye, that they do. And I with them, if it is any matter to you. They have been generous with me in difficult times."

"I hope that does not mean that you have borrowed money from them, nor sold them stock in your company!" Colin said with blunt urgency. Minna sat stiffly, her apprehensive blue eyes going from one to the other of them.

Etienne showed rare anger, his fist clenched on the arm of his wheelchair. "And if we have? Is it your concern? You have tried for years to buy into our company! You long for Canadian furs now that your American ones have petered out! Your animals have been hunted too much, and everyone knows they are emptying from the plains. And now you dare to come here and question—"

"Nay, Etienne, do not let us quarrel about this!" urged Colin, his hand out in pleading. "Father is deeply concerned. I do not know how he manages to hear the whispers in the market, but he comes home with news that months later proves correct. And he has heard that Canada West is backed by some men who are not scrupulous in their dealings. If you join with them, they will take your all!"

"I am not so stupid as to allow such a thing to happen," responded Blaise angrily. "I think this is just a ploy. Ludwig Gunther has longed for years to take over my company! Well, MacCameron's is not for sale!"

"He would buy you out, or he would back you to maintain your own company." Colin presented the choice positively. "He loves Minna and his grandchildren. He believes in the future of Canadian furs. And it is true—the American fur traders are gradually emptying the lands of the fur-bearing animals. Our plains and forests are becoming barren. But it is not for this—"

"I say it is!" said Blaise, furiously. "I say that Ludwig has wanted for many years to get a connection up here, to enable him to bring our furs over the borders to New York, for him to resell at a big profit to himself! What Minna does proves that! Her furs go over the border, and she gets but a small profit—"

"A large profit, Father," said Minna gently, but with firmness. "And Father had nothing to do with the dealings. I deal with Roderick Dindorf only. We have always kept our operations separate, you know this."

"Well, well, I do not approve of women in business," said Blaise, ignoring the look of pain in her face. "My own wife a shopkeeper! If it did not give her such amusement, I would not permit it!" he added grandly.

Etienne looked upset, but Stephen reached up and gave his mother's hand a sly squeeze and a little shake, as though for encouragement. Colin did not miss that movement. Stephen was on his mother's side.

"Let me present the matter as Father told me," said Colin with unusual patience for him. "Rumor has reached New York that Canada West is a branch of a London firm that wishes to rival the Hudson's Bay Company. Their ambitions are cunning, and they have managed to snatch up more than ten independent companies such as yours. If they have managed to get stock in your company—"

"I say nothing," continued Blaise stubbornly.

"Then all I can add is this: beware of them, and be cautious in your dealings with them," said Colin. "If you wish aid, Father and I stand ready to offer it."

"At your price!" taunted Blaise. "Ludwig Gunther wants Canada furs."

"Yes, he does. And stands willing to pay a very fair price

for them," said Colin. "Let us have done with the matter. I came for a wedding."

"And another try at getting our company from us!" Blaise could not resist a final jab at his American rival's son.

Colin compressed his lips but changed the subject. "May we have some of your excellent coffee, Minna? And I would see your fine warehouse and store before I depart."

He and Minna went off together to the warehouse after luncheon. Wolf and Eugenia came with them, radiant, hands clinging. Colin deduced that the wedding night was a success, and he was happy for them. Their happiness only reminded him, however, that his troubles at home were coming to a head. Odette had heard about the affair between Jacquetta and Colin. And if she so chose, Odette could use her knowledge of the affair to prevent Colin from seeing the children. If Colin could not persuade Odette to give him a divorce, and Jacquetta to marry him, then he would have to give up the only woman who had drawn and attracted him, amused and desired him, for many long years.

He was glad to forget the problems in admiring Minna's neatly kept account books, her beautiful store with the glass cases of Oriental porcelain, ivory, lacquer ware, gilded trees with jade leaves, and flowers of precious stones.

Colin also spent some time with Wolf and Eugenia during the next few days. He helped them choose supplies, advising them on pots and pans and blankets, knives and rifles and ammunition. And he became much more closely acquainted with Eugenia and came to appreciate her splendid courageous spirit, as well as her humor and warmth.

He told Wolf, "You have a wonderful wife, my son. Cherish her, and care for her, for she is a treasure. It is a rough life you are going to; make sure she has the comforts she will need. Especially uphold her in her womanly needs, for privacy among so many men. She has been gently bred."

Wolf listened carefully, not rebelliously as he often had in the past. "I will take good care of her, Father," he promised solemnly.

"And come to see us in New York. There is always a job waiting for you there," added Colin with a smile. "I do not mean to compete with the MacCamerons for your services. I just wish you to know and remember that you are my son, my heir, my cherished lad. We are not to become strangers."

*   *   *

They clasped hands before they parted. Colin thought, as
the canoes shoved off amid cries and songs, laughter and encouragement and bantering, that his son had grown up over-
night. And little Eugenia, how beautiful she was, bravely smiling in the sunlight, waving her hands to them, as she sat among
the bundles of goods in the long canoe. "God keep them safe,"
he whispered as they pulled away.

"Aye," said Blaise softly, beside him. "They do not know
what they do."

At first Wolf was happy in the days of traveling, the brief
nights of rest. Yet knowing that Eugenia was uncomfortable,
hiding her discomfort, uneasy among those eighty-some men,
he began to become aware of the problems facing them. Stephen stood between them and some of the more rowdy voyageurs, yet Wolf heard the words spit, "Indian squaw! Half-
breed!"

It made his heart sore and angry. He was the more protective
to Eugenia, and she to him. They took part in the singing, in
carrying the canoes around the portages, in the cooking and
cleaning and sometimes in the paddling. They were part of the
group, and Stephen was already a firm leader.

Most of the men were Frenchmen, some half-breeds like
himself. Some were pure French, and these seemed to feel they
were above the rest. The Cree Indians were silent and kept to
themselves, not speaking to Wolf and Eugenia, even when the
pair tried their Cree language on them.

Only an elderly Blackfoot Indian trapper was friendly. And
he was so filthy dirty, so greasy, and smelled so strong that
Eugenia found it difficult to hide her repulsion. Yet he could
tell stories of the old days, of the hunting, of legends and the
lore of his people, tales that held them all entranced. Stephen
kept hiring him each season, though the other men protested
that the "old one" could not earn his keep, being too elderly,
too slow, too past his prime.

"Howling Loon had traveled with my father and with my
grandfather, from the time of his youth," said Stephen in slow
stately words, with a firm mature tone that was quite unlike
his lively mischievous air at home. On the trail he was the
leader, and he felt his responsibility keenly and showed his
maturity and understanding. "Howling Loon travels with me

333

so long as his legs can move, his brain can comprehend, and his hand hold a rifle. I am honored that he gives his loyalty and his trust to the MacCamerons. He comes."

So that was that, and although the younger men grumbled, the older ones nodded, satisfied. Stephen MacCameron was not one who would discard them when they were old and less rapid and could not carry sixty pounds, but only forty or thirty.

The days and nights went by, and they plunged further into the wilderness. Wolf and Eugenia lay together at nights, in their blankets, but were usually too weary to make love, and could only hold each other. Sometimes they whispered their impressions of the day, and at times they joined in the singing around the campfire and helped in the cooking. Yet, Wolf thought, they grew no closer to the Cree Indians of the party.

Stephen also was apart from them. He was the leader. It was he who said which way they would go, and how many hours they would paddle until they came to a smoke rest, where they would draw up on a bank to light their pipe, then continue on the way.

Stephen must feel his loneliness, the loneliness of a leader, thought Wolf curiously, watching the man who was his age, and his relative, yet so different from him. Different? Yes, with his red-gold hair, his blue eyes, his authority, his laughter, his ease, his sense of command. He was, Wolf realized, the product of two very different people—Etienne, the French voyageur, and Minna, the warm but sternly practical German.

And Wolf himself? The product of a German father and a shy Indian mother, also part French. No wonder he felt so pulled in various directions.

It was late October when they arrived at the fur trade post which was their destination. From there the men would scatter to a place of their own choosing, to hunt, trap, and live through the winter. Stephen would remain at or near the post, to take command there, to count the furs, and especially insure the loyalty of their own Indians against the efforts of other fur traders to buy the precious Far North furs of white ermine, dark rich mink, polar bear, and wolverine.

Wolf and Eugenia set up a cabin for themselves. The young woman set to her housekeeping eagerly. Wolf sensed she wanted something practical to do, to keep her mind from troubling her. He himself went out with the Indians to hunt, fish, trap.

He found his own cousin at once, a chief of a local tribe.

334

Named Strong Wind, the Cree was tall, taller even than Wolf, of commanding appearance, and about twenty-eight years of age. He was grave, yet he had a silent humor about him, recognized only in the shine of his black eyes.

Wolf and Eugenia were invited to the chief's lodge early in their stay. They went to a feast there with high hopes, doubts, worries. They were greeted with courtesy and given the place of honor next to Strong Wind. His wife waited on them, handing choice bits of meat from the pot to Eugenia with her own greasy fingers and chatting with them patiently in slow speech so they would understand.

There was singing and dancing followed by story telling. An old woman told the story of Rippling Waters, and how, despite her love for him, her Frenchman had left her. She told how the young woman had given birth to the beautiful Morning Star. Many years later another trapper had come, one kind of heart. The old woman sang the story of how the bear had attacked Colin, how his dog Wolf had rescued him, how the Indians had come to attend him, how he and Morning Star had loved and created a child between them. This child of their love was here and they welcomed him.

It was odd, embarrassing, and yet touching to hear the whole story. And Wolf noted that no one gave the name of that French trapper, Blaise MacCameron. Yet they all knew it. They knew that the fur trade post named MacCameron was that of the old man, his grandfather. Was it from kindness that they refrained from saying this? Or was it the wish to keep their good money flowing in? He wondered.

Sometimes Wolf went hunting with the Blackfoot trapper, Howling Loon. He had a reluctant liking for the man, who was a clever trapper, though elderly now, and slow of walk and speech. The liking grew, for Wolf found the man honest and honorable, and loyal to a fault, for he would not hear one word against the men who had employed him all his life.

"They good to old Howling Loon. They pay him in good season, they pay him in poor season. They take care his woman, until day she die. They grieve over his son and help to bury him. I live in this land, and it is a good land. The animals die with nobility. I respect them. One day I die here."

Wolf learned much from the old man, including how to lay a trap for a vicious wolverine, and take him too, Howling Loon taught him to ignore the huge, baying wolves. They were only curious, just like pet dogs, he assured him. Only a rabid wolf, or one made fierce by a long winter of hunger, would attack a human being. Some could be tamed to set into dog teams, and he told a long story of a wolf he had tamed to run with his team many long moons ago.

The man smelled like a skunk, and the illness in him was killing him. His language was not that of the Cree. But how much the old man knew! The scent of the bear, the movements of the beaver, the ways of the otter and the mink.

Eugenia had found her people also, a branch of the same Cree people. Often she went to be with them, to cook with the women and learn their ways. She would come home with new ways to cook cornbread, to boil meat and vegetables so they did not taste like glue, to add herbs to tea to give it a fresh clean taste and guard against the winter illnesses.

Yet Wolf sensed she was not happy. She was more grave this winter. She was good with him in bed, when they would make love and laugh like children over their happiness. But coming home early, seeing her at the campfire bending over the hot iron pot, seeing her flushed earnest face, he knew she was not happy.

Nor was Wolf. In his buckskins, his long hair flowing about his shoulders, he had gone into the trading post one day soon after his arrival. No one knew him. He stood inside the door, then came up to the counter. The old man who kept the books glanced at him, then glared and scowled.

"Wait outside until you are called, Injun," he said. "What's your name?"

"Wolf," said Wolf Gunther coldly.

"Well, Wolf, wait out there. You a half-breed?"

"A quarter-breed," said Wolf bleakly, his hands on his rifle. The old man stared at his hands, and the young assistant came up behind the counter and put his hand on the pistol at his belt.

Wolf went outside, burning angry. He stalked up and down outside the cabin. Other Indians came and went, still those running the post did not call him. They were making him wait for his insolence.

Stephen MacCameron came along and saw him. "Hey there, Wolf. What are you doing?"

"Waiting to be called as an Injun," said Wolf bleakly, with a wry twist of his mouth.

Stephen put his hands on his hips, and pondered, his eyes on the face of his dark cousin. "Want me to introduce you, and fire them both?"

Wolf shrugged. "Not if they are good help."

"Well, come on in and meet them. I want to see them turn red," said Stephen dryly and put a friendly hand on Wolf's shoulder. He must have felt the tension in him. They went into the cabin together, and the old man snapped, "You'll have to wait," to Wolf.

Stephen said quietly, "I think I told you to treat all Indians decently and politely, MacGregor."

The old man swallowed. Wolf watched the Adam's apple go up and down several times. "Yes, sir, Mr. MacCameron," he said, biting out the words. "What d'ja want, Injun?"

"Sack of flour. Sack of sugar. Half pound of bullets."

The young assistant counted it out. Stephen waited, lounging against the counter. They got out the tally book, the old man dipped the pen into ink. "What's the full name?" he asked.

"Wolf," said Wolf.

"I said full name!"

"Wolf Gunther," said Wolf. The man began to scratch it down, then scowled, as the realization of just who the mistreated young man was began to dawn on him.

"Gunther?" he asked.

"That's right," said Stephen easily, a devil in his blue eyes. "Wolf Gunther. Son of Colin Gunther. Grandson of Ludwig Gunther, the big fur man down south in American land. And a cousin of mine."

The man did not turn red. Instead he went pale and clutched at his stomach, dropping the pen which spattered ink all over the page. "But he's—he's—" He stared at Wolf's long hair and the casual buckskins he wore, now dirt covered from hunting.

"My cousin," repeated Stephen. He straightened. "You know, MacGregor, you never know who's coming in here. Good idea, isn't it, to be polite to every damn human soul?"

He helped pick up the goods and carry them out with Wolf, his shoulders shaking as they walked up the hill to Wolf's cabin.

"You got a damn crazy sense of humor, Stephen," grumbled Wolf. But he was beginning to smile a little, some of the hate draining away. "That man's face! I'll never forget it."

They began to laugh, and they continued laughing as they dumped the goods down in the cabin. But they did not tell Eugenia what had happened, and the humor in Wolf was rather a sour one. He treated MacGregor from then on with formal politeness, though the man fawned on him.

Life in the wilderness gave Wolf further lessons about who he was, and how he felt about himself. Out hunting one day with Howling Loon, the older man seemed very quiet, almost lazy quiet, half asleep. Wolf finally turned on him. "What's the matter with you today, man? You do not wish to hunt with me?" he demanded.

The old man shrugged. "I wait to see if you can hear with Indian ears," he said mildly.

Wolf listened. He listened, intently, then turned in exasperation to the old man. "I hear nothing!"

"Indians follow us. Blackfeet Indians. More than a dozen of them. We going home, they mean us no good."

The old man had directed them in a circle, and now, though seeming to go forward, they headed for the post. Wolf had not realized that either. He felt embarrassed, angry, and ashamed. He kept turning to look back and finally glimpsed one body as it slid behind a thin tree, and stood motionless.

"How did you know they were there?" he asked when they arrived back at the small circle of cabins that surrounded the post.

The old wrinkled face was blank. "The wind tells me. A crackle of a branch. A shadow behind me. The feel on the back of my neck."

Wolf was so depressed that night that Eugenia finally begged him to tell her what troubled him. She sat at his side on the blanket before the hearth, her slim hand on his knee. She said, "Wolf, we are so close, but tonight you are far away. Tell me, I beg you. Do not let anything come between us."

He bent his head. "You are right, Eugenia. I am bitter and ashamed of myself. I thought to take my place with my cousins and I cannot. It is not born in me, to move like an Indian, to almost magically sense someone behind me." He told her what had happened that day and ended, "You see, I am not Indian. Yet I am not white. What am I? Who am I?"

"I feel the same way," said Eugenia. "We have been here for almost six months now, and I feel more and more distant from the Cree. I do not fit in. I go less and less to the Indian women. They are kind, yet they giggle behind their hands at my foolish ways. I learn, but even a child half my age knows more about herbs and preparing a rabbit. And I hate to skin them, I hate the blood on my hands. Wolf, who am I, then? Am I only the civilized shell of a girl I was in Montreal? Is there nothing deeper in me? I always thought that one day I would be with my real people, and know who I am, and what I am, and be fulfilled."

Wolf nodded. "Yes, yes, yes! This is how I felt in New York. Always watching, waiting to find who I am. Someday, I thought, I will go to my people, and belong. But I do not belong here."

"When we go to dinner with—them..." said Eugenia in a low soft voice, her head drooping, "I am ashamed because I can scarcely bring myself to eat the bits of meat they give me with their fingers. Yet Stephen can eat and thank them, politely."

"Aunt Minna told me of her pleasure in the nights here. She watched the stars, she hunted at night, she revered the northern lights," reflected Wolf.

Words tumbled from their lips, and they talked and talked until dawn. They had both felt stifled here, not free. They were different from these people, who were supposed to be their own people. Strong Wind mocked at them a little as he explained customs. He was kind, but cool to them. They were, after all, half-breeds. They were not full Indians, like himself.

"Then where do we belong?" asked Wolf as dawn lighted the windows of the small cabin. He lay on the blanket, his head on his young wife's lap, and she stroked his long hair tenderly. "Where do we belong? Who are we? What are we? Nothing, and nobody?"

She was silent for a time, sleepy-eyed, grave. Her hand smoothed his head, smoothed the beard-thickened skin on his face. Then she bent to kiss him, gently.

"Oh, my Wolf, how foolish we are," she said.

"Foolish, my darling? How? Why?"

"We are who we are. I am Eugenia, you are Wolf. Our parents loved us, love us still. Our grandparents are concerned for us. Our cousins enjoy us as we enjoy them. We have friends who laugh with us, and miss us, as we miss them. We are part of the city, we are part of the plains and the forests. We have a piece of the heavens and the stars, our own small section of the earth."

He sat up and took her slim hands in his. There was wisdom here. He groped for it, earnestly searching her glowing, golden face. Her black eyes gleamed in the dying firelight.

"But where do we belong, my love?" he asked.

She smiled at him and held out her arms. "Where we are,

my Wolf. Where *we* are. We belong together, wherever we are. We go where we will, and the stars will be there also. We look up, and the heavens bend over us. So long as we are together, the world is beautiful for me. Do you not feel this also?"

He stared, he laughed in pleasure, he held her tightly in his arms. "Oh, my wise one," he whispered to her. "Oh, my love, my darling, my clever bright shining one!"

They sat, holding each other closely, rocking back and forth on the hearth rug of bearskin, and laughed in happiness that brought them close to tears.

Chapter 28

Wolf was relieved as the snows melted away in April, 1828, and the fur packs were piled high in the warehouse inside the stockade. He and Eugenia would be going home to Montreal soon. And he would be glad—glad!

He had met his Cree people and was not one of them. He was secretly ashamed of their dirty ways, their filthy clothes, the scratching for lice, their casual debts. To a youth raised mainly in the city, they seemed to have no pride, no wish to become better than they were. And he had been so proud to call himself an Indian!

He did not know what he would do when he returned home to Montreal. Should he go to New York and work for his father and grandfather? Would they expect him to go to the American West for them? Could he hide his contempt for his own people, the Indians, and find some white identity for himself?

April showed blooming flowers on the plains, and the grass was turning green. Stephen began to gather up the packs and count them, frowning. "There are few this year," he muttered. "Only the Cree brought furs to us. I wonder—"

The traders were coming in, some with goodly packs, others with few. Howling Loon watched and listened, his faded black eyes dreamy, his wizened old face wise with a wisdom he did not reveal to them.

Then early one morning the guard sounded the alert, and all the wooden gates of the palisades were swung shut. The men came running from various parts of the fort. Wolf jumped out of bed and pulled on his boots, then his pants and shirt. Eugenia leaned up on a sleepy arm.

"What is it, Wolf?"

"Trouble. Get dressed, but stay inside," he warned. He yanked the wooden window shut and barred it. "Get out the rifles and pistols and lay out the ammunition."

He grabbed his rifle and powder flask and hurried out. The men were gathering in the center of the stockade.

Stephen was giving them orders in a calm, clear voice. The men stood about, listening. The Cree Indians, Strong Wind among them, nodded, and turned to climb the walls and hide behind the thick posts at the corners. The trappers took up other posts, some near the barred gates. A couple went to the corral to guard the horses.

Wolf asked, "What is it? What has happened?" Other men had burst from cabins like seeds squirted from a lemon and were running to them. Stephen waited till the rest had come.

"Blackfeet Indians, about a couple hundred out there, seem to be mad about something." A shot was fired, and they all flinched involuntarily.

Stephen was directing the men. "Watch for fire arrows. Some of you get water from the well and wet down the roofs. Wolf, take a couple of men over to the gate and watch what's going on out there."

Wolf chose several men, and they followed him. The old Blackfoot Indian, Howling Loon, limped along with them.

Wolf asked him as they went, "What is it? Why do the Blackfeet attack us?"

The old man shrugged. "I do not know. I feel trouble this winter, not know what it is."

It was not often that the old man admitted to ignorance, and it seemed to gall him. He was scowling, his wrinkled face screwed up, his eyes half shut against the brightening sunlight.

More shots were fired, and some found their mark. The Indian women and Eugenia, turned into nurses, settled the men in a safe cabin near the center of the fort, and did what they could to remove bullets, smear on herb salve, bandage, treat the fever with cool cloths. Sometimes the wounds were such that there was not much anyone could do.

Stephen was everywhere, directing the men, relieving them when they tired, always keeping a cool manner. The attack went on spasmodically for two days and two nights, and moved into a third day. The Indians shouted, raced their horses about, and fired angrily into the trade post.

Finally the firing seemed to quiet down. Eugenia went to her cabin and was just changing to a clean dress after washing. She heard a sound behind her, and whirled about, the dress hanging on her shoulders. To her horror the window was being slipped open. Someone outside had broken the bar that held it shut. It must have been sawed quietly from outside.

As she stared in horror, the window was pushed aside, and a painted face peered in, the feathered headdress brushing against the small window.

Eugenia screamed, piercingly. She could not reach for the pistol at her hand. She felt paralyzed.

Two Cree Indians from within the fort burst into the room, and fired. The Blackfoot Indian, his face bloody, fell back. The Indians peered over at him, shook their heads.

They shut and barred the window, getting a fresh round log to bar it. By this time Wolf had come, to find Eugenia shaking and weeping.

Strong Wind, one of the two Cree Indians who had saved her, gave Eugenia a pitying look which held some contempt in it.

"She is all right," he said in the Cree tongue. "Not hurt. Good loud scream!" And he grinned a little, and strutted out, his man with him.

Wolf held her closely to him. His shaking hand went over and over her loosened hair and her back.

She finally drew away a little. "I am sorry, Wolf. I was so—startled—so scared—"

He shivered. "If anything had happened to you—" He was cold with fear. "You will be better at the hospital room. You must be with others."

As he led her out, Stephen came over to them and touched her gently on the shoulder, his face concerned. "All right, Eugenia? That was a bad experience for you."

She nodded and tried to look more calm. She wiped her face of the tears, but she was shaking with shock. Wolf gave her hot coffee to drink, and two of the Indian women talked to her practically. Their men were near. They would not let harm come to her.

She went back to work in the hospital. They had about a dozen patients, three of them gravely wounded.

Wolf and Stephen talked quietly that evening, wondering what had caused the attack. Howling Loon came up and was listening to their conversation. "It is beyond us. We must ask them why they attack, we have done nothing to them," the old man said practically.

"I have called to them, but they do not answer me," said Stephen.

"Let me go tomorrow morning. I talk to them," said Howling Loon. He had been injured in the side, but said little of it, shaking his head at any concern. He was old, but tough, he said. He had put on a bandage, and that was enough. The bleeding had been halted.

That night the Blackfeet Indians attacked again. It was unusual for them to fight at night. Indians rarely did. Eugenia watched with burning sleepless eyes, as the Cree Indians, mixed with a few fur traders of the French and the half-breeds, manned the palisades. They all fought together, saying little, helping each other.

One would fire, then step back to cool his rifle, and reload. As he did so, another would step into his place, wait, then fire and step back. When one tired, he would come to the ground, climbing down the rickety ladders, and lie down on the earth, to sleep for a time. Then he would waken, eat a little, drink some water, and go up on the palisades again.

Eugenia had another view of the Indians then. So calm, so strong and confident, they fought coolly. One died in silence, falling from the wall to the ground to hit it with a thump. His woman bent over him, rocking back and forth in silence, not wailing aloud in anguish, for to do so would reveal to the enemy outside that they had hit and killed a man.

It was odd, she thought, between bathing the forehead of a feverish trader and changing the bandage on the leg of a Cree Indian. The men were different. They were not close friends, yet when the attack came, they fought against a common enemy as a close unit, scarcely needing words. Stephen directed them, telling one man to get some sleep, another to cook some meat for them, and sending another for a fresh keg of black powder. But mostly they directed themselves, seeing where the greatest need was, climbing the walls to fill the gap, firing into the darkness.

Slowly the city-reared woman had come to admire her people, the Cree. They might be filthy, they might be crude and vulgar and greasy of hands. But they had dignity, loyalty, and the ability to fight with honor and courage. She watched her cousins, and she watched Wolf's relative, Strong Wind, as they fought with cunning and patience.

Strong Wind came near to her as she went out to get food for the wounded. "Is this how you saw our wilderness, my sister?" he asked, and that slow twinkle came into his black eyes. "The peace, the quiet of the stars? The beauty of the plains?"

She smiled for the first time in days. "You tease me, my brother," she retorted easily. "I know there is beauty here, in the blue white of the snows, in the yellow of the spring flowers, in the glory of the northern lights. But when one has red eyes that burn with gunpowder, it is difficult to see beauty!"

He grinned quietly to himself, well pleased. He even chuckled a little in response to her spirited answer.

Morning came, and the sun was red, burning away the white fog that lay on the grass. They could see the hundreds of Blackfeet Indians that lay outside in the tall grass and hid behind the thin trees. They had their campfires lit, they moved about, they talked, they shook their fists at the fort.

Stephen watched, frowning. He did not understand why they had attacked his fort. All knew MacCamerons for fair dealing. If it had been a matter of cheating, he would know about it.

Howling Loon came up to him, limping a little, his wrinkled face more weary, but the black eyes alert. "I go this morning," he said. "They would fight on a long time, stubborn and not changing. Talking must be done."

"You wish to go, elder brother?" asked Stephen gently. "It could mean your death."

"I am old. Death comes more easily to one of my age and many experiences," said Howling Loon with a little sparkle in his eyes, his head up proudly.

Together they went to the gate. Howling Loon shouted to them in his strong voice. "This is one of your brothers. I am Howling Loon of the Blackfoot people. I wish to come among you."

A long pause. Then a strong voice came, one of the chiefs, "Come out, and let us show you how to make a man die!"

The voice was angry. Stephen frowned.

Howling Loon replied, "We do not know why you attack the fort of MacCameron. The MacCameron fort and the traders have always treated the Cree and the Blackfeet and any who come with fairness and good value for the furs. What is your complaint?"

"Death answers death!" came the reply.

Stephen muttered to Howling Loon. "I do not understand this. What death?"

"What death?" yelled Howling Loon.

Some of the Blackfeet Indians came together, their head-dresses showing their chiefdom. They talked together. Then an older one turned toward the fort and called. "Come out, and we will speak together with calm!"

Stephen hesitated, but Howling Loon called back at once, "I come to speak with my brothers. I, Howling Loon, long known among you. I speak with truth. The MacCamerons trust me, my own people trust me. The gate will be opened for me to come to you."

They muttered, but the old man, standing erect before the gate, nodded to the Cree Indians holding the huge log that held the gate shut. They pushed it opened enough for him to slip through the wooded gates, then barred it once more.

Stephen watched from the top of the palisades, his rifle loaded and ready in his hands. If they slaughtered the old man, he would get at least one of them.

The ranks of Indians closed about the thin erect figure of the old trader. Stephen saw him raise his empty hands, to show he carried no weapon. They talked, vigorously, waving angry fists. He nodded, he looked at them. They sat down on the earth, and talked for a long time.

Inside the post all was quiet. Everyone knew the old man had gone out alone to talk to the enemy. They walked about quietly, or rested, unable to sleep, lying about in the shade as the sun moved higher in the blue heavens.

Finally Strong Wind lifted his hand to Stephen, who came up again on the palisades and looked toward the large crowd of Blackfeet Indians. The old fur trapper was coming alone toward the fort.

As he came close, he lifted his head and saw Stephen. He stopped. "They wish to speak with you, chief of the Mac-Cameron," said the trader and spat a wad of tobacco on the ground. He seemed quite calm now.

"I'll come down," said Stephen. He climbed down the ladder and went to the gate. Wolf strode beside him, worried.

"I'll come with you, and a dozen others," said Wolf. "Do you trust them? They'll murder you!"

"Not if they wish to talk," said Stephen. "Stay inside, stay calm. If anything happens, you are in charge. Listen to Strong Wind's advice," he added, and he looked at the Cree Indian chief.

Both men nodded, Strong Wind's face impassive. Wolf wanted to protest, but something in Stephen's attitude made it impossible. He went to the gate with his cousin and watched as the Cree Indians allowed him out, alone and unarmed.

Stephen met Howling Loon. The old trapper said, "Two of their men were murdered about a month ago, nearby here. Said it was three trappers. None of ours, I feel sure. But they want to talk to you about it."

Stephen nodded and walked forward slowly with him. His arms swung free, showing he held no weapons. Four of the chiefs came to meet him. They carried rifles over their arms.

One was still angry, the others more calm. The eldest spoke as they met.

"You are MacCameron, chief of the post?"

"Aye, that I am. Stephen MacCameron, son of Etienne MacCameron, grandson of Blaise MacCameron, who built this post many moons ago. Always we have dealt fairly with the Indians of the plains and the mountains."

Stephen spoke in a slow, dignified manner, his red-gold hair bare to the sunlight.

They eyed him curiously. "We remember your father, oh one of fiery hair. And we remember your grandfather. They spoke truth to us."

Stephen motioned to their fire. "We will sit and talk of this matter that troubles you and me also."

They sat down together. No pipe of peace was offered. The eldest chief spoke again. He told a long story, sometimes in the Blackfoot tongue, and Howling Loon translated every word. It seemed that two of the Blackfeet had been caught alone at a trapline and murdered. Three Indians had seen the killers from a distance and followed their tracks. They wanted those men, to avenge the deaths of their tribesmen.

Stephen thought. About a month ago two strangers had come to the fort. He had bought their furs, thinking they had especially fine furs for such greenhorns, who didn't even know how to treat their horses. The men had accepted their pay, then rushed on without remaining to drink or sleep.

He said this to the chief. "I have still the packs of furs they sold to me, those two strangers. Their marks are on the furs. Will you come to the fort and look at them? If those furs are with your marks, I will give them to you again, and make apology for accepting the furs from thieves. I say to you, however, I did not know they were yours, nor the work of murderers."

"We know what those men looked like. We would see inside your fort and see if the men are there."

Stephen nodded. "You may come, the chief among you and the men who would know the strangers."

They agreed, and came with him, about a dozen of them crowding after him and Howling Wolf. Stephen explained to the Crees and Frenchmen in the fort what had happened, and they nodded. Strong Wind said, "I remember those men. I follow them five, ten mile. They go south, they meet a third man. They hurry much, look behind them often."

347

The Blackfeet searched the fort and found no one they wanted. They acted in a polite manner. Stephen ordered the packs of furs brought out, and the one man shouted and pointed to the marks. "This is the mark of my brother!"

The Blackfoot identified four packs of furs with his brother's mark. The Indians muttered, their faces dark with rage. Stephen said calmly, "I sorrow with you. I will return these packs to you, or pay double value to you for them. It is my fault for taking the word of strangers. They have gone, or I would have turned them over to you for punishment. What else can I say and do, my Indian brothers?"

They finally agreed he could do no more. They settled down. Most of the Indians drifted away as the chiefs smoked a peace pipe with Stephen and with Wolf. They looked curiously at the dark Indian features of Wolf Gunther.

Some of the Indians returned again and brought packs of furs with them. To show that they were friends again, they sold their furs to Stephen, and they brought fine furs, ermine, white and blue fox, glossy, dark mink, the rare wolverine, and even several white polar-bear skins.

He gave them good value, in trade goods and in silver coins, which pleased them much. The dead were buried decently, and the injured treated with herbs and medicines. Then most of the Blackfeet departed.

Since it was now late May, Stephen decided to depart with the furs, leaving the fur-trade-post men in command until the next autumn. Most of the Cree Indians drifted away. A few would return to Montreal with them, to help carry the furs, paddle the canoes, and carry the goods in portage.

Eugenia came to Stephen. "I think Howling Loon will not make the journey, Stephen," she said, worry in her dark eyes. "He has insisted on being carried outdoors, into the open grass, on a blanket. The wound in his side has turned green, and he will not allow it to be cut."

Stephen put his hand on her shoulder. "I was afraid of this, Eugenia. His days are numbered. Send Wolf to me, and we will talk to the old man."

Eugenia followed Stephen's wishes, and together the two young men went to the place where Howling Loon lay under the shade of a sparse, stunted tree on the great plain. He lay where he could see the white snows on the blue mountains to the west.

"You sent for us, Howling Loon," said Stephen. He and

348

Wolf squatted down in the shade. The sun was hot that day.

The old man blinked his wrinkled eyelids. He said nothing for a time, then gave a great sigh that seemed to come from his feet up through his throat.

"I travel no more to the rising sun," he said, and his voice was feeble.

"I feared that, my friend," said Stephen. "You have worked hard and long and wisely all your days. You go to your final rest, having served all of us as your friends and companions."

A faint smile eased the old face. He blinked again, as though finding it hard to see.

"I remember the old days," he said after a long pause. Stephen waited patiently for the words that came with an effort from the thin wrinkled throat. "I remember when the plains were full of buffalo, and deer ran in great herds from us with our arrows. I remember when the rivers ran full and tasted sweet."

Another long pause.

"I slept a long time," he said. "I dreamed a long dream."

"What was this dream, Howling Loon? Will you share the story with us?"

"Yes, the dream, the last story," he murmured. He seemed to gather strength. "I dreamed a great dream. I saw again the mink in great numbers, I saw others playing along the streams, I saw beaver cutting down huge trees and building their dams."

He gazed up at the blue sky.

"The night comes," he whispered. "It grows dark. I dreamed a long dream. The plains emptied. The buffalo went away to the north and came no more. The deer disappeared into the mountains and no longer came to play among our trees."

"Few come now," said Stephen quietly. "Do you wish a pipe, my brother?"

"No pipe," said Howling Loon with regret. "It chokes my old throat. The dream, lad. The dream. The plains were empty. No beavers came to the drying streams. No mink played there. No otters were sliding down the snow and ice into the waters, and playing their games. The furs were gone, my brother."

"You have seen the great packs of furs that the Blackfeet brought to us," said Stephen quietly. "You saw their furs, how fine they are, from the great white North."

"Yes. Fine furs. Beautiful furs. But I remember, Stephen MacCameron, I remember the days when the South was full of mink, and beaver, and wolverine, and wolves. No longer

349

do the wolves howl at night in the American South. The land of the Sioux grows empty. The buffalo, no longer do they fill the land from sunrise to sunset."

He stopped, panting for breath, the rattle in his throat stronger. He groped for Stephen's hand with his own frail one. Stephen found it and held it firmly.

"Take a care, my brother. Be wise. Or the North also, like the South, will lose the little brothers of us. The mink will go, and the beaver, and the otter. Where do they go? To the sky, never to return to the earth. If our trappers are not cautious, and take too much each year, our little brothers will all die. All die—all gone—"

"We will take care," said Stephen. "I know what you mean, my brother. I also have seen what happens in the South."

"I love this land," said Howling Loon. "I love this full rich land. My vision is of a desolate land, stripped of animals, no good to man. A land with no more of my little brothers, no more. Protect my little brothers, MacCameron. Protect—"

He paused, his voice choking. Stephen felt the hand grow limp. He waited, but the voice came no more. Stephen reached forward and gently closed the faded eyes staring blindly up at the blue skies he had so loved and at the white snows on the mountains.

"Is he—dead?" asked Wolf.

Stephen nodded. He rose and said, "I will get some men to dig his grave here. He loved this land. He shall remain in this place."

Stephen went back and gave the orders. The old trapper was buried where he would have wished. His words lingered with Stephen.

A desolate land with no little brothers, no more mink, beaver, otter, wolves, buffalo, deer. No more animals—unless they took care. Each year buyers wanted more and more furs as the demand from Canada, from England, from America, from Europe, grew greater and more insatiable.

But they must not give in to that demand. They must hunt and trap with more care, taking only some of the furs. The little ones must be left to breed, to live, or one day there would be none left. The land would be empty. Then what would the Indian do? No furs, no meat—no life for them either.

The packs were counted and loaded into sixty-pound weights. The stores of flour, sugar, and dried meat were loaded onto the sturdy backs of the Indians and the French voyageurs.

Eugenia and Wolf put on their trail clothes, and their boots, and loaded up their packs also.

And one early morning they started out once more, Stephen MacCameron in the lead, waving farewell to the few men they left behind to take care of the fur trade post.

They walked to the first rivers, then prepared to launch the canoes they had placed there in the autumn. Some needed fresh pitch and tar patches of birchbark. They worked a day or two, and then started out again, into the rivers, down toward the lakes, along the watery passageway to the East, to Montreal. The winter was over, the working year was over, and soon they would be home once more.

They sang as they went, and this time there were some new songs, about the battle with the Blackfeet, about the incidents of the winter, about the hunting, about the little furry animals they had caught. They sang, and joked, and told stories, and worked together as comrades, Wolf and Eugenia among them. They were comrades together, for they had wintered in the cold North, and endured.

Chapter 29

A little more than halfway home, Eugenia realized that all was not well with her. She counted, scared, and knew what had happened. She was almost two months pregnant. She finally told Wolf.

He was happy and terrified all at once. "Oh, my God, Eugenia, and the journey will be more difficult as we come to the rapids!"

"I know, Wolf." Tears shone in her dark eyes, and she squeezed his hand convulsively. "I don't want to lose the baby."

Wolf went to Stephen, and the young leader swallowed with fear. He had never had this problem before. He put his hand on Wolf's shoulder. "Let us talk to Eugenia," he said. Her condition was very much outside his experience, but he was gentle and thoughtful of her. "Eugenia, if we are very careful with you, travel shorter days, and you carry no packs, do you think you will be all right?"

"Oh, yes, Stephen, thank you. I hate it, not to carry my share—"

"That is the least of our worries," he smiled at her cheerfully. "I want you to promise me, to tell me at once if you feel ill, or dizzy. We will stop at once."

She promised. Stephen quietly told the others, and their sympathies were roused. A baby! And such a nice woman she was. They would do all they could to help.

Wolf was relieved of his packs also, over his protests. His first duty was to Eugenia. Always another man, a different one each day, hovered near them and watched over them. The work days were shorter. The men started later, politely turning from her as she was sick at her stomach, comforting with offers of hot tea and a biscuit first thing in the morning. They stopped earlier in the day, and often the sun had not yet set when they dragged the canoes ashore and made fires for the night.

The journey was much longer, and it was August before they reached Montreal. But Eugenia was well, the baby safe inside her, and she was grateful to them. She would have the child in late January, probably. She was not shy about shaking the hands of each of them, the French voyageurs, the half-breeds, the Crees, as they landed on the wharves.

Blaise had come down to greet them, having been alerted by a watchman. His face was old and lined, thought Stephen curiously. He seemed to have grown much older that year Stephen had been gone.

"Don't take your furs to our warehouse," he said at once bluntly. "Take them to Minna's warehouse. We'll open it up for you. Will the men wait? Minna will give a good price."

"Of course," said Stephen at once. "What's wrong, Grandfather?"

"I will tell you tomorrow. It is a long sad story," said the old man rather grimly. He and Stephen and Wolf directed the men to take the furs to the warehouse close to them on the wharves, the large one that Minna owned. Further away, Stephen could no longer see the sign of MacCameron's on the family fur warehouse. Another name stood there—Canada West!

Wolf and Eugenia rode in a carriage Blaise had sent as soon as he learned of her condition. They went at once to her parents' home. The Chantals greeted them joyously.

Stephen stayed to see the canoes unloaded and the men paid. He asked them to return the next afternoon. They would be glad of an evening with their families, time to laugh and eat and drink. Then he and Blaise climbed the hill, slowly on foot, back to the big house where Etienne and Minna lived.

"Will you not give me some clue, Grandfather?" asked Stephen.

Blaise smiled with an effort and shook his graying red head. "No, I will not spoil your homecoming. Henri has planned a musical evening. It shall be a party for you and for Wolf, and for Eugenia, if she feels well enough to come."

Stephen wiped his forehead. The August day was warm, but it was not only that which made him sweat. "I was never so glad to arrive home," he said fervently. "If she had miscarried—I would never have forgiven myself. We spared her all we could, carried her up and down cliffs, made her comfortable in the canoe, yet—" He shivered.

"You have done well, Stephen," said Blaise, his hand on his grandson's shoulder. How tall and strong and mature he looked, this lad of only twenty-one. How much more could he take? Etienne was no longer able to take command, and Blaise himself felt old and weary. And Minna had done too much—she looked gray and tired. On this young man, scarcely more than a boy, rested their future.

At home Minna gathered Stephen into her arms as well as she could. She was a tall stately woman, but the lad towered over her now, and his arms were long and bronzed and hard with tough muscle. "Oh, Stephen, oh, how glad I am to see you." She studied his face, the bronzed face with bright blue eyes, the quick grin that lightened it, and smiled back. All was well with her eldest boy.

It was a joyous evening. After a huge dinner the guests began to arrive. Henri had reluctantly offered to call off the musical event, but Stephen had said, "Nonsense! Nothing finer to celebrate my return. I hunger for more music than my men can make!"

He was weary, nevertheless, as he finally relaxed from the strain of the journey. He longed to sleep for a week, yet he was worried about the news that his grandfather would tell him tomorrow. He knew by the look on his mother's face that it was grave. And his father remained in his bedroom, propped up in a chair, unable to come downstairs. Etienne was even more weak than when Stephen had departed.

Stephen had trimmed his hair and beard hastily with scissors and the aid of his brother Kendall. Smart in his trim blue silk suit, Kendall's dreamy eyes showed his happiness that his brother was home. He spoke of his studies, his tutor, the university he was attending. Stephen felt no envy of his studious brother. That life was not for him.

"And you are thinking of the priesthood, Kendall?" asked Stephen.

"Aye, Stephen," said Kendall simply. "The more I live and learn with the good fathers, the more I wish to be like them. The world holds little appeal for me; boisterous living, drinking, dancing. No, it is the books, the wisdom of their speech, their philosophy, their faith—"

Stephen nodded. He did not understand the life, but he had taken instruction and become a Roman Catholic when he was fifteen. The faith was strong in him, and he needed it, to have faith in a Higher Being, trust in God, knowing he was never strong enough in himself. "God be with you then, my brother."

They went downstairs together, Stephen wearing an unaccustomed stiff linen and lace shirt, with his green silk suit which Minna had had cleaned while he was gone. The smart black shoes felt odd after months of wearing boots or moccasins.

He stood in a corner after greeting the guests, mostly musicians, friends of Henri from his musical school. He knew some of them, had met the others, and smiled at them all. They seemed so young, so giggly, amused over little things, eating heavily of the trays of food that Minna provided for them. The two drawing rooms were crowded with them.

He did note one solemn-eyed young lady. She must be about eighteen, he thought. Her looks reminded him of those of his grandmother, Yolanda. She had great solemn black eyes, an oval face, a demure gravity. Unlike the the cute bubbly blonde beside her at the piano, she was not beautiful. She was not pretty, and her face was almost a sallow brown, and her hair of blue black was drawn back too severely from her face into a bun. Yet there was something about her, the grace of her shy movements as she went to the golden harp and seated herself, the bend of her head as she played, the enchantment of her music as she drew sounds from the strings with long graceful fingers—he could not take his gaze from her as she played.

He had met her before at one of Henri's musicals. She was Rosine Peguy, of French descent, her father rather wealthy, a merchant. Her mother sponsored many musical events in Montreal, and her married sister Celeste was a glorious dark-haired beauty with two small children now.

He applauded when she finished. She flushed with her efforts before the crowd, but her audience was a friendly one.

"Well done, Rosine, lovely. Your own composition? Beautiful. You have much talent." They encouraged her, and with a blush she settled into a chair not far from Stephen's stance. They all listened while Henri played one of his new compositions at the piano.

They applauded him respectfully, recognizing his unusual talent. He was the most gifted of them all, they whispered. Only sixteen, he was entered at the conservatory in piano, violin, and composition.

Stephen's thoughts drifted to the night before, the last night on the river. They had paddled through the night, anxious to return home. Eugenia slept peacefully among the cushions they had arranged for her, Wolf watching over her. The men had sung softly to the river, and to her, to keep her sleeping. How strange—the night before on the river, and tonight in a warm drawing room, windows opened to the night air, candles flickering on the silks of blue, green, purple, rose and lilac. The laughter and the civilized sounds of piano and harp and violin.

355

The exotic foods, the wines.

"Stephen!" Henri's excited voice was imperious. He had risen and turned to his brother. "Sing for us! You have listened all evening. But for now, no more of Beethoven and Bach! Sing one of the songs of the voyageurs! Sing of the river and the wild West!"

The others took up the clamor, turning to the tall bronzed man with red-gold hair who stood so silently in the corner. He was dressed as they were, yet there was some breath of wildness about him, some devil in his blue eyes, some scent of the pines and spruce and smoky campfire.

Stephen grinned and strode forward, giving his mother a smile as he went past her, sitting in such a stately fashion in her purple silk gown with the pearl trim. He stood at the piano, and Henri seated himself again.

"The song of the women left behind," he said, tongue in cheek. Minna shook her head at him, eyes laughing. Henri grinned and touched the chords.

His strong baritone filled the rooms, drifted outside to the night air, and rang even upstairs where Etienne sat in his lonely chair and listened with pride and longing to his strong eldest son. Minna's eyes went soft with memory. The Chantals next door fell silent in their eager speech, to listen and remember.

"The women we left behind us, oh, the lovely Yvonne," sang Stephen, his blue eyes roving about the room, resting his gaze first on one lovely face and then another. "Remember the kisses of Veronica, the blush of pretty Marie—"

He went on to the end, and they cheered. Rosine Peguy had been staring up at him solemnly, listening in fascination to the deep tones, the rolicking rhythm of the boat song to which they had often paddled the wide remote rivers of the North. As he completed the song, and laughed at their response, the cheering and the clapping, he ducked down and dared to kiss her red mouth. Just a touch, and she jumped back, almost overturning on the red hassock where she sat.

He touched her cheek. It was warm and flushed. Her mouth had been unexpectedly sweet, soft and fragrant—a scent of violets? Her gown was lilac colored, and she wore lace demurely at her throat, fastened with a cream and gold cameo. His gaze lingered on her mouth, her cheek, as though he would kiss her again. Then he straightened, to their cheers and curious stares.

"Sing again," Henri urged his brother. His thin cheeks were

356

flushed, his eyes bright with pride. "Sing the song you made up. I have written something for the piano to go with it. 'The Evening Song,' Stephen."

"Very well, one more," said Stephen. He moved back to the piano, and his face sobered a little as Henri's deft fingers rippled into the melody. He had indeed created a beautiful accompaniment to the simple chant. Stephen waited, then at Henri's nod he began to sing, in French, 'The Evening Song' he had made up on one voyage.

> Far from home, I light my faithful pipe.
> Woodsmoke burns my tired eyes.
> Against closed lids I see my wife's dear face.
> I reach my hand to touch my son.
>
> Oh, far from home, the winter has been long.
> White were the nights in frozen snow.
> Northern lights reminded me of God,
> The moan of wolves the devil sent.
>
> Far from home, oh, let me come at last
> To rivers dear and lakes I know.
> Guide me, dear Lord, and let me not meet death.
> I beg of Thee—let me come home.
> I beg of Thee—let me come home.

The last notes were deep and low, as low as his baritone voice would go. The words throbbed into the silence. There was a hesitation, and he saw tears shining in his mother's eyes. And Rosine's face was glowing, her eyes bright.

Pause, then wild applause. "Again, again," they cried out, but he shook his head, smiling, and went to perch on the arm of his mother's chair. Her hand went to his hand, and she pressed his fingers.

"Beautiful, my dear," she said, her eyes bright.

Blaise and Yolanda were seated beside each other on the couch. Stephen saw in satisfaction that they were holding hands, hers under his, half hidden by her smart black lace and silk dress. He was glad that they were close again, after the years of trouble.

The evening ended soon after. The guests drifted out, calling their thanks and good nights, some singing as they made their way down the street.

Stephen slept deeply that night and wakened early to troubled thoughts. He rose and went down to breakfast to find Minna there before him.

"You rise early after such a journey," she said.

Wolf came in the back door, easily, as one accustomed to their welcome. "Papa Chantal has talked to me," he said. "He has told me some of the troubles." His eyes met Stephen's, and the red-haired young man knew that the problem facing his family was a serious one.

They sat down together but had scarcely started drinking the hot sweet coffee before the sound of Etienne's wheelchair was heard. Stephen jumped up to help him roll it along the hallway. Kendall had helped him down the stairs. The brothers looked at each other keenly, Kendall's gentle eyes worried.

Blaise and Yolanda soon came, and then all gathered in the drawing room. "There is no hiding the fact, Stephen, no glossing it over," said Blaise, the first to speak. "The MacCamerons are bankrupt."

"Bankrupt!" Stephen turned from one to the other, dazed. "It cannot be. I do not believe it—"

"It was Canada West," said Etienne wearily. "That Patrice Scudery, and his right-hand man, Leonard Richier—pretending to be so helpful, so friendly—always willing to give us a loan."

"Taking stock in the company in return," said Minna, shaking her head. "Thank God the bankers refused to honor their demands for the warehouse and store that are in my name."

"That is why I asked you to take the furs there, Stephen," said Blaise urgently. "Scudery has charge of my warehouse. He took it over soon after you left. Every pack of furs, every shipment of trade goods was taken into my former warehouse. They even changed the name on it! Blast them all! Damn them. They cheated me for years—"

"But—all? All?" asked Stephen, bewildered. "I cannot comprehend. That warehouse, it belongs to us all. What about my stock? What about the payment to the men—the fur posts in the West?"

"Scudery claims them all," said Blaise wearily. "I refused to permit him to send me this past winter to claim them. But he threatens to send his men there this autumn. My God, how can I stop him?"

Wolf spoke for the first time. "Papa Chantal said to me that they fired your bookkeeper and chief clerk and replaced him with a man of their own a while ago."

358

"Yes, that was done," said Stephen, nodding. "It took place before our last journey. But what difference. Oh, Father, have they cheated us all?" His anger was rising.

"Cheated us? How could they? No, it was done legally. I did not know how deeply in debt I was to them. Always they advanced whatever money I requested. Fool that I was, not to demand to see the figures more often." Etienne rubbed his head wearily, and Minna gave Stephen a look of warning. Etienne was more fragile than ever.

They had to leave off the discussion to go down to Minna's warehouse, count the furs, and pay the men. The work went on for days. Minna was always there, as well as Yolanda, and the two worked with practiced speed. Blaise and Stephen stood on the outside, apart from the work, longing to help.

However, Scudery and his men stood about, urging the Indians and the French to come to his warehouse, "Canada West," and sell there. "Better prices, men! Higher prices!" They called out. "Do not go to the Minna MacCameron warehouse, she will cheat you!"

Stephen turned on them, furious, but Blaise stopped him. "No, just tell your men quietly that they will receive a fair price within. Tell them you wish them to sell to your mother, not to Canada West, which no longer belongs to the Mac-Camerons."

Stephen did so, over and over. Scudery and his men watched in anger and made sure that Stephen and Blaise had nothing to do with the financial transactions inside the warehouse. "For if you dare," warned Scudery, "I shall have the bank take over that warehouse and all those goods also. That will prove that you own shares in it, and then it is mine also!"

"No, the finances of that are completely separate," said Blaise, his old hands shaking with rage. He held his graying red head high, but inside he was aching with hurt, Stephen knew. That was all that kept Stephen under control.

The French trappers and the Indians were bewildered, but they followed Stephen's directions and sold to Minna. She gave them good value, rolling out the furs, eyeing them keenly, offering the best money or goods for them. They each had an account in her neatly kept account books, and Yolanda entered whatever Minna told her without question. The men went away satisfied. They had enough for their families, and enough to supply them against the voyage of the coming winter.

After the hectic work of several days matters calmed down.

But Stephen had come home so late, because of Eugenia, that it was already time to prepare against the next voyage West. He talked long and late to his family. It was finally decided he should go West, try to maintain the fur trade posts, and keep the Cree and Blackfeet Indians loyal to the MacCamerons.

"Fortunately Scudery and his men do not have enough trappers to man the posts. They will have to wait at least another season. And the courts have not yet officially turned over ownership of those posts to Canada West. I shall fight them," sighed Blaise. "By the time you return in the spring, you may find us all in order once more."

Stephen loaded his canoes, packed up, and left them with a heavy heart. He had hoped for so much more since the wealth of the furs was good, and his most recent trip had gone well. And to return to find the MacCamerons bankrupt except for his mother's separately owned warehouse and store—it was a terrible shock. From wealth to poverty, he could scarcely believe it.

Wolf did not come. Eugenia was expecting her child in the winter, and he would not leave her. And Stephen thought that his once-wild cousin was not as enamoured of the West as he had been.

Wolf seemed more mature and thoughtful these days. Before Stephen left, they had a long walk along the waterfront and a talk of a few hours.

"I have received several letters from my father and Grand-father Gunther," said Wolf as they started down the cobble-stoned streets. The September wind blew in their faces, off the river, and the sounds of the rivermen singing and chanting, and laughter and teasing came to their ears.

"Oh, I have hardly asked about them," said Stephen. "Are all well there?"

"Yes. Father has obtained a divorce from Odette," said Wolf, grimacing at her name. "I hated her. I am glad it is over. It seems that her father had a heart attack and wished to retire from the store. Odette wanted the store kept for Gerald, her son. So Colin made a bargain with her. He bought the store for Gerald and put in a manager until the boy is of age. In return, he got a divorce and complete custody of Juliette. I told you about Juliette, and how they treated her."

"Yes, yes. I am glad your father has her. Poor child! What terrors she endured."

"I think Father cares much for another woman," said Wolf

thoughtfully. "And I believe he will marry again. In any event I should like to invite him and Grandfather Gunther to come up here sometime soon."

"Of course. I only wish I could be here to greet them."

"That is not my only purpose, to see them again," said Wolf. They stood now on the windswept pier, and both gazed across at the loading of the great colorful canoes, the plaid-jacketed men who sang and shouted as they set great bundles into the canoes. "I am very suspicious of that Scudery. He is a bastard and a cunning one, I am thinking."

"So do I, but what can anyone do?" sighed Stephen.

"Grandfather is a very clever man with accounting," Wolf told him. "I used to go to the warehouse with him. He would peer at the pages of a clerk and find any mistake in minutes. He and Grandmother Agatha were both good at the books. They kept their own for years."

"And you think—" Stephen turned to face his cousin.

Wolf Gunther nodded, his black eyes narrowed. "I think Scudery must have cheated. No other way could he have obtained control so rapidly of what your Grandfather Mac-Cameron owned. But how? The courts believe him, the bank believes him. So it must have been cleverly done. I want to send for Father and Grandfather Gunther, and ask them to help."

The two men walked on in silence. Stephen finally spoke. "Blaise will be furious, he is so jealous of Ludwig Gunther. And Etienne still hates Americans, since the war."

"They are related, after all. And they would do anything for Minna. Both adore her. May I ask them to come, Stephen?"

"My God, I don't know." Stephen walked along in silence again for a time. Wolf could be quiet as an Indian at times, his face blank, his eyes dark and expressionless. He waited for Stephen to speak again.

Stephen kept thinking. How he hated to be cheated out of his inheritance! All the MacCameron money gone, the warehouses, the fur trade posts. All that was left was what Minna in her cleverness had kept. Her shop went well. All Montreal craved her beautiful imported Oriental porcelains, ivory, lacquer, silks. She was clever—very much like her father, he thought.

But what if they called in Ludwig Gunther, and he settled the matter by taking over their business? That would make Blaise even more angry, he was afraid. Ludwig Gunther and

Blaise MacCameron had been bitter rivals for years, in spite of occasional moments of friendship.

Yet—to be cheated like this, and by supposed friends! That grated. He thought of Scudery's shrewd look, of Leonard Richier's red-faced joviality as he tried to direct Stephen's own men to *his* warehouse, the Canada West warehouse. Damn them all! It could not have been done honestly. It had been too fast. Blaise had nothing left but his house!

He stopped then and held out his hand to Wolf. His cousin grasped it strongly, and the two gazed at each other. "Yes, Wolf, write to your father and grandfather. Tell them the whole story. Ask them to come. No, damn it, beg them to come! Tell them we need help. Tell them you and I suspect we have been cheated. Ask them to come as soon as possible. Damn it, I wish I could remain and help!"

"You are needed out West. We shall need good furs. Offer good prices, as always, Stephen," urged Wolf. He sounded so much older that Stephen stared at him, unable to believe he was the same wild young man who had come to them. He seemed so much more like Colin and like Ludwig, a true Gunther, and like Minna also, only black of hair and eyes instead of blond and blue-eyed. "Make good deals, tell them of the troubles, tell them we wish their loyalty and they will be well repaid for it. Take more coins along with you, good blankets. Aunt Minna had stocked up on plenty. Take good knives with you, more iron pots and copper kettles. I noticed many of the Indians wanted more, their women asked for them. They wear out quickly over the campfires."

"Yes, I'll do that," Stephen agreed, fired up. His blue eyes shone. "I'll take the best damn stuff I can get. Take double amounts of pots and pans, things for the women. And good knives. And I'll make damn sure the men at the post give good value. I'll bring back some great furs in the spring!"

"Good, good, *ja, ja* said Wolf. And Stephen started. He sounded just like Ludwig! "And it would help if you also wrote a letter to Grandfather Ludwig, to explain what has happened. I do not know all about the stock deals, the money loaned. It would help if you write to him before you depart."

"I'll do it," said Stephen. They continued along the wharf, talking eagerly, planning.

Chapter 30

In response to the letters from Wolf and Stephen, Colin, Ludwig, Jacquetta, and Juliette arrived in Montreal in October. Blaise had been reluctantly relieved that they were coming. "Though I swear to God I don't know what anybody can do," he had growled to Wolf.

Minna made room for them all, with delight. The fact that her beloved brother Colin had married again, and to such a delightfully different woman, pleased them all. Jacquetta arrived sparkling in an orange traveling gown, with a dark brown cloth coat trimmed with mink. And she was already expecting a child. She blushed to admit it.

"That was hów I got her to marry me so quickly," said Colin to Minna, the old wicked mischief in his blue eyes.

"That's how you got me to marry you at all!" rejoined Jacquetta, making a face at him. "I'll keep my house, though," she threatened. "I need peace and quiet to write my books. And you promised to tell me all about the fur trade, so I can write a novel about that!"

Jacquetta and Eugenia held long talks, mostly about babies, and Minna was satisfied that for all her bold talk, Jacquetta adored Colin and would have married him anyway.

Colin had brought his daughter Juliette with him; it was her first journey away from home. The nine-year-old girl shrank from all the men and boys of the household. Her wide violet eyes were startled when any of them spoke to her. Minna understood, since Colin had told her of her terrors in Odette's house with Gerald.

Therese, thirteen, wise for her years, and very practical and motherly, took charge of her. The first morning when Juliette came downstairs timidly, glancing about in hunted fashion, Therese had gone to her and taken her hand.

"We will have breakfast, then I'll show you my dolls," she had said firmly. From then on they remained together much of the time. Both of the young girls were fascinated by Eugenia and Jacquetta and the talk of babies to come, and wide-eyed, often stayed near them to listen.

The men had much business to discuss. They spent hours in the back drawing room, Minna joining them, to talk of what had happened. Old Ludwig Gunther was stiff with arthritis, but his brain was as quick as ever, and his experience was valuable to them.

He questioned over and over what had happened. Scudery would allow no one to see the books at the warehouse, so that manner of investigation was closed to them, unless the courts would order the books open.

Colin contributed keenly from his own experience. "It sounds to me that they did give you stocks in Canada West in exchange for your stocks and your warehouse and goods. Where are those stocks?"

"Worthless pieces of paper!" grumbled Blaise furiously. "They are in some lockbox or other. They say we get no payment for them until affairs are straightened out."

"Let's see them anyway," said Colin. Blaise brought his over the next day, and Etienne hunted out his from a strongbox. Stephen had none, having been underage when the deals were made. Minna had kept out of their arrangements.

Ludwig Gunther looked them over, studying each one, the dates on them, and the value printed on them. He grunted from time to time, scribbled down notes. Blaise watched him uneasily, and Etienne leaned his head back against his chair back and closed his eyes. He seemed to have drifted away from them all, much of the time. He had not the strength to attend to any business. He lay awake much of the night for the pain in his body. Yet he never complained. Minna brought him a fresh cup of hot tea with herbs in it, and he thanked her with his gentle patient smile. How he had changed, thought Minna lovingly, anxiously, as she smoothed back his graying hair.

Wolf went to sit beside his grandfather and studied each paper as Ludwig did. Ludwig gave him a sharp look and began to explain what each mark meant.

Blaise grew restless as they proceeded. It all seemed nonsense to him, he grumbled. "Fool papers, what do they mean? They'll give me no money on them! Just take away my stock, my warehouse, my furs—"

Minna soothed him. "Let Father study the matter, my dearest." Yolanda joined them, coming to bring in a tray of cups, followed by a maid with a pot of hot strong coffee.

Ludwig continued to sit at Minna's desk and go over the papers. He muttered to himself, then motioned to Colin. "Look at these, lad, and see if you think what I do."

He gave up his chair to Colin and sank into an armchair, accepting his large cup of coffee. He added cream and more sugar lavishly. "Got a sweet tooth in my old age," he grinned at Minna. She leaned to press her pink cheek to his aging wrinkled face.

"Dear Father, how good it is to see you again. And Mother does well in spite of her ailments?" Minna asked, the concern in her eyes revealing emotion that her light tone tried to mask.

"Ay, *ja, ja*, she does well, longing to come with us, she was. But her bones would have hurt the more. Will you come in the spring to her? She longs to see you again," he assured her, patting her arm.

"Perhaps when Stephen returns," she said with interest. "It is several years now since we have come. We could come for a month, if I can leave Etienne."

"Surely you will go, Minna," said Etienne, his quick ears picking up what she said. "We are not so feeble, all your menfolks, that we cannot manage without you!"

They were teasing each other affectionately when Colin lifted his head. Wolf tensed as his father stared at his grandfather. "Papa, I think—they moved too fast, the fools!" Colin's voice was excited.

Ludwig nodded slowly, complacently, a broad grin on his face.

"Us?" said Blaise, sitting up straight. "We are fools?"

"No, no," Colin assured him quickly. "Scudery and Canada West. Greedy hasty fools! They could not wait to get hold of the warehouse and stores. Look. The first stocks were issued in return for moneys borrowed against the warehouse. Then the next ones against the stores. But none against the fur trade posts! Not a post! You still own those. Do you owe him any more money?"

Colin gazed at Blaise eagerly. Blaise shook his head.

"Not a penny. He offered to loan me more to start a new warehouse. I said, no, damn your eyes! Not a penny more. And this house belongs to Minna, the other house to Yolanda. I signed that over to her years ago. Minna advised it, the smart one! Or I would have lost that also." Pain flickered in his blue eyes. He plucked restlessly at his jacket.

Ludwig rumbled in his deep voice, "Well, they did move too fast. Must have been anxious to do as much as possible before Stephen returned, and Wolf. So. They have the warehouse and stores. But you have your houses, your fur trade posts, and the stocks. Ha, ha, ha!" He slapped his knees heartily. "Well, we have them, eh, Colin?"

"If you are thinking what I am thinking, Father," said Colin. A wild gleam had come into his eyes. "Hudson's Bay Company!"

Blaise started at the mention of his old enemy. "What do you say? What do you say?"

Ludwig settled down to explain. "I have heard rumors in New York. Hudson's Bay Company is buying up all the independent traders and companies they can get their hands on. They want a monopoly on all the fur trade in Canada. They would then shut off trade with the United States. We would starve for furs. And every independent would have to work for Hudson's Bay, if he wanted to work at all."

"What does that have to do with Canada West?" asked Wolf. He put his hand on the stock papers on the table. "Would these be worthless, then?"

"Ha, ha, ha!" laughed Ludwig Gunther, and Colin grinned in excitement. "Just the opposite! Let me take those stocks to New York, handle them through an agent, and you will be rich again. We'll sell out to Hudson's Bay and start over again on our own!"

Blaise, Etienne, Minna, and the others stared at the old man in shock and amazement and incredulity. "Man, ye're daft!" Blaise finally said, shaking his red-gray head. "Sell—to Hudson's Bay. After all the years I've spent fighting to keep what is my own?"

Ludwig Gunther was shaking with such excitement that Colin worried over him. "Let me explain, Father," he said. Ludwig nodded wearily, and Minna filled his coffee cup again and brought tobacco for his pipe.

"Canada West is evidently trying to form a strong rival to Hudson's Bay, grabbing up all the independents. Then in the future, they will sell out to Hudson's Bay, at the highest price they can wangle. They are in a rush, since they know Hudson's Bay is getting many of the independent traders already. Scudery must be in charge of this operation, but he is careless. He issued stock that is common stock in Canada West. That means, you can sell it to whom you please for whatever price you can get for it. At this time Hudson's Bay would be very anxious to buy into Canada West, to help them get control of the new firm, and wreck them from within. Scudery says it has no value to you. Well, he cannot give royalties and dividends for it, but you can sell it!"

Colin repeated his explanation for the benefit of them all. They could not take it in. It was a complex deal with which they were not familiar. But Ludwig Gunther and now Colin had been working with just such deals in New York City and heard often about more.

"And what then?" asked Blaise, setting down his long pipe. "I cannot see what we do then. Do I take the money and start my own company again? And what if they cheat me again?"

"I propose," said Ludwig Gunther, "to go into partnership with you. As we talked of doing years ago. Colin, explain."

Colin started. His father must be feeling his age. The excitement of the morning's talk was wearying him.

He began again. "Well, Father and I have talked of this before. Wolf and Stephen work well together. We need the furs in New York, we can get the Oriental porcelain, silks, ivories, and so on, for Roderick Dindorf is no longer able to operate his firm. We have talked of buying his firm, he is agreeable. So we have the goods you want, including the trade goods of iron and copper pots, the blankets. Three-way trade, the furs of the West, the porcelains and silks of the Orient, the trade goods of New England. From New York and Montreal, we can control the business. Father even thought of calling it MacCameron-Gunther Fur Company."

He paused to get their reaction. They were all staring at him, Minna's hands gripping together in excitement. He smiled at his sister. "This was just as Minna began it years ago," he said. He added with affection, "She was smarter than all of us. She set it up, in her own way, and it has gone well. If we issue stock in our company, Canada West cannot get control of it—not unless one of us sold out to them, and we are not about to do such a stupid thing! If any money is needed to buy stock"—he glanced at Blaise—"the money would be loaned from the company and paid back in due time from furs and trade goods. We would all own all, through stock. The fur trade posts, which Canada West did not get. The warehouses here in Montreal, and in New York. The stores, here, in New York, in the American West, in Canton, and Macao. The sailing ships which bring the Oriental goods to us, the furs to them. The China trade is still open, though troubles occur from time to time. We can still deal with the hong merchants, though Mouqua died a few years ago. What do you say?"

"I am stunned," said Blaise, shaking his head.

Etienne shook his also. "I cannot understand it all."

"Well, the first thing is to get your permission to sell this Canada West stock to Hudson's Bay Company for the highest price we can get. The money will go into the new company, MacCameron-Gunther, and we will be in business. Colin will be finance manager. I have no longer the strength to take on the everyday jobs," admitted Ludwig. "Wolf and Stephen can handle the operations in Montreal."

"We could take turns going West," said Wolf slowly. "It is not fair to Stephen to make him go every time."

"When I am old enough, I shall go," piped up young Michel, blue eyes blazing. "I want to go with Stephen, and learn the trade!" At eleven he bubbled with energy and excitement, and mischief, just as Stephen had done, thought Minna, and as had she herself.

"Ah, *ja, ja*, you're a MacCameron and a Gunther," said Ludwig and rubbed his hand affectionately on the young lad's head. "Ye shall go, my lad. And with Wolf and Colin increasing the family, and Stephen to hear from, we'll be having another generation to continue the work. I'll be glad of that! A man likes to see his work go on, eh, Blaise?"

"That he does, that he does!" Blaise's face had eased of his gray worried lines, and he looked younger already. He called for some champagne, and they drank to their new company, though it would be a time before it was formally set up.

The stocks were turned over to Colin for safekeeping. He departed with Ludwig, Jacquetta, and Juliette, promising to keep the MacCamerons informed of developments. "Though not a word of this around Montreal!" he warned. "Don't tell a word, or we'll be in the soup. We want Hudson's Bay to pay as high a price as possible, thinking it comes from some third party."

Letters flew back and forth by messenger that winter. Colin managed to sell the stock for a quarter of a million American dollars to the Hudson's Bay Company. On hearing that news, Ludwig rubbed his hands in glee and sat down to write to Blaise at once. "Ah, *ja, ja*, how he will laugh and cry and have a drink to it!" he exclaimed again and again.

Wolf's child had arrived in January, a small black-eyed, curly haired doll whom they named Angelique. Everyone adored her. Therese sat with her by the hour, blissfully. How much better than a porcelain doll was this live wiggly one!

When Stephen arrived home early in June, having hastened home driven by his worries, he found them all exultant, wild with delight. Incredulous with all Ludwig and Colin had done, Stephen promptly began his courtship of Rosine Peguy, swept her off her feet, and married her within the month.

No sooner was the wedding over than a great procession formed to go to New York. Minna hated to leave Blaise and Etienne, but Yolanda and the Chantals promised to take good care of them. So she set off with all her brood: Stephen and Rosine, Kendall, Henri, Therese, and Michel. Wolf came with his Eugenia and little Angelique. They took three great barouches and all the trunks went in two other wagons.

They were welcomed happily by Colin and his new wife, and their new baby son, Theodore, born in April. Ludwig and Agatha were ecstatic, in a quiet way. Agatha sat with the two babies, Angelique and Theodore, in her arms, one in each, beaming over her spectacles, rocking back and forth.

"Ah, I feel young again," she said over and over. "Two little ones! How happy I am!"

Juliette was a little more sturdy now, her cheeks more full, her violet eyes brighter and more sparkling. She loved her new stepmother, Jacquetta, so brisk and understanding. And when Therese came in shyly, Juliette went up to her, took her older cousin's hand, and said, "Come and I'll show you *my* dolls!"

It was a joyous month they spent together. Wolf and Stephen spent many days down at the warehouse and in Ludwig's offices, going over the books, listening to explanations of how the whole work of the new MacCameron-Gunther Company would proceed. Kendall, Henri, and Michel listened in on the sessions, with more interest than they had realized they would feel for the complicated mechanism of the world of business.

The women sometimes joined them in their business sessions. In the great drawing room of the Gunther home, where the two clans gathered, the adults spoke of the work, and the children listened. Agatha would tell of the days when she handled the books and offer practical advice about that, and also of housekeeping to Eugenia, Rosine, and Jacquetta.

Minna was encouraged by her proud son, Stephen, to tell how she handled her warehouse and store, and what goods she found sold the best. She explained how she kept the books there, what work Yolanda had done, how they divided the duties between them. She told what goods the women of Montreal most wanted and suggested that silks brought to New

York be made up into some gowns before being sent to Montreal. "New York modistes are smarter than the ones in Montreal at this time," she added thoughtfully. "And there is some prestige in saying a gown is from New York. We can take the measurements in the store, and send them to New York, to be made up specially. That would increase our business."

"Yes," said Stephen. "I think that would be a good way to increase business. I told you about Howling Loon and his dream. When I was West this year, I told the trappers, we do not want all the otter trapped, all the mink, all the beaver. We must trap more wisely and try to leave the mothers and young. If we take too many year by year, they will all be gone."

Ludwig Gunther would have protested. But he studied Stephen's eager young face and finally said, "You may be right, Stephen. Already we have seen signs in the American West that the beaver are disappearing. All the otter and mink are gone from Pennsylvania and the Ohio country. The wolves themselves are disappearing, and it is long since a bear was seen in the East. Yes, if we do not protect the young and be more conservative about trapping, our business will be finished in another decade or two."

They discussed this matter seriously, and how they could encourage the trappers to conserve the mothers and babies of the species. There were certain seasons when the animals mated. Why not encourage no trapping at that time?

Eugenia shyly added her piece. "I noticed that the Indian women liked to weave, and some obtained the wool of sheep and goats, to dye them with herbs and roots. They spin the threads and make their own looms. Could we not encourage the Indian women to do more of this, and thus earn pots and pans, and needles and such that they wish to buy?"

This was a new idea to them. "Who would buy the Indian weaving?" asked Colin.

"I would," said Jacquetta spiritedly, not releasing his warm hand which had captured hers as they sat together on a silk sofa. "I would love to have some weaving done by Indians, to hang on the walls of our rooms. They would be like medieval tapestries, only they would be original designs of our country!"

The children sat on hassocks or curled up on the floor, at the feet of their elders, absorbing all the ideas that were flying about. They seemed to sense that this was the beginning of a new era in their families, the Gunthers and the MacCamerons. Joining together, contributing their abilities and their brains, they could build even higher an empire founded on furs, but enriched by their appreciation of the various heritages from which they had sprung: German, French, Scottish, and Indian.

Of course there was music in the evenings. Henri often played the piano, and Rosine the harp, Kendall played a sweet flute, Minna played the harpsichord or the piano. Even Ludwig took out his battered flute and played along. Stephen and the others sang or played musical instruments.

"How I wish Blaise and Etienne could be here to listen," Minna said wistfully to Colin. "They would enjoy this so much."

"Could they not come, Sister?"

She shook her head simply. She glanced at her own father. In a low voice she said, "Blaise is more feeble now than Father. I fear the both of them will make few trips now. But the younger ones can travel back and forth, we must arrange it, Colin. I will not be strangers with you any longer. The years when we did not speak or write were painful for me."

He squeezed her hand and said no more. By the bitter pained look that came to his face, and by the way he glanced at his son Wolf, Minna knew he was thinking of his first wife, the lovely shy Indian girl Morning Star. She was sorry for those hard years for him.

However Jacquetta had changed him. He was more relaxed now, he laughed more, and his smile at his new wife was sweet. Jacquetta was a quick-spoken, merry woman, full of many interests. She still wrote novels and kept up her separate house where she often entertained guests from Europe. Her baby was a new fascinating interest, and she carried him on her hip as Minna had shown her that the Indian women did. She would never be a conventional society woman of New York. She made her own pace, she believed what she honestly thought. And she adored Colin, ruffling his graying hair, teasing him, giggling at his remarks like a child. She had taken over Juliette as her own child, giving her firm advice, taking a keen interest in her hairstyle, her clothes, her books, her dolls, her schooling. Juliette could come to her stepmother with any problem, and Jacquetta would sit right down and talk to her about it.

The burden of dealing with Colin's children by herself was off Agatha. She could relax and drift into older age, yet look younger than she had for years. If a dinner party was planned, Jacquetta would handle the management of it, easily, gaily.

Otto and William and their wives and children came more often, attracted by Jacquetta's literary parties or musical evenings, to which all the smart New Yorkers longed to be invited.

For Rosine and Stephen, Jacquetta planned a musical day. She invited fifty guests, all of them musicians, and they made music from morning breakfast to a finale in the evening at about eleven. Anyone else would have been exhausted. Ludwig and Agatha crept away to their rooms at nine, and the babies were put to bed by their nannies. But the guests and the young hosts enjoyed the rare event, with guests coming and going all the day, refreshments continually renewed on the buffets, and the drinks lavish.

Time passed all too quickly. Minna gathered up her little troupe, and they went home again to Montreal. All through the winter letters went back and forth by messenger. Wolf had gone West this time, and in the spring he returned with a rich haul of furs. He had done well his first time alone, and he glowed with relief and joy at Stephen's praise.

Colin brought his family North that summer, and they remained for two months, to visit and work. The Canada West company was going under since Hudson's Bay Company was buying out more of their stockholders and their independent traders. The MacCameron-Gunther Fur and Trade Company was growing bigger, stronger, and branching out into stores of silk gowns, silk slippers, an entire store of ceramics from the Orient and from Europe, and jewelry stores in Montreal and Quebec.

Colin added up the books and audited all the accounts that summer of 1830. He announced to them, casually, though deep pride behind his voice, "We have made a profit this first year of one hundred and thirty thousand dollars!"

Blaise practically collapsed in his armchair. Etienne sat and beamed, helplessly gripping the arms of his wheelchair. Stephen grabbed Rosine and danced around the room. Wolf and Eugenia joined them, laughing, emitting war whoops that rang through the house.

Minna sat on the sofa and smiled blissfully at Yolanda. Her mother-in-law, looking so splendid and regal, gave her a wicked wink. In her expression was much that reminded Minna of the hard years, the difficulties they had gone through.

But the Gunthers and the MacCamerons had passed successfully through those difficult times. In the future would be more difficulties, probably, more cares, more worries, as time always produced for anyone who lived life to the fullest.

They would endure. They had managed to live adventurously, dangerously, as Minna had in the wilderness. And they had endured, and gone on to greater heights.

Stephen and Henri came in with trays of glasses, and the younger ones brought bottles of chilled champagne. With the cool bubbly white wine, they toasted with pride:

"To the adventurous, the thrill of challenge.

"To the daring, the excitement of the chase.

"To the courageous, victory!"

Stephen's voice rang out with the words, and they laughed, and drank, some with tears burning in their eyes.

Small Theodore, staggering from one adult to another, his sturdy legs having just learned what it was to walk, paused to stare up at his father, Colin. Blue eyes wide and wondering, he blinked at the cheers and the laughter.

Colin caught him up in his one big arm and held the champagne glass to the baby's lips. "Here, my son, drink. You will one day know what this day means to us all! And on your head will be the responsibility that we know now! You shall know the adventure, you shall travel the wild trails that we know now—"

Theodore licked at the bubbly glass, and Jacquetta scolded Colin and took the baby onto her own lap. He watched and clapped his baby hands. Excitement! A true Gunther, he loved it already.

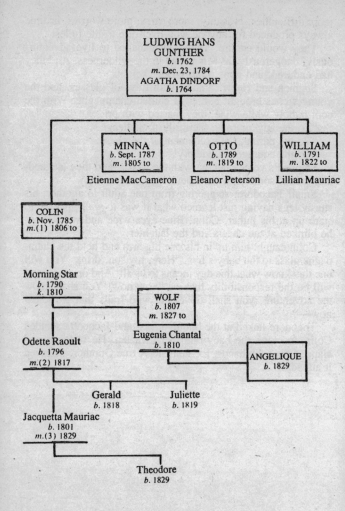

THE GUNTHERS

THE MacCAMERONS

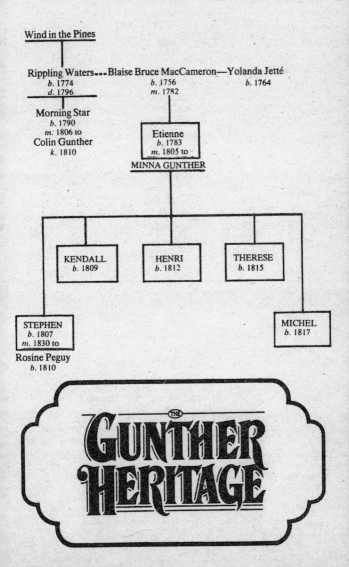

Wind in the Pines

Rippling Waters ··· Blaise Bruce MacCameron — Yolanda Jetté
b. 1774   *b.* 1756   *b.* 1764
d. 1796   *m.* 1782

Morning Star
b. 1790
m. 1806 to
Colin Gunther
k. 1810

Etienne
b. 1783
m. 1805 to
MINNA GUNTHER

KENDALL
b. 1809

HENRI
b. 1812

THERESE
b. 1815

STEPHEN
b. 1807
m. 1830 to
Rosine Peguy
b. 1810

MICHEL
b. 1817

THE GUNTHER HERITAGE

THE BORODINS

WAR and PASSION

LESLIE ARLEN

The grand saga continues… as a dynasty's dreams are born anew!

$2.75   0-515-05481-X ☐

Also available: Book I, LOVE and HONOR

$2.75   0-515-05480-1 ☐

Available at your local bookstore or return this form to:

 JOVE/BOOK MAILING SERVICE
P.O. Box 690, Rockville Center, N.Y. 11570

Please enclose 75¢ for postage and handling for one book, 25¢ each add'l. book ($1.50 max.). No cash, CODs or stamps. Total amount enclosed: $_____ in check or money order.

NAME_____

ADDRESS_____

CITY _____ STATE/ZIP_____

SK-2

★ ★ ★ ★ ★ ★

JOHN JAKES' KENT FAMILY CHRONICLES

Stirring tales of epic adventure and soaring romance which tell the story of the proud, passionate men and women who built our nation.

☐ 05862-9	THE BASTARD (#1)	$2.95
☐ 05894-7	THE REBELS (#2)	$2.95
☐ 05712-6	THE SEEKERS (#3)	$2.75
☐ 05890-4	THE FURIES (#4)	$2.95
☐ 05891-2	THE TITANS (#5)	$2.95
☐ 05893-9	THE WARRIORS (#6)	$2.95
☐ 05892-0	THE LAWLESS (#7)	$2.95
☐ 05432-1	THE AMERICANS (#8)	$2.95

Available at your local bookstore or return this form to:

JOVE PUBLICATIONS, INC.
BOOK MAILING SERVICE
P.O. Box 690, Rockville Centre
New York 11570

Please enclose 75¢ for postage and handling if one book is ordered; 25¢ for each additional book. $1.50 maximum postage and handling charge. No cash, CODs or stamps. Send check or money order.
Total amount enclosed: $_____

NAME _____

ADDRESS _____

CITY_____STATE/ZIP_____ SK-17